Worth Killing For

As the son of a bookshop owner, Max Luther grew up immersed in literature, reading the likes of Roald Dahl and the Biggles books, before discovering crime fiction in adulthood. A lover of fast paced stories, whether on the screen or the page, he decided to try his hand at writing one of his own. *Nowhere to Hide*, a crime thriller starring private bodyguard Alex Drayce, is the first.

Also by Max Luther

Alex Drayce

Nowhere to Hide
On The Run
Worth Killing For

WORTH KILLING FOR

MAX LUTHER

CANELO

First published in the United Kingdom in 2024 by

Canelo
Unit 9, 5th Floor
Cargo Works, 1–2 Hatfields
London SE1 9PG
United Kingdom

A CIP catalogue record for this book is available from the British Library.

Print ISBN 978 1 80436 584 7
Ebook ISBN 978 1 80436 591 5

Cover design by Andrew Smith

Cover images © Shutterstock

Look for more great books at www.canelo.co

Printed and bound in Great Britain by Clays Ltd, Elcograf S.p.A.

1

For my mama, Mary.

Prologue

The grenade made him nervous.

He'd set it up just as he was taught all those years ago, when he'd been given his introduction to a hitman's tools of the trade. It was a rudimentary technique in the grand scheme of things: the fragmentation device was strapped to the underside of a rusty old Peugeot with black tape, pressed tight to the fuel tank. He'd attached a wire to the pin, which ran along the exhaust system all the way to a rear alloy, tied off to one of the spokes. Theory being that when the target started his car and drove off, the wheels would turn, the slack in the wire would tighten, and out would come the pin.

Boom. Nice and simple.

But as Reaper sat in the driver's seat of his own vehicle, he questioned himself. The nagging doubts and negative thoughts grew louder in the quiet space. It was an old grenade, one of six dozen purchased from an associate in Albania and smuggled into London by his boss's firm. He couldn't afford for it to be a dud. He couldn't afford for the wire to snap, or for the primer to fail, or for the pin to seize up. He wished he'd demanded something more reliable from the man for whom he worked, but he knew reliability came with additional risks: a precision, custom bomb was a hard thing to make; it required a rare skillset, so scarce that often the people who were capable of making such devices could be identified from how they'd been constructed – a signature, if you will. But still, surely an organisation as powerful as theirs could do better than gaffer tape and string?

Reaper shook his head and pushed these thoughts aside. The point was moot; the job was on. He brought his hands up to his thick black beard, cupped them in front of his mouth, and blew warm air through his numb fingers. Having the hot air blowers on would have been heaven, but he didn't want the engine running. Parked fifty metres away from his target's car, he had a direct line of sight down the dimly lit street, lined either side with modest town houses. Even from that distance, a car engine idly ticking over at such an early hour, on such a quiet residential side street, would have been like emitting smoke signals. It would have drawn attention, and he didn't want attention. He just wanted to watch his target climb into his car, drive off, and pull the pin out. Simple as that.

They needed this man dead.

Condensation gathered on the windscreen, thanks to his warm breath in the cold space. He cursed as he wrapped his scarf over his mouth, trapping the moisture with every exhale. Misted-up windows were a sure sign that something warm and breathing was lurking on the inside, and he wanted to be invisible. A ghost. An unseen observer of what was to come.

He tracked his eyes down the row of terraced houses all the way to his target's front door: white UPVC with a small glass window at head height, glowing from an interior light for the past twenty minutes. Reconnaissance had shown his target had a similar morning routine to most other men in their forties: shower, dress, breakfast, and off to work. Every other day that week he'd left at various times between 6:35 a.m. and 6:40 a.m. A man of routine: the easiest type to kill.

Reaper glanced at his watch: 6:38 a.m. Any minute now. His focus returned to the house. He froze, breath held tight. He'd seen something, he was sure of it. Something at his target's front door.

Movement.

–

Jason Martin braced himself against the cold as he opened his front door, the colourful, busy Christmas wreath rattling. He stepped outside, turned the collar up on his jacket, and spun around to face his wife. Melanie pulled the lapels of her dressing gown tight around her neck, mimicking her husband in an attempt to block out the chilly morning air. Before he leaned in for the kiss, he noticed the glow of the icicle fairy lights, strapped to the guttering above his head, reflecting in the hard frost that covered every exposed surface. He gazed up and remembered the afternoon he'd spent at the top of a ladder just a couple of weekends ago, when he'd seen his life flash before his eyes more than once. He looked at his wife.

'We need to remember to switch those off before we go to bed. No point lighting up the street overnight.'

Melanie didn't hide her irritation. He couldn't blame her; he knew very well what an irritating cheapskate he could be. It was something he was working on, but it wasn't easy when you were trying to make ends meet while raising a young family.

'I just don't want to be forking out unnecessary money when the energy bill comes,' he continued in response to the tiresome expression on her face.

'Set a reminder in your phone,' she said. 'Then you won't forget.'

He nodded, leaned in, and kissed her on the cheek. Over her shoulder he saw their two children, Joshua and Christopher, shuffling up to the front door in their pyjamas to stand either side of their mum. They were eight and twelve. Four years difference didn't sound significant when Jason said it in his head, but looking at his kids it felt as significant as the difference between BC and AD. Totally different perspectives on life, apparently. Something to do with hormones, no doubt. Joshua was happy and alert, smiling despite the hour and the fact he was off to school soon. Christopher, on the other hand, appeared barely awake. His eyes were half shut and his hair was a mess. It would probably cost Melanie a twenty-minute argument to get him to smarten himself up before he left the house. He spent most of his time grumpy, dopey, or sleepy: none of the good dwarfs. And he wasn't even a teenager yet.

Jason wrapped his scarf even tighter around his neck as he reluctantly pulled away from his warm wife. He glanced down at his two kids. 'Make sure you guys work hard at school. We've got parent–teacher meetings for both of you coming up soon.' His eyes fell on Christopher. 'I don't want a repeat of last time.'

'Will do, Daddy,' Joshua said as he scurried off to the kitchen, the giant Santa on the back of his pyjama top waving from his sleigh. 'Love you.'

'Love you too, Son.' Jason saw Christopher start to turn around. 'Love you, buddy.'

A grunting sound was all he got in return as Christopher pulled his hood over his head and sloped off to the kitchen for his breakfast, covered head to toe in grey digital camouflage, too cool for Santa this year. Jason sighed, then kissed Melanie on her cheek, her dirty blonde fringe tickling his forehead.

'Love you, darling,' he said.

'Love you too, sweetheart. Stay safe.'

'Always.'

He walked to the pavement, taking care not to trip over as he blew a kiss over his shoulder. She blew him one back and then shut the front door, the wreath rustling and jingling once again. He patted himself down to check he'd left the house with everything he needed for the day. Phone, wallet, and car keys pretty much covered it. He navigated a zig-zag route along the pavement to avoid the slippery patches of ice and frozen dog muck, cursing his lazy, irresponsible neighbour, who refused to pick up after his spaniel, as he did a hop, skip, and a jump to his car door.

He drove an old Peugeot. Had done for the past three years, ever since his brother-in-law had convinced him to buy the heap of useless metal from him. Jason would like to say that getting him from A to B was its only redeemable feature, but it even struggled with that simple, basic task on the best of days. On such a cold morning it was easier getting Christopher out of bed than it was getting that car moving.

He fished around for his keys and eventually found them, pressing the unlock button from within his pocket so he could keep his hands warm. The hazard lights flicked on and off and he heard the doors unlock. He reluctantly took his hands out of his pockets to enable him to open the driver's door, wincing as his bare skin touched the cold metallic handle. He quickly climbed inside and shut the door, pulling the lapels of his coat tightly around his neck and grimacing at the temperature. It felt even colder inside the car than outside.

Not surprisingly, the engine didn't start on the first attempt. After some vigorous encouragement, and a lot of swearing, it finally coughed itself to life. He set the climate control to as hot as it would go, which did nothing but blast cold air into his face. He crossed his arms and wedged his hands into his pits, tucking his chin down and compressing himself as tightly as he could in the vain hope of creating warmth. He didn't want to move until the heating had kicked in, but he had no choice. He needed to get going, otherwise he'd be late for work. For motivation, he told himself that the engine, and subsequently the blowers, would warm up a lot quicker once the vehicle was on the move. He buckled himself up, sighing as he did so. After releasing the handbrake, he began to pull out into the road.

With a panicked jerk, he stamped on the brakes.

His wing mirrors were frosted up, blinding him to any traffic approaching from behind. He yanked the handbrake up and twisted around in his seat to try to get a view of the road, but it was no use. The rear window was just as bad as the mirrors.

What the hell, he thought to himself. *Maybe I could risk it just this once?*

His road was always quiet at this time in the morning, and not a single car had gone past while he'd been sat there. The odds were pretty good that he could just pull straight out without checking and not hit a thing. He reached once more for the handbrake and set the throttle, not wanting to get back out into the cold and dance around the dog muck again. He tried to focus on the odds. They were in his favour. He should just go for it.

But then again.

'Bloody cold weather!' he cursed as he relented to his better judgement, climbed out of the car, CD case in hand, and marched around to the passenger side to scrape the thin layer of ice from his nearside wing mirror.

Which is when he saw something that made him stop dead.

It was an easy thing to miss, nothing but a slight glint to catch the eye, like a silky strand from a spider's web. But now that he'd seen it, it was the most obvious thing in the world to him. He couldn't take his eyes off it. A thin plastic wire was tied to one of the alloy spokes on his rear wheel and trailed off somewhere under the vehicle. He dropped down into a press-up position and followed it until it disappeared underneath a bulging mass of black tape. He examined it closely with nothing more than his eyes, not daring to reach out and touch it. Most people wouldn't have known what it was even if it had been pointed out to them.

Jason knew exactly what was in front of him.

Panic swelled. For years he'd worried they'd try something, ever since Lily had been killed. But not this. Dear God, not this. And outside his home of all places. Those bastards. What if he'd taken the tube to work, and left the car for Mel to use to get the kids to school? Jesus Christ; it didn't bear thinking about.

If he hadn't seen it with his own eyes, he would never have believed it. His imagination would never have stretched this far. But it was true. It was right there in front of him. They'd come for him, just as he'd feared. He needed to call for help.

The panic turned into anger as he scurried away from the car, back to his house, his hand delving into his pocket as he reached for his phone.

Reaper watched the whole thing play out: the walk to the car; the hazard lights flashing; the engine starting. He'd even gone as far as closing his eyes, expecting the bright flash of the explosion.

But it never came.

Something had gone wrong.

When he opened his eyes, Jason was walking around the car with something in his hand. He watched Jason scrape his wing mirror for a few seconds, then he seemed to pause for a moment, as though startled, before he dropped to the ground and looked underneath the vehicle.

Shit.

It took Reaper a second or two to believe it. You could run a thousand people through the same setup and every single one of them would drive away without spotting the wire. But not his guy. The odds must be ten thousand to one, at least. Jason Martin had just won the lottery.

As Jason walked back to his house, Reaper quietly opened his door and stepped out of his vehicle. He began jogging towards Jason, using the row of parked cars as cover. He'd been relying on the grenade, but he had a backup plan. Of course he did. It was the reason for him freezing his nuts off, so he could watch the whole thing play out and fix anything that went wrong.

He picked up the pace, reached into his coat pocket, and removed his revolver.

—

Jason fumbled with his phone, sending it clattering to the pavement as he rushed back to the house. His feet skidded on ice, his toe catching the device after the second bounce, kicking it across the tarmac right up to his front door. He hurried the rest of the way and bent down to pick it up, cursing to himself when he saw the cracked screen. In a panic he lit it up, a wave of relief hitting him when he discovered it still worked. He hurriedly tapped three nines into the keypad, deciding at the last second to make the call on his doorstep, rather than inside where Mel and the kids would be able to overhear the conversation. He didn't want to worry them; this was his burden, and his alone. After pressing the call button, he came to a stop in front of the wreath and lifted the phone to his ear.

It never made it.

The force of the blow was formidable, as though a giant had punched him in the back, knocking the wind out of him and dropping him to his knees. He collapsed onto the doormat and rolled onto his side, sapped of energy. He turned his head and glimpsed his attacker: a dark figure stood in the road, too far away to have reached him with his fist. He saw what was in the figure's hand and remembered hearing a loud bang when he'd been punched.

And then he understood.

Hot blood poured down his back, warming his skin as it soaked through his clothing. He tried to lift the phone up to his ear, but soon realised his hand was empty. He spotted it a second later, right next to his wallet which had also fallen to the ground. He tried to reach for it but couldn't move. The pain burst out of him like a broken dam, flooding his ability to think of anything else.

Footsteps approached from the road. Jason managed to face his attacker just in time to see the man's eyes, peering at him over the top of a scarf that covered the lower half of his face.

'You bastard!' Jason shouted, using his last measure of strength to sit up and lunge at the man. He managed to get a grip of a trouser leg and pulled him off balance, causing him to stumble. Jason clamped a hand around his ankle and dug his nails into the man's flesh, clawing at his skin.

His attacker kicked him away, the explosive movement enough to dislodge the scarf around his mouth, exposing the smile beneath, his joyful expression at total odds to what Jason

expected of a man trying to commit murder. The maniac
pointed the revolver at Jason's head and watched him make
another attempt to grab his phone. It was just out of reach,
his fingertips only just brushing the case. As a last resort he
shouted out a description of his attacker, hoping the operator
had answered at the other end. But he barely managed to utter
a single syllable before the next crack of gunfire.

—

Five bright flashes lit up the area like paparazzi bulbs. Reaper's
heart was racing, his skin tingling with excitement. He
inspected the front of his trousers; judging by the mess, he'd
placed the barrel far too close to Jason's skull.

Noises from within the house made him run for it. The front
door opened. A woman screamed, the howl of which echoed
down the two rows of terraced houses, chasing him all the way
back to his car.

—

Melanie was unable to take her eyes away from her husband's
catastrophic head injury and the unimaginable amount of
blood, spattered up the white front door as though an abattoir
cleaner had thrown a full bucket at it at the end of a hard day.
Jason's arm was reaching out for his phone, encapsulating his cry
for help. It was an image so terrible, the shock of it meant she
didn't see Jason's killer run to a car and drive off. All she could
focus on was the horror of her husband's body, lying there on
the doormat, steam rising from his warm blood as it pooled
around him, his phone just out of reach, along with his wallet,
which had landed open, revealing his identification card, which
displayed a white crown on a black background.

The logo of the National Crime Agency.

1

Five months later

Alex Drayce jogged down the steps into Green Park tube station. Wind blew into his face as the trains forced the mild spring-city air out of the network of tunnels. He hustled through the labyrinth until he found the northbound platform for the Victoria line and leapt onto a train just before the doors closed. He dropped his rucksack on the floor so he wouldn't take up any more shoulder room than necessary; his frame already occupied the space of three normal-sized people. He undid the cable lock – a keepsake from his career in the police – strapped to the Molle webbing on his bag. It was made to thread through the breech on his weapons before storing them in the armoury. Nowadays he used it as a theft prevention device, and secured his bag to the vertical handrail he was holding on to. You could never be too careful with something that contained everything you owned in the entire world.

He'd decided to remain standing for a couple of reasons: firstly, it was approaching morning rush hour, so there was only one seat left on the busy carriage, and there would be plenty of people crowding in at stations further into the city who'd need it more than he did; secondly, he'd not long ago walked out of Heathrow after an overnight transatlantic flight from the USA's West Coast. It felt good to be on his feet, giving the muscles in his legs something to do. He tentatively touched the dried cut to his cheekbone that he was certain would leave a scar. His head and back ached, but not just from the jet lag. Recent events in the Californian desert had left their mark.

10

He was on his way to Islington Police Station to meet Detective Chief Inspector Paul Territt: the senior investigating officer in charge of his wife's reopened murder investigation. It would be a surprise visit, having established who the SIO in the case was via Julie Adler: an old friend from his days in the police who now worked for the National Crime Agency. Drayce hadn't been in the country long enough to warn Territt he was coming, and he didn't want to wait days for an appointment. He had things to be getting on with.

Unlike Julie, Territt was not an old friend of Drayce's. Drayce had never worked with him during his time in the Met, but he'd heard of the man's reputation from when Territt had been a detective sergeant. As Drayce understood it, the careers of numerous good cops had been stalled or terminated because of the lies that man told to get ahead in his career, setting people up for failure so he could discipline them to get in favour with the brass.

As Drayce stood there, the carriage floor vibrating under his feet, he told himself he would have to ignore his prior knowledge of the man's feeble character for the foreseeable. Things had been building up in Drayce's head while he'd been in America, and now that he was back home, he was in a rush to find out what the police had discovered about the man who'd murdered Lily. He gripped the rail tightly as the train moved off beneath London's busy streets. He pulled on it, felt his back muscles gently stretch. His white t-shirt tightened across his back. The sound of Rice Krispies bathing in milk popped off around his shoulders as the threads strained at the seams.

He eased off and stood up straight.

Something had caught his attention.

There was a subtle change in body language from a guy sat nearby. He was in his forties, with a hard life behind him. Drayce could see the cuffs of three different pairs of tracksuit bottoms peeking out above his scuffed white trainers: the mark of the city's drug addicts – a way for them to keep their emaciated bodies warm as they roamed the streets, day and night.

Cold eyes lurked within haggard features that hid underneath a bulky grey hoodie, over the top of which was a black bomber jacket pitted with cigarette burns. Those eyes regularly glanced at another passenger: a teenager with Down syndrome, several seats further up the aisle, who clutched a wallet to his chest with both hands, the edge of which showed a thick stack of cash inside.

Drayce watched the hooded man's reflection in the windows, which were as black as Turkish coffee thanks to the backdrop of the tunnel walls. The man was trying, but failing, to hide the fact he was staring at his intended victim. His narrow, beady eyes scanned the carriage, assessing if anyone was watching him, but always returned to that wallet, licking his lips. Drayce clenched the rail as the train slowed on the approach to Oxford Circus. The teenager with the swollen wallet stood up and moved towards the nearest doors. Drayce kept a close eye on the man watching him.

Stay in your seat. Don't do it.

But his silent orders were ignored. The man stood up, pulled his hoodie even further over his head to hide his face, and followed the teenager off the train.

Drayce studied the Underground map above the window. Islington was still four stops away, meaning he didn't want to get off the train yet, especially not to get embroiled in something that had nothing to do with him. What he wanted to do was get to Islington Police Station as soon as possible, so he could sit down with Territt and discuss something that was *very* personal to him.

But now that he'd seen a potential threat follow a vulnerable kid off the train, he had a dilemma to contend with. He wasn't the kind of man who could nestle in the comfort of ignorant bliss. The naive mind tricks that many people played with themselves just weren't going to work for him. He couldn't tell himself the lad *probably* wasn't going to get robbed; that it was *probably* just a coincidence the man with the hoody had got off at the same station as him; that he *probably* wouldn't follow him; that everything would *probably* be all right. Because Drayce knew better. Eighteen years in the police, working in cities across the country, had honed instincts that told him the worst *probably was* going to happen.

He unlocked his bag and stepped off the train.

The grey hoodie hovered among the other floating heads in the crowd. Drayce gradually closed the gap between them as they meandered through the white tiled corridors up to street level. The white glow of the cloudy English weather enveloped him as he got to the top of the steps, walked out into daylight, and pushed his way through the morning crowds on Regent Street.

The kid with the wallet was stood in front of the windows to Niketown with wide eyes and a smile. The guy in the grey hoodie stalked his target from the edge of the road, the wide pavement giving him ample distance behind his prey, allowing him to remain hidden from view. Drayce watched the thief glance around, showing his experience by keeping his chin tucked in to prevent the CCTV cameras from getting a decent shot of his face, no doubt checking for any police presence as he built himself up for the steal.

If the kid had been more in tune with his surroundings, and more aware of the dangers that lurked in the city, he might have spotted his tail in the shop window's reflection. As it turned out, he was oblivious, the only thing on his mind a pair of bright yellow trainers with black ticks, displayed on the feet of a slender manikin, which he admired with awe as he fingered the edges of the bank notes in his hand.

Drayce slowed his walking pace down to a meandering crawl, doing his best to blend his six-six, twenty stone frame amid the crowd as he stalked the stalker. In the back of his mind, he hoped the guy would abandon the idea and move on, negating the need for Drayce to be violent before he'd had his first coffee of the day. He stopped short and pretended to look at something on his phone, giving the robber one last chance to fight the malevolence in his heart.

Walk away, Drayce begged the man silently. *Please, just walk away.*

No such luck.

As the thief approached the kid from behind, he was probably thinking of a place to run to where he could count the money safely. Maybe he was considering which of the city's many dealers he'd call to score the gear he so desperately needed. Whatever was going through his mind, it could only have lasted four, maybe five paces, before his brain abandoned the plan, forced instead to prioritise the overwhelming trauma of what had just run into him.

Drayce slammed his forearm into the man's neck and continued with the momentum, driving him along the pavement all the way to the next junction, as though a car had mounted the pavement and collected the guy off his feet. Drayce gathered up two big handfuls of his bomber jacket and manhandled him around the corner, his toes barely touching the ground, a naughty toddler being dragged along by an angry parent. There was scaffolding built up along the front aspect of one of the buildings, at the bottom of which were wooden boards covering the shop windows, with just a single dark entranceway cut out for the workmen. Drayce dragged the man's half-conscious body inside and dumped him in the shadows. He appeared drowsy and weak from the blow to his neck. Drayce hammer-fisted him in the exact same spot to put him out cold.

As Drayce stepped back into the daylight, the other pedestrians either hadn't noticed what he'd done or didn't care, because nobody was paying him any attention; the soundtrack of the city hummed along as usual. He walked back onto Regent Street just as the kid strolled through the doors of Niketown, still smiling, with his money still safely in his hands.

The needs of his conscience settled, Drayce hurried back to the Underground.

2

Islington Police Station was a large fortress of a building, three floors high, which took up a sizeable plot on the corner of Tolpuddle Street and Penton Street. CCTV covered every aspect, and razor-sharp curves of aluminium sat atop the walls of the compound to give any escapees, or would-be rioters, second thoughts about climbing over. Drayce made his way along the pavement, past the large blue metal gates that blocked access to the rear yard, which gave the impression they could stop a tank. Across the road was a police van, the back doors wide open as a man from a commercial cleaning company – who seemed far from pleased about his career choice – chased vomit and blood out of the cage: the aftermath of a busy night shift for the borough's cops.

Drayce stepped under the middle arch of three at the entrance to the enquiry office. As the automatic doors opened in front of him, he was greeted with the familiar atmosphere of a busy nick in times of crippling austerity.

To his left was a lone enquiry officer, stood behind a large grey desk which a sweaty middle-aged man was trying, but failing, to lean across, waving a stack of documents and opened envelopes at her off the back of a tirade of abuse. Behind this 'gentleman' a cue of three had formed, everyone giving off a similar vibe of impatience and intolerance. To Drayce's right were benches bolted to the floor that ran the width of the room, crammed full of similarly unhappy 'customers', sitting shoulder to shoulder with scowls on their faces. The unmistakeable smell of body odour and unwashed clothes hung in the air. Drayce tossed some gum into his mouth to help fill his nose with something a little more pleasant and joined the end of the queue to wait his turn.

Ten minutes later, the enquiry officer had skilfully dealt with every single request made by the line, all of whom were either signing on as part of their bail conditions or their legal requirements under the sex offenders register. Drayce waited for the last cockroach to scurry out and stepped up to the desk.

'How can I help?' the lady asked, her mouth turned down and a frown on her face as she no doubt took a dozen incorrect guesses as to how and why Drayce had sustained his facial injuries. A rectangular badge said her name was Janet, pinned to her chest below a stern and unforgiving expression; there was no chance of a smile on the horizon. Not that Drayce was expecting one; this wasn't Fortnum and Mason.

'I'm here to speak to Paul Territt.'

Janet shot him a look you might expect from the king's butler if you told him to *fetch the old man*. 'I think you mean: *Detective Chief Inspector* Territt.'

'I'm not Job anymore. The rank structure means nothing to me.'

She seemed a little taken aback by this revelation. 'Well, I would have thought that being an ex-officer you would have more respect for—'

Drayce chuckled, stifling the flow of her sentence. 'The exact opposite, I'm afraid. My view of senior management is cursed by knowledge and experience. And I'm now a self-employed, tax-paying civilian, so if you wouldn't mind getting Paul down here to update a murder victim's husband, I'd be grateful.'

Startled, Janet stared down at the long line of post-it notes stuck to her desk by various officers who had appointments that day. 'Name?'

'Alex Drayce.'

'Is he expecting you?'

'Not exactly. I've been expecting a call from him, but thought I'd avoid any more of a delay and pay him a visit in person.'

A bored sigh, a slow turn of her head and shoulders, then, 'I'll go see if he's free.'

'Much appreciated.'

Drayce dumped his rucksack on the empty bench and took a seat, trying to ignore the framed portrait of Lily mounted to the wall on the other side of the enquiry desk. Uniform pristine, she stared at him across the room with her green eyes and pearly white smile on the fresh, young face of her attestation photograph. A lump formed in his throat; he quickly and firmly swallowed it down.

In memory of Detective Constable Lily Drayce were the only words in a font big enough for Drayce to read from where he was sat. But it didn't matter. He knew what the rest said, had been consulted on the words, had been present when it was mounted, and wasn't keen on reading it again. He focused on her face and allowed the sadness to come. He could feel it wash over him, threatening to drown him, but he'd handled the grief for long enough now to know how to stay afloat.

All this time he'd thought he'd been dealing with the loss, but he hadn't. He'd just been surviving. When he'd been told the police had a suspect, he'd soon realised the anger had gone nowhere. It had been building up under the surface ever since she'd died, and would stay there forever if he ignored it, festering like an infection, killing him from within. Now that he was taking action, rather than waiting for the police to find the evidence as a good citizen should, the anger felt more in tune with an energy reserve powering him on, rather than a crippling sadness dragging him under. Like a tank of rocket fuel, the quickest way to get rid of it was to burn it up. Only one way to do that.

'Mr Drayce?'

A slender woman was stood in front of him, dressed in smart, dark-coloured trousers and a light blue V-neck sweater. She clutched a folder to her chest and stared at him with what appeared to be concern. God knows how long she'd been stood there. Hopefully only a few seconds. Drayce hadn't heard the door open, too deep in his thought process. He snapped out of it and smiled at her. His face felt flushed, and his heart raced. A bead of sweat broke free and ran down his temple. He wiped it off with the back of his trembling hand. He wasn't sure how much longer he could hold the adrenaline at bay. He needed to put it to use.

'That's me.'

'I'm DC Gardner,' the woman said. Her pupils zig-zagged across his face as she examined the cut to his cheekbone, but she was clearly too professional to mention it. 'It's nice to meet you.'

Drayce stood up and slung his bag over his shoulder. They shook hands. Her skin felt soft, but her grip was strong. 'Nice to meet you too, DC Gardner.'

'Follow me. We'll find somewhere private to talk.'

Drayce followed her down a corridor, past a stationary cupboard, through a couple of closed doors, and finally into one of the interview rooms reserved for witnesses and victims of crime. It was small and windowless, the grey walls, floor and ceiling all competing for who could be the dullest. There was an old wooden table with three plastic chairs, two facing the one, the edges of the tabletop dented in numerous places, exposing the chipboard beneath the veneer. The short walk had done Drayce some good. He'd taken some deep breaths and felt as though his heart rate was down to a normal level. He dumped his bag on the floor and took the seat that was on its own.

'Territt busy?' he asked.

'Yes, but that's not why he isn't here.' She shut the door and took one of the other seats. 'I've been assigned as your family liaison officer, so I wanted to be the one to sit down with you right from the beginning.'

'Makes sense,' he said. 'Sorry to drop by unannounced, but an old colleague gave me the heads up that you'd reopened Lily's case, so I thought I'd come see you.'

'Yes, I've been meaning to invite you in, Mr Drayce.'

'Please, drop the Mr. Alex is fine.'

She smiled. 'And you can call me Lucy.'

Drayce nodded.

'I've heard a lot about you,' Lucy said.

'Hopefully some of it good.'

'All of it, actually. You built quite the reputation in this city. Many were sad to see you go.'

'And I'm sure just as many popped a bottle of champagne before the ink on my letter of resignation had dried.'

'Hard not to make enemies when you're the kind of man who stands his ground.'

Drayce smiled. 'Who've you been talking to?'

Lucy let the question go unanswered. She placed her phone and the folder, thick with paperwork, down on the tabletop, pulled her chair up, and adjusted the blue Metropolitan Police lanyard that held her warrant card around her neck, folding it underneath the collar of her white shirt as she would a tie. She swept both hands over her black hair to tuck the loose strands under the tightly packed bun at the back of her head. When her collar shifted, Drayce saw there was a mark on the side of her neck, red and angry, which ran in a horizontal straight line. A strangle mark, he thought on first impression. She'd tried to cover it with make-up, but her collar had rubbed it away. Drayce realised he was staring, so he blinked hard to snap himself out of it.

'I wasn't sure if you'd been trying to get hold of me or not,' he said. 'Sorry if you have. I can be a hard man to track down.'

Lucy waved Drayce's apology away as she leaned into her back support. 'I should have been in touch before now, so I'm sorry you've had to come to us. The delay has been because we wanted to make sure we had something meaningful to tell you when we updated you, so I waited a while after it happened, until we'd established the facts.'

Drayce felt the confusion crease his brow. 'Waited a while after what happened?'

Lucy's eyes widened. Silence hung in the air, as uncomfortable a feature as smoke in an explosives factory. She placed a hand on her forehead. 'I thought that's why you'd… I mean, I thought if you'd been told about the reopening of Lily's case then…' Her complexion reddened. She wiped her hand across her brow and lowered it to her folder. 'Right, let's start from the beginning.' She opened it and flipped over a couple of plastic wallets full of A4 paper. 'Can I get you a drink? A cup of tea or coffee perhaps?'

'No thanks.' He stared sharply at the folder, its top page full of short sentences, each one organised as separate bullet points. 'I'd rather we just get on with it.'

'Of course.'

Lucy shook away her fluster. Her phone danced on the tabletop. Drayce clocked her fingertip pattern as she tapped in her PIN. He had no idea why, but such observations had proved to be useful in the past. She read the message with a sense of urgency then dropped it back on the table, carelessly, and plainly out of anger. Bad news, it would seem.

'Why is the investigation based here?' Drayce asked. 'I know Lily was murdered in this borough, but aren't homicide investigations in these parts run from Barking?'

'Normally, yes. But it has to do with why your wife's case has been reopened.'

Drayce leaned forward. 'I'm all ears.'

Lucy focused on the page in front of her. 'A man by the name of Jason Martin was murdered in December last year, on the doorstep of his home address here in Islington, and we have reason to believe his death is connected to your wife's. The incident room for Jason's murder was run out of this nick, and the decision was made to base your wife's investigation team here also, so everyone could work side by side.'

She pulled a dozen sheets of A4 paper from the folder and spread them out in front of Drayce, who ignored for a moment what had been placed in front of him, and instead noticed the distinctive layout of a DNA report left behind in the folder. It was facing Lucy, therefore upside down to Drayce, but despite being unable to read it properly, he nonetheless knew its significance. He made a play of checking a message on his phone and snapped a photograph of the desk without Lucy twigging.

With his phone back in his pocket, they both sat in silence while he read what Lucy had presented to him, going back several times to re-read important parts. Lucy had just included the bare bones: everything he needed to know, nothing more. It was, after all, a live murder investigation. The finer details had clearly been held back, but it painted quite the picture, nonetheless.

'You think he spotted the wire?' Drayce asked.

'Either that, or he checked under his car before getting in,' Lucy replied.

'He have reason to be that paranoid?'

'Evidently.'

'What was he working on?'

'Nothing we know about, and nothing we're likely to know about in the near future. The NCA aren't telling us much.'

'They not want his killer caught?'

'They have a habit of keeping their cards close to their chests.'

'Even when those cards might help identify someone who kills police officers?'

'We don't think it has anything to do with his current case load.'

'I see. Which brings us neatly on to why you've connected his murder to Lily's.'

'She and Jason used to work together when they were detectives here in Islington. He left to work for the NCA after she passed away.'

'Murdered,' Drayce said. He locked eyes with Lucy. 'She didn't pass away; she was murdered. Don't ever sugar coat anything for my benefit. I deal with the truth, nothing less.'

Lucy bowed her head slightly. 'My mistake. Won't happen again.' Her phone vibrated. This time she sensibly ignored it.

Drayce looked back at the report. 'You were saying.'

'Story goes he made it pretty clear how angry he was with the senior management. Didn't think enough resources were assigned to finding her killer. He became quite the pain in the brass's backside when they refused to do more. On paper he left of his own free will, but word has it they hounded him out of the job.'

'Sounds about right,' Drayce said, thinking of his own run-ins with senior management during his career in the police. 'Where'd they find the suspect's DNA?' Lucy narrowed her eyes. She wasn't a poker player. 'Let's cut to the chase, Lucy. They may have had a working relationship once upon a time, but that can't be the reason you've connected the two murders. There must be a DNA link. It was the only solid evidence found at Lily's scene.'

Lucy adjusted her seating position. She licked her dry lips. 'They found skin cells under Jason's fingernails. It seems he may have lashed out at his killer.'

'Lily did the same. That's where they found her killer's DNA: skin cells under her fingernails and blood on her hands. I take it I was right? The two match?'

Lucy nodded.

'Okay. But there's no need to panic, Lucy.'

'Who's panicking?'

'You're getting nervous. I can tell. You're accustomed to families being told information of that calibre and instantly expecting guaranteed justice. But you don't need to worry about that with me. You need to keep me informed, but I understand this changes very little.'

Lucy eyeballed him quizzically. 'Why's that?'

'That DNA hasn't turned up anywhere else. If it had, you'd have kept everything under wraps until the suspect had been located, arrested, charged and remanded, enabling you to give me the full bells and whistles good news that my wife's murderer was finally behind bars. The fact you haven't done that tells me this DNA has only ever shown up at Lily's and Jason's murder scenes, and you still have no idea who it belongs to. Am I right?'

She nodded. 'Yes.'

'So let's hope there's more than the DNA to work with in Jason's case.'

'The detectives haven't found much yet.'

'Witnesses?'

'None.'

'CCTV? This *is* London, after all.'

'There were a few Ring doorbells on the street, but the killer was careful. He stayed out of sight of all of them. There is a privately owned camera that overlooks the entire street, but it doesn't work.'

'Ever? Or just on the day in question?'

'Just that day.'

'Does it point in the right direction?'

'Yes.'

'Then it's a bit convenient it was broken at such a crucial time, don't you think?'

'The investigators thought the same, so they checked it themselves. They seized the hard drive and examined every crumb of data stored on it. There's no footage from the morning in question.'

'Who owns the camera?'

'Why?'

Drayce smiled. 'I have an inquisitive mind. Can't help myself.'

Lucy rested her hands on the desk and laced her fingers together, a barrier of sorts. 'I can't tell you those kinds of details,

Alex. I'm sorry, but that report has been compiled for your viewing, and I can't stray from it.'

Drayce stacked the sheets of paper together and handed them back to her. 'Well then, now that I've read it, there isn't much point in me hanging around.' He took hold of his bag and got to his feet.

'Wait.' She grabbed his arm as he walked past and stood up to face him. 'Don't go yet.'

'Don't worry, Lucy, you've done nothing wrong. But you said it yourself. That report is all you can tell me at this stage.' When she let go of his arm, he leaned on the table, took her pen, and wrote his number down on page one of the report. 'Call me if your team find anything else.'

He stood tall again and considered Lucy carefully. She obviously felt him leaving in a hurry was a failure on her part, but undoubtedly understood there was very little she could do to stop him.

The door to the room swung open and Paul Territt stepped into view, then knocked on the door, which immediately struck Drayce as the wrong order in which to do such things. He was wearing a sharp suit and had a floppy head of brown hair that covered his ears like something out of the seventies, the composition of someone who enjoyed fast food too much and their exercise not enough, and the complexion of a man who had become accustomed to drinking a bottle of wine most evenings. He hadn't aged well since Drayce had last seen him but was doing his best to hide it. His smile was fake in more ways than one. A dazzling mouthful of veneers were displayed.

'Hello, sir,' Lucy said, with a flustered tone to her voice. 'This is Alex Drayce. Lily's husband.'

Sir. On the rare occasions Drayce had rolled that word around his tongue in the past, it had always tasted foul.

'Of course, of course,' Territt said, without breaking the smile. He stepped well inside of what Drayce would class his 'personal space', and seized Drayce's right hand with both of his, shaking it vigorously. His eyes widened when he spotted Drayce's facial injury.

'Been in the wars have we? I can see your life hasn't got any easier since leaving the job.'

'You could say that.' Drayce's manners forced him to be friendly. 'It's nice to see you again,' he lied as he looked down at Territt.

'Likewise. I'm the SIO in charge of the joint investigations into the murder of your wife and Jason Martin.'

'I know.'

'I hope the report we wrote for you has helped bring you into the picture as to why we're linking the two.'

'It has.'

'And I hope Lucy has explained why we've had to be so selective with the information we've disclosed to you.'

'She has.'

The smile grew wider, somehow. 'Rationing our words today, are we?'

'I find people who talk too much to be untrustworthy.' Drayce paused for a count of three to let the barb sink in and take hold. The veneers vanished, Territt's wrinkled smoker's lips clamped tighter than a cat's arse. He let go of Drayce's hand, his tongue flicking out as he forced the smile to come back. A moist glint of saliva lingered on his lips like venom. He glanced at Lucy and winked; Drayce felt his stomach turn.

'She's marvellous, this one.' Territt jerked a thumb in Lucy's direction without looking at her. 'Could have used her on my *personal* team, but there's no pulling her away from her FLO duties. Loves helping grieving families. Shame really. She makes a bloody good cup of tea.' Another glance; another wink.

'It's time I left,' Drayce said, catching sight of Territt's snake-like grin as he walked past.

'Well don't be a stranger,' Territt said. 'We're here to help guide you through this whole daunting process.'

Drayce nodded at him and turned to Lucy. 'I'll be in touch.'

'I think I'm the one who's supposed to say that to you,' Lucy said.

The tail end of that last word was cut off as the door closed behind Drayce. Seizing the opportunity now he was alone, he marched down the corridor, through a couple of doors back the way he'd come, and slipped into the stationary room he remembered passing on his way in. He scanned the shelves. Bingo. A large plastic exhibit bag and a handful of nitrile gloves found their way into the back pockets of his jeans. He hurried out to the corridor before he was noticed.

'Alex?' he heard Lucy call out, as the sound of her voice passed through at least a couple of closed doors behind him. 'Just wait a minute.'

He made it all the way out onto the street before she caught up with him and skipped ahead to block him.

'Just wait a second, would you?' She held out a business card. 'Take this in case you want an update before we next speak, or if you just want to talk.'

'You shouldn't tolerate him speaking of you like that.'

Lucy appeared taken aback. 'He's my boss.'

'Even more of a reason to keep him in line.'

Drayce noticed her take a deep breath. 'Let me worry about how I'm spoken to.' She held the card higher. 'Please, take it. I'm here to help you through this.'

Drayce examined the card. He didn't need the kind of help she was referring to; he was a long way past needing anyone's *support*. But he was a man on a mission, and having someone close to the investigation was bound to come in handy. He thanked her, took the card out of her hand, and walked away.

Lucy made her way back through the building to a quiet corridor that led to nothing but the property store, a cleaning cupboard, and her destination of choice: a drying room used by the nick's officers to hang wet kit. It was several hours until the next shift would be in for handover. She wouldn't be disturbed in there.

It was noticeably warmer a few seconds after she shut the door behind her. Stiflingly so. She loitered among the boots lined up next to the radiators, and the body armour that hung from coat hangers hooked around the thick iron water pipes that ran horizontally across the room. The smell of damp Kevlar and sweaty socks hung in the air. Lucy took out her phone in a hurry. She didn't want to be in there any longer than necessary.

She read the message that had pinged through while she'd spoken to Alex. It was another from Barnaby, wanting her to call him. He'd been playing these games for months now: always too busy to speak on her rest days; demanding she call him while she was at work. She needed to think of a way to settle things between them once and for all. It couldn't go on like this for much longer, at each other's throats every time they spoke. Maybe she could suggest they only communicate through their solicitors? But wouldn't that just drag it out for longer? All she wanted was a clean break, and it was evident he was no longer in love with her – God knows she wasn't with him – so why was he prolonging the agony? She tapped the call icon next to his name and put the phone to her ear, a heavy sensation pulling down on her stomach as she did so.

'You took your time,' Barnaby said when he answered.

'You know I'm at work.'

'I'm far too busy to keep track of your schedule.'

Lucy dug her nails into her palm. 'You don't know what busy is. And it's funny how you only want to talk when I'm at work. Almost as though it's planned that way.'

'It's not my fault you've resorted to doing a peasant's job that makes you work a *shift pattern*, for crying out loud. Where on earth is your dignity?'

Lucy wiped away the sheen of sweat from her top lip. Her face flushed. Neither were because of the heat. 'Just get on with it. I have crimes to investigate, criminals to put away. You know the sort of thing. Basically, the exact opposite of what you do.'

'I got your letter.'

'And?'

'It's out of the question.'

'It's my money.'

'Not quite. Under the law, it's *our* money. And there's a procedure to follow.'

Lucy closed her eyes and pinched the bridge of her nose. 'Why are you still dragging this out? Both of us could have moved on with our lives by now. You can keep kicking the can down the road, but once you run out of tarmac, you'll be left with the options of either paying me my money out of your own pocket, or selling the house.'

The line went quiet for a moment. Even the sound of his breathing made her angry.

'No,' he said, eventually.

'What do you mean "no"? You don't have a choice.'

'We'll see about that.'

'You spiteful little weasel!'

Barnaby laughed, the public-school arrogance coming off him in waves. Lucy had to move the phone away from her ear. Her nails were still digging into her palm, so hard they may have drawn blood. She clenched her teeth. When that wasn't enough, she kicked a pair of boots across the room.

'You chose to move out,' Barnaby said in the tone of a bad winner.

Lucy could almost hear the smile on his face, as though the words had become tainted with it as they passed his lips. She pictured him at his desk, in his wanky pin-striped 'power suit', checking his hair in the mirror. Who the fuck kept a mirror on their desk? She should have known he was a dickhead the moment she found out about it. But then again, looking back, there were plenty of warning signs she should have picked up on long before the mirror.

'I chose to move out because you made my life hell,' she said. 'The insults, the violence. You controlled everything. I couldn't stand living under the same roof as you any longer. But that doesn't mean my share of the equity is any less.' A thought pushed its way to the forefront of Lucy's mind. 'And I want my grandma's figurine back.'

'What on earth are you talking about?'

'Don't play stupid with me. The ballerina figurine my grandma bought for me when I was a child. I want it back.'

'You've already moved out, remember? You collected all your belongings.'

'But it wasn't there, was it? You hid it.'

'Don't tell such lies. Why would I bother hiding such a stupid piece of tat?'

'It's not tat! It's extremely dear to me. And you hid it from me because you knew it would hurt me.'

'You're being ridiculous. You must have lost it.'

Lucy stamped her foot, her heel making a loud *crack* against the concrete floor. 'Unbelievable! Is there a depth you're not willing to sink to?' She paced back and forth across the small room. 'I should have known marrying a defence solicitor would land me in bed with a snake!'

'Don't be jealous of me because I did something with my law degree, unlike you, running around the city with your stupid little badge. Given out many parking tickets lately?'

'Fuck off, knobhead. I investigate murders and support the families of the victims. And if you're trying to paint yourself as some great success story, you're living in a dreamworld. The company you claim to run was placed at your feet with a bow on it.'

'I think you'll find it's my name above the—'

'Don't give me that "it's my name above the door" bollocks. You were handed on a silver platter a well-established firm of solicitors that has been doing business for several decades. Your grandfather did the hard work, your father less so, and now you're reaping the rewards with your feet on the desk. You couldn't have had it any easier, you entitled little prick, with a little prick!'

Another bout of silence. This time her 'soon to be ex-husband if it killed her' was no doubt taking his turn to bite down in anger. Lucy was glad of the reprieve from the sound of his voice.

'You know what? Fine,' she said in response to his silence. 'Be a lowlife, if that's how you want to behave. We'll see who has the last laugh.'

She cancelled the call before he could reply and flung the phone across the room in a blind rage. She screamed as it left her palm, bounced off a set of body armour, and hit the wall and then the floor with two audible cracks. She stood there for a few seconds and stared at it. Her eyes tracked the cracks that now covered the broken screen like a spider's web, her chest heaving, panting uncontrollably, on the verge of hyperventilating. As the anger subsided, and her breathing settled, she collapsed onto her knees, fell forward onto the palms of her hands, and broke down into tears.

4

Drayce spotted Julie Adler as soon as he stepped into the cafe.

He'd messaged her immediately after leaving Islington nick and they'd agreed to meet at a Starbucks in Vauxhall, on the corner of Bondway and South Lambeth Place, a short, convenient walk from Julie's office at NCA headquarters. She was sat at a table close to the entrance, nursing a giant Americana. Black suit, white shirt, blonde hair tied back in a ponytail, she looked as professional and switched on as ever. A paper bag that had once contained a sausage cob, and a plate with the crumbly remnants of a giant muffin, bracketed her mug of coffee. She smiled and stood up as Drayce approached, her svelte physique a complete mystery when you knew her diet. The perky corners of her mouth melted when she saw his face.

'Jesus, Alex. What happened to you?'

'Bit of a run-in with the locals in Vegas.' He grinned, set down his rucksack, and gave her a hug. 'It's just a scratch. Nothing I haven't healed from before.'

'You need a holiday.'

'No time for that.' He took a seat opposite her. 'I've got things to take care of.'

Julie's expression sobered. 'Well, in that case, you'll need some caffeine.' She stood up and set off for the counter. 'Wait here. My treat.'

Drayce sat quietly among the noise and the scent of fresh coffee. All around him the city ticked by at its usual, unstoppable pace. Heads and shoulders darted by the window. People chattered on phones, typed on laptops, giggled across tables. An

Uber Eats rider sauntered in, filled his giant square rucksack, and hurried out. A pair of electricians, up on ladders, worked on something in the void above the ceiling. Normally, Drayce enjoyed watching the world go by. But it was all white noise to him now. Would be until he'd righted the wrong that had invaded his life three and a half years ago.

Julie set down a flat white in front of him, dragging him from his thoughts. Drayce thanked her and took a sip: far too hot. He put it down and waited for Julie to emerge from her vat of black liquid energy before getting down to business.

'Thanks for meeting with me at such short notice, Jules.'

'Anything for you, Alex.' She smirked, then blew on the surface of her coffee. 'So, you meet with Territt?'

'I did.'

'He still the same sexist pig I remember him being?'

Drayce nodded. 'He is. But I'm hoping to stay out of his way. They've assigned me an FLO, and she seems to be one of the good ones.'

'Her name?'

'Lucy Gardner.'

Julie gazed up. Drayce imagined her dragging the name through a database of contacts made over a thirty-year career in the Met. 'Don't know her.'

'I've only met her once, but I got a good vibe. I think she's trustworthy.'

'Just be careful. If Territt's in the picture—'

'I know. I'll be cautious. And he'll be kept at arm's length.'

'Further than that, Alex.'

'You know what I mean. I won't let him near me while I do what needs to be done.'

Julie's expression turned serious. 'Speaking of which—'

'Tell me about Jason Martin.'

Julie blinked, caught off guard by his interruption. 'The NCA officer who was murdered last year?'

'What did he do for the Agency?'

'He worked in Strategy. The Government Relations team. He spent his time convincing the Home Office and Treasury of why the NCA's vast budget was so necessary.'

'Strange route for a career detective to go down. I'd have thought they'd want to work him as an investigator.'

'They did, but word has it he wasn't interested. Desired something a little steadier after his career in the police. Apparently, he made a promise to his wife that his days of constantly coming home late were over. Strategy's an easy life. Routine hours, no danger. I think it suited him. He had young kids, after all.'

'Yes, he did.' Drayce wrestled with thoughts of the man's grieving family. 'And if he was no longer an investigator, it's unlikely his murder was related to his role in the Agency.'

'Not unlikely: impossible. The only conflict he had in Strategy was with the bean counters in the civil service, and they're hardly the grenade under your car, shoot you in the head, types.'

'Which leaves his time in the Met as the period when the motive for killing him spawned.'

'Unless it's more personal than that.'

Drayce shook his head. 'No. It's connected to his work in the police.'

Julie's eyelids narrowed. 'Why so sure?'

Drayce took a breath. 'DNA found at the scene matches that of Lily's killer.'

Julie's jaw sagged, her mouth hung open. 'What?'

'They worked together when they were detectives in Islington. The same person killed them both, three years apart. Why?'

'You're asking me?'

'I'm asking myself. It's what I need to answer if I'm to identify him.'

Julie put down her mug and leaned forward. 'You? How *you're* going to identify him?'

Drayce locked eyes with her. 'How did you honestly think this was going to play out?'

'Alex, you need to let—'

'Let Territt find her killer? Are those really the words that were about to pass your lips?'

'Look—'

'If the police were capable of finding him, they already would have.'

'Just give them time.'

'They've had this man's DNA for three and a half years and achieved nothing.'

'They have rules to follow, Alex. Investigations take time.'

'They've had enough time, and whatever they've been doing clearly isn't working. Not for me. Not for Lily.'

'She wouldn't want you doing anything crazy.'

'She'd want her killer caught.'

'And he will be. Let the police do their work, the correct way. Their approach is best, their methods tried and tested. Let them catch him by following the rules, Alex. You don't need to put yourself at risk.'

'Yes, I do. It's my job as her husband. The *correct way* has been tried and found to be sorely lacking. A new approach is needed. A new method. A new set of rules!'

The cafe went silent. Drayce didn't realise how loud he'd become, his emotions getting the better of him. He felt his face flush with anger, found he was gripping the edge of the table, knuckles white. Julie watched him. Her eyes told him to cool it. Others in the vicinity stared, then quickly got bored and returned to what they'd been doing.

'You asked to meet with me for a reason,' Julie said, calmly. 'I think, deep down, you wanted a friend to talk some sense into you.'

Drayce leaned forward and lowered his voice. 'I asked to meet with you because I wanted to know if an NCA investigation could be behind all this – something Lily and Jason were perhaps working on with the Agency when they were Islington CID, that Jason continued when he made the switch to you guys after Lily was killed – but his role at the time of his death rules that out. You've saved me some time, stopped me getting distracted by Jason's job in the NCA. It's his time in the Met that matters; the work he did with Lily. That's all I needed from you, Jules. Now it's up to me to hunt this man down, and there's nothing you can say to change my mind.'

'Alex, how on earth do you plan on discovering the identity of that person's DNA if the police can't? Think about it.'

'I am *thinking* about it. It's all I've been *thinking* about for the last three and a half years.'

'Well then surely you've come to the conclusion that your only option is to let the police run through their investigation.'

'No, I haven't reached that conclusion at all. I have plenty of options.'

'Such as what? Going door to door sticking a gun in people's faces?'

'That'll do as a starting point.'

'Jesus, Alex…'

'Put yourself in my shoes. How much time is enough? They've had three and a half years. Should I wait another three? How about six? Maybe ten? When does it get to the point where I can step in and demand justice?'

'The police are already doing what needs to be done.'

Drayce shook his head. 'No, they're not. They're doing what *they* need to do, following the rules they *must* follow, because that's what society demands of them. Well, what's good for society isn't always good for the individual. Better ten guilty men go free than one innocent suffer. That's what Blackstone said, wasn't it? Well, what about this innocent?' He pulled his necklace out from under his shirt and opened the locket.

Julie stirred uncomfortably when she saw Lily's face. 'Alex, I…' She shook her head. 'You've got to let the police handle this.'

'It's past that now, Jules. They had their chance to find the justice my wife deserves. Now it's over to me to hunt it down and take it.'

'I'll say it again: how do you plan to do that if the police can't? You don't have access to their systems, their workforce, their intelligence. You're one person, Alex.'

'So was Mariya Oktyabrskaya.'

'Who?'

'Google her.'

Julie rolled her eyes. 'Listen—'

'No, you listen. Cops have rules to follow; I don't. They have pensions, and careers, and reputations to protect; I don't. Whatever needs to be done, I can do. I can bleed information out of the people involved. And I will. From the first to the last, all the way up the chain, until I get the name of Lily's killer.'

'I won't let you.'

'Yes, you will. Because you know I'm right.'

Julie didn't reply.

'It all sounds crazy to you, because you're not feeling what I feel. But please, Jules, try to understand. I *must* find this man, and I can't let correct procedure get in my way. You of all people should understand.'

She placed a hand on his. 'I do.' Her voice had softened, her expression too. 'I'm just looking out for you. I don't want you to get hurt.'

'I'm not the one who's going to get hurt.' Drayce pulled his hand away, sank his coffee, stood up, and swung his rucksack over his shoulder. 'Thank you for meeting with me.' Julie assessed him from her seat, concern and fear plastered across her face. 'I'm sorry you had to listen to all that.'

'It's okay.'

'I'm not myself right now. And I don't think I will be until I've righted the wrong they committed.'

He walked to the exit. Reached the door. Stepped outside.

'Alex?'

He turned around.

'I do understand. I really do.' Julie stood up. Her eyes glistened. 'I just care about you, that's all. But if you think I can help,' she waved her phone at him, 'I'm here for you.'

Drayce nodded, thanked her, and walked away.

5

Drayce found a nearby hotel and booked himself a room. He dumped his rucksack next to the bed, stripped off his clothes, grabbed his toiletry bag, and took a shower. Some of the blunt trauma injuries he'd sustained in America were still sore and stung like sunburn when the powerful streams of hot water hit them. Closing his eyes, he tilted his head back and let the warmth cascade down him. He grabbed his bar of Mr Bassett's Grappler's Soap and washed himself from head to toe, taking care around the cuts to his cheekbone and scalp so as not to break the scabs.

Shower finished, he towelled off, brushed his teeth, then padded back to the bed. Somewhat rejuvenated from his long transatlantic flight, squished into an economy seat like an adult in a child's car seat, he sat on the edge of the mattress and contemplated taking a nap. The knowledge gained from his meeting with Lucy gave him the confidence that things would progress quickly, at least from his side of things, if not the police's. Drayce would have to recharge his batteries if he hoped to handle what was coming next.

A bulge on the inside of his rucksack caught his eye. He unzipped the top and pulled out the item: three photographs in black frames, stacked together, linked by hinges, the corner of one of the frames taped after it was damaged by a clumsy Mexican gangster on his recent job in the States. He unfolded them and laid them across his lap. Each was a portrait of Lily. Wedding; honeymoon; first anniversary. Big beaming smile, bright green eyes, brown hair tied back on one, let loose on the other two. Drayce swallowed the lump in his throat, surprised himself with a smile. The time they'd had together was perfect, the memories glorious. The man who took her could never spoil that.

Exhausted from his activities across the Atlantic, he set an alarm for thirty minutes and lay down, the photographs clutched to his chest. Vivid images flashed behind his closed eyes. His breathing slowed; his heart rate settled. As he sunk deeper into the mattress, part of him left the hotel room to embed footprints in a world already lived.

-

Lily held high the tail of her wedding dress – strapless, with long sleeves made of lace and a plunging neckline – and carefully negotiated the wooden steps down to the room behind the hall where the ceremony had just taken place, her bright white figure in contrast to the rustic surroundings, the converted barn that had hosted the ceremony beautifully constructed of exposed brick and oak beams.

Drayce clutched her free hand and watched every move she made with a smile on his face.

'Soooo,' she said through pursed lips, exhaling as she expelled her nerves. 'I guess we're married now.' She grinned at him, her smoky eyes even more beautiful than usual, which Drayce would have said was impossible, if he wasn't witnessing it himself.

'I guess so.'

She giggled. 'What now?'

'We take a minute to let it sink in while the guests get their drinks.' He led her to a table in the corner of the room. Two flutes of champagne and a tray of finger food had been laid out. Drayce tried the honeyed sausage and grilled haloumi.

Lily screwed her face up. 'Ugh! Squeaky cheese.'

'You're missing out.'

'I'm not hungry.' She necked her champagne in one. 'Ah, that's better.'

They both laughed.

'I suppose we should go out there and mingle with our guests,' Drayce said.

Lily grinned at him, mischief in her eyes. 'There's plenty of time for that. Our guests can wait.'

She placed her champagne flute down and flung herself at him. He caught her around her thighs and held her up, her legs clamping his waist as her arms wrapped around his neck. They looked into each other's eyes.

Lily's grin turned into a beaming smile. 'I can't wait to spend the rest of my life with you.'

'There's no one I'd rather have by my side.'

Lily placed the flat of her hand against Drayce's cheek. 'Right back at you, big guy.'

They closed their eyes and kissed. The world around them vanished, both totally lost in the moment. After some time had passed, their lips parted. Drayce stared into her green eyes, their noses touching. He felt hypnotised.

'You make me so happy,' she said.

'And you me.'

'That's what it's all about, after all.'

Drayce smiled. 'That's certainly part of it.'

Lily cocked her head to one side. 'And the rest?'

Drayce paused a beat. 'I suppose the rest is what that happiness is grounded in. The thing that gives our lives meaning.'

'Well look at you. If I wasn't mistaken, I'd say you were on the verge of expressing your feelings, Mr Door-Kicking-Gun-Toting-Tough-Guy.'

Drayce smiled. 'Maybe I am.'

'Well don't let me stop you. Open up. Tell me how you feel.'

Drayce wasn't sure how he felt, but he spoke regardless, airing his thoughts out loud. 'I read somewhere that the problem with the mere pursuit of happiness, is that when storms come along in life, happiness disappears, and then you're left with nothing.'

Lily's eyes narrowed. Her cheeky grin returned. 'Have you been buying those self-help books again?'

Drayce chuckled. 'Happiness is wonderful; God knows there's enough suffering in the world without us turning down opportunities to be joyful. But ultimately, it's fleeting. It's much better to ground your life in that which gives you meaning.'

Lily couldn't keep the smile off her face. She looked as though she was struggling not to laugh at him. 'Well, hello, Mr Stoic! So tell me: why is *meaning* so important to you?'

'It makes me a better man.' He paused, gazed into her eyes. 'And now, a better husband.'

'Now *that* I can drink to.' Lily leaned back in Drayce's arms, reached for the table of drinks and snacks, topped up her champagne flute, and lifted it in the air as she came level with Drayce again. She took a sip, then poured some into Drayce's mouth, being clumsy on purpose. She pouted her lips at him as it ran down his chin. 'Whoops!'

They both laughed.

'Come on then,' she continued. 'What is it that gives your life so much meaning, Mr? And I want specifics!'

Drayce gazed deep into her eyes. '*You*, silly.'

She held him even tighter. 'Good answer. But why me?'

The answer came easily. The truth rolled right off his tongue. 'Because before you, I didn't know if the effects of my upbringing would ever allow me to connect so strongly with someone. Because you've convinced me I'm worthy of all of this. Because you're everything I've been looking for my whole life.' He paused. Took a breath. 'Because I love you.'

Lily's smile faded, her face adopting a more serious expression. 'I love you too.'

She chucked her champagne flute across the room, clamped his face with both hands, and kissed him passionately. Once again, they were lost in the moment, but this time, there was no stopping. Her hands moved to the back of his head, her fingers running through his hair, pulling his head back, biting his lip. She pulled his tie off and ripped his shirt open, several buttons pinging across the room, her nails clawing his chest. She swiped the food and drinks off the table behind her. Drayce laid her down on it.

Lily was right, Drayce thought.

Their guests could wait.

—

Drayce bolted upright to the sound of his alarm ringing. His chest heaved, mouth drier than a cracker in a heatwave. The towel had come loose, now wrapped around one leg, still damp. The photo frames had fallen to the floor. Hurried beads of sweat tickled his face. His skin was stuck to the sheets. He avoided the photo frames as he swung his feet to the floor, switched off his alarm, leaned forward, and breathed deeply. He closed his eyes again, grasped with all his might onto the dying whispers of the dream. Eventually they faded. He opened his eyes. His breathing settled. His jaw, his fists, his whole body clenched tight. The room blurred through tears.

Lily had been everything to him: his world; his universe; his entire meaning on this giant ball of rock, spinning through eternal darkness. And she'd been taken from him. *Torn* from him.

That terrible injustice could not go unanswered any longer.

He'd kill for her; die for her.

Maybe one; perhaps the other.

Drayce took another shower, got dressed, and left the hotel room.

Time to find out which.

6

The walk through the city had warmed Drayce up. He shrugged off his wolf-grey ThruDark Hybrid jacket, tossed it over his arm, and knelt on one knee, pretending to tie the laces on his dark brown Altberg boots as he examined Jason Martin's front door from the pavement.

The address had been in the report Lucy had shown him, along with details of what had happened there. As Drayce had read it, vivid images of what had occurred appeared front and centre of his imagination, but now that he was stood right in front of the house, he had a far greater appreciation of the horror. There was a large stain on the doorstep, only just visible, like the faint shadow a man's figure might cast on a cloudy day. A shiny new Ring doorbell was fixed to the brickwork, with additional cameras and security lights mounted to the fascia; the words 'barn door' and 'already bolted' sprang to Drayce's mind. The front door was also new, the occasional thin slither of manufacturer's tape still dotted around the edges of the frame as it had been pulled off carelessly. The family had obviously felt a replacement was necessary.

Sometimes, you just can't get things clean enough.

Drayce stood up, put his jacket back on, and walked away. If Jason's family were in, he didn't want to risk activating their cameras, causing them to be frightened by a giant stranger staring at their front door. After what they'd been through, that sort of thing would terrify them. He continued up the street and examined the area carefully.

There was indeed just one camera, as Lucy had mentioned, which was easy enough to spot. It was mounted to the front aspect of a pub – The Tavern (how original) – at the end of the street, pointing down to the entrance. As Drayce got closer, the angle of the camera came more and more into focus. Yes, it was aiming at the pub's entrance, but it was also inadvertently aiming down the street, right towards Jason's front door. It looked new, perhaps installed in the last year or so. There was no weather damage, no mildew, no pigeon crap. It was wired in, so dead batteries couldn't be an excuse. It appeared expensive, too. Drayce recognised the company name on the sign mounted next to it. They were reputable. Strange for something like that to start giving up so early on in its existence. Especially unusual for it to stop working at such a critical moment.

Drayce reached for the handle. Locked. The door was old and wooden, carved at a time when things were made to last forever. It had been painted black to hide its age. Drayce banged on it with the bottom of his fist. An angry face appeared at an upstairs window of the pub, so briefly that if it wasn't for the swinging blinds, Drayce might have believed he'd imagined it.

A minute later he heard the door being unlocked. When it opened, Drayce was greeted by the same face from the window, whom he presumed to be the landlord. The man was wearing a black tracksuit, climbed into in a hurry. White labels flapped in the breeze, the top inside out. He realised his mistake as he moved to zip it up but was unable to. Turning the collar up around his neck would have to suffice. He shivered in the open doorway. His grey hair was buzzed short, so bedhead wasn't an issue, but the bags under his bloodshot eyes and the pillow creases across his unshaven cheek gave testament to him being woken up. He glared at Drayce, his top lip curling.

'The fuck d'you want?'

'The landlord. You him?'

'The fuck else would I be?'

'Certainly not the maître d', with that vocabulary.'

'You what?'

'It's French for… never mind. I need a quick word, if it's not too much trouble.'

'What about?'

Drayce flicked his head up. 'Your camera.'

That second word seemed to throw water over the flames, extinguishing his aggression. His top lip uncurled; his bottom one quivered. 'What about my camera?'

'Better off having this chat inside, if you don't mind.' Drayce smiled, trying to look friendly, but was aware it was charged with more hostility than charm. 'I just have a few questions. I won't need much of your time.'

The landlord hesitated then moved aside, allowing Drayce in. Drayce heard the door shut behind him, stealing the daylight from the gloomy interior. The blinds were closed, the LEDs from behind the bar the only illumination. It was a small place, made even smaller by the haphazard configuration of tables and chairs. Drayce turned, analysed the landlord's body language. He was wary, which was understandable; a man like Drayce turning up at your front door would make most people nervous. But Drayce's presence wasn't the only factor. The landlord had been aggressive to start with. It was only after Drayce had mentioned his camera that his attitude had changed. But why? Drayce was confident he knew, but it was time to find out for sure.

'What's your name?' Drayce asked.

More hesitation, a flap of his bottom lip, fingers twirling the drawstring on his tracksuit bottoms. 'Lenny.' He rested his fidgeting hands on his pot belly. 'My name's Lenny.'

'Lenny, you need a more creative name for this place. You might as well have called it "The Pub".'

Lenny shrugged. 'Not had the place long, have I. Only took over the tenancy last year.' He glanced around the dark, gloomy space. 'Work in progress, innit.' Lenny focused on Drayce. His eyes scanned up and down his body, assessing him as he nervously moved his weight from one foot to the other. 'Fucking big cunt aren't yer?'

'I've been called worse. Listen, I'm going to be completely honest and open with you, and I expect the same in return. Deal?'

Lenny nodded.

'In December last year, something very serious happened just down the road from here. Your camera would have caught it.'

'The murder? It weren't working. It—'

Drayce held up his hand, palm facing Lenny. 'Remember what I said about us being honest with each other?'

Lenny nodded, faster this time. 'Yeah, but…' He froze, eyes locked with Drayce. 'Wait, aren't you part of that other lot that came here?'

Just as Drayce had suspected. 'What other lot?'

Lenny closed his mouth, lips sealed tight, eyes full of worry. Drayce took a step closer to him, forcing him to back up until he hit the front door.

'Let me explain something to you,' Drayce said, close enough to smell Lenny's rotten morning breath. 'Because I think it's only fair you're put fully in the picture before you decide how you want to play this. I know your camera wasn't broken, and so do the police. They just can't prove it. Which leaves only two other possibilities for why there's no footage from the day of that murder. Option one is that this "other lot" who came here were bad men. Maybe they came in numbers. Perhaps they had weapons. Maybe they were blunt about it and put a gun in your mouth, or were subtler, and instead showed you pictures of unsuspecting family members going about their daily business. They threatened you, they terrified you, so you did as they asked, and switched off the camera. With me so far?'

Lenny's response was more a spasm than a nod.

'Option two, if it's true, is more of a problem,' Drayce said. 'You're one of them. Maybe they're the local villains, who pay you off from time to time to look the other way. Perhaps it's worse than that and you're on their payroll, full time, helping them cover up their criminality any way you can.' Drayce placed his palms on the door, either side of Lenny's head, and leaned in. Lenny had nowhere to go; he looked as though he was trying to melt into the wood. 'So, which is it, Lenny? Are you a victim, or a villain? And please think carefully before you answer. I help victims; I hurt villains.'

'The first one,' Lenny said, struggling to get the words out fast enough.

Drayce pushed off the door and stepped back. 'Who are they?'

'I don't know.' Lenny's top lip stuck to his teeth and folded back in on itself. He ran his tongue around his gums as though trying to generate some saliva. 'They woke me up one morning, about a week before that bloke down the street was killed, and wrote a date down on a little slip of paper. They told me to make sure my camera wasn't recording that day.' Lenny closed his dry mouth and swallowed, grimacing as he did so.

'Go get a glass of water,' Drayce said. 'It'll help.'

Lenny nodded, scurried around to the other side of the bar, and poured himself a shot of whisky. Not exactly what Drayce had recommended, but if it helped him talk, that was all that mattered.

'How many of them were there?' Drayce asked.

Lenny winced against the burn of the drink. 'Err, three of 'em, big fuckers like you, and they had guns 'n all. Look mate, I didn't know what they were gonna do. If I'd have known they were gonna kill some bloke, I'd never have done it.'

'Perhaps. Or maybe, if you'd known they were killers, you'd have been even more inclined to do as they asked. You don't seem the type who's willing to die hard.'

Lenny didn't reply to that.

'How precise was this note they gave you?' Drayce asked.

'Erm, well, I can show you if you like?'

'You kept it?'

'Yeah.'

Drayce waited; Lenny didn't move.

'Go get it,' Drayce snapped.

Lenny reached into a drawer underneath the till and came back with a yellow post-it note screwed up in his hand. Drayce took it off him and unravelled it. The date was first, then the bracket of time: six a.m. to eight a.m. It had been handwritten in black ink using a ballpoint pen, the letters thin with a diagonal slant.

'And this was written by one of them?' Drayce asked.

'Yeah. It's from my notepad, using my pen, but yeah, one've them lot wrote it.'

Drayce read it again. He was no expert, but he was confident it was a good enough sample of handwriting to link to an individual, as and when he had something to compare it to.

'Why did you keep it?' Drayce asked.

Lenny shrugged. 'Well, to begin with I wanted it as a reminder of when I needed to turn the camera off. Then afterwards I just screwed it up and threw it in that drawer, just in case they came back later and accused me of getting the timings wrong. I wanted to be able to show them that note and say "look 'ere, see that, that's what you asked me to do and I did it, so if I did wrong, it's only 'cos you told me wrong".'

Drayce stuffed the note in his pocket and glared at Lenny. 'Do you know how much all of this would have helped the police if you'd have been honest with them?'

'Yeah. I'm sorry. I just…' Lenny's thought process died off, replaced by more pressing considerations. 'Are you gonna show it to 'em?'

Drayce said nothing in response to that question. Instead, he asked one of his own. 'Did you look out of your window?'

'What?'

'You'd been threatened into turning your camera off during a very specific two-hour period. You must have been curious about what was going to happen on the street that they didn't want to be recorded.'

'Erm, well…'

Drayce spoke through clenched teeth. 'What did you see?'

Lenny puffed his chest out. 'Who said I saw anything?'

Drayce felt his face turn fierce as the red mist descended. He wasn't sure how much time passed – a few seconds at least – but when the mist cleared, he had Lenny up against the door by his throat. Lenny's heels clattered frantically against the wood as his legs dangled in the air, his arms flapping uselessly against the giant hands clamped firmly around his neck. His eyes began to bulge out of their sockets. When his face turned purple, Drayce let go. Lenny landed on his feet, bent forward, and had a coughing fit so violent it was a wonder an entire lung didn't fly out.

Drayce gave him a few seconds to get his breathing under control, then said, 'Get cocky with me again and your feet won't touch the ground until I'm happy you'll never take another breath. Got it?'

'All right, all right, fuckin' 'ell.' Tears ran down his cheeks, mucus down his chin. 'I looked out the window.'

'And?'

'I saw one geezer shoot another.'

Drayce took out his phone. With Lenny's level of descriptive talent, he'd need to take notes. 'What did the trigger man look like?'

Lenny stood up straight with his hands on his wheezing chest, but carried on staring at the ground, avoiding eye contact with Drayce.

'Don't go all shy on me, Lenny,' Drayce said.

'I don't want these people coming back. They said they would, if I ever talked to anyone. I don't want no trouble.'

'Bit late for that. You're an accomplice to a murder. You're already balls-deep in their world, fella.'

Lenny lifted his chin, eyes pleading. His hands left his chest and clapped together as if in prayer. 'Please don't tell the police what I did.'

'Listen—'

'They'll send me to prison. I can't go to prison.'

'Look—'

'This pub's my life. I don't wanna lose it. Got an ex-wife bleeding me dry, won't let me see the kids. Please mate, I can't handle no more—'

'Don't worry about the police,' Drayce said quickly, to stop Lenny interrupting him again. 'Worry about me.' He glared into Lenny's eyes. 'I want these men. I want all of them.' He raised his phone, hovered his thumb over the screen. 'What. Did. The. Trigger man. Look like?'

Lenny's eyes darted everywhere, his expression giving away how hard he was working to recall what he'd seen. 'Right, well, let me see. He was middle-aged, I'd say. Maybe early fifties. Perhaps late forties. Hard to tell.'

'Describe him.'

'I am doing.'

'No, you're not. What you're doing is giving me a very wide parameter of his age. So wide it's almost completely useless. I want to know what he looked like, his physical features. And the more specific you can be, the better.'

'I was getting to that.'

'Well get there quicker.'

'Fuck's sake.' Lenny sighed. 'Right, he was a white bloke with black hair. He was wearing a black coat and had a scarf wrapped around his face. Better so far?'

Drayce smiled. Once again, it was more menacing than friendly. 'Much.'

'Good, 'cos I'd hate to upset…' Lenny paused his sarcastic speech when Drayce balled his right hand into a fist. 'Anyway, that's about all I can remember. Oh, he seemed quite tall I guess, taller than your average bloke, anyway.'

'Picture him next to the guy he shot. Taller, or shorter?'

'Erm, taller, I'd say. But not much. Maybe only by a couple of inches. He looked well-built 'n all. But that might just have been the thick clothing he was wearing.'

'Tattoos? Scars? Anything unique about him?'

'It was fucking winter, mate. Freezing fucking cold. Geezer was wrapped up for Antarctica. His scarf did slip though. I did notice that.' Drayce stayed silent, not wanting to interrupt Lenny's thought process. 'He had a beard. Yeah, I remember that now. Big, black beard. And his nose looked kinda funny. Flat, like, you know? As though it'd been broken a few times.' He clicked his fingers, his eyes widening in a eureka moment. 'I'll tell you who he reminded me of. That baddie from one of the original Superman films. What was his name?… Non! That was it. Non from Superman Two. Geezer looked just like him.'

Drayce nodded as his fingers frantically tapped the screen. 'Anything else?'

'There was something wrong with one of his eyes. The left one, I think.'

'His left, or your left as you were looking at him?'

'Erm… his left.'

'What was wrong with it?'

'Hard to explain.'

Drayce's jaw clenched. 'Try.'

'It just kinda drooped a bit, you know? Like there was a line drawn down the whole thing, through his eyebrow and eyelids, to his cheekbone, pulling it all down, making it sag in the middle.'

'A scar?'

Lenny shrugged. 'Yeah, could have been. I was a distance away though. Hard to tell what it was.'

Drayce saved his notes. It was better than nothing, but he didn't want to keep piling the pressure on. Pretty soon either Lenny would start making things up on purpose to keep Drayce happy, or his mind would subconsciously fabricate an image that had never existed. Eyewitnesses are unreliable creatures. Time for a change of topic. He opened a new notes page.

'Right, let's move on. What about the three men who threatened you into turning off the camera?'

'What about them?'

Drayce frowned. 'Describe them.'

Lenny shrugged, his bottom lip curling out. 'Well, I could, but I don't have to.'

'And why's that?'

Lenny smiled, showing two rows of yellow teeth. ' 'Cos I got 'em on video.'

7

'Show me,' Drayce said.

Lenny led the way through a door behind the bar. Drayce followed him out of the reasonably presented public space of the pub and into the poorly maintained staff areas, his shoulders brushing against corridor walls stained yellow by cigarette smoke high up and blackened by rising damp low down above the skirting board. The wallpaper peeled back in several places. Drayce pivoted sideways to fit past several cardboard boxes full of packets of crisps and crates of soft drinks.

They turned a corner and went up a flight of stairs to a spare room, decorated with nothing but a bed with a bare mattress, and a chair pushed up to a wooden table which had a computer monitor, keyboard, and mouse on it. Wires trailed down the chipboard wallpaper and across the dirty beige carpet to a computer tower. The monitor's screen was on, split into four segments, each quarter offering a different view. The top two were feeds from cameras mounted outside; the bottom two from ones indoors. Drayce recognised the top right to be from the camera at the front. Top left showed a beer garden at the back of the pub, and the bottom two both overlooked the bar and seating area from different angles. Drayce watched Lenny take a seat at the desk and place a hand on the mouse.

'The outdoor ones are big and obvious,' Lenny said. He pointed a finger at the bottom two feeds. 'But these are hidden. I wanted to have cameras inside for the safety of me and my staff after we had to bar a couple of local meatheads, but I had to hide 'em in the end, 'cos having 'em big 'n obvious was too much bother. Nearly cost me some business, truth be told. A lot of the regulars weren't comfortable having a camera pointed at 'em when they were tryin'a wind down in their local boozer.'

'Understandable.'

Lenny clicked on a search bar and typed in a date and time. 'After they left, I saved the footage, just in case the coppers rumbled what I done. Then I could show 'em this and say "look 'ere, I was threatened. Had no choice".' He smiled at Drayce, as though he expected him to be impressed with how he planned to shirk his responsibility for the part he played in Jason Martin's murder.

'We always have a choice,' Drayce replied.

Lenny's smile fell off his face. He turned back to the screen and tapped the return key.

The four quadrants changed to the time and date Lenny had specified back in December of the previous year. The angles were identical, presumably because the cameras hadn't been touched since. But the details were different. Outside there was snow on the ground. Not much, just the icy compacted stuff left on the pavements where the grit and salt hadn't reached. The entire scene was dull, no doubt due to the whitewashed cloudy December sky. It was as if the contrast had been turned down in the way you can with your television, sucking the colour out of the screen. Inside, the tables and chairs were in different positions, as far as Drayce could tell, but other than that the recorded footage from the internal cameras wasn't much different to the present-day feed.

Apart from the three men.

Lenny was right: they were big. One stood directly in front of him with piercing eyes, jabbing a finger on his chest, his facial muscles contorted and his lips snarling as he conveyed the necessary threats. The other two were stood either side of Lenny, staring down at him, heads nodding with each finger jab. There was no sound. The whole scene played out like a silent movie.

'That's them,' Lenny said, as though it wasn't obvious.

Drayce assessed the trio. The one giving the speech appeared to be in charge; he had that aura about him. From the way he towered over Lenny, Drayce put him in the five ten- to six-foot category. Similar for the other two. They had the physiques of strong men, even when Drayce factored in the extra bulk from their big winter coats. He watched the recording play out, saw them shuffle their feet, move their heads, and generally alter their positions every few seconds. No one stays perfectly still; it's not natural. Drayce bided his time, waiting for the right moment.

'Pause it there,' he said.

Lenny did as he was told, but he was too slow.

'Can you skip back, frame by frame?' Drayce asked.

'Course.'

The footage juddered slightly with every click of the mouse, reversing back to the spot Drayce had seen.

'Stop there,' Drayce said.

He reached in front of Lenny's face and took a snap of the paused recording with his phone. He stared at each of them in turn, taking his time. Having a photo of them was useful, but he wanted to commit them to memory, so he'd recognise them in a heartbeat when he eventually tracked them down.

'Think any of these men could be the trigger man?' Drayce asked.

Lenny shook his head vehemently, as though he'd already spent some time thinking that question through. 'No chance. They don't look anything like him. And they don't even have beards.'

Drayce kept his eyes on the screen; if he looked at Lenny, he might not be able to resist the urge to slap him.

'Maybe our shooter had enough wherewithal to disguise his usual appearance by purchasing a fake one?'

The room went silent, nothing to hear but the hum of the fans in the computer tower.

'Well, yeah,' Lenny began. 'Course. But even without the beard, none of them look right. I mean, the shooter had jet black hair, for a start.' His chubby index finger wagged at the screen. 'The geezer barking at me's got short brown hair, the one to my right's blond and swept back like he's in a boy band, and the other's some sort of gingery colour. Don't fit the image I remember, mate.'

'Heard of hair dye?' Drayce asked.

Lenny went silent.

'What about accents?' Drayce asked, pinching the flesh between his eyes.

'Scouse,' Lenny replied, in his most confident tone yet.

'All three?'

Lenny nodded. 'Yep.'

Drayce made a note of that in his phone. Even a man like Lenny would struggle to mistake a scouse accent for another.

'Strong? Slight?'

'As fucking scouse as I am cockney, mate. Them cunts made John Bishop sound like Roger Moore.'

'I've been meaning to ask: what *is* a cockney doing running a pub in Islington?'

'We do move around yer know? We're not fucking oak trees, mate.'

Drayce smiled.

'I'm assuming none of them were stupid enough to mention their names?' Drayce asked, to bring the conversation back on track.

Lenny met his gaze. 'You assume right.'

Drayce nodded. 'All right. I think I've got everything I need.'

He put his phone away and walked out of the room, confident there wasn't much else to be gained from talking to Lenny, who hurried after him, his little legs jogging to keep up as they descended the stairs.

'What you gonna do with that note?' Lenny asked. 'You ain't gonna give it to the coppers are ya? Please, mate. I'm begging.'

Drayce stopped when he got to the front door and turned to face him. 'Yes, I can tell. You should do less of it.' Lenny frowned, his eyes lost. Drayce pressed on. 'That note's staying with me until I've found those three men. As soon as that happens, I'll burn it. Sound good?'

Lenny's eyes shifted as his brain processed his options. He nodded.

'Good,' Drayce said. 'Believe me, Lenny, I don't want the police involved in my plans any more than you do.' He noticed the marks around Lenny's throat. 'And for what it's worth, I'm sorry I put my hands on your neck.' He turned, opened the door, and stepped into the daylight. 'If it makes you feel any better, you got off lightly compared to what I've got planned for the three scousers.'

8

On Berkeley Street, Mayfair, in an office overlooking the dancefloor of his nightclub, Daniel Sullivan walked the room, holding court, all eyes on him. The thick pile rug silenced his footsteps, as though he was gliding around the other seven men who were sat at the oval glass table in the centre of the room, its surface mirroring the glittering mass of light from the chandelier above. He fidgeted with the buttons on his suit, which had been cut by the best tailor in London; by deduction, the best tailor in the world. The dark-brown wool followed the curves of Sullivan's body to perfection, a suit of armour, making him feel like a king.

'You've got nothing to worry about, gentlemen,' he said. 'Your investment has never been safer.'

He paused at the floor-to-ceiling window and admired the group of dancers who were practising for the private party being held there that night. Each girl was wearing a comfy tracksuit as they clung to, spun around, and slid down the poles that were scattered around the venue. Their high-heeled footwear hinted at the kind of outfits they'd be wearing later. No point practising a dance routine in anything other than the shoes you'll be wearing for the performance, he'd been told. He promised himself he'd find the time to enjoy a drink from that same vantage point in several hours when the doors opened and they were performing their routines wearing significantly less. Most of the girls he knew well, but a couple were new. He'd invite them up to his office at the end of the night, pour them some drinks, let them know what he expects of them: the perks of being the boss. He blinked hard, pulling his mind back into the room.

'We're going from strength to strength,' he said as he turned back to the seven men and resumed his circuit. 'The money you put into the operation three years ago is now worth more than five times what it was. And can anyone at this table remember a time when a single quarterly pay-out was missed?' He stopped behind his seat at the head of the table and met the stern eyes of the men he was addressing. 'Didn't think so. And they'll only continue to increase as we develop closer bonds with the Chinese. You'd be crazy to pull out now.'

'The risks you're taking are what's crazy.' This from John Ryan, three seats down the table on Sullivan's right, his scruffy jeans and decades-old leather jacket camouflaging his true wealth. He was unshaven, three days at least, his cheeks coated in salt and pepper stubble. His thinning hair was a similar shade, although it was edging closer to the grey end of the spectrum with every day that passed. Sullivan had always thought him to be a scruffy bastard. What was the point in being a high-ranking multimillionaire in the biggest Organised Crime Group in Liverpool if you weren't going to enjoy the trappings.

'It's a miracle you're still a free man,' John said as he glanced at the others, then back at Sullivan. 'It's a miracle we all are after the way you've behaved.'

Sullivan gently patted his blow-dried hair with both hands, freshly dyed the night before, checking it was as it should be: swept back on the sides, a large flowing quiff on top. He smiled to appear relaxed. The strain he felt in his facial muscles suggested it conveyed the opposite. 'Risks are a necessary part of our business, John. You know that.'

'But too much risk is detrimental.' John waved a fat, hairy finger in Sullivan's direction. 'You need to be more subtle in the way you operate, and not so flamboyant for Christ's sake. This club; the fancy suits; the gold watches. Tone it down, Daniel. You do good work, but you're at risk of becoming an embarrassment to us.'

Sullivan felt his body's temperature spike. 'That so, John?'

'You know it is.'

Sullivan gauged the reaction of the others. 'Is that how you all feel?'

A wave of nods and agreeable murmurs came back at him.

'We operate in the shadows for good reasons,' John said. 'And the way you react to things shines a light on us all. Killing the bizzies, for fuck's sake! What were you thinking?'

'I was thinking I wanted business to flourish, not wither. The way I react is what's kept my operations in this city afloat. You do things how you want up north, John, but London belongs to me. In case you'd forgotten, three and a half years ago the "bizzies", as you call them, caught wind of a unit I was running in Islington. If I hadn't responded to the police investigation in the way I had, they'd have carried on gathering evidence against me, linked our joint north–south operation, and we'd all have been finished.'

'*Responded to the police investigation?* That how you describe having one of them stabbed to death in the street, is it?'

'She'd have brought my entire empire down. I had to get rid of her.'

'And how d'you think the bizzies will react now another of their own is dead?'

'They'll continue doing what they do best: scratching their heads, hoping the killer lands in their lap.'

'Don't be so naive, Daniel!'

'It's been four months, John.' Sullivan held up as many fingers to the men at the table to emphasise his point. 'Four whole months and they've got nothing. If they had any evidence worth a damn, we'd already be in prison. We got away with the first one three and a half years ago, and we'll get away with this one. There was nothing else for it, John. He was getting too close and had to go, just like the first.' He lowered his hand and locked eyes with his northern counterpart, daring him to rock the boat again. 'You invested in me for a reason: I run this fucking city. I decide what comes in and out. We've all been in this together from the beginning, getting rich, and gaining power and influence along the way. All of us have blood on our hands. I've lost count of the bodies we've left behind. Adding a couple of London pigs to the tally doesn't matter one fucking bit. They're only a problem when they're alive, sniffing around. Dead, they're an irrelevance.'

'When we went into business together, we agreed assassinations would come to everyone at this table first, for approval.' John's face reddened. He was almost out of his seat. 'This is the second time you've taken it upon yourself to leave me out of the decision!'

A single knock on the door made all seven heads turn. Sullivan knew who it was by the tone, which was always the same: the type of ominous sound the Grim Reaper might make as he rapped his knuckles against a victim's door. Perhaps his knock was how the man got his nickname, although Sullivan suspected it was for other reasons.

'Excuse me,' Sullivan said, grateful he'd been given a reason to step out of the room.

The man he'd expected was stood facing him on the other side of the door, wearing a black suit and tie. Sullivan shut the door behind him and gestured for Reaper to walk down the steps with him to the floor below, far enough to be certain they couldn't be overheard by the men in the office.

'Problem?' Sullivan asked as they paused in the empty corridor.

Reaper's left eye drooped from an old knife wound. He stroked his dark beard, three lines of scar tissue visible on the back of his hand. 'There might be.'

'Explain.'

'I've just had a phone call from the landlord of The Tavern in Islington.'

Sullivan's irritation transformed into worry in a heartbeat. 'And?'

'He's had a visitor. Some big fella asking questions about the camera.' Reaper checked over both shoulders. 'He mentioned the job.'

'What about it?'

'He wanted to know if the camera had recorded it.'

'And what did the landlord tell him?'

'Same thing he told the police, so he says. It's broken. Technical glitch. Happens from time to time.'

'You believe him?'

Reaper shrugged. 'He's not brave enough to fuck us around without a serious incentive, and I can't see how one man could outweigh the threat we pose. But it's possible he might have told him something he shouldn't have.'

Sullivan frowned. 'He know anything about this man?'

'Not a thing, so he says. Gave me a decent enough description of him, though. Sounds as though he'd stand out in a crowd.'

'When did this happen?'

'Just now. The landlord called me as soon as the man left. If we hurry, we might catch him on the street.'

Sullivan put his hands in his pockets. His eyes traced the pattern in the polished oak floorboards as he thought through his options. 'Who'd you use for the original visit about the camera, before you did the job?'

'Sean, Ronan, and Liam.'

Sullivan met Reaper's eyes, the iris as dark as tar. 'John Ryan's lads? From Liverpool?'

'That's them.'

'They're good boys.'

'That they are.'

'They still in London?'

Reaper nodded. 'I sorted them out with a place to stay and told them to stay close for a few months. Said we might need them again.'

'Call them. Tell them what this man looks like. Then tell them I want him found. I want to know who he is and why he's asking questions.'

'You not want me to do it?' Reaper's tongue flicked out between his teeth and licked his lips, a darkness revealing itself in his eyes. 'I'd enjoy bleeding him for information.'

Sullivan regarded his assassin with concern, a tiger in an old, battered cage, the bars fractured, close to buckling, a loss of control possible at any moment.

'No,' Sullivan told him, his stern gaze hopefully enough to make the wild man heel. 'I want them to do it. They're not linked to me directly, and I like to keep you for the most important jobs only. But you're to give them their instructions and see to it those instructions are carried out precisely. Understood?'

Reaper's disappointment was unmistakeable. 'Understood.'

Sullivan jerked a thumb behind him. 'There are some nervous shites in that room for me to contend with. I need smooth waters, at least until they feel confident enough to fuck off back up north and leave us alone to run our city by ourselves.' He jabbed a finger on Reaper's chest. It felt hard and cold, like stone in winter. 'And when problems do rear their ugly heads, it's your job to ensure they're cut off. You hear me?'

Reaper nodded. 'I hear you. You concentrate on the business; I'll see to it this man, whoever he is, is dealt with.'

Sullivan nodded back, checked his tie was straight, then turned around, forced another smile onto his face, and walked back into the room to resume the diplomacy.

9

Drayce sat at a table outside The Tavern. Back to the wall, he faced the pavement. He stared at his phone, at the photograph of the three men who'd threatened Lenny into turning his camera off the day Jason was murdered, and realised he was contemplating a fork in the road. One direction was as clear as day, leading down the official path where he'd hand the image over to the police. But that path was long and steep, a slow climb. Days, maybe weeks of enquiries; tight lips, closed doors, no comments. The other direction was the unofficial path, which was dark and dangerous, cliff edges on either side, jagged rocks and alligators at the bottom of the drop. But it was much shorter, tempting Drayce to take the risk for a faster result.

Lenny had been confident that none of the men in the photo was the man he'd seen murder Jason. But those men would know the murderer, Drayce was sure of that. And even if they didn't, they were certainly a link in the chain of people who had conspired to have Jason killed, a chain Drayce could follow all the way back to the killer.

Lily's killer.

Drayce shivered despite the bright sun, his adrenaline kicking in again. He dropped his phone in his pocket and focused on his breathing. No point getting riled up yet. It was early days. There was too much work to do for him to be heating up this soon in the game. He took in his surroundings while he calmed himself. The street was alive with the morning's activity. A group of mums crossed the road with their kids in pushchairs; a bright yellow commuter cycled past, his GoPro mounted on his helmet like a periscope; an Amazon Prime van raced around the corner, the driver constantly switching his gaze between the road and his sat nav.

A black Mercedes pulled up to the kerb.

It stopped with a sense of urgency, right in front of where Drayce was sat. He heard the ABS kick in. The windows were tinted, but thanks to the beaming sunshine, he could tell there were three men inside, their heads tilted in his direction. He got the sense their lips were moving, a conversation being had; something serious, Drayce felt, considering how fast they'd come to a halt. Heads nodded, the trio coming to an agreement. The burbling engine cut out. Doors opened.

All three got out at the same time, each pair of eyes staring at Drayce as they did so, brows furrowed, eyebrows crooked, as though they were each contending with a complex mathematical equation they needed to work out.

Is it, or isn't it? Drayce imagined them thinking as they assessed him.

They stepped onto the pavement, lined up side by side no more than five feet in front of Drayce, giving him a proper view of their faces. If forced to guess, he'd put all three in their late twenties. He took out his phone, brought up the photo of the three Liverpudlians, and held it up to compare.

Well, isn't that interesting.

He put his phone away and waited for their introduction.

'You been inside that pub there have you, big fella?'

This from the guy on the left. He wasn't as big as he'd looked on camera, but he was set with thick muscles, his neck even wider than his head, like Mike Tyson in his prime. He wore a grey sweater with an ugly swirling pattern on it similar to a set of curtains from the seventies, his black jeans ripped at the knees. He was a mess, but the outfit had probably cost him a fortune – Drayce had never understood fashion. The guy's hair was dark brown, shaved close at the sides and left bushy on top in a tangle of curls. His nervous transference of weight from one foot to the other made a couple of the strands bounce off his forehead continuously. He had the appearance of the world's most ridiculous model.

'I asked you a fucking question.'

Drayce looked him in the eye. 'I heard you.' He glanced behind him at the pub door, frowned, then turned back to the trio. 'Lenny called you, did he?'

'So what if he did?' the man in the middle asked. He was the biggest of the three, but only just. He'd opted for the opposite end of the fashion spectrum to his model friend: a tightly fitted tracksuit, the white tick on the leg and trainers the only addition to the otherwise all black outfit. He had a face full of red stubble, almost long enough to qualify as a beard. From a distance it could be mistaken for sunburn.

'I'll have to buy him a gift,' Drayce said. 'Something to say thank you.'

'Come again?'

'For calling you. He's saved me a lot of work. Might have taken me all day to track you down otherwise.' Drayce took out his phone again, opened the photo, and tilted the screen in their direction. 'You boys made a big mistake.'

The three men exchanged a look.

'What business is it of yours?' the one on the right asked as he adjusted his black leather biker jacket. His face was ghostly white, and there was only a couple of inches of forehead separating his dark eyebrows and his closely shaved head of hair. He was a barrel of a thing, the sort of burly, squat physique that would get some real speed up if he were rolled down a hill. He reminded Drayce of Uncle Fester.

'I wanted to know why he turned his camera off,' Drayce said as he put his phone away again. 'If he hadn't, it would have recorded a man's murder.' He eyeballed each of them in turn. 'Might have been good enough to identify the killer if he didn't do as you asked.'

'I suppose,' Tracksuit said. 'The victim a friend of yours, was he?'

Drayce shook his head. 'No.'

The model took a step forward. 'Then why the interest?'

'It's more than an interest.'

'How so?'

'I want the life of the man who pulled the trigger.'

Uncle Fester slipped a hand inside his jacket. When it reappeared, the knuckle duster glinted in the sun. 'You'll get fuck all and be grateful.'

'Ah, good,' Drayce said. 'I was getting bored of the flirting. Was hoping things would start to progress.'

'You're not asking any more questions about that murder, you hear?' Tracksuit said. 'You're done.'

Drayce grinned. 'I've not even started yet.'

The expressions on all three faces contorted into angry scowls. The niceties were over. The model and Uncle Fester moved with brazen arrogance, blocking Drayce in on either side of his table. Tracksuit stayed where he was and lifted his top. The wooden handle of a machete poked out of his waistband.

'We're sending you packing, big fella,' the model said. 'And we'll make sure you're in no state to come back.'

Drayce assessed the situation. The duster was closest to him, but the machete was the real threat, hence why he'd deal with Tracksuit first. Drayce glanced down at the table legs: they weren't attached to the bench he was sitting on.

'Hand over your phone,' Uncle Fester said.

Drayce gripped the table from underneath. 'No.'

Tracksuit took a step closer, the front of his thighs now just a few inches from the table.

'You'll do as you're told!' Tracksuit shouted. 'Or I'll chop you into pieces you bastard!'

The table levitated just as Tracksuit's hand moved to the machete's handle. Drayce curled it up into his chest and launched off the bench, ramming it into Tracksuit's waist, pinning the weapon to the man's body as he drove him backwards and slammed him against the Mercedes, rocking the vehicle on its springs.

With the model in easy reach, Drayce slammed an elbow into his chest to give him something to think about, then turned to face Uncle Fester and clenched his fists, unloading on him before he could bring the duster into play. A couple of blows glanced off Drayce's chest and shoulder, but he was too busy going to work to feel them. He cut Fester below both eyes with jabs, buckled him in half with a straight right to the body, then put him down with a left hook to the temple.

Drayce heard the table legs scrape across the concrete behind him. He spun around. Tracksuit was trying to push it away with help from the model, who was pulling from the other side. While the model's hands were full of table, Drayce ran at him and slammed an elbow into his neck at full stride, dropping him like a stone. A swift kick to the edge of the tabletop ensured Tracksuit stayed pinned to the Mercedes. Drayce glared at him and his desperate attempts to pull the machete free, then placed his hands on the edge of the tabletop, ground the balls of his feet into the pavement, and drove forward with all his weight.

Tracksuit winced, a strand of spittle spilling out from the corner of his mouth. His face was red, his expression pained. Sweat poured down his face. Drayce knew the pressure of the table driving into his soft tissue must be painful, but even so, it seemed an overreaction. A thin trail of blood trickled out from under the table and diverted several times as it collided with the numerous cracks in the pavement. Tracksuit must have cut his own leg during his efforts to free the massive blade from his trousers. Drayce pushed the table a little harder, driving the wedged blade even deeper into his flesh.

'The shooter's name,' he demanded.

Tracksuit took a few rapid, shallow breaths, then managed to reply, 'Go. Fuck. Yourself.'

Sirens started somewhere in the distance. Drayce saw a few curtains twitch. The odd face or two appeared momentarily at upstairs windows. The affray had caught the eyes of the pub's neighbours. One of them had obviously dialled three nines. Question time was over.

'Suit yourself,' Drayce said to Tracksuit. 'We'll be seeing each other again soon enough.'

Drayce reached across the table, took a handful of Tracksuit's neck, and squeezed his carotid arteries until the man's eyes rolled back into his head and his upper body slumped onto the table. Drayce stepped back and assessed the volume of the sirens: wouldn't be long before the police showed up. A day or two in custody would spoil his plans. Better get to work.

He hurriedly searched all three men. On the model he found a bank card in the name of Sean Maack, on Tracksuit he found a driver's licence in the name of Ronan Kelly, and in Uncle Fester's jacket pocket was a credit card in the name of Liam Walsh. He pocketed all three, took out his phone and made a note of the names as he walked around the Mercedes, opened the driver's door, and peered inside. A mobile phone was perched upright in one of the cup holders. Drayce took it, knowing there'd likely be communications on there with the next link in the chain. He illuminated the screen: Enter PIN. An idea took shape for how he could get around that obstacle.

The sirens were loud now, maybe only a few streets away. Drayce walked calmly so as not to draw attention to himself, leaving the three men squirming as they regained consciousness. Flashing blue lights reflected off windows up ahead. He ducked down an alleyway to get off the street. Just before he vanished out of sight, he took a quick glance behind to see Liam 'Fester' Walsh and Sean 'The Model' Maack bundle Ronan 'Tracksuit' Kelly into the back of the Mercedes and drive off.

Probably for the best, Drayce thought. Questioning them again would be much harder if they were in police custody. He backed away, deeper into the shadows of the alley, saved the notes he'd made on his phone, then switched to the keypad, and took out Lucy's business card.

10

The cafe in Covent Garden was busy, just as Drayce had hoped. He was sitting with his back against the wall, at a table in the corner of the room, with a view of the entrance. He'd ordered a steak with his coffee, not because he was particularly hungry – it was only eleven a.m. – but because it came with a sharp knife. He'd asked for an ashtray, which he'd seen other customers clutching on to as they smoked outside, not because he smoked, but instead because it was a heavy lump of glass that would get through several skulls before it broke.

That little skirmish outside the pub had changed things. He'd chosen his path, no going back. They knew his face, and next time it wouldn't be dusters and blades, it'd be guns and twice the number of bodies. It was imperative he be careful from now on.

Lucy arrived on time, as Drayce knew she would; an FLO never kept their families waiting. He first saw her when she passed the big glass windows, and waved as she walked inside. His smile was reciprocated, but there was an effort to it. He wondered if his blunt ending to their introduction at Islington nick was to blame for her perceived hostility, but then he saw faint smudges of mascara around her cheekbones. She'd been crying. There was evidently some trouble in her life.

'Thanks for meeting with me at such short notice,' he said as she approached the table. He stood and pulled her chair out for her.

'No problem. It's my job.'

'Fair point. Listen, I'm sorry I was sharp with you when we parted ways earlier this morning.'

'It's fine,' Lucy said as she sat down. She kept her coat on even though it was warm in there and held onto her handbag, which she clutched on her lap: the body language of someone who wanted this meeting over with as soon as possible. 'You're going through a lot. And believe me, I've had a lot worse from other victim's families.'

Drayce sat back down. 'I'm sure you have, but nonetheless, I was out of order walking out the way I did.'

'Really, it's fine. What did you want to discuss?'

'Can I get you a coffee first? You hungry?' He gestured at the fatty remains of his steak. 'I've already eaten, but—'

'Just a coffee would be lovely, thank you.'

Drayce stood up. 'What sort? They've got a list of about a hundred on the wall, and the guy on the till looks as though he takes his job very seriously, so I should probably at least try to sound as though I know what I'm talking about when I go up and order.'

She smiled. 'A flat white, please.'

Drayce walked up to the barista and ordered two flat whites, but apparently it wasn't as simple as that. Questions were fired back at him regarding his choice of coffee origin and type of milk, along with several more in relation to a variety of optional syrups and spices. He told the guy he didn't care where the coffee was from, and he wanted good old-fashioned cow's milk, pointing out that the other 'milks' on offer – almond, oat, soy – were juices.

'Juices?' the barista asked.

'Yeah. I mean, think about it.' In response to the confused look on the barista's face, Drayce said, 'Almonds don't have nipples.'

The barista regarded him with disgust and hurriedly began making his order, presumably to be rid of the strange giant as soon as possible. When the coffees arrived, Drayce carried them back to the table. Lucy had taken off her coat and slung it over the back support of her chair, her handbag now propped up on the table.

'Here you go,' he said.

'Thank you.' She dropped a sugar cube into her drink and stirred it. 'So, what did you want to discuss. Not much has changed since we first met. I still can't tell you anything that wasn't in the report I showed you.'

Drayce took a deep breath. 'Actually, it has nothing to do with Lily's murder.'

Lucy stilled the spoon, silencing the tinkle of metal against ceramic. Her eyes locked onto his. 'Oh?'

'I wondered if you'd do me a favour.'

She let go of the spoon entirely. The handle rattled against the lip of the mug. She folded her arms. 'What sort of favour?'

Drayce took out the phone he stole from the heavies' Mercedes. 'A friend gave me this just before I called you. It's her husband's. He's out of the house until noon and forgot to take it with him, so she grabbed it and called me, wanting my help.'

'Help with what?'

'It has a PIN lock on it. She wants to get past it and knows I'm ex-Job, so she thought I might be able to unlock it for her, or might at least know someone who could.'

Lucy's eyelids narrowed; it appeared she could smell his bull-shit.

'I'm not sure I like where this is going,' she said.

'Just hear me out. My friend suspects her husband's cheating on her, has done for months, but he normally takes his phone everywhere with him. This is the first chance she's had of interrogating the device.' Drayce made a play of checking his watch. 'He'll be back home in less than an hour.'

Lucy placed her palms on the tabletop and stood up. 'You dragged me here for this?'

'Listen, I'm sorry I didn't tell you why—'

'You lied.'

'Not exactly. I told you I wanted to discuss something with you. I never mentioned the case.'

'Oh my God,' Lucy hissed as she pulled her coat off the back support and turned to leave, toppling the chair over as she hurried to the exit.

Drayce darted around the table. 'Wait a second. Let me finish.' He followed her outside, ignored the rubberneckers at the other tables, and ran ahead to cut her off. 'I'm sorry, but I needed to explain it face to face.'

'I'm not interested,' she said, as she shrugged her coat on and side stepped to go around him.

He mirrored her like a dancer to keep her path blocked. 'You might be when you've heard what I have to say.'

She folded her arms. 'You know I can't just hack into someone's phone for you. It would be illegal. If anyone found out—'

'Nobody would.'

She avoided eye contact with him. He gave it a couple of seconds, then said, 'She's been desperate to catch him out for years. She's in a horrible situation.'

'Well then she should leave.'

'It's not that simple, and you know it. Not with the house, and the kids. She wants evidence of his infidelity to put in front of her solicitor before she escapes, because it'll give her more power in the divorce proceedings.'

'None of this is my problem.'

'The cheating isn't the only reason she needs to get out of the relationship.' Drayce let the implication of that sentence hang thick in the air. 'He's never been a pleasant man, but things are getting worse. He controls all the money, tells her who she can and can't see, tells her what to wear, what to eat, what to do.' He held up the phone. 'I don't want her to be dissuaded from leaving him just because she can't get past his PIN. If she continues down the road she's travelling on, she'll be a serious victim one day. I'm trying to stop that from happening.'

Lucy looked at the phone, then she met Drayce's gaze. 'I don't appreciate being emotionally blackmailed.'

'I understand that, and I'm sorry I've resorted to coming to you with this, but I'm just trying to do what's right.'

Lucy didn't reply. She unfolded her arms and placed her hands on her hips, defiant, and just as frosty as before. The look on her face said *Keep pushing it and see what happens, mate.*

'You can have this thing unlocked in five minutes back at the station,' Drayce said. 'No one ever has to know.'

She stuck her neck out and glared at him. 'Not happening.'

Drayce lowered the phone and rubbed the stubble on his cheek as he evaluated her body language. She was tough; no way would she budge with his current tactic. He needed a different angle.

'What if I were to do you a favour in exchange?' he asked.

'I don't need any favours.'

'Perhaps *need* isn't the right word, but I think you could use one.'

'What are you talking about?'

He flicked his eyes down at her left hand. 'There's a very slight indentation around your ring finger.' She quickly glanced down at her hand, clearly shocked he'd noticed. 'I saw it when you spread the report out in front of me back at the station. On its own it wouldn't mean much; lots of people take off their engagement rings and wedding rings at work. But then your phone repeatedly buzzed with messages, and you appeared desperate to read them, did read one, in fact, so I knew it wasn't work related, because you'd ignore work stuff during an FLO meeting. Which means those messages were clearly of a personal nature, and were obviously stressing you out, making them difficult to ignore. Then I saw the red mark on your neck, which is the sort of friction injury clothing leaves behind when someone grabs hold of you and drags you around.'

Lucy's hand shot up to her neck, covering the mark.

'And then you turn up to our meeting here in this cafe with marks where your mascara has run,' Drayce continued.

Lucy's other hand moved up to her face, furiously wiping her cheeks with her palm.

'Maybe I'm wrong,' Drayce said. 'But I'd say you've been through a violent relationship, and now you're going through a nasty divorce.'

Lucy stuffed her hands into her pockets and eyeballed him, defiance personified. 'So what?'

'Like I said, I can help you. Maybe your ex is the arsehole, or perhaps you're both being as difficult as one another. I don't care which. I just want this phone unlocked, and I'm willing to do you a favour to make that happen.'

Lucy stayed silent for a moment, as though weighing up her options. Drayce gave her all the time she needed.

'What kind of favour?' she eventually asked.

'You're a cop; I used to be one. We've both seen how devastatingly painful domestic situations can be made by an angry, vengeful partner. I'm going to go out on a limb and say your ex is a he, and that he's the problem, making the process as difficult as possible, for no other reason than because he's a spiteful arsehole. Stop me if I get something wrong.'

Lucy said nothing.

'This ex of yours is behaving the way he is, partly because it's in his nature, but also because he has nothing to fear.' Drayce watched Lucy's face carefully as he tested the water with each sentence, feeding off her reaction to his guesswork as he tried to find where the truth lay. 'I'm guessing he's the one with the chips stacked in his favour. Wealthy family? Expensive solicitors? Made life together unbearable until you moved out, giving him control of the home you jointly own?'

Lucy didn't reply, but it was clear he was on the right track.

'If any of that's true,' Drayce continued, 'then the chips are all stacked in his favour, and if he's the malevolent sort, he'll sit back, take his time, and watch you suffer. I'm offering you a way to switch the dynamics of your dying relationship. You don't have to be the one in fear.'

Lucy lifted her chin. Drayce saw her chest expand as she took a deep breath.

'Explain,' she demanded.

'I'm offering to pay him a visit, to explain to him that it's in his best interests to give you a clean break so you can move on with your life.'

Lucy frowned. 'Are you saying what I think you're saying?'

'I need this phone unlocked; you need your ex out of your life.' Drayce watched Lucy's eyes drop to the phone, then flash back up at him, as though tossing it around inside her mind. Nearly there. 'Let's help each other.'

Lucy took her hands out of her pockets and let them hang either side of her waist. Drayce lifted the phone up again, like a baited hook, and waited for the bite. She moved a hand towards it.

'I'm willing to forget this conversation.' Lucy punched her hand past the phone and jabbed a finger in his face. 'Only because of who you are and what you've been through. But don't you ever step over the line again.'

She barged past him and marched down the street. Drayce put the phone back in his pocket and watched her go, knowing it was pointless trying to stop her again.

–

Lucy walked as fast as she could, weaving around other pedestrians, huffing and puffing with exertion and anger until she turned a corner and was out of Alex's sight. She fumbled inside her handbag for the pack of wet wipes she always carried with her, pulled three out at once, and stared at her reflection in a shop window as she furiously wiped her cheeks.

'How dare he,' she muttered to herself. 'How fucking *dare* he!'

She couldn't tell if the wipes were making a difference or not because the reflection wasn't great, but she used all three and rubbed as hard as she could. Finished, she balled them up together and threw the wet lump into the nearest bin, overhand, whipping some real sting in its tail. She lifted her shirt collar to make sure the mark was covered.

Was she really that transparent? She'd spent half an hour with the man, half a fucking hour, and he'd read her like a book: the ring; the mark; the messages; the tears. She'd always complained men hadn't taken enough notice of her, paid enough attention to her, but this was taking the piss. Then there was his request to unlock his friend's phone, something she could get into real trouble for if anyone found out. Not that she'd ever seriously consider the notion. Why would she? What did she care if his friend was stuck in a bad relationship?

Join the club, sister.

And as cheeky – no, cheeky didn't do it justice – as fucking-bold-as-brass as his first attempt had been, it was his last that had spooked her the most: his offer to 'pay' Barnaby 'a visit'. But the shiver she felt down her spine after he said those words, and the cold dread that had seeped through her pores, wasn't because he'd offered to threaten violence towards her ex to get him to back off.

It was because she'd nearly accepted.

She began walking again, wanting to get further away from Alex before she was tempted to go back. She crossed three junctions. Her phone buzzed. She took it out of her handbag, still surprised it worked with a cracked screen. She opened the message. It was from Barnaby. No text. Just an image. She tapped on it and stepped to the side of the pavement as it downloaded. What could it be? Scanned copies of the divorce papers, ideally. It opened, blurry at first, then in razor-sharp focus in the blink of an eye.

It can't be.

The bastard. The evil fucking bastard.

The ballerina figurine she'd asked to have back, which had been given to her by her grandma, who had paid for her first pair of ballet shoes and tutu when she was six years old, and watched every class, smiling the whole way through, lay smashed in pieces, on the tiled floor of the kitchen in the house Lucy once shared with a monster. A laughing emoji was superimposed on the top right corner of the photo. Lucy's hand shook, gently at first, then so powerfully it made her drop her phone. She didn't move to pick it up, just stood there, absorbing the pain, determined not to cry in public. The seizure faded, then her whole body shook, just the once, as though expelling a demon. Breathing hard, she picked up her phone, the screen already cracked from earlier, its corner now dinted, and walked back the way she'd come.

This time she didn't move for people; they moved for her. When she reached the cafe, she hit the door with something: an arm, a leg, her head perhaps, she had no idea. It clattered against the wall, drawing the attention of the other customers. She ignored the looks she was getting and approached the table.

Alex was in the same seat as before, waiting for her, as though he'd known all along she'd come back. She stopped short and assessed him. He was literally twice the size of anyone else in the vicinity. The legs on his chair were bowing, the back incapable of supporting a damn thing that man had to offer. It was merely a feature in his presence, his shoulders three times its width. Then there were his hands, strong enough to roll up a steel frying pan; his jaw, which, if you were fast enough to land a punch, you would break your hand on; and his messy, cauliflowered ears, testament to thousands of hours of full-contact martial arts training.

Visualise such a man kicking down your front door, knowing there was nothing you could do to stop him. Perceive the helplessness. Imagine the terror.

Well, Lucy knew someone who wouldn't need to picture it in his mind.

He was going to get the real deal.

She sat opposite Alex, picked up her lukewarm coffee, and necked the entire cup.

'You better go order me another,' she said as she slammed the cup back on the table and looked Alex dead in the eye. 'Then we need to talk.'

11

The taxi ride back to Islington nick was a quiet one, in total contrast to the second round of coffees in the cafe. Drayce hadn't yet worked out why Lucy had changed her mind so quickly, but he'd felt palpable relief when she barged through the door, stomped over to the table, and reclaimed her seat. After he'd refreshed her coffee, she'd spoken in the rushed, energetic way an angry and determined person does when they want to make something happen, the end of each word close enough to kiss the beginning of the next, the conclusion of every sentence merging with the birth of the following. Drayce had simply watched and listened to the machine gunning of words as Lucy dictated everything: the terms; the rules; the outcome. Drayce's only contribution was to nod whenever she allowed herself the briefest of pauses to draw breath. If she unlocked that phone for him, he'd play the game however she wanted it to be played.

Drayce turned his head away from an air freshener clipped to a vent in front of him, which blew a toxic mixture of something resembling disinfectant mixed with potpourri. It made him squint and take shallow breaths, dubious it was any better than what it endeavoured to protect him from. He prepared his credit card and scooted to the edge of his seat when they were still minutes away, eager to escape the smell. He watched Lucy clutch the phone he'd stolen from the Mercedes, pulsing her grip as though she was working a stress ball. He'd expected to feel bad for lying to her about who the phone belonged to and why he wanted it unlocked, but he didn't. Such a thing was low down on the scale of what he was prepared to do to find the man who murdered Lily.

Having sat in silence with her own thoughts during the entire journey, Lucy came alive and shot out of the cab as soon as Drayce had paid the fare, for reasons other than the air freshener, he suspected. He knew she'd want to hack the phone and hand it back as quickly as possible, as though the less time she was in possession of it, the lower the risk of being caught with it.

Drayce thanked the driver and stepped out onto the pavement to the sight of DCI Territt holding the front door of the station open for Lucy. Drayce stepped to the side of the arches where he was out of view and leaned against the wall, back to the entrance, hoping the man wouldn't notice him.

'Alex?'

No such luck.

Drayce turned to face him. He didn't know what to say, so he said nothing, hoping Territt was too busy finding Lily's killer to waste his precious time with small talk.

Territt thumbed a gesture towards the door he'd just held open. 'You here with DC Gardner?'

Drayce nodded, slowly, to buy some time, wishing he'd asked to be dropped off around the corner, out of sight. Despite his low tolerance for men like Territt, he was acutely aware of how careful he needed to be with this guy. He didn't want to risk getting Lucy into trouble after she'd been good enough to agree to unlock the phone.

'Yes... we just met for coffee to discuss some things about Jason and Lily's history together in the job. I thought it might help me to understand more clearly what my wife was going through at work in the days and weeks leading up to her murder.' He paused it there, hoping it'd be enough to placate Lucy's boss, but Territt just stood there, confused and sceptical as he glanced over his shoulder at the door Lucy had just walked through, then back at Drayce. Clearly, more was needed. 'I've booked a room in a hotel not far from here, and Lucy needed to get back to the office, so we shared a taxi.'

Territt's expression softened somewhat as he looked Drayce up and down. Drayce clocked a subtle nod directed his way.

'Makes sense,' Territt said, who then jabbed his other thumb towards the opposite side of the road. 'Want a lift to this hotel of yours?'

Drayce followed the thumb. A gleaming white Jaguar F-Type was parked across the street. The registration was TA71 LOW. Territt was grinning like a Cheshire cat with cream on its whiskers.

'She's a beautiful ride,' Territt said in response to Drayce's silence. 'I like to take her out of the city once a month, if I get the chance. Really open her up.'

Drayce tried his damnedest to appear impressed. 'That sounds great, but I'm okay, thank you. Hotel's only just around the corner.'

Territt nodded, his smile making way for a more serious character. 'Listen, Alex, I understand your desire to be close to the investigation, but you're not a police officer anymore.'

Drayce didn't like the direction this conversation had taken.

'We've got to make sure there's a distance kept between you and the enquiries that are being conducted,' Territt continued.

'I understand that.'

'Now, I'm not suggesting there's anything inappropriate about your discussions with DC Gardner—'

'I should hope not.'

'So long as everyone's aware of where the line is drawn.'

'I certainly am,' Drayce said, wanting to add *There's a whole other line you're at risk of crossing with this line of questioning, pal.*

Territt held on to his serious face. 'The report we showed you was carefully put together to ensure that line wasn't crossed. I'd hate for you to be tempted to bleed any more information from DC Gardner.'

Drayce hoped Territt couldn't see the sweat building on his forehead. 'I'm just here to see justice be done for my *murdered wife.'* He put emphasis on those last two words, hoping it would remind Territt he was talking to a murder victim's widower.

'We never did work together when you were in the job,' Territt said, carrying on his train of thought as though Drayce hadn't spoken, 'but I know of your reputation.'

And I of yours, Drayce wanted to say. He tried to keep the clench in his jaw out of his expression. 'What of my reputation?'

The smile returned, but only briefly. 'You were a very good officer, Alex, of that there's no question. But by all accounts, you were a man who did what he thought was right, regardless of… the rules.'

On thin ice, with cracks echoing around him, it was imperative Drayce treaded carefully. 'You have no reason to worry about me,' he lied.

'I'm sure, Alex, I'm sure. But you understand why we must be careful. You're a highly trained former Counter Terrorist Specialist Firearms Officer, whose life was devastated by the murder of his wife. The temptation to take independent action to find your wife's killer must be overwhelming, which is why that distance between you and the investigation must be kept.'

Drayce managed a smile he hoped would come across as genuine. 'It was just coffee.'

'I know, I know.' Territt closed his eyes and sighed. 'Oh dear, I've let my mouth run away with itself. I honestly didn't mean to suggest we need to keep our eye on you.'

Territt's smile returned, wider than before, the implication of that last sarcastic sentence obvious. Drayce struggled to remember a time when he'd seen such an astute display of passive aggression. He suspected it was something Territt had spent his entire career perfecting.

'I'm just being open and honest about our reasons for being so guarded with our enquiries,' Territt said.

Drayce nodded. 'I get it. Don't worry, Lucy's taking good care of me, but she's keeping me at arm's length.' He managed another smile. 'I best get back to my hotel room. I've got things to sort.'

'Of course, of course.' Territt assessed the traffic before stepping into the road. 'You take care.'

'Likewise.'

Drayce walked up the street as Territt climbed into his Jaguar. As Drayce rounded the corner, he caught sight of its sparkling white reflection in a shop window, heading off in the opposite direction. He ducked into a corner cafe that afforded him a view of the nick's entrance, bought a bottle of water, took a seat by the window, and waited.

Territt's line of questioning had unnerved him as much as it had infuriated him. Voicing his none-too-subtle concerns that vigilantism might occur, to a family member of a murder victim, was a hellishly inappropriate thing for Territt to do, and was something he undoubtedly only felt confident to say because Drayce was a former officer with a reputation for being resoundingly disliked by the senior management, due to his propensity to go against the grain if it was tilted the wrong way. Territt knew that if Drayce complained, it would fall on deaf ears. Therefore, Drayce had eaten his fury at being so blatantly disrespected, consuming it rather than venting it, leaving behind an aftertaste that told him the SIO in charge of his wife's reopened case was clearly keeping a close eye on him, and that in return, he must do the same. He opened the bottle of water and sipped it slowly while he breathed deeply to bring his heart rate down.

While waiting for Lucy, he examined the photograph he'd taken on his phone, sneakily, of the paperwork Lucy had left in view during their meeting. He flipped the image of the report the right way up and zoomed in, praying it was what he thought it was. Gratefully, the clarity was sharp enough for him to read the text. Exuberant, he thumped the table with the bottom of his fist.

Noticing the funny looks he was getting from the staff, he gathered himself and focused. It was the DNA report from Jason Martin's murder scene. He skipped past the summary which explained what the tissue was and where it had been found and focused on the important part: the DNA profile of Jason Martin's killer – more importantly for Drayce: Lily's killer. The cops were having trouble linking the DNA to a person because they had no suspects in the case, and nothing in the national database to match it to. But Drayce wasn't burdened with their legal restrictions. He slid a hand under his lapel and felt the bulge of the exhibit bag in his jacket pocket. He hoped it would come in handy down the line.

Lucy reappeared from the nick. She came to a halt on the pavement and checked up and down the street. Drayce suspected she'd want to off-load the phone back on him as soon as possible. Instead of leaving the cafe in a hurry, Drayce waited. Seconds later, he was glad he had.

Territt's white Jaguar came flying around the corner and pulled up next to Lucy, the window buzzing down before it came to a stop. A brief conversation was had. Lucy appeared taken aback by whatever was being said, shrugging a few times as she spoke through the open window. Drayce could smell his name in the air.

Less than a minute later, the Jaguar flew off again, pulling a U-turn as Territt headed off the way he'd come. Questions bombarded Drayce's mind. Had Territt sat nearby the whole time, waiting for Lucy? Maybe he'd called someone in the nick and asked them to give him the heads up when Lucy was preparing to leave? Drayce was now markedly aware of how many pairs of eyes might have been on him since his return to the Met's bubble. Territt had obviously seen Drayce as a threat right from the reopening of Lily's case. Drayce would have to proceed with extreme caution from this point on, conducting enquiries in the shadows while looking over his shoulder at every turn, allowing minimal contact with Lucy. Maybe none would be the smarter choice.

Once he'd collected the phone from her, that is.

He called her from his seat in the cafe and told her to walk down Penton Street towards The Lexington pub. Cutting her off before she could ask any questions, he waited until she passed the cafe, then gave it thirty seconds while he checked for Territt's Jaguar. When it didn't reappear, he left the cafe and caught up with her.

'What's going on?' she asked, as she turned at the sound of his approaching footsteps.

'Not here.' He directed her down a side road where they had some relative privacy. After making sure there was nobody in ear shot, he asked, 'What did Territt say to you just now?'

Lucy regarded him with suspicion. 'Why do you want to know?'

'It was about me, wasn't it?'

'No,' she answered, far too quickly in Drayce's opinion. 'It was work related.'

'I see.' Drayce tried to hold eye contact with her, but she appeared reluctant to look at him; uncomfortable with lying, he suspected.

'Here's your friend's phone.' She forced it into his hand, desperate to relieve herself of it. 'I've reset the PIN to 1234. Thought even you'd remember that.'

Drayce slipped it into his pocket as he frowned at her. He understood the resentment she felt towards him for making her betray the rules she'd promised to adhere to, but still, she could lose the attitude. Rules are meant to be bent; it's the only way things get done.

'You've done the right thing,' he said.

'Don't contact me again unless it's regarding the case.'

'I won't.'

Lucy walked out of the alleyway. As she got to the pavement, she stopped, turned her head slightly, and spoke to Drayce over her shoulder. Even though he could only see half her face, the softening of her expression was unmistakeable.

'Tread carefully, Alex.'

Drayce stopped walking as soon as the Liverpudlian thugs' house came into view.

According to the messages he'd read on their phone during the tube journey, the Victorian semi-detached house in Ealing was an Airbnb property and had been rented for a few months while the trio were staying down south. Other than the address – which the messages made clear had been arranged for them by a boss in their firm, who resided in London full time – there was frustratingly little information on the phone. The men were guarded in their communications. Not to worry, though, Drayce thought. He'd get what he wanted from them, one way or another.

After checking for Ring doorbells and CCTV cameras, he darted up a neighbour's front path. He'd been hypervigilant of his surroundings since Lucy's warning, taking a convoluted route on the tube to ensure he wasn't being followed. He was confident Territt hadn't put anyone on him yet, but if he ever did, Drayce wanted to know about it the moment the first surveillance officer's footsteps mirrored his.

He slipped through an unlocked gate and came to a halt as he approached the neighbour's back garden. He scanned the windows and surrounding area for movement. Happy he wasn't going to disturb anyone, resulting in a three nines call to report a prowler on the street, he vaulted the fence and landed in the back garden of the trio's temporary home.

It was mostly a stone patio, with some decking and a shed at the far end. The blinds on the house were shut, as were the windows, with no cameras in sight. Drayce hurried to the back door as he slipped on a pair of nitrile gloves, knelt to be out of sight from the neighbouring properties, and put his ear against the painted wood. He held his breath. Nothing. If they were home, they weren't talking, or watching television, or listening to music, and Drayce didn't think they were the reading-a-book-by-the-fire types.

Consequently, he felt safe to continue.

He examined the door. Because of his size and strength, he'd been the method of entry specialist on his CTSFO team in the police, so he knew precisely what he was looking at. It was constructed of solid wood and had multiple locking mechanisms on both sides, handle and hinge; something strong and modern judging by the fittings, which would hook deeply into the frame: a hell of a thing for him to force his way through. Discounting brute force, he focused on the lock. It had a standard Euro-profile barrel, old and discoloured, without a kite mark: not anti-drill, bump, or snap.

He walked to the shed, shouldered open the flimsy door, and began the search for what he'd need. As suspected, there was a variety of tools and gardening equipment. He selected a heavy pair of pliers and a small screwdriver and returned to the back door. He clamped the pliers over the exposed section of the barrel and violently pulled it to the left, then the right, snapping it in two. Removing the half that was held firm in the pliers, he peered into the exposed gap, and got to work with the screwdriver, fishing around for the locking mechanism. There was some resistance, smooth and even. Then a click. He tried the handle.

Bingo.

The inside darkened as Drayce closed the door behind him. Thin shafts of light shone through gaps in the blinds, highlighting the dust that swirled through the air. He was in an open-plan kitchen diner. Where a dining table should be was a two-seater red leather sofa facing a similarly upholstered armchair, with a metal coffee table in-between. The smell of last night's meal and the unmistakeable sweet tang of stale cigarettes and weed hung in the air. An ashtray overflowed on the coffee table. Dirty plates were stacked in the sink, empty foil takeaway cartons strewn across the counters. Drayce didn't move, just listened, his ability to detect movement within the house far more accurate now he was inside.

Silence.

The kitchen diner led to a hallway, off which was the living room and an under-stair cupboard, none of which contained anything that interested Drayce. He paused at the bottom of the stairs and listened carefully again. Still no movement. He padded upstairs, planting his feet on the far sides of each step to avoid emitting a creak. A tall bookcase faced him at the top of the stairs, the literature replaced by empty, colourful vases, and framed 'artwork' displaying meaningless sentiments such as 'live, laugh, love'. Four doors led off the landing. Drayce worked his way around. He pushed the bathroom door: clearly unoccupied; then the first bedroom: empty; second: empty. He approached the third and final with caution, conscious that if there was someone lurking in the house, he was about to confront them. He booted it open.

Nobody.

The three Liverpudlians had a room each. Drayce rooted through the men's possessions, disregarding almost everything as meaningless, until he found a small piece of paper, torn from a notebook and left folded up on a bedside table. It was a food shopping list, jotted down just before Sean Maack went to sleep, judging by the designer clothes in the wardrobe. If the list was just for him, he must be pre-diabetic and a borderline alcoholic, Drayce surmised. But the items on the list didn't interest Drayce.

The handwriting did.

Drayce folded it back up and put it in his pocket.

He continued the search and found a bulging black gym bag under Ronan Kelly's bed, a machete resting on top in a black sheath. Drayce dragged it out, tossed the machete on the bed, and unzipped the bag.

My, my, he thought to himself. *Wasn't expecting that.*

As he zipped the bag back up, his head snapped in the direction of the landing.

Someone was unlocking the front door.

13

Drayce froze.

How long before they realised there was an intruder? He pictured the damage to the back door's lock, calculated the distance between it and the front door. He heard the handle turn, then a sucking sound as the door opened, the plastic draft excluder separating from the frame. Three distinct voices muttered to one another; Drayce could discern enough of the conversation to know it was certainly the Liverpudlian men. If they headed straight for the kitchen diner, he had roughly ten seconds before they noticed the gaping hole where the barrel should be, and perhaps another three before they grasped its significance.

Drayce had thirteen seconds before he lost the element of surprise.

He listened carefully as they entered the house. Rubber soles squeaked on laminate floor. He moved to the door, each step taken with painstaking care, heel to toe, silent thanks to the thick carpet pile. His legs seized as he got to the landing.

One of them was climbing the stairs.

Plan A was out of the window; Drayce would have to improvise. He stepped back through the bedroom doorway as the shadow of the man's head crept up the top step, then watched from behind the frame as it slithered across the landing, swaying to the rhythm of a relaxed gait. A cough; something wet dislodged from his throat; a scratch of stubble. Plainly, the man thought he was alone up there. A black Nike trainer appeared, then a matching tracksuit.

Ronan Kelly.

Drayce set his feet in a fighter's stance, ready to launch an attack as soon as Ronan came within reach.

'What the fuck is this?'

The voice came from downstairs, at the back of the house, muted through the floor, but plenty loud enough for Ronan to hear.

The thirteen seconds were up.

Ronan stopped immediately and turned around.

'What is it?' he called out, the volume testament to his vicinity. He was an arm's length from the door frame, Drayce estimated. Drayce moved slightly closer, taking care to stay out of sight.

'Get down here!' the voice shouted.

Ronan took his first step back to the landing.

He didn't manage a second.

Drayce wrapped an arm around his neck, elbow under his chin, and cinched it tight with a gable grip, his other forearm wedged behind Ronan's shoulder, locking the strangle hold in place. Ronan startled, but to his credit, only for a split second. Realising he was in a fight, he attempted to do something about it. Drayce amplified the pressure as he dragged Ronan back through the bedroom doorway, his flailing arms and legs making an inconvenient racket as they clattered into the frame. Drayce sat him on his arse in the middle of the room, squeezed even harder, and pressed his chin towards his chest, stealing any remaining space from his carotid arteries.

Ronan's desperate writhing withered to nothing.

Drayce laid him down carefully as he listened to the rest of the house. Hurried footsteps drummed a dull beat downstairs. The others must have heard the commotion. Drayce searched Ronan and found a pistol in the small of the man's back. Bad news. If Ronan was now armed, it stood to reason the other two would be.

Two pairs of feet climbed the stairs, far more cautious than Ronan had been. Pistol in hand, Drayce grabbed a mirror from the bedside table and crept to the landing, halting near to the top of the stairs, out of sight of Liam Walsh and Sean Maack, who by the sound of it were only halfway up, proof of their wariness since they'd found signs of an intruder and heard a struggle.

'Ronan?' Sean called aggressively, a hint of trepidation in his voice. 'You okay up there?'

Drayce edged the mirror past the corner of the landing and contained the expletive that fought to pass his lips. Both men were indeed armed, a pistol in the hand of each. They locked eyes with Drayce in the reflection and raised their weapons, needing a split second to register that there was nothing for them to shoot at. Their expressions transformed from shock to anger in the blink of an eye, their footsteps becoming frantic. Drayce dropped the mirror and stood back.

There was only a second or two until they reached the landing, at which point a cluster-fuck of a shootout would begin. Opening fire was a last resort; Drayce wanted time to question these men, and even if the gunfire didn't kill them, it might attract the attention of the neighbours, and subsequently the police. The bookcase caught his eye. Worth a shot. He picked it clean off the floor, turned to the top of the stairs, and just as Sean appeared on the landing, threw it at him.

The deafening racket of the six-foot-tall piece of solid wooden furniture drowned out the men's gasps and whimpers as it clattered down the stairs, riding the two men all the way to the bottom and culminating in an almighty crash. Through the racket of glass vases shattering and wood splintering came the murmurings of two men in utter shock, dazed and confused, possibly a little concussed.

Drayce peered around the corner of the landing, gun up. They were trapped, legs squirming from underneath the book-case, their top halves pinned at the bottom of the staircase, their pistols discarded a few steps up. Drayce walked down and retrieved them, tucking both in his waistline. He trampled over the bookcase to get downstairs, the men crying out in pain as he did so. A long crack ran up its entire length, from top to bottom. Drayce placed a foot on one side of it, slid the fingers of his free hand through the gap, and ripped the bookcase in half. He aimed Ronan's pistol at the two men. They were conscious, but only just, their eyes struggling to hold focus.

'We need to have a little word, fellas,' Drayce said.

Movement at the top of the stairs caught Drayce's attention. He whipped the pistol up on aim as Ronan staggered into view on the landing, dazed and confused, the same machete as earlier held out in front of him, retrieved from the bed where Drayce had left it. The two men locked eyes.

'This is a bit like rock, paper, scissors,' Drayce said. 'Except in this game, the gun in my hand trumps everything.' He pulled one of the others from his waistline and aimed both at Ronan. 'And now I've got one in each hand, so guess who wins?'

Ronan seemed to understand his position; the machete fell silently to the carpet.

'Now get downstairs,' Drayce said. 'The four of us have a lot to discuss.'

14

Drayce held them at gunpoint and directed them to sit down on the two-seater sofa in the kitchen diner: Ronan on the left, Sean squished in the middle, and Liam on the right. From behind, Drayce leaned over the back of the sofa and searched them for more weapons, the muzzle of one of his newly acquired guns pressed into the back of their necks as he did so.

The injuries Drayce had caused them in their earlier fight outside the pub had been compounded by their latest scuffle. The wound to Ronan's thigh had been clumsily bandaged since their first introduction, and fresh blood now seeped through his tracksuit bottoms, glossier than the dried stuff from earlier. Dark bruising stained the side of Sean's neck from when Drayce had elbowed him, and the cuts below Liam's eyes had been glued shut; a clumsy DIY job, Drayce deduced. Both men clutched their chests protectively, no doubt suffering from a cracked rib or two. They had the appearance of three naughty children, lined up outside the headmaster's office, waiting to be lectured.

Drayce kept a close eye on them from the kitchen counter, the edge of which he leaned his backside against, one wrist propped up on the microwave, the other on his belt buckle to steady the pistols he was aiming their way. Boiling water rumbled in the background, the kettle building up to a crescendo. No one had said a word for nearly five minutes. Judging by their expressions, the three gangsters were wondering what the hell was going on.

At the click of the kettle, Drayce spoke up. 'We got off on the wrong foot earlier. Thought I'd make a round of brews as we wipe the slate clean.' His eyes flashed down to the guns in his hands. 'You mind if I put these down?' They shook their heads, confusion personified. Drayce raised his eyebrows, curled one corner of his mouth up into a half grin. 'Not going to do anything stupid, are we, fellas?' They shook their heads again. 'Good boys.'

Drayce laid the guns flat on the counter, pointing their way. He was confident the three gangsters wouldn't make a move, but if they did, he could have those guns back in his hands and in play in half a second. They wouldn't even be out of their seats before bullets flew their way, and judging by their demeanour, they understood this.

Drayce made four cups of tea and lined them up on a tray, alongside a packet of chocolate Hobnobs he'd found in a cupboard.

'My favourites,' he said with a smile. 'Sugar?' They shook their heads. 'Biscuit?' Same response. Drayce frowned, the smile evaporating. 'You three lost your voices or something?'

'No sugar,' Ronan said. 'No biscuits.'

Drayce shrugged. 'Suit yourselves. But a cup of tea's not the same without a biscuit, if you ask me.' He stuffed one in his mouth, whole, then slipped one of the pistols on the counter back into his beltline, and aimed the other at the three men as he carried the tray of drinks to the coffee table one-handed. He kicked the overflowing ashtray off the surface, sending it skidding across the floor, spewing the contents in its wake. The sudden violence, coupled with the ear-splitting raucous of smashed pottery crashing through the silence, made the three gangsters flinch.

Drayce set the tray of drinks down in the ashtray's place and took a seat in the armchair, facing the trio. The gym bag he'd found upstairs was down by his feet. He rested the bottom of the pistol's grip on his thigh, pointed the muzzle across the table, and took his time to finish the remains of the biscuit in his mouth. The three scousers were statues.

'Drink up then, lads,' Drayce said. 'Be rude to let them go cold.'

The three men cautiously leaned forward. As they sat back and raised the cups to their lips, Drayce began the interrogation.

'You've got some priorities to put in order.' He made eye contact with each of them in turn. 'You need to decide what's more important to you: your own lives, or the lives of the people you work for.' Sean's lips quivered. 'Not yet,' Drayce told him as he lifted the index finger of his free hand to his lips, silencing the man. 'You need to listen first. And please, listen carefully. Take seriously everything I say. It'll benefit you in the long run.'

Drayce moved the pistol's position slightly, to remind them of its presence.

'It's simple,' he said. 'I know, that you know, the identity of the man who shot Jason Martin dead on his doorstep. And I want you to tell me who that man is.'

'Why's it so important to you?' Liam asked.

Drayce turned his attention to him and him alone. His eyes bored into the man's soul. 'That's a good question, Liam, and I understand why you're intrigued to know, but the truth is, it's none of your business.' All friendly pretences fell from Drayce's expression. 'It's between me and the man who shot Jason. The only question you need to answer, is whether you're willing to die to protect him.'

The three men exchanged nervous glances.

'So, let's make a start, shall we?' Drayce said. 'Who sent you to The Tavern?'

A few beats of silence passed.

'No one,' Liam said.

Drayce tilted the muzzle his way. 'Don't lie to me.'

'I'm not.'

'So what were you doing there?'

'Nothing important.'

Drayce took out his phone and showed them the photo he'd taken of the CCTV footage. 'Looks like a pretty heated conversation for something that wasn't important.'

Liam shrugged. 'Landlord ripped us off the night before. Overcharged our credit cards for a few rounds of drinks. Should have added up to around a hundred quid in total, but the thieving bastard added a zero. We paid him a visit to get our money back.'

Drayce smiled. 'Is that a fact?'

Liam nodded. Drayce assessed the other two. They did the same, backing up their friend's lie.

'There any sound on the video you took that from?' Liam asked, his confidence growing, taking the lead on their defence.

'No,' Drayce said, because what was the point in lying. Sound recording in a busy pub was a waste of time, and Liam obviously knew it.

'Prove me wrong then,' Liam said, with a smirk that made Drayce's blood boil.

Drayce took out of his pocket the shopping list he'd pinched from the bedside table. He unfolded it and placed it on the empty tray, facing Sean. 'You write that?' No reaction. Drayce took out of another pocket the note with the date and time that had been left with Lenny. He laid it down next to the list. 'Notice anything?'

No reply. Liam turned his head towards Sean, fire in his eyes.

'The handwriting's the same,' Drayce said. 'You wrote the note, Sean.' He addressed Liam again as he cocked the hammer on the pistol. 'Lie to me again, Liam. I dare you.'

Liam sipped his tea and sat back with a face of stone. Drayce was running out of patience.

'I know you threatened the landlord into switching the camera off during these times,' Drayce said, jabbing his finger down on the note.

'We don't give a fuck what you think you know, big fella.' Liam's smirk had returned. 'You have no idea who you're dealing with.'

'I know exactly who I'm dealing with. That's why I'm here, pointing a gun in your face.'

'Not done much with it yet though, have you?' Liam nodded at the weapon. 'You even know how to use that thing?'

'Keep talking like that and you'll find out.' Drayce switched his glare between the three men. 'For the last time, I want to know who the killer is.'

Liam leaned forward, demanding Drayce's attention. 'Why you got such a hard-on for that pig?'

Drayce locked eyes with Liam. 'If I were you, I'd think very carefully before you put another foot over the line you've just crossed. Because if you keep stumbling along on your current path, you might not like where it leads to.'

Liam rested his elbows on his thighs, his mug hovering beneath his chin. 'Fuck you! We're telling you nuttin.' He blew on the surface of his brew, a cocky smile on his face. 'And fuck that pig cunt who died squealing in the street.'

Drayce's world slowed down, sounds muffled, as though he'd fallen into deep water. Liam's last sentence was referencing Jason Martin's death, but it was Lily's face Drayce pictured upon hearing the words – the love of his life, a serving police officer, attacked in the street with a knife. Something in Drayce's mind shifted. He heard a pop in his ears, as though from a change in pressure, making way for the steadily increasing buzz of tinnitus. His vision blurred, face flushed, body heating up. The dam was cracking. Couldn't hold it in much longer.

He pulled the trigger.

The gunfire was muted in his fuzzy ears, but Sean and Ronan jumped in their seats, mouths open, aghast, faces ashen with glossy fear in their eyes as they stared at their friend.

A clean red hole the size of a five pence piece now sat between Liam's eyes, which had lost all signs of life. Drayce was barely aware of the contents of Liam's head that now decorated the wall and ceiling in a chaotic splatter. A fine red mist hung in the air between the men. A torrent of claret poured out of Liam's nostrils, off his chin, showering his leather jacket as the tension in his body vanished. His mug fell from his hand and smashed on the floor before he toppled face first onto the coffee table, the epicentre of a dark red pool expanding across the cracked glass.

Liam wasn't smiling anymore.

Drayce turned the gun to the other two.

'Wait!' Ronan shouted. 'Just wait!'

'Talk,' Drayce said. 'The faster you speak, the sooner I calm down.'

'He's called Reaper, that's all we know.'

'What's that supposed to mean?'

'I'm telling the truth! It's what he goes by!' Ronan looked to Sean for support.

'It's a nickname, or something,' Sean said. 'No one knows his real identity.'

'And you pair work for him?'

'We mostly work for an associate of his up in Liverpool – a business partner. But we done good work for Reaper recently, so he's used us quite a bit down here. No one knows who we are in London. We can move around easier. Back home, the bizzies terrorise us. Makes it hard to get things done.'

'How do you contact him?'

'We don't. He messages us. And before you ask, the number's withheld.'

'How do I find him?'

'You don't. He finds you.'

Drayce lifted the pistol level with their heads, moving it from one to the other. They both shut their eyes and brought their hands up.

'We're telling the truth!' Ronan pleaded.

Drayce considered his next move. No use turning up the heat on these two; he was confident they were now telling him the truth. And besides, he needed to leave someone alive for the next part of his game plan to work. He regarded the giant exit wound to the back of Liam's head, the tip-tap of blood steadily trickling off the side of the overflowing coffee table. Extreme, but it had done the trick, greasing the wheels with the other two. Now they were taking him seriously. Hopefully the same would be true for the next link in the chain.

Drayce stood up. 'Next time Reaper contacts you, tell him I'm coming for him. Tell him there's nowhere to hide.' He picked up the gym bag. 'And I'm taking this with me.'

Ronan and Sean both nodded frantically, the muscles in their necks twitching as though in a spasm. Their eyes suggested they couldn't believe they'd been spared.

Drayce eased the hammer, put the gun away, and walked out of the front door.

The fitting room, located in the back of one of the oldest, most exclusive tailors on Savile Row, had the whiff of a traditional London gentleman's club, Sullivan pondered. Handmade rugs decorated the polished wooden floorboards, which, even though they had been laid nearly two hundred years ago, did not emit a single creak underfoot as he shifted his weight in front of the mirror, twisting from side to side as he examined the fit of the navy cashmere trousers.

Tartan wallpaper displayed a pattern of colours which complemented the cast-iron radiators and solid hardwood furniture arranged along the walls. The door creaked as the tailor – a grey-haired old man with keen eyes sat above half-moon glasses – returned momentarily with the tie Sullivan had chosen, before leaving to collect the jacket. Two cigars sat in the rests of a large stainless-steel ashtray, each emitting tall, thin lines of smoke that slithered in the air, the movement that of cobras rising from a basket. Either side of the ashtray was a crystal glass tumbler, each with a double measure of whisky. The drinking of alcohol in the fitting room wasn't just tolerated by the tailor, it was encouraged; the man was somewhat of a whisky connoisseur and took pleasure offering recommendations to his customers from the drinks cabinet he kept on site. But smoking was a wholly different matter. The effect it had on the garments, the terrible odour it infected them with, meant even royalty were banned from indulging when in the shop.

Not so for Daniel Sullivan.

The tailor let him do as he pleased.

Sullivan focused on his reflection in the full-length mirror as he tied the dark green garment around the collar of his white shirt, Reaper in view behind him, sat in a leather wingback, watching his boss try on the outfit he'd commissioned specifically for the meeting that evening. Reaper reached for his whisky as he appeared to assess their surroundings.

'How much does a suit from this place set you back?' he asked before he sipped the dark brown liquid to the tinkling of ice cubes.

'About three times as much as the flat you were born in,' Sullivan replied. 'Worth it, though. Need to look sharp tonight. With the Chinese coming to discuss the future of our partnership, security needs to be on point, Reaper.'

'It's in hand.'

'Good. I want to show them the scale of the money I can make for them in this city. The party's going to be a flash affair. We need to show off our success. Give them confidence in the relationship we've struck with them.'

'I've got a hundred good men lined up to secure the club, more than a dozen of whom are elite enforcers, hand-picked from around the country. Plenty of guns for each of them. It'll be the safest place on planet Earth.'

Sullivan folded down his collar, did up his top button, and cinched his tie. 'I don't want Ryan anywhere near it.'

Reaper smiled. 'I don't think it's his scene. Besides, it seems he wants to keep a close eye on the operation while he's down from Liverpool. After your meeting, he went straight to the unit.'

Sullivan turned his head and stared at Reaper out of the corner of his eye. 'That a fact?'

'I got a call from Tommy. Ryan and a bunch of his scouse pals are marching around like they own the place, barking orders at the workers, wanting to see the merchandise. They're slowing the operation down.'

Sullivan turned fully to Reaper. 'Call Tommy back and tell him to keep the old bastard in one place until we get there. I'm not having him set us back. He's only an investor with us. He might run things up north, but the capital's my operation.'

Reaper set his drink down and stood up. 'Will do.'

Sullivan faced the mirror. In the reflection, he saw Reaper take out his phone and leave the room. The tailor reappeared to take his place.

'Your jacket, sir.'

Sullivan held out his arms, allowing the tailor to thread them through the sleeves. He shrugged the navy wool jacket onto his shoulders and assessed himself in the mirror while the tailor adjusted the fabric, running his hands over Sullivan's shoulders and upper back, the smile on his face evidence that the material was seated just right. Sullivan fastened the single front button and admired himself. His upper body had transformed, angles now as sharp as a knife, as well defined as a Roman sculpture. Shoulders accentuated; waist hidden; generous lapels giving shape to his featureless chest. A suit of armour. Fit for a king.

Worth every penny.

The tailor circled him, judging the suit from every angle. He crinkled his nose at the overwhelming scent of tobacco in the air, but the look on his face told Sullivan he was happy with his work.

'Perfect, isn't it?' Sullivan asked.

'Indeed it is, sir.'

'I'll settle the bill in cash.'

The tailor bowed his head submissively. 'As you wish, sir.'

The door clattered against the wall. Reaper marched in, his hard leather shoes tapping a fast beat on the floorboards. His phone was still clutched in his hands, his knuckles white, a wildness in his eyes. Sullivan glared at the tailor, who bowed his head once again and left the room, shutting the door behind him.

'The fuck has Ryan done?' Sullivan asked.

'Not Ryan,' Reaper replied. 'That man's under control. Tommy's got it in hand.'

'What then?'

'I've just taken a call from Sean.' Reaper ran his fingers through his beard. 'We've got a problem.'

16

Drayce found himself back on Jason Martin's street, tucked down an alleyway in-between two houses, roughly thirty metres away from Jason's front door, with a view of The Tavern beyond.

Drayce had been careful with his movements after leaving the two surviving gangsters. Everything he'd uncovered so far suggested Lily and Jason were victims of organised crime, so Drayce was sure the murder of Liam Walsh wouldn't be reported to the police; that kind of thing just wasn't in their rulebook. Providing the neighbours hadn't heard the gunshot and dialled three nines – unlikely, as it was only a single shot from a small calibre handgun, which, even if there was someone in the nearby vicinity to hear, could easily have been mistaken for a door slammed shut – there would be no statement, no scene, no police activity whatsoever. The next tier of the organisation would be informed, and an appropriate plan of action would be decided upon, one which Drayce hoped would slot nicely into his chosen method of identifying their chain of command.

Hunt with bait; give these men a reason to come after me.

Of course, Territt was still a concern, or at least a potential one. The anti-surveillance tactics Drayce had employed to ensure he wasn't being followed meant it took him a long time to make the journey back from Ealing to Islington. But needs must. He couldn't afford to fall victim to one of Territt's surveillance teams. Not with what he was getting up to.

He stayed in the shadows, thinking through his options for how to make use of his time while the OCG got their act together. He wondered why he'd felt an instinct to go back to the street on which Jason was murdered. He had no further use for Lenny, but he might for Jason's family. Tricky void to cross, though. He hadn't known Jason, so he was a stranger to the man's wife. Didn't even know her name.

The only connection he had to work with?

Hi, my wife used to work with your husband. She was also murdered. Fancy a chat?

Pathetic didn't do it justice.

But still, gut instinct had brought him back, made him contemplate knocking on her door, armed with nothing more than the hope she might know something he could use to help him find the man who'd killed both their partners. He knew from experience that an officer's spouse was often the person they offloaded things onto at the end of a hard day. Maybe Jason consoled in his wife, spoke about the pressures of his case load, let slip a key piece of information that could establish why someone wanted him dead. If Drayce could convince her to talk to him, maybe he could coax something out of her, and make her remember a key detail that might lead him somewhere.

He stepped out of the alleyway and crossed the street.

Drayce sensed he was being watched as soon as he stepped within range of the Ring doorbell. He pushed it and waited. After a delay brought on by understandable apprehension, a shy voice spoke to him through the device's speaker.

'Can I help you?'

Drayce's lips parted, his tongue fumbling the first word. How on earth should he begin this?

'I'm sorry to bother you.' He licked his dry lips, took a big breath. *Oh, what the hell. Just get on with it. Telling the truth is rarely the wrong decision.* 'My wife used to work with your husband. In the police.' A pause, swallowing his doubt. 'She was murdered three and a half years ago.'

Drayce was met with dead silence, not even the sound of her breath fluttering against the microphone. He stood like a statue, muscles seized up, breath held. Just as he was beginning to feel he'd made a terrible mistake, the front door opened. A woman dressed in black jeans and a cream sweater appeared, blonde hair tied back, expression all business.

Without saying a word, she stood to one side and held the door open for him.

17

It had been a long time since Drayce had been in the company of a murder victim's widow. He was a little out of practice, but the basics were hard to lose: be polite, prioritise listening over speaking, and whatever you do, don't spill the tea.

Two out of three wasn't bad.

A brown line ran down the side of the white porcelain in his hands. He turned the mug, the steaming liquid constantly teetering close to the edge, until the evidence of his clumsiness was out of Melanie's view. He tried sipping it to bring the level down, but it was too hot. His legs clamped together to hide the small, brown splash mark between his thighs, hoping his jeans would soak it up before it stained the white leather. Conscious of the heavy metal guns in his jacket pockets, he tried to position himself so the bulge of their shape wasn't obvious. It wouldn't exactly earn Melanie's trust if she registered he was armed – a contender for understatement of the year, Drayce thought.

Melanie took a seat in the armchair opposite, cradling her mug as she watched Drayce. Her back was ramrod straight, shoulders locked back, eyes bright and alert as she scratched a nail across the lip of her mug, more noticeable than it should have been thanks to the silence of the house, her two children at school until later in the afternoon. The only other noise was a clock on the wall, its tick unfeasibly loud, filling the space as the sound of a ticking bomb would. Drayce got the impression she was tumbling around in her mind everything he'd just told her. He'd wanted to lay out exactly what the police had informed him of, believing honesty to be the best means of gaining her trust. He knew she'd have been assessing him from the moment she'd spied him through her Ring camera, and having taken the risk of inviting into her home a stranger with the presence of a Viking marauder, it seemed she might be as desperate for answers as he was.

'Why haven't the police told me about the DNA link?' Melanie frowned at him as she asked the question, lips tight, the corners turned down, hostile to the new information he was bringing into her life.

'You'll have to ask them,' Drayce replied. 'Maybe they've got plans for your FLO to sit you down to discuss it.'

'But why the delay? They told *you* straight away.'

'Actually, no they didn't. They sat on it for months. I was the one who went to them, after an old friend told me of the developments.'

Drayce sipped his tea, bringing it down to a safe level.

Melanie's scratching intensified to scraping. 'It's not good enough.'

Drayce shrugged. 'In their defence, there's little point in getting your hopes up until they can link it to a suspect.'

'We could have had this conversation months ago if they'd told us straight away. Maybe, between the two of us, we could have found a link ourselves.'

'There's no point wasting further time obsessing over what could have been. We're having the conversation now. That's all that matters.'

Melanie looked away sharply.

Drayce sipped his tea and waited.

'I don't know what any of this means,' she said. 'How can two murders that happened three years apart be linked?'

'The answer lies somewhere during their time working in the Met. They were in Islington CID together. There must have been something they were working on, something they discovered that made them a big enough threat for a group of criminals to kill them.'

Melanie faced him, tears threatening. 'But why the time lapse? If the killer needed them both dead, why wait three years before killing Jason?'

Drayce glanced at his cup as he considered her question. 'I don't know. I've racked my brains trying to think of something Lily might have told me, anything about work that might shine a light on a motive, but there's nothing.' He locked eyes with Melanie. 'Think hard: did Jason ever talk to you about work?'

She shrugged. 'Occasionally, but not often.'

'Did he ever mention a case that was bothering him, or give you any reason to believe he'd been threatened at any point?' Her eyes glazed over as though her mind was searching for an answer. 'Did he ever bring any work home with him? Laptops, phones, case files, notebooks. Anything at all.'

Melanie's eyes lit up. Her lips quivered, pursing as though about to say something. Drayce leaned forward, on the edge of his seat, praying for a revelation. But as quickly as she'd morphed into it, she snapped out of it. Her lips pulled tight, her expression returning to the hostile poker player of before.

'No,' she said.

Drayce leaned back into his seat, deflated. He nodded once, finished his tea, then stood up. 'Thanks for the brew. And thank you for your time.' He handed her the empty mug and stepped towards the hallway.

'Is that it?'

Drayce stopped and turned to face her. 'You were expecting more?' She remained silent, a bewildered expression on her face. He shrugged. 'I've asked the only questions I need answers to. No point wasting any more of your time.' He continued to the hallway, paused at the phone table where he'd earlier clocked a notepad and pen. He wrote his number down on the top sheet, tore it off, and handed it to Melanie as she joined him. 'Call me if you think of anything.'

She nodded, eyeing him cautiously, as though slightly dumbfounded at his hasty departure. 'Sure. Will do.'

'Sorry for bringing all this back up for you. I know how hard these past few months must have been.'

Her lips pulled tightly in a thin, toothless smile.

Drayce opened the front door and put one foot out. He paused. Turned back to Melanie. 'Before I go, can I use your bathroom? That cup of tea has gone straight through me.'

'Of course. Upstairs, second on the left.'

'Thanks.'

Drayce climbed the stairs. On the landing, he waited until he heard Melanie take the mugs into the kitchen and, certain she wasn't loitering in the hallway, began his search. With only a limited amount of time before the toilet excuse ran out, he made haste, treading lightly so as not to creak any floorboards.

After identifying the kids' rooms, he ignored them, thinking it unlikely their father would hide anything there. Same deal with the bathroom. He reached inside the airing cupboard on the landing, running his hand along the top of the boiler, the shelves, and anywhere else a USB stick or memory card might be hidden.

Nothing.

The carpets were all tucked tightly into the skirting board and trims, giving no indication Jason had lifted the edges to conceal small items underneath. In the main bedroom, Drayce focused on the empty wardrobes and drawers that had once housed Jason's possessions, checking for false backs concealing a void.

Again, nothing of interest.

The spare bedroom was sparse, other than a fold-out bed pushed against a wall, stacked next to which were half a dozen cardboard boxes, which Drayce quickly ascertained were full of old clothes and unloved children's toys destined for a charity shop. As the only room in the house with wallpaper, he checked the corners for signs of a SIM or memory card pushed between the paper and plaster.

Nothing.

He glanced at his watch. Time was running out. He walked gently to the bathroom, flushed the toilet, and plodded loudly downstairs.

Melanie was waiting in the hallway for him. He assessed her body language: nothing to suggest she'd rumbled him. He smiled, thanked her again for her hospitality, and walked out onto the street.

The sun hit his eyes immediately, forcing him to squint. He crossed the road and loitered for a moment in the shade of a house. As feared, he'd gained little by talking to Melanie, but it wasn't entirely a lost cause; she now had his number and might remember something she'd be willing to share with him. He glanced up the street, one way then the other, trying to decide where to go from here. His only real option was to make himself obvious to the people who would soon be coming after him. He took one last glance at Melanie's home, patted the guns in his pockets, and set off on foot.

The hairs on the back of his neck stood to attention. He stopped. Turned back. Something wasn't right. His mind, his body, his subconscious, were warning him. He rotated on the spot, assessed his surroundings for a threat. Nothing. The nervous feeling intensified, his gut trying to tell him something. He looked back at Melanie's house. The hairs settled; his anxiety calmed. He cocked his head to one side, as though changing the frame might bring into focus what his brain was trying to tell him. His discipline kept him there, bathing in the confusion, emboldened by an unrelenting trust in his instincts. Something slotted into place, his brain finding the next gear as it searched through his hard drive, evaluating everything he'd seen in the house and desperately trying to make sense of it.

His head snapped up when he worked it out, his neck rigid, the realisation hitting him like a brick to the face.

He marched across the street and banged on Melanie's front door.

18

Sullivan's base of operations had changed locations many times over the years – staying in one place for too long was dangerous. It was currently southeast of the city, right where the sprawling mass of London breaks up and gives way to the green landscape of Kent. An industrial unit on the bank of the Thames, it was an ideal location for processing shipments. Across the North Sea from the continent, a short journey down the river, and here is where his organisation's variety of merchandise ended up, to be processed before it was disseminated across the capital. Located between a concrete supplier and a busy recycling yard, it masqueraded as a pallet company, thousands of them stacked three floors high around the perimeter of the yard to block the view of the unit from the road – a handy by-product of the goods that were smuggled in.

Sullivan left Reaper to his phone call, stubbed his cigarette out on the ground, dropped the butt in the metal case he kept for such needs – no good leaving his DNA on site should there ever be a police raid – and walked past the line of vans queuing for the loading bays. Several shipments had been dropped off that morning, meaning the warehouse was starting to fill. Having the product sat still was risky. Ideally, it should be constantly kept moving right from purchase to sale, the vans filled up and fucked off as quickly as possible. They were wholesalers, not a storage company. He'd have to remind Tommy of his priorities.

Sullivan's presence washed over the workers like a CEO marching across the factory floor. Everyone picked up their work rate as he passed by. His handmade leather shoes clipped the concrete, an early warning someone of importance was approaching. He saw Tommy, river side of the unit, stood by the yard crane as he barked orders and threw his arms around to hurry everyone up. He settled down once he caught sight of Sullivan.

'Hello, Boss,' Tommy said with a nervous smile. He ran the fingers of both hands through his shoulder-length brown hair, clearing several strands that had clung to his sweaty face. 'Wasn't expecting a visit from you while the unit's full.'

Sullivan nodded. Under normal circumstances, he preferred to keep his distance from such a large bulk of seriously illegal assets. But needs must. He frowned at Tommy, making it clear this wasn't a social visit. 'Where's Ryan and his pals?'

Tommy licked his lips, blinked the worry out of his eyes. 'They're in the warehouse, checking things over. Been under my feet all afternoon, following me around, asking questions, distracting me. I wasn't sure if it was legit, so I called Reaper...'

Sullivan raised a hand. 'That's why I'm here. I'll handle them.' He jerked a thumb back in the direction he'd just come. 'You just concentrate on getting those vans filled up and fucked off fast, you hear me?' Tommy's head jerked up and down. Sullivan jabbed a finger at the stack of small containers under the miniature yard crane. 'I want these products turned around so fast the van tyres barely stop moving, from the moment they come into the yard, to the moment they leave. Understand?'

'Yes, Boss.'

'None of what's come in today can be stored in the warehouse. It needs to be on the road straight away.'

A jerky nod. 'Boss.'

'Good lad. Now get back to work.'

Sullivan walked to the warehouse entrance, leaving Tommy to shout at the workers, his voice twenty decibels higher now he'd had a dressing down from the boss. The young man's angry tones soon made way for the soft murmurings of John Ryan and his band of not so merry men. Sullivan brushed aside the plastic curtains and stepped inside.

Sixty metres long by forty wide, the ceiling vaulted, thirty metres high, this was where non-perishable goods could be stored for a short time before their journey to the customers. The turnaround was quick; nothing remained on site for more than a week. More than three hundred crates were stacked up in rows and columns, containing everything from the purest class A drugs to unregistered firearms. John Ryan and his six associates were huddled in front of the first row, mumbling to one another. Heads turned at the sound of Sullivan's foot fall.

'That long-haired faggot grass me up, did he?' This from John, throwing Sullivan a scowl above a smile.

'What you doing here, John?' Sullivan stopped short of the group, keeping them all in sight.

'I'm keeping an eye on my investment.' He opened his arms and glanced at the men either side of him. '*Our* investment.'

'You're getting in the way, is all you're doing. Slowing things down.' Sullivan flicked his head back to the plastic curtains. 'Half those containers should already be on the road. Instead, they're stacked halfway to the ceiling, all because you've been distracting Tommy from his job.'

'That what he told you?'

'Didn't need to, John. It's obvious. Now gather up your boyfriends and get the fuck off my site before I lose my temper.'

The six bristled, muscles bunched up, hands clenched. John took a step forward. 'Are you threatening me?'

Sullivan shook his head. 'It's a warning, not a threat. You want to risk ruining the gravy train just because you don't like me? Go ahead. It'll be you that suffers, not me. Your associates back home won't take too kindly to you cutting their profits short by disrupting the operation down here with your arrogance.' Sullivan felt his glare sharpen, the creases around his nose and eyes deepen. He wielded a rigid finger in John's direction. 'You might be a big swinging dick in Liverpool, but here in London, you're fuck all! We agreed to invest in one another's smuggling operation to improve our returns, but you don't see me up there, sticking my nose around your port, wanting to know what's going on. You send me my percentage every quarter, and I send you yours, as arranged. At no point was it agreed that either of us would have any business on each other's site. We need to trust each other if our arrangement is going to continue.' He held his arms out wide, palms facing the seven men, fingers splayed. 'But if you want to piss all over that trust, gentlemen, and you'd prefer trouble instead? Well then, it's trouble you'll get. Just don't be surprised when the other ranks within your organisation side with me in the aftermath of the bloodbath.'

Ryan clenched his jaw, widened his stance, his dominant hand delving deep into his jacket pocket. Sullivan braced himself for the sight of a weapon, the beginning of the end. So be it. The bastard wouldn't get out alive. Reaper'd see to that.

Screams broke the tension: a woman, terrified and hysterical, somewhere out on the loading bay. Her voice cut through the air like a knife, echoing around the giant expanse of the warehouse. Sullivan ignored John Ryan and his cohort and marched back through the plastic curtains.

The smell hit him before he caught sight of the source. The doors of a container were held open by two workers, their mouths and noses pressed hard into the crease of their elbow as they turned their faces away from the interior. A young Vietnamese woman no older than twenty stumbled out, tears streaming down her cheeks, shaking violently. Her fingers clawed at her throat as she muttered an incoherent ramble of words, her eyes roaming the room, lost in grief. Panic in her face, her shoulders rocked back and forth, chest heaving as though trying to breathe but unable to. Her lips were blue. Her eyes rolled back in her head and she collapsed to the damp concrete floor, lifeless.

'What the fuck is going on?' Sullivan asked. 'Is she dead?'

One of the workers stepped forward to check her pulse. He nodded.

'Fuck's sake!' Sullivan exclaimed.

He stomped forward, made it within twelve feet of the container before he had to pull a jacket lapel over his nose. Tommy had made it a little closer and shone a torch inside. His eyes widened, mesmerised, as though in a trance. He quickly aimed the beam of light at the ground, his free hand coming up to his mouth as he stifled a gag. Sullivan grabbed him by the shoulder and spun him around.

'Why the fuck did you open the doors? You know they're supposed to stay closed until they arrive in the city.'

'One of the lads heard banging.' He flicked his head towards the once hysterical woman, now a corpse. 'Must have been her. He opened it to check on them and… Well, good job he did. Would have done our reputation no good opening these doors in front of the customers in Chinatown to the sight of that fucking horror show.'

Sullivan dropped his arm, unconvinced it was doing anything to block the smell from his nostrils. He snatched the torch out of Tommy's hand and approached the mouth of the container. He peered into its black interior, afraid to illuminate it just yet. The stench got stronger with every step, gases so potent they made his eyes sting. Gradually, his sight adjusted to the darkness. The inside of the container took shape. He levelled the torch with the container's back wall, bringing the space to life. He stopped dead, a hand clamped to his mouth to stifle his gag reflex.

A child's ankle caught his eye first, jeans pulled up to her knees, the colourful flowers embroidered on her socks and her ghostly white skin in total contrast to the backdrop of the shiny black floor. He couldn't see her top half for the rest of the bodies, twenty or more in a space you'd struggle to fit ten, piled high as they'd scrambled for an airhole near the top. Each man, woman, and child had evacuated their bowls as the life had been pulled out of them, the floor swimming with urine and faeces, hence why it glistened in the torch light. With the entire grisly scene lit up in front of him, the reason the legs of the child's jeans were pulled up to her knees became apparent to Sullivan: she'd kicked out manically in her desperate attempts to free herself from the crushing pressure of the bodies on top of her. He turned off the torch and threw it at Tommy. It hit his chest with a *thud* and landed in his open hands.

'Those fucking greedy Triad bastards!' Sullivan said. 'They know they're not supposed to pack them in like that! The fuck were they thinking, stuffing that many bodies inside a container with one tiny airhole!' He waved a finger in Tommy's face. 'If they think they're keeping all the money they took off this lot, they can think again. They'll be sending me the full amount, plus an extra ten percent for cleaning up their mess. Unless they want me to cut them out of London's market, the fucking idiots!'

'Yes Boss,' Tommy replied with a swift nod, clearly unsure of how to deal with Sullivan's outburst.

'What do they expect me to do with a stack of bodies? They think they can cream the profits their end and leave me with dead assets, is that it?'

'Problems, Daniel?'

Sullivan's head snapped round to the sight of John Ryan, stood by the plastic curtains, hands in his pockets, a sly smile edged across his face.

'Never you mind,' Sullivan replied. 'Just don't forget your way to the exit, John.'

Sullivan marched past Tommy and carried on outside to the Mercedes. As he walked across the yard, he slipped a cigarette between his lips and lit the tip. Reaper was coming off the phone as Sullivan approached.

'What's the matter?' Reaper asked, reading his boss's demeanour.

Sullivan blew a cloud of smoke in the air as he waved a hand dismissively. 'Let's just get out of here. Our Triad associates have fucked up, and now I've got calls to make and lives to threaten if I'm to ensure it doesn't happen again.'

Reaper gestured with his phone. 'Hate to bring more problems your way, but…'

'Let me guess. No one knows who this mystery man is, right?'

Reaper nodded. 'I've put Sean's description of him out there, but nobody's coming back with anything useful.'

Sullivan opened the car door and put one leg in. 'One of our competitors?'

'Doesn't feel like it. If any of them wanted to make a move on us, they'd send more than one man, that's for sure. This feels different. More personal.'

Sullivan paused, pulled his head back out from under the car's roof. 'How so?'

'Sean told me this guy said he was coming for us. That there's nowhere to hide.'

Sullivan lifted his leg out of the car and stood up straight. He pulled on his cigarette, the tip glowing red as he squinted through the rising smoke and peered at Reaper over the car door. 'What do you make of that?'

Reaper shrugged. 'Sean says he's obsessed with finding the man who killed Jason Martin.'

The two men locked eyes. A tiny flicker of worry shot down Sullivan's spine. 'In that case, he needs netting, quickly. Send the boys after him again. Tell them not to be so soft this time.'

Reaper shook his head. 'I don't think it's as simple as that. This guy killed Liam. Shot him in the head from less than three feet away. Whoever he is, he's not fucking around.'

'Okay, send ten men after him. Fifteen if it makes you feel better. We've got an army in this city. Just make sure this time they snatch him off the streets and get him somewhere where they can find out what the fuck it is he's up to. You hear me?'

Reaper nodded and turned his back to make another call. Tommy appeared from one of the unit's loading bays and ran up to the vehicle.

'Boss,' Tommy said, breathless. 'About this container.'

'Close it up, get it back on a boat, then tell them to sail the thing out to sea and dump the lot of them in the ocean.' Sullivan moved to get in the vehicle, changed his mind, and stood back up. 'But not near the Thames Estuary – I don't want patrols increasing in our gateway. Tell them to take the boat south to the channel and dump them there. By the time they wash up on shore, it'll be thought of as nothing more than another failed crossing.'

Tommy nodded, turned, and ran back to the unit. Reaper cancelled his call and re-joined Sullivan next to the Mercedes.

'It's done,' Reaper said.

'Good.' Sullivan tugged hard on his cigarette. 'Let's hope we've soon got this stranger in a net.'

Reaper smiled. 'With the calibre of men I've sent on the hunt, he won't stand a chance.'

19

When Melanie answered the door, she had the appearance of a different person, no longer the confident woman who invited Drayce in the first time and watched over him like a hawk. Her eyes peeked up at him, head bowed, arms folded in front of her chest as though trying to contain the secret. Drayce heard the air huff out of his nostrils, felt his heartbeat thud in his chest. He forced himself to settle down.

'I left too soon,' he said, the words a growl through clenched teeth.

She stood to one side and let him in without saying a word. Once the door shut behind him, he glanced at the staircase, then faced Melanie.

'You lied to me,' he said.

She locked eyes with him, challenging his aggression with her defiance. 'Jason made me promise not to tell a soul.'

'And you stuck to that, even after they murdered him?'

Her eyes glistened; her lips quivered. 'I didn't know what to do. We never talked about a plan for if… if…' Her chin dropped to her chest, shoulders rocking in time with her sobs.

Drayce's fiery anger at being lied to, which had caused him to walk away and almost miss what he was sure would be a treasure trove of useful information, withered to a lazy flame. He took a deep breath, flooded with compassion for the grieving widow in front of him. He put a gentle hand on her shoulder.

'I need to see it,' he said.

Melanie looked up at him. Thick goblets of tears clung to her eyelashes. She nodded, sending a teardrop cascading down the front of her sweater. 'Help yourself. I'll stay down here.'

She turned away and walked out of sight.

Drayce went upstairs to the spare bedroom. His phone buzzed with a message. He checked the screen: Lucy. She wanted to meet for lunch at The York pub in Islington 'to discuss something important'. She could wait. He moved the cardboard boxes out of the way of the far wall and ran his hand along the ceiling, down the wall, and across the skirting board. His fingers hit something. He went over the same area again and felt the white plastic raised a millimetre or two above the rest in two locations, six inches apart, as though a section of the board had been cut vertically then placed back together, leaving it not quite flush. He put the palm of his hand in the centre and pushed. The cut-out section of skirting board depressed. He felt some slight resistance, heard a clunk, and to his astonishment, a door in the wall flapped open a couple of inches.

Drayce stood up. When he'd turned back to the house, his subconscious had told him something wasn't right. The dimensions on the outside didn't add up to what he'd witnessed on the inside. The spare bedroom should have been longer. A fake wall had been put up to hide something. But what?

Drayce opened the door.

The small, windowless space was dark and gloomy, lit by nothing more than the faint light that shone through from the bedroom. Drayce peered inside. A small wooden table was to his left with a chair pushed up to it. A lamp craned over a stack of paperwork a half inch thick, neatly stacked together on the desk. A fountain pen stood erect in a stand, a queue of spare ink cartridges lined up alongside. Above the desk was a corkboard, mounted to the wall. A dozen or more newspaper clippings were pinned to its surface. Drayce's eyes were drawn to Lily's face, front and centre of the biggest. He stepped inside and shuffled to the desk awkwardly, his size making it difficult to navigate the cramped space. The other clippings were articles written by investigative journalists, detailing the alleged activities of an organised crime group in London, warning of their growing influence, both in the capital and across the continent. Drayce recognised the top sheet on the stack of paper: the opening page of a Metropolitan Police case file, screenshotted at work then reproduced on a cheap home printer. Drayce flicked the pile like a pack of cards. There must have been a hundred sheets, a mixture of printed files and Jason's own handwritten notes.

Drayce sat down, switched on the lamp, and began reading.

-

Half an hour after Drayce climbed the stairs, he trampled back down with Jason's notes clutched in his hand. Melanie was manifestly alerted by the thud of his boots on each step; she hurried from the kitchen where she'd loitered and made it to the hallway just in time to catch sight of him striding from the foot of the stairs to the front door. She moved with purpose, no longer tearful, having had the time to subdue her emotions and strengthen her resolve.

By reminding herself of the reasons why she'd kept that room a secret, Drayce presumed.

'I've never set foot beyond that wall,' she said in a rush as he wrenched the door open. 'Whatever you found, it has nothing to do with me.'

Drayce stopped in the open doorway and turned his head to the side as acknowledgement of her words. 'You expect me to believe that?'

Out of the corner of his eye, he saw her wringing her hands in front of her chest, a terrified, pleading energy emerging.

'It's the truth!' she claimed.

'You've known that room was there all along, and you chose to keep it a secret; to lie to the police; to lie to me.'

Hesitation, brief but unmistakeable. 'I had no choice.'

'Yes, you did. And you chose poorly.' Drayce turned to face her properly. 'So now that we've established you're a liar, are you sure curiosity didn't once get the better of you?'

'I'm sure. Jason told me the less I know the better, and I trusted him. If he said I wasn't to know what was behind those walls, then that was good enough for me.'

Drayce was wary of uttering these next words to a woman still in the clutch of grief. He took a deep breath. 'And since his death?'

Melanie stood a little taller, her posture strengthening. She lifted her chin. 'I've come close a time or two these past few months. But if the knowledge behind those walls frightened a seasoned detective so much that he kept it hidden from the world, I knew how dangerous it must be, and in turn how at risk the lives of those who were cursed with it were. I wasn't going to jeopardise mine and my children's safety just because I was curious.'

'But then the secrets behind those walls would die with your husband, along with justice for my wife.'

Melanie stiffened through defiance. 'If that's the price to pay for the safety of my family, then so be it.'

Drayce felt himself deflate, at a total loss as to how Melanie could ignore what they had done to the man she loved. 'I understand your desire to protect your children, but they murdered your husband. What about justice for him?'

'Survival is more important than justice.'

Drayce folded Jason's notes in half, stuffed them into his jacket pocket, turned away, and stepped through the open door, unsure whether what he was witnessing from Melanie was fear or cowardice. Either way, he was revolted by it.

'Not to me, it isn't,' he said.

Melanie scurried to the doorway and called out to him with more than a hint of desperation in her voice. 'You're putting me and my children in danger! The men who killed Jason will come after us!'

Drayce halted in his tracks and stared at her over his shoulder. Melanie leaned back, her expression fearful, as though she'd seen something in his eyes. Something dark. An energy she had probably never seen before in a person.

'By the time I've finished with them,' he said, 'there won't be anyone left alive to come after you.'

20

Drayce caught a train to Watford, the hometown of Lily's parents. After reading the notes he'd found behind Jason's false wall, he wanted to speak to his wife's own flesh and blood, to seek reassurance he was doing the right thing by ploughing forward on his own. Having already killed a man, he was in too deep to turn back, but the revelations he'd discovered in Jason's home had risen the danger to a new level. Lucy's words sprang to the forefront of his mind. It was imperative he tread carefully from now on.

Lily's parents lived in a four-bedroom mock Tudor semi on Belmont Road. The front door was old and wooden, the top half opaque glass, the bottom a freshly painted sky blue, the same as when he'd last visited. Drayce stared at a slight indentation at the top, a dimple the size of a golf ball, triggering an avalanche of memories to come crashing into his mind.

–

'I think this might be the first time I've ever seen you nervous,' Lily said with a smile as she gazed up lovingly and admired Drayce. They were navigating the short path to her parent's front door, his hand held in both of hers.

'This is the first time I've had cause to be nervous in a long time,' he replied.

Lily pulled a face. 'You arrest terrorists at gunpoint, Alex.'

He shrugged. 'But that I'm in control of. *This…*' He nodded at the looming front door. 'This I have no control over.'

Lily rolled her eyes. 'It's just Sunday lunch.'

He chuckled nervously. 'It's not *just Sunday lunch*. It's expectations; it's first impressions; it's step one in the most important—'

Lily yanked him to a halt and clamped a hand over his mouth. 'You're overthinking it. Just be yourself and they'll love you.' She took her hand away from his mouth, kissed him, and smiled. 'Just like I do.'

His giant mitt clamped firmly back in both of her hands, she led him the rest of the way down the path. He caught sight of something thin and black flicking haphazardly around his right foot. His shoelace.

Lily reached for the doorbell.

'Wait,' he uttered, the word stumbling over his tongue in a rush. 'My shoelace.'

He hurriedly bent over but was halted in his tracks a moment later when his forehead struck the front door like a mallet, creating a loud, booming *clunk* that reverberated through the walls. He rubbed his head and groaned like a grumpy bear. Ignoring his sniggering girlfriend, he stepped back and bent the rest of the way down to tie his laces.

Lily looked on with a hand over her mouth to stifle her laughter.

'Well,' she said as she removed her hand and exposed her grin. 'I guess there's no need for me to ring the doorbell anymore.'

A large silhouette appeared on the other side of the opaque glass, growing larger still as it approached the door. It swung wide open before Drayce had a chance to finish what he was doing and stand up.

'Hello, love,' Lily's father said to his daughter. Drayce peered up. His eyes tracked the body of the man stood in front of him. Sam Carleton was everything he'd imagined the retired Royal Marine would be from Lily's description. His brown hair, greying at the sides, was combed to perfection, and his clothing.

– a pair of smart trousers with a precise crease down the front so sharp it might cut flesh, and a light blue shirt, pristinely ironed – was immaculate. Soldiers had spent less time preparing their attire for parade. He glanced down at Drayce with sharp eyes. 'We're not deaf you know. Just a light knock would have been enough. No need to bash it down.' He smiled. 'You're not at work now, son.'

Sam extended a hand.

Drayce rushed to tie off his laces and stood up. He shook the hand of his girlfriend's father and smiled in the hope he was doing enough to hide from his face the embarrassment he felt. He tried to ignore the dimple in the door in the hope he wouldn't draw Sam's attention to it.

'Make way, Samuel,' came a voice from over Sam's shoulder.

He turned to make way for Elizabeth – Lily's mother – whose face beamed with delight as she came into view.

'Hi, Cherub,' she said, her arms branching out wide before wrapping around Lily.

'Hi, Mum.'

Elizabeth met Drayce's eye from over her daughter's shoulder. 'And you must be Alex.'

'It's lovely to meet you, Mrs Carleton.'

She narrowed her eyelids and pouted her lips as she gently parted from Lily. 'Less of that. You'll call me Elizabeth.'

Drayce's smile widened as he bowed his head just a fraction. 'Elizabeth.' He held out his hand.

'Well, well, aren't we the formal type. It must be all that discipline you've learnt in the police.' She batted his hand to one side, stepped in, and hugged him tightly, her arms around his waist on account of him being too tall for her to reach above his shoulders. 'It's lovely to meet you too, Alex.' When they parted, she gazed up and appraised him for a moment. 'My, my, so handsome.'

'Mum!' Lily rolled her eyes, but evidently couldn't keep the smile off her face.

'What?' Elizabeth glanced at her daughter. 'He is.' She turned back to Drayce. 'A little on the rugged side for my tastes, but first impressions are good.'

Drayce felt his face flush and knew he was blushing.

'Oh my God,' Lily said as she rubbed her forehead in exasperation. 'This is precisely the sort of conversation that is normally held back for after we've left.' She put her hands on her hips and pulled a face at her mother that suggested she was trying to frown through the smile but was clearly finding it difficult to hide her amusement. 'We haven't even crossed the doorway yet and you're already embarrassing me.'

Elizabeth giggled as she turned and walked back inside. 'Well, you better come in then. I haven't even got started.'

Sam held the door open for Lily and Drayce, who knelt to take his shoes off.

'No need for that, lad, just come on through. It's probably safest if we limit the amount of times you undo those.' He smirked. 'Wouldn't want you getting a concussion.'

Sam laughed at his own joke as Drayce walked down the hallway. His once flushed face turned paler by the second as he followed his nose to the kitchen, feeling completely out of his depth for the first time in years.

—

The knife and fork clattered loudly against the plate as Sam finished his last mouthful and laid the utensils to rest. 'Delicious, darling.' He dabbed his mouth with a napkin. 'Best one yet.'

Elizabeth shrugged the red wool throw off her slender shoulders and left the table to put dessert in the oven: a deep, round apple pie the size of a small car's tyre. She gave her daughter's shoulders a loving squish as she passed behind her.

Lily leaned back in her seat, the palms of her hands resting on her midriff. 'I couldn't eat another bite.'

Drayce politely placed his knife and fork down on the plate, side by side, north to south, as Old-Man-Jack had taught him many years ago, at the end of one of the many meals he'd cooked for Drayce when he'd been living above the boxing gym in Nottingham. The memory brought a smile to his face. He wondered how Jack was doing and promised to himself he'd find the time to visit the only father figure he'd ever had.

'Is that it?' Elizabeth said, inspecting Drayce's plate as she returned to her seat and wrapped the throw back around her shoulders, pulling it tightly across the front of her neck. Clearly, Lily's mother felt a chill with ease. 'A man your size can surely manage more.'

Drayce caught her eye and realised she'd been watching him for a while. His unsatiated appetite must have been written all over his face.

'Well…'

'Here.' She handed him a serving spoon. 'It all needs eating.' She flicked her head towards Colin, their black labrador, curled up by the Agar. 'If you don't eat it, Colin will, and he's on a diet.'

'*Should* be on a diet,' Sam interjected.

'Yes, yes,' Elizabeth said with a dismissive wave of the hand. 'He *should* be on a diet. But you try resisting that face.'

Colin's head rose, his big, round, glassy eyes looking pleadingly at the table of leftovers. Drayce understood Elizabeth's struggle. If Colin was his, he'd get whatever he wanted.

'Thank you,' Drayce said as he took the spoon and lifted his knife and fork to make way for a second helping.

Elizabeth caught her husband's eye. 'Put a pot of coffee on, would you, dear?' Sam gingerly stood up and made his way to the filter machine on the counter. 'And use your stick.'

'I don't need that wretched thing to get around my home,' he grumbled. 'I've fought in three wars during my lifetime.' He reached out and took hold of the counter's edge to steady himself. 'Marched across deserts and streets and mountain ranges, so I'll be damned if I need a bloody walking stick to make it across the kitchen.'

Elizabeth rolled her eyes in response to her husband's stubbornness. Her gaze settled on Drayce, watching him fill his plate, her elbows resting on the table and her fingers steepled. 'So, Alex, where did you grow up?'

Drayce felt his body lock tight, the spoon pausing midway through the mound of mashed potato. He'd been dreading this line of questioning and had naively hoped the topic of his upbringing wouldn't come up. He caught sight of Lily in the corner of his eye, glancing nervously between him and her mother.

'Alex…' Lily began, her lips faltering as her brain struggled with how to construct the rest of that sentence.

'It's complicated,' Drayce said. He broke free of his temporary paralysis and continued loading his plate. 'My parents both died when I was very young.'

Elizabeth's steepled fingers shot apart. She clasped them to her chest, one hand over the other, right above her heart. 'Oh, Alex. I'm so sorry. I shouldn't have—'

He looked her in the eye and smiled to ease her discomfort. 'Don't be silly – you weren't to know.' He glanced down at his plate and began loading his fork. 'I grew up in children's homes all over the country, but mostly in the north. Spent the majority of my teens in Nottingham until I joined the police in Manchester.' His weighty fork hovered in mid-air. 'Not exactly a traditional upbringing, but it made me the man I am today.' He quickly shovelled the food into his mouth, grateful he had an excuse not to talk for a bit after blurting out such a stupid cliché.

'Sounds like you've had a hard life,' Sam said, his eyes carefully assessing the man in his daughter's life.

Drayce shrugged as he finished his mouthful. 'Harder than some; easier than others. We play the cards we're dealt. I had no control over it, so I didn't worry about it.'

'Well,' Elizabeth interjected with a grin. 'That's all in the past now. What matters is the future.' She reached across the table and placed a hand on her daughter's arm. 'Come with me, my love. I want to show you something I've been making for you.'

Lily caught Drayce's eye as she stood. 'Mum's taken up a new hobby.'

'I've started knitting.' Elizabeth pulled a face. 'God, I feel old!'

They sauntered down the hall together, their arms linked, giggling to one another. When they went out of sight, Drayce felt the power of Sam's eyes on him. The big, retired marine leaned forward and propped his elbows on the table. He balled his right hand into a fist, wrapped the other around it. Drayce sensed they'd been left alone on purpose.

'I hate to get all "old fashioned" on you, Alex. But I'm an old-fashioned kind of man.'

Drayce met his eyes. 'Okay.'

'I realise today is the first time we've met, but I understand you've been courting my daughter for a while.'

Drayce nodded. 'That's right.'

'Then you need to know something – something that might seem obvious, but needs saying, nonetheless.' Sam paused, his gaze breaking momentarily as he scanned the table. He was choosing his words carefully, Drayce surmised. Or had probably chosen them a while ago and was taking the time to make sure he got the prepared speech right. Drayce kept his mouth shut and waited. 'Her whole life, it has been my responsibility to keep her safe. Anything she's ever needed, any threat or danger that has come her way, I've dealt with it, whether she knew about it or not. Not a moment has gone by when I haven't been fully focused on keeping my girl safe from the many things in this world that pose a risk to her.' He locked his fierce eyes on Drayce. 'So, when a new man enters her life, I wouldn't be doing my job as her father if I didn't make it perfectly clear how important Lily's happiness and wellbeing are to me. You make her happy, you keep her safe, and you and I will be best friends.' His Adam's apple bobbed in his throat as he swallowed, his left hand squeezing his clenched right. 'But if you're ever the cause of her pain; if you ever let harm come her way...' He let the statement trail off, allowing the silence to communicate the rest for him.

'I understand,' Drayce replied.

'Take good care of my girl.'

Footsteps descending the stairs broke the tension in the kitchen. Elizabeth and Lily appeared moments later.

'What do you think?' Lily asked Drayce, her face beaming above the multi-coloured wool scarf that was wrapped around her neck and shoulders. She turned on the spot to give him a fuller appreciation of what her mother had made for her, her long, brown, silky hair swaying across her face.

'I love it,' Drayce replied. He admired her beauty for a moment, thinking not only of how lucky he was, but also of how there was nothing on this God-given Earth that could ever get through him to harm her. His safety, his wellbeing, his life, would all come secondary. He turned back to her father and whispered, 'You have nothing to worry about.'

Drayce noticed Elizabeth catch her husband's eye as she walked past the table to check on the apple pie, a knowing glance exchanged between the two of them.

21

Drayce reached back and rubbed the top of his traps, digging his fingers into the sore muscles, which were still knotted and aching from everything he'd demanded of his body in the States. He pressed the Carletons' doorbell, its high pitch buzzing through the glass. A silhouette appeared. A key turned. Drayce braced himself.

Sam filled the doorway, arms crossed; muscles bulged despite the man's age. Serious eyes lurked beneath bushy grey brows as they assessed the visitor. Pressed brown chinos, ironed shirt, bright white hair pristinely combed, there wasn't a single thing about the ex-marine's appearance or demeanour that hadn't been brutally whipped into shape. He stood guard, assessed the man on his doorstep, his face so red it could stop traffic. Drayce extended his hand.

'Hello, Sam.'

'Alex.'

Lily's father didn't move, didn't even glance down at the olive branch. Drayce lowered his hand.

A shadow swept along the corridor. Drayce smiled when Elizabeth came into view.

'For the love of God, Sam, move out of the way.' Strong hands barged their way through and forced her husband out of the door. 'What kind of a welcome is that for our son-in-law?'

Elizabeth stepped outside and admired Drayce, hands clasped in front of her chest, eyes wide. She smiled in wonder. 'Oh, Alex.' Gentle arms found their way around his waist and hugged him tightly, her voice muffled against his chest. 'How long has it been?'

'Too long,' Drayce replied, avoiding Sam's glare. He put his arms around Elizabeth's shoulders and hugged her back.

She broke free and gazed up at him, clamped her hands on his cheeks, cupped his face. There were tears in her eyes. 'It's so good to see you.'

Drayce swallowed the emotions that were building. 'You too.'

She eased her hold on him when she noticed the week-old cut to his face. 'Oh dear. Sweetheart, what have you been up to?'

'Just a few bad days at work. Nothing to worry about.'

'What brings you here?' Sam asked, arms folded again.

Elizabeth shot him a look that could stop a charging bull. 'Never mind what brings him here. He's here, and that's all that matters.'

Drayce looked Sam in the eye. 'I've been doing some work in the city and—'

'Don't you dare explain yourself to that grumpy old fool!' Elizabeth took his hand and led him inside. 'Come. You must be hungry.'

'Actually, I—'

'I'll fire up the grill and grate some cheese. We'll have tuna melts.'

Drayce thought about the steak he'd eaten not long ago but didn't want to derail his mother-in-law. She'd always found joy in feeding the people she cared about. Drayce looked down at his boots. 'Shall I take off my—'

'No, no, don't bother with that. Everywhere downstairs is tiled, remember? No use for carpets when you share your home with a labrador.'

There was no stopping her, Drayce realised. He rode the wave all the way to the kitchen, the air heating up substantially as he made his way through the house. Elizabeth felt the cold more than anyone Drayce had ever known, the central heating cranked up even on the approach to summer.

'Here,' Elizabeth said, pulling a chair out at the dining table in the middle of the room. 'Take a seat.'

'Thank you,' Drayce replied as she shrugged off his jacket and draped it over the back support, wiping his brow with the back of his hand as he slowly acclimatised to the stifling temperature. The pistols in the pockets clattered against the wooden legs. Drayce peeked at Elizabeth to assess whether she'd noticed; if she had, the sound of two heavy metal objects in his possession certainly didn't cause her to be suspicious – she scurried around the kitchen, seemingly oblivious as she gathered everything she'd need to make a spot of lunch for her son-in-law.

The home of Lily's parents hadn't changed one bit since Drayce's last visit. He glanced at the solid oak cabinets that lined the kitchen, mounted above black granite countertops that were polished to a high gloss. Everything was immaculate. Drayce heard the front door close. Colin raised his head above the lip of his bed in front of the radiator, noticed the guest, offered a double wag of the tail, then put his head back down.

'Samuel, come and brew a pot of coffee,' Elizabeth called out. She took a break from busily gathering the required kitchen utensils to fuss Colin's head. 'He likes it there, bless him. You like it where it's warm, now you're an old boy, don't you, Colin.'

Sam appeared with his usual slow and steady gait, face a grimace. Even a decade later, he clearly still despised his wife's choice for their dog's name. Drayce had always thought it was perfect.

Sam ignored Drayce as he followed Elizabeth's orders. The walking stick he'd always hated and refused to use was propped up next to the whisky cabinet, an item of furniture he'd always loved and refused to leave alone. He shot Drayce a hostile look and fired up the coffee machine with some reluctance.

'Tell us, Alex,' Elizabeth said as she laid two baguettes on a chopping board and sawed at them lengthways with a bread knife. 'What have you been up to since we last saw you?'

'Working, mostly. I've just got back from the States.'

'Ooh, whereabouts?'

'LA and Vegas.'

'Plenty of people in need of a bodyguard over there I imagine.' She glanced at him out of the corner of her eye as she fetched butter from the fridge, her gaze assessing the marks on his face. 'Dangerous place, America.'

Drayce nodded. 'It can be.'

'And I suppose when you protect people for a living, the dangerous places are where the work is. Isn't that right, Samuel?'

Sam responded with a noise that might have been indecipherable English but could just as easily have been a groan.

Elizabeth eyed Drayce as she buttered the baguettes and jerked her head at her husband. 'He'd know all about being sent to dangerous places from his time in the military.' She raised her voice. 'How's that coffee coming along, dear?'

The reservoir had been filled and Sam was now pouring coffee grounds into the basket.

'Not long,' he replied, as he closed the lid and pressed a button.

'How long's—'

'Five minutes, maybe.'

'Good. Come sit at the table.'

Sam took his time, ignoring Drayce until he was seated opposite him. Once he'd shuffled his chair forward, he propped his elbows on the table, wrapped his left hand over his clenched right fist, and rested his chin on top, eyes locked on Drayce until the food was served.

The two men ate in silence as Elizabeth sipped her coffee and chatted away, reminisced, and asked questions among the speech without pausing for answers. Drayce smiled and nodded in the right places and told her how delicious the food was once he'd finished. At no point did he notice Sam take his eyes off him.

Elizabeth reached across the table and took Drayce's hand in both of hers. 'It's so good to see you, Alex. After all this time.'

'I'm sorry I haven't visited in a while.'

'You don't need to be sorry about a thing.'

'It's just… hard. To see you, I mean. It reminds me of Lily. Of everything I lost.'

'Everything *we* lost,' Sam corrected, prompting a stern look from his wife.

Elizabeth's eyes glistened again when she turned back to Drayce. She bit her lip in an obvious attempt to hold back the tears. 'Well, you didn't lose us, dear. And you're always welcome. Anytime. Any reason.'

She glanced at her husband, his face as hard as stone, eyes still locked on Drayce, lips parted in a snarl.

'Why are you here?'

'Samuel!'

'We deserve an answer. This isn't just a social visit; I can tell. The man has something to tell us.'

Drayce gently pulled his hand away from Elizabeth and focused on Sam. He met the man's eyes. 'You're right.'

'Well, spit it out.'

Elizabeth slapped the table. The cutlery jumped. 'Samuel, I swear—'

Drayce caught Elizabeth's eye and raised a calming hand. He turned back to Sam. 'I've found information in relation to Lily's murder.'

It was as though their world had suddenly stopped. Both were statues.

'In… In… Information?' Elizabeth stuttered. 'What kind of information?'

'You mean evidence?' Sam asked him.

Drayce nodded. 'Yes. But there are complications.'

'What do you mean *complications*?'

'The information is about the people who are responsible for her death.'

Elizabeth gasped, pulled a hand to her mouth.

'But,' Drayce quickly added, 'it doesn't identify her killer.'

'Have you been to the police?'

Drayce took a deep breath. 'No.'

Sam shot out of his chair. 'You idiot! You mean to say you've kept this to yourself? For how long?'

'I came straight here as soon as I found it.'

'Why?' Sam roared.

Despite being separated by a wide table, his breath still billowed across Drayce's face like a hairdryer. Drayce stood, squared up to the man. 'I need your blessing for what I plan to do next. She was your daughter. You deserve a say.'

Sam frowned. His eyes searched Drayce's face. 'What are you talking about?'

'Sit down, Sam. Let me explain.'

'Don't tell me to sit down in my own—'

'Oh, for the love of God!' Elizabeth's voice cut through the air like a sword, so sharp that her husband, the retired marine, hardened by six tours split between Northern Ireland, Kosovo, and Iraq, startled. Her eyes were daggers. 'Sit down, Samuel!'

Sam did as he was told.

Drayce reclaimed his seat.

'Tell us what you found,' Elizabeth said.

Drayce did just that. He took out of his jacket pocket the folded wad of papers he'd found on the desk in Jason Martin's secret room and laid them out on the kitchen table. Once he'd finished explaining what it all meant, he sat in silence and waited for their response.

'I don't believe it,' Elizabeth said.

'I know it's hard to get your head around,' Drayce replied, 'but this is all accurate information. Jason was a highly trained investigator with years of experience. He knew what he was doing.'

'So, he carried on with the investigation after leaving the police?'

'Precisely.'

'In secret? Collating these notes behind a fake wall in his home?'

'Yes.'

Elizabeth turned to her husband. His red face had paled. 'Samuel? Say something.'

Sam stayed silent, a thousand-yard stare cast down at the papers.

'All of this might be enough for me to identify Lily's killer,' Drayce said. 'But not if I take it to the police.'

Elizabeth frowned. 'Why not?'

'There's a reason Jason stole these documents and carried out his own investigation at home. He clearly didn't trust the giant machine that is the Metropolitan Police with this information. Which leads me to believe perhaps I shouldn't either. Added to that is the fact that Lily's murder was ordered by an extremely powerful and wealthy criminal organisation. The police must act within the law, which weakens their position. Organisations such as this,' he tapped a finger on the sheets of paper, 'cover their tracks well and can afford the best solicitors on the planet. If I hand this over to the police, the criminals will close ranks and hide the man who murdered Lily.' Drayce clasped his hands together on the table. 'But if I go after him myself, I can play by my own rules, leaving him with nowhere to hide.'

'You're talking about breaking the law?' Sam asked. 'Becoming a vigilante?'

'Yes.'

'You can't do that, Alex,' Elizabeth said.

'Yes, I can. I owe it to Lily.'

'Let the police carry out their investigation.'

Drayce shook his head. 'It won't work.'

'You can't just break the law, Alex. There are rules—'

'The law's a joke, being laughed at by the likes of Lily's killer. I enforced and obeyed the law for nearly two decades, as did Lily. We both followed the rules. So did you, your whole lives. And look where it got us: mourning the death of a daughter and a wife who was brutally murdered in the street.'

The punch came out of nowhere, thumping Drayce's right cheek. Elizabeth gasped. Drayce rocked back in his chair, heard the crack of his shoulder blades as they hit the edge of the kitchen counter behind him.

Sam retracted his fist, teeth clamped firmly together as his chest heaved. Air huffed through his nostrils, mimicking an angry bull.

Drayce's chair settled back in its default position. He shook his head, tasted blood, and stared calmly at the man who'd hit him. The ex-marine may have been retired and in his sixties, but he punched like a professional fighter in his twenties. Elizabeth was silent, hands clamped over her mouth. Drayce took a breath and summoned the courage to describe the elephant in the room.

'Sam, I know you blame me for not keeping your daughter safe—'

'No,' Elizabeth said. 'That's not—'

Once again, Drayce held up a hand, palm facing her. 'Please, let me finish.' He searched Sam's eyes. 'I know you blame me, and I understand why.' Sam looked away. A glimmer of shame danced across his face as the truth registered. He unclenched his fists. 'I blame myself too. I wasn't there when Lily needed me, and it was my job to keep her safe. I must live with that. And I'm struggling. I know you're hurting, but you're not the only one. The life was ripped out of my heart when your daughter died. I've just been existing ever since.' Drayce swallowed the lump in his throat. 'I can never make it right, because I can never bring her back, but what I can do is make the people responsible pay for what they did.'

A moment of silence passed. Sam's expression softened. He struggled to meet Drayce's eyes.

'One man committed the act,' Drayce continued, 'but there's an entire organisation behind that man, an organisation too powerful for the neutered law in this country to be of any consequence.' He felt his face redden, his blood anger, the fire in his soul taking over. Another fracture formed in the dam, a loud *crack* echoing across the valley as the immense power of what he was holding back threatened to burst free. 'They're out there in the world, right now, right this second, living their lives, while our Lily rests in the ground. I can't live with that.'

Elizabeth took her husband's hand, the one he'd hit Drayce with, and stroked his swelling knuckles. 'What exactly is it you want our blessing for, Alex?'

Drayce felt the locket swing against his chest. He turned his wedding ring around his finger. 'They think they got away with it. I want to remind them they haven't. No one gets away with anything. Not really. Whatever energy you put out there, the universe always finds a way of sending it back to you, days, weeks, years later, multiplied a thousand times.'

He switched his gaze between Sam and Elizabeth.

'When they killed Lily, the energy they sent out into the world was so horrific, monstrous, and painful, that when the universe does hurtle it back at them, their entire world will be destroyed.' Drayce's legs trembled, the dam cracking further. 'That energy's in me. I want to let go of everything I've been holding on to for the last three and a half years. I want to snap. I want to hurtle their wrongs back at them a thousand times. Everything they know, everything about their way of life. With your permission, I'll destroy it all. I'll turn their world into ash.'

Elizabeth and Sam stared at him, mesmerised. Eventually, Elizabeth reached across the table and took his hand. 'You've always made the right decision, Alex. Whatever the choice, you've always chosen well. Lily trusted your judgement implicitly, as do we.' She gazed at her husband; his expression mirrored hers. He gave her a slight nod of the head, almost imperceptible. 'So, whatever you need to do.' Eyes glazed; tears built. 'Whatever you think is for the best...' She tried to speak further, but couldn't, her breath lost in the anguish.

In the quiet of her suffering, her husband wrapped an arm around her. He reached across and gripped Drayce's shoulder with the same hand he'd punched him with just moments ago. The two men locked eyes. Sam was trembling as well, as though something in him was about to break, two men holding back unimaginable pain. But he held it together, resolute no matter what, for the good of his family. His fingers felt like steel. Drayce's arm was going numb. Sam's eyes widened, an understanding reached between the two of them without the need for words. But Sam spoke them regardless.

'Do it,' he said. 'Make them pay.'

22

Drayce left Lily's parents' house an emotional wreck. He walked, or more accurately staggered to the train station, sat on a bench, closed his eyes, and slowed his mind. To help distract him from the cluster bomb of information threatening to overwhelm him, he replied to Lucy's message and agreed to meet her.

Two possibilities sprang to mind when he considered her motivation for reaching out to him: either she was having cold feet about their agreement regarding her husband, or she'd got wind that Territt had put a team out on the streets to spy on Drayce. He hopped on his train back to London and crossed his fingers it was the former.

Forty minutes later, Drayce spotted Lucy from across the street. He'd asked the taxi driver who had picked him up from the station to drop him short of the pub in Islington, in case he was walking into a trap. She was sat alone outside, as expected, at a table nestled under the overhanging branches of two birch trees. An empty plate sat in front of her, knife and fork lined up on top. The honking, belching traffic streamed by continuously.

No sign of an arrest team.

Drayce crossed the street, still nervous about her motivation.

As he caught her eye, the folded stack of paperwork wedged into his inner jacket pocket jabbed him in the ribs, reminding him of the most pressing issue. He took a couple of deep breaths to settle his nerves and prayed they wouldn't show on his expression. With what he'd found hidden in Jason Martin's home, he'd need to utilise every ounce of acting talent he possessed if he was to keep his anger at bay. And it wasn't as though the paperwork was the only thing stressing him out; he was more than mildly uncomfortable meeting a serving police officer with loaded guns in his pockets.

Lucy nodded at the seat opposite her. 'Sit down. We need to talk.'

Warning bells rang, but Drayce did as he was told. The expression on Lucy's face suggested it was probably for the best.

'Sounds serious,' he said. 'Am I in trouble?'

'Not yet. And I hope to keep it that way.'

'How about a *thanks for replying to my message so quickly and meeting with me at such short notice.*'

Lucy stared at him without saying a word. She didn't even blink.

'Can I at least order a drink first?' Drayce asked.

'Sure. The waiter will be over soon.'

'Table service at a pub?'

'Did you fall asleep in 2005 and wake up this morning? Or have you just spent too long outside of London to remember how things are done properly?'

Drayce huffed and cupped his chin with the palm of his hand. His fingertips drummed a beat against his temple. 'Please tell me why you asked to meet with me. It's just, as much fun as it is to sit here with the world's most efficient mood hoover, I'd quite like to crack on with the rest of my plans for the day.'

'I've been thinking about our agreement.'

'What about it?'

'We need to discuss boundaries.'

'All right. What do you have in mind? And before you say it, don't worry, I wasn't planning on killing your husband.'

Lucy's head darted side to side at the busy tables around them. She lowered her voice. 'Don't even joke about that! And he's my ex-husband, actually!'

'Not until the divorce is finalised. Which is where I come in.'

Now it was Lucy's turn to huff. The air burst out of her nostrils, the sound that of a disgruntled dog.

'What boundaries?' Drayce asked, wanting this meeting over with as soon as possible.

'You can't hurt him.'

Drayce looked away, scratched his neck. 'At all?'

Lucy shook her head. 'If it ever got out that it was me who sent you after him…'

Drayce put up a hand. 'All right, I won't hurt him.'

'You promise?'

He scratched his chin. 'Define hurt.'

'Alex!'

'All right. I promise. I'll just have to be a little more creative than usual.'

'Words only.'

He raised his eyebrows. 'You want to tie my hands behind my back while we're at it? How am I supposed to—'

'I don't care how you do it, just as long as you don't injure him.'

'You don't want to make it easy for me, do you?'

'What I don't want is to be arrested and lose my job. Frighten him as much as you need to, just don't break the bastard.'

Drayce shrugged. 'Fine.'

A waiter came over with a smile and a menu. Drayce didn't need either. He ordered a bottle of water. The waiter sauntered off, unimpressed.

Lucy cast judgement his way. 'Last of the big spenders.'

'I've already eaten.'

'Didn't fancy anything a little stronger?'

'I want to stay sharp.'

'Any particular reason?'

Mind your damn business, Drayce wanted to say. But instead, he went with, 'I don't drink during the day.'

Lucy stood up. 'Whatever gets you through life. I'm off to the bathroom. Think through what I've said.'

Drayce watched her go and pondered how he might put a double-barrelled twelve-gauge shotgun in her husband's mouth while he explained precisely how the divorce is going to play out. Probably wouldn't injure him, providing Drayce didn't pull the trigger.

Lucy should have been more precise with her words.

Her phone caught his eye, flat on the tabletop, peeking out from behind her drink. Drayce scanned the pub doorway she'd only just disappeared through. Jason's paperwork dug into his ribs; his memory of the contents flashed in front of his eyes. Could save him a lot of work, if he was quick enough. How long did he have? Certainly a couple of minutes; probably no more than five. Best get a move on.

Grateful he'd spontaneously memorised Lucy's PIN during their first encounter, he opened the screen and found the app that would do the job he was after. He typed in the details he'd memorised from earlier and hit search. Bingo. He memorised the information that came up, always keeping an eye on the pub's doorway. Being sure to erase any evidence of his activity, he placed Lucy's phone exactly where she'd left it just before she reappeared.

'There's something else that's been bugging me,' she said as she approached the table and reclaimed her seat, clearly none the wiser.

Drayce tried to look relaxed. 'Do tell.'

Her eyelids narrowed. 'What you said in the cafe: the way you worked out everything to do with my ex. It doesn't sit right with me. Even in an episode of Poirot, your powers of deduction would have fallen on the wrong end of the believability scale.'

Drayce forced a smile onto his face. 'What? You don't see me as a match for Poirot?'

'Only if he started making notes in crayon.'

That one made him laugh for real. 'I went back to the nick after our first meeting.'

Lucy couldn't hide her shock. 'You did what?'

'I spoke to the enquiry officer.'

'Which one?'

'Janet. Nice lady, once you break the ice.'

'Hard one to get on the right side of. The cops at Islington call her Amen, because she's always got to have the last word.'

Drayce nodded. 'Yeah, I got that impression when we first met, but she soon came around. Started out as friendly chit chat, reminded her I was ex-Job, and before I knew it, she was telling me all the nick's dirty secrets. By the way, who's The Microwave? She really doesn't like the bloke, whoever he is.'

Lucy stared at Drayce, lips parted as though about to speak, eyelids narrowed as though trying to work him out. 'You're lying. She wouldn't have told you anything personal about me.'

'No, you're right.' A smirk crept onto his expression. 'I must have just worked it all out by myself.'

Lucy stiffened; no one liked to be the subject of gossip.

'Don't feel bad,' Drayce said. 'In my experience, nobody has secrets in a police station.'

Lucy necked her drink, stood up sharply, and snatched her phone from the table.

'Fucking nosy cow!'

'Bit harsh. I might be the size of one, but…'

She threw him a sarcastic look. 'You're not funny.'

'It's been said before.' Drayce felt guilty for angering her. 'Listen, don't leave yet. Stay for another drink.'

'I can't, I've got things to do. I just wanted to see you in person briefly, to make sure we both understand where the boundary is when it comes to Barnaby.'

Drayce shared the expression of a man who'd swallowed a fly. 'That's his name? Barnaby?'

'Don't. It wasn't the only dickhead warning sign I ignored.'

Drayce nodded. 'I see.'

As the waiter brought over Drayce's bottle of water and a glass with ice, Lucy half turned to leave.

Drayce stood up. 'Hang on. You going to tell me who The Microwave is before you leave?'

She shrugged. 'Just some young know-it-all probationer at the station who Janet doesn't like.'

'But why The Microwave?'

The hint of a smile broke out on Lucy's face. 'Because he's been in two minutes and he's already done.'

–

From their positions, they watched their target fill his glass. Conor swept his long grey hair out of his face, took out his phone, and called Reaper.

'We've found him.' He sank a little lower in the front passenger seat of the silver BMW and peered around the B-pillar. 'He met some woman at a pub. Now she's left and he's drinking alone.'

'Good,' Reaper said. 'Let him finish his last drink, then follow him when he leaves and take him at the first opportunity. But remember, don't kill him. We need him alive if we're to find out his identity and his motivation for sticking his nose where it doesn't belong.'

'Understood.'

'Call me back when you've got him somewhere quiet, and I'll arrange to come meet you.'

'You want him still in one piece when you get there?'

A pause for deliberation. 'Yes. If he needs to be tortured, I'll be the one to do it.'

Conor smiled at his boss's love for excessive violence. 'I'll ring you back within the hour.' He cancelled the call and turned to face Brendan, his driver. 'Tell the others to get out of their cars and position themselves on the street. Our boy's on foot. When he leaves the pub, I want us all around him, ready to leap on the bastard.'

Brendan nodded, took out his phone, and made the call.

23

The sun broke free from behind a cloud just as Drayce finished his second glass. Dazzled by its glare but unwilling to turn away, he shut his eyes and let the rays warm his face. The speckled shade of the overhanging birch tree, coupled with the ice, had kept the second half of the bottle cold up until now, but with the warmer turn of the ever-unpredictable British weather, time was running out. He finished the water while it was still an acceptable temperature. Were his jacket not concealing such important documents and weaponry, he'd have removed it to take advantage of the sunny spell.

When the waiter collected the empty bottle and glass, Drayce asked for the bill. While he waited for him to return with a card machine, he took out his phone to summon an Uber. The information he'd surreptitiously stolen from Lucy's phone would help him with his next move on the board, but the person he planned to visit, and the questions he needed to ask, would heat things up substantially. Extreme caution was required when he approached this next link in the chain.

He tapped on the app, hovered his thumb over the screen.

And froze.

The urge to look up at the man who had assessed him as he'd walked by was strong, but Drayce was stronger. He resisted and kept his head down, eyes buried in his phone. Under normal circumstances, the attention of a stranger wouldn't mean a thing, but right now, Drayce was living the very antithesis of normal. Paranoia was his friend, his survival mechanism. He lifted his chin and tapped his fingers on the table, playing the part of the impatient Londoner who wanted to pay his bill and get on with the day. He watched the guy in his peripheral vision. The man was in his thirties, face cursed with the hardened appearance of a person who'd spent a great deal of their life consumed by anger. His dark hair was cut short. He wore jeans and a leather jacket, both of which looked fashionable and expensive. Same for the boots. A thousand pounds on a casual outfit meant he wasn't one of Territt's cops.

Drayce breathed a sigh of relief.

Now the only question that needed answering was whether Drayce's gut instinct was correct. Was the guy interested in him, or not? He watched and waited. Another came into view from up the street and seemed as though he'd been spat out of the same twenty-first century gangster factory as the first guy. He swaggered past the man on his phone. They noticeably avoided one another, like opposing magnets unable to get too close. Unnatural. Drayce pivoted his head and scanned his surroundings.

Thirty yards behind him were another pair from the same production line, loitering with no apparent purpose. Across the street, two more fit the mould, hanging around the bus stop. They'd been there a while, and plenty of buses had come by.

Drayce took a deep breath, closed the Uber app, and put his phone away.

A taxi was no good to him now. He needed to stay on his feet, mobile and ready to react, not cocooned in a metal box controlled by a stranger. He'd hoped for a response of this nature, and the organisation hadn't let him down.

Time to make the most of it.

He paid his bill, stood up, and headed down the road. They might try and take him here, on a busy street, but if Drayce was a betting man, he'd put his money on them waiting for a better opportunity.

Time to give them one.

He approached the entrance to Angel tube station. The shiny windows at the front of the bank Drayce passed reflected his background beautifully. The three pairs all followed, staggered, with twenty metres between Drayce and the closest. He entered the tube station, touched his credit card to the contactless sensor, and jogged down the escalator. A glance over his shoulder at the bottom showed no sign of the nearest pair.

Drayce ran through the walkways, his hurried footsteps clipping against the red and grey stone slabs. Out of sight of the people following him, he assessed the theatre for the game they were about to play. With shiny domes at every junction to see around the corners, and advertising boards with glass screens covering the walls, it made a successful ambush unlikely; both a positive and a negative for Drayce. He would have to be more creative. He marched to the southbound platform, stood out of sight behind a corner between two junctions, both of which led back to the main walkway, and waited.

The weight of the guns in his jacket pockets was a constant reminder of his potential to cause harm in this forthcoming scenario. Discipline was paramount. With the number of cameras dotted around the station, a shootout would undoubtedly result in arrest and prosecution. He clenched his giant hands into fists. The guns would have to stay where they were.

Eyes locked onto the reflective domed mirror, he spotted the first pair before they spotted him. They exchanged a glance and split up on the walkway: one to the northbound, the other south. Drayce locked eyes on the corner and planted his feet in a fighting stance.

As the man stepped onto the platform, he saw Drayce immediately. Aghast, eyes wide, mouth open in a silent scream, the man fumbled with his jacket, no doubt an attempt to arm himself. But he was too slow. Drayce's fist impacted his chin with a *crack* just as his hand slipped into a pocket, spinning his head as his jaw hinges tore from his skull with the *snap* of ligaments. The energy shockwave travelled down his entire body, twisting his shoulders, torso, and waist. His legs buckled.

He hit the wall, cracked an electronic advertising screen, but was caught in a pair of giant hands before he reached the floor.

Drayce dragged him along the platform, smiling at the other travellers to try to put them at ease, all of whom were backing away. He sat the man down on a bench, folded his arms across his chest, and checked his airway. Still breathing. He pulled his cap down over his eyes and assessed his work: probably be hours before anyone tried to wake him, and it might be a full twenty-four before he woke up naturally after a punch like that.

Drayce slipped off his jacket to change his appearance, folded it up next to his unconscious mate, then jogged back to the junction and eyed the mirrored dome.

The second pair appeared on the walkway. They looked left and right but didn't appear to clock Drayce in the domed mirror, lurking on the southbound platform. They separated to cover both sides, but then the other half of the first pair reappeared from the northbound and shook his head.

All three walked towards Drayce.

He hustled closer to the corner and turned his back on them. The tracks rumbled and a steady gush of air passed through the tunnel, indicating the next train was imminent. Drayce listened to their approaching footsteps and held his nerve. At the last moment, he spun around and grabbed the guy at the front, using his hefty leather jacket as leverage to pull him towards the tracks. His forward momentum, amplified by the force of the throw, was too much for him to stop. He stumbled over the yellow line and toppled over the edge with a scream.

The others, startled, sprang into action. Drayce ran at the one closest to him, slipped the punch that came his way, and fired back a left hook to the man's cheek. It landed with a clap of flesh, followed by the crack of something in the man's neck. He fell sideways into his mate, who caught him in his arms, unable to hold him as the flame of his consciousness withered to nothing. Drayce made his next move while the man's hands were full, blasting him on the chin with a straight right that could fell a tree. Both men hit the ground, motionless.

Drayce took a deep breath, legs quivering with adrenaline. He turned. Fingers and thumbs clawed at the edge of the platform. The train was close now, noise building, the air forced through the tunnel flattening the man's hair across his forehead as he heaved his chest onto the concrete, his pained expression one of exertion and fear. Drayce walked over, gripped his lapels, and bicep curled him into the air, his feet dangling over the tracks. He stared into the man's eyes, nostrils flaring, teeth glinting like fangs.

'Who sent you?' The man pressed his lips together, defiant. Drayce glanced to the dark tunnel entrance, the thundering train only seconds away. The third line hummed with electricity. Drayce locked eyes with him again. 'Was it Reaper?' The man's unblinking eyes widened. 'Who is he? If you don't tell me, I'll hold you here until the train rips you out of my hands!'

Sweat poured down the man's face, the terror evident. He parted his lips, but before a single syllable left his mouth, he glanced over Drayce's shoulder and smiled.

There wasn't time to turn. Drayce took the punch to the back of his neck, an electric shock firing up his spine into his brain. He stumbled forward from the force of it, vision blurring, the smile on the face of the man he was holding vanishing as his weight toppled Drayce's balance the wrong way, causing them both to tumble over the edge of the platform.

The impact onto the trainline stunned Drayce, his knees and elbows stinging, head throbbing. He sucked air through his clenched teeth, clung on to his consciousness. The vibration on the track dragged his mind into focus. He raised his chin, the electrified third line mere inches from his face. A glance to the tunnel: lights, heading their way, fast. He rolled off the man underneath him and glimpsed the platform. The last pair stared down at them both, eyes cold and unforgiving. They seemed far away, the edge unreachable. Drayce rolled again and clambered to his knees, locked eyes on the edge of the platform. No time. The train's red and white body burst free from the tunnel, an unstoppable two hundred tonne missile.

Drayce's world went black in an instant.

–

Conor turned away and stepped back behind the yellow line as the train rocketed past and flew straight through the station without stopping. He brushed his long grey hair out of his face and checked his hands, relieved to see no signs of blood splatter from the impact. The speed of the train must have contained it all on the tracks. He glanced at Brendan, the two men sharing an expression of disbelief. How had the shit hit the fan so quickly? One minute, they're calmly following their target into the Underground; the next, two thirds of them are all fucked up. He turned on the spot and surveyed the scene.

The other travellers had fled the station when the violence had begun. Of the team, two were unconscious, slumped against the wall, another out cold on a bench, and now a fourth had been annihilated by a train. And their target, the one Conor had been told to deliver to Reaper alive?

Obliterated into a thousand pieces.

What an unbelievable fuck up.

'Fuck's sake!' He scowled at Brendan. 'Why d'you hit him so hard?'

Brendan shrugged. His shoulders bulged like giant boulders. 'Thought he was gonna throw O'Brian in front of the train.'

Conor held up his hands and flicked the switch to turn his face into full sarcastic mode. 'Ah, well, you sure stopped that from happening, didn't you? Thank God you punched him *towards* the massive fucking train, instead of dragging them both *away* from it.' He flicked his head in the direction of the tracks, noticed Brendan's expression, who was no doubt imagining the frenzied splattering of blood and offal that would be down there. 'We need O'Brian's ID before we go.' The big slab of a man stared blankly back at him. Conor jabbed a finger up at his face. 'Don't play stupid with me you big cunt! This is your fault, so you can get down there and fetch it. We need to be off, fast, you hear?'

Brendan peeked warily at the tracks. 'Maybe he didn't have any on him.'

'Yes, he did. His wallet was in his back pocket. Credit cards; debit cards; driver's licence. He paid for lunch, remember?' Brendan's shoulders slumped. 'Since when did you become such a pussy?'

'I'm not a pussy.' His eyes flirted with the edge of the platform. 'It's just… I've seen what trains do to people. That fella we threw off that bridge a few years back, remember?'

'I do.'

Brendan shrugged. 'Not sure I want to see that again, is all I'm saying. And there'll be two of 'em down there, all mangled up like a butcher's front window.'

Conor lunged towards him, the urge to lash out almost unbearable. He settled for shaking his fist in his face. 'Fucking get down there now you dopey prick, or you'll look worse than them by the time I'm finished with you!'

The big man delved his fingers beneath his mop of brown hair, scratched his head, and wandered off, unwillingly. Conor turned his back and tried to wake the others.

'Fucking idiot,' he muttered under his breath. 'It's like working with cramp.' When he got to the pair on the floor, he bent down and slapped them both across the face, twice each. Both men stirred. 'Come on you soft bastards. Wake up. We need to get out of here.'

From the edge of the platform came a scuffle of boots; a clatter of limbs; a yelp of terror.

Conor turned sharply.

Brendan had vanished.

'Brendan?' Conor walked towards the tracks, slowly. His eyes scanned the lip of the platform. 'You okay?' He bent at the waist, trying to peer over without getting too close. 'Speak up you clumsy bastard!' He knelt, hands flat on the stone, fingers curled over the edge. *That's strange*, he thought. *No blood*. He leaned forward gingerly.

A hand shot out of the dark and grabbed him by his jacket. The scream that left his mouth was stolen by the wind generated from his fall. He hit the tracks headfirst, heard the crack of his own skull against iron. Blood poured down his face, the ground no longer solid. Everything spun as though he were drunk. Strong hands rolled him over. He blinked, the world a blur, until the figure of a giant towering above him gradually began to sharpen.

—

Drayce assessed the damage. The man's eyes were all over the place, but other than a cut to his forehead, and a nasty concussion, he'd be all right. Drayce bent over and slapped him across the side of his face that wasn't covered in blood, forcing his eyes to focus.

'I take it you're the last one?' The man didn't reply. Drayce gripped him by his collar and made him sit up. 'See them?' Drayce pointed to the two unconscious men in the drainage pit at the side of the track, where Drayce had hidden as the train had shot past. He'd dragged the bloke who was on the track at the time with him, saving his life. He didn't want anyone dying here, in such a public place. Too much attention from the authorities would come his way if they did.

'You're going to help me wake them up and get them back on the platform before the next train comes,' Drayce told him. 'Understand?'

The man nodded. His expression suggested he was only vaguely aware of what was happening. Drayce stood up, pulled the man to his feet and dusted him off, relieving him of the .357 Magnum revolver in the small of his back as he did so. He dragged the two out of the pit and shook them until they were roused, then leapt onto the platform before they got any stupid ideas about having another pop at him. The guy on the bench was still dreaming in another dimension, and the two on the floor had dragged themselves into seated positions, their faces in their hands as they tried to deal with their head injuries.

Drayce reclaimed his jacket from the bench and returned to the edge of the platform. From his elevated position, he lifted all three men from the tracks, one by one. They staggered about, unsteady on their feet. Drayce spoke to the one with long grey hair. He appeared to be the oldest. No indication of seniority, but it was the best Drayce had to work with.

'Tell your boys to pick up their mates and get out of here. Our little scuffle will have been viewed on the station's CCTV. The police will be here any minute.'

The man jerked his head at the others as an apparent instruction to get on with it. They scurried off to collect the other three. The guy with grey hair glared at Drayce. His hand slipped round to the small of his back. Realisation clouded his eyes. Drayce shook his head.

'This isn't my first rodeo, fella. Now collect your friends and get moving.' The man did as he was told but moved off with a swagger. Drayce caught him by his arm as he took his first step, clinched him by his neck and pulled him in close. The fear in the man's eyes was real. Drayce enjoyed it for a second, then put his lips close to the man's ear.

'Go back to the man who sent you.' He growled the words. Menace, anger, and revenge all fuelled the fire that was lit beneath them. 'Tell him she was my wife.'

Drayce pushed him towards the others so hard he nearly fell, then set off at a march, breaking into a jog as he got to the elevator and hurried out of the station with sirens echoing nearby.

24

Islington nick buzzed along as usual. Doors crashed and feet stomped; radios blared as fingers tapped on keyboards. Laughter from the parade room; screams from custody. All of it hummed along in the background and drummed through the walls as Lucy sat at her desk and tried to focus on her work.

She had a report to write following her FLO meeting with Alex that morning, and she still hadn't done it. She'd managed half a page in the last hour, her mind constantly drifting to what she'd done for Alex, and what he'd agreed to do for her. She slapped her desk in frustration, leaving behind a sweaty handprint. She always got clammy when she was stressed. She stood up and walked to the kitchen for a glass of water, drank it at the tap, refilled it, drank that. Closed her eyes. Breathed. She poured water into her cupped hands and splashed her face, leaned on the edge of the sink and gazed at her dull reflection in the polished steel, wishing she lived a different life, one without a psychopathic husband, divorce proceedings, and illegal favours done for a dangerous man, who in return had promised to ensure Barnaby gave her a clean break.

Her phone rang.

Speak of the Devil.

'You've got a nerve,' she whispered, before she glanced over her shoulder and scanned the kitchen to make sure she was alone.

'Have I?' Barnaby asked in that horrific, pompous tone that set Lucy's teeth on edge and made her want to stab him in the eyes.

'Calling on the same day you send me a video of an ornament with priceless sentimental value, smashed to pieces on the kitchen floor? Yeah, I'm pretty sure the saying fits the circumstances. But then, you always have been your bravest self on the other end of the phone, haven't you?'

He laughed. Lucy shut her eyes, gripped the edge of the sink with all her strength, and felt a nail snap as pure, undiluted rage burned through her veins. She'd never hated a person with such conviction.

'Just tell me what you want,' she snapped.

'You've already answered my question, Lulu. I wanted to make sure you'd watched the video.'

'You've called to gloat?'

'Well, I wouldn't go as far as that, but I thought it pertinent I witness your reaction.'

Lucy could hear the smile on his face; it infected the words as they passed his lips. She stayed calm. Demanded it of herself. 'You'll get no reaction from me. I'm long past venting at you over the phone. You've made a big mistake. That ornament was the last item connecting the two of us. And now you've destroyed it, cutting the only real tie you had to me.'

He tutted down the line. 'Oh dear, Lulu. Losing our tiny little mind, are we? Have you forgotten about the equity in the house you were so keen to get your filthy hands on? Hmm? If so, I'll send the paperwork over and you can make it official.'

'I've got a plan for getting my fair share of that.'

'Really? Well please, do tell.'

Lucy smiled. 'I want it to be a surprise.'

'I shall wait with bated breath, my dear Lulu. In the meantime, you can contemplate a life of *me*, till death do us part, as you vowed.' His tone changed, each word sharpened to a razor's edge. 'I didn't just call to gloat. I called to tell you I'll *never* go away. You will *never* be rid of me. How *dare* you think you could just up and leave our marriage! The embarrassment of it all! My parents—'

'Bollocks to your parents!' Lucy swallowed, her throat dry. 'That narcissist of a father of yours, and your cold-hearted mother are part of the reason why you're such a cruel, selfish, spoilt little turd! And you may have had a strong hold on me when we lived together, but in case you haven't noticed, you don't frighten me anymore. So go ahead and gloat at your vile attempt to break my heart using my grandma's precious gift to me. It does nothing but weaken your character even further, if that's possible.' She paused to take another breath. Her tongue stuck to the roof of her mouth. The silence on the other end of the line was deafening. 'And get my money counted out. Make sure it's ready and waiting for me. I'll have someone swing by to pick it up.'

She cancelled the call, refilled her glass and swigged it back, then blocked his number, having said everything there was to say. *Alex can sort the rest.*

After she'd recovered from Barnaby's ice-cold promise that she'd never be rid of him, a sense of clarity washed over Lucy. The guilt vanished. The man she was sending Alex after had proven himself worthy of whatever ill fate befell him.

With a clearer mind, she returned to her desk and opened her laptop. About to continue with her report, she paused suddenly and minimised it.

Something had to be checked first.

She reached into her handbag and took out the notes she'd made as she'd unlocked the phone Alex gave her. She opened the relevant programs and ran searches on both the number and the IMEI. Her fingers tapped the tabletop, a ripple from little to index, broken nail snagging the wood like a claw as she waited nervously.

Three results.

She clicked the first: IMEI registration. She frowned.

Huh, that's strange. Why is the phone registered to a corporation in Dubai?

She glanced at the next result. Her spine tingled as though something had scurried up the back of her neck, making her scalp crawl. She clicked on it: an NCA intelligence report, restricted access. She clicked on the third: an Interpol intelligence report, restricted access. She leaned back into her chair and stared at the screen. The room felt hot. She slammed her laptop shut, wiped her brow with the back of her hand.

'What are you up to, Alex?'

25

Sullivan leaned his forearms on the conference table, in an even worse mood than when he'd sat there earlier that day and examined a different collection of faces gathered in his office. The light from the chandelier cast shadows beneath their facial features, hardening the appearance of the men he'd summoned. He stared at everyone in turn, starting with Ronan on his left, to Sean, Conor, Brendan, and ending with O'Brian on his right. The only person Sullivan ignored was Reaper, who lurked in the background and watched his cohort of feckless shite from the shadows. Sullivan would speak to him privately. Other than Reaper, the group presented as though they'd been tossed into a gladiator pit with a pair of knuckle dusters each and told to fight for their lives. Their faces were bruised and swollen, movements rigid from blunt trauma to their limbs and torsos. From the accounts they'd given, the man responsible for their injuries had walked away unmarked. Unacceptable. Totally fucking unacceptable.

No one had so much as cleared their throat for over a minute. The only sound came from the music that was being played for the dancers, who were rehearsing for tonight's party, the noise reduced to almost nothing thanks to the soundproofing. It hummed gently through the bulletproof glass wall that separated the office and the dancefloor below, a dull, persistent, mind numbingly repetitive drumbeat. The silence his men were exhibiting – a hand-picked collection of the hardest leg breakers in London, mixed with a couple of John Ryan's best enforcers – along with their nervous, frigid body language, told Sullivan they were shitting their pants. And so they should be. Hard men or not, they knew who the boss was, were aware they'd fucked up, and understood the consequences.

After all, they were the ones who often introduced said consequences to others on Sullivan's behalf.

He waited as he glared at each of them in turn, one after the other and back again, daring someone to open their mouth.

Conor swept back his long grey hair and took up the challenge. 'I think I speak for all of us—'

'Shut the fuck up!' Sullivan roared. He locked eyes with Conor, who did as he was told. 'You're in no position to speak about anything. I've heard what you've had to say, how a single man, a fucking nobody, ran rings around the lot of you.'

'He can't just be a nobody,' Ronan said.

Sullivan risked whiplash as he turned to face him. 'Is that so?'

'With all due respect—'

Sullivan's hand shot up, a razor-sharp finger aimed Ronan's way. 'Choose your next words very carefully, boy.'

Ronan raised his hands, palms facing Sullivan in surrender. 'We're not beginners in this game, Mr Sullivan. It's why you employ us. So, for this man to do what he's done to all of us, makes me confident we're not just dealing with some average Joe off the streets. The man's been trained.'

'By whom?'

'I don't know. The way he fights shows a skillset in martial arts, and the vicious way he executes techniques tells me he has a lot of experience putting it into practice. Then there's the way he handled the guns he took off us. He manipulated those weapons as though they were his own, so he knows how to shoot a pistol, and that's a rare skill in this country.'

Sullivan cupped his chin with his palm, tapped a finger against his cheek. 'Well, he's not police; they don't send one man to deal with the likes of us, and when they find guns on people, they tend to arrest them, not shoot them in the face and then disappear.' He clenched his fist, cracked his knuckles. 'What about other organisations?'

'Who'd have the balls?' Reaper said. He stepped out of the shadows, between Brendan and O'Brian, a hand on each of their back supports, his head and shoulders immersed in the light from the chandelier. 'You run this game, and you've got all the biggest outfits in the world on side. No one would fuck with you.'

'Well, clearly this man fancies his chances.'

'He knows you sent us,' O'Brian blurted out, head cocked to the side where Reaper was standing.

Sullivan stuck his neck out, eyes wide. 'Come again.'

'Reaper. The man knows he sent us. Told me so while he was dangling me over the train tracks. Which means he knows about your organisation, somehow, so perhaps he is from another gang.'

'No one outside of us knows about Reaper. I keep him in the shadows for a reason. The police don't even know he exists.'

Twitching movements, sharp and nervous, caught Sullivan's attention out of the corner of his eye. Ronan couldn't sit still. There was a sheen of sweat on his face and neck. His eyes were transfixed on the bare glass tabletop, as though terrified to look up.

'Something on your mind, Ronan?' Sullivan asked.

Ronan glanced up momentarily. He had the appearance of a frightened little boy. 'We told him.'

Sullivan turned to face him properly. 'Told him what, exactly?'

Ronan's Adam's apple jolted up and down. 'That Reaper sent us. We should have told you before now, but—'

'But what?'

'Well, after we told him—'

Sean thumped the table with his fist, the glasses on the surface dancing in response. 'There's no fucking *we* about it, you lying cunt, you!'

'Fine!' Ronan said. 'After *I* told him, I panicked. Didn't know what to do. Didn't think it would matter, to be honest. It's not his real name, so it's not gonna help the man in any way.' He lifted his chin, faced Sullivan, his expression pleading for forgiveness. 'I had no choice. I had to give him something. He'd just shot Liam in the face, for Christ's sake!'

Sullivan sat in silence, lost for words.

'If I hadn't fed him something, he'd have killed us too,' Ronan explained, 'and we wouldn't have been able to come back here and tell you so much about him.' He glared at Sean. 'And sitting still, saying, doing, fuck all, was the worse option.'

Sean stared daggers back at him.

Sullivan took a deep breath. 'No, it wasn't, Ronan. You should have kept your mouth shut.' He caught Reaper's eye and jerked his head in Ronan's direction.

'No!' Ronan shouted, stumbling as he tried to push his chair back from the table to stand up, the seriousness of their communications dawning upon him. Reaper blocked his chair with one hand, the other disappearing behind his jacket lapel as he grinned at the pleading man. 'Please,' Ronan implored him. 'Don't do this!'

At odds with his intention, Ronan's begging only seemed to spur Reaper on, the assassin's eyes widening, excitement building as the gun appeared in his hand and was pressed to Ronan's temple. Stilled in horror, Ronan did nothing in the split-second opportunity he had to alter his fate.

The gunshot made everyone jump. Ronan's head snapped sideways from the force of the bullet. A filthy oval pattern of blood, bone and brain matter splattered across the window that looked down to the dancefloor. Despite the gore, the embedded bullet was visible, having passed clean through Ronan's skull, it's mushroomed brass body the epicentre of a spider's web pattern of cracks. On the other side, preparations for tonight's party carried on undisturbed. Sullivan was glad he'd soundproofed the room and chosen bulletproof glass, mirrored on the other side.

Reaper's gun pivoted to Sean, a maniacal smile still plastered across the professional killer's face. A swift shake of the head from Sullivan was enough to stop him in time.

'You should have told me,' Sullivan said to Sean.

Sean visibly shook. His eyes darted between Sullivan and the gun. Smoke from the fired .45 round hung in the air, gently swirling around the group of men, its presence highlighted by the light from the chandelier. A fine mist of Ronan's dark red blood had left its mark across Sean's face, flickers from an artist's paintbrush. His hands gripped the edge of the table, a man clinging on for dear life. 'I know.' His breath was a lifeless whisper. 'I'm sorry.'

Sullivan scrutinised him for a moment. 'You kept your mouth shut when a gun was pointed at you, and you stayed loyal to the man next to you. I can live with that.' He made brief eye contact with Reaper, who reluctantly put the pistol away, his smile wilting. 'But in the future, you tell me everything. Understand?'

Sean nodded with all the vigour of a prisoner accepting conditions that would get him off death row. 'Yes. I understand.'

Sullivan's chair creaked as he leaned back and addressed the entire group. 'So, where do we go from here?'

'It all seems personal to this fella,' Sean said, with a calmness that surprised Sullivan, considering a man had just been shot dead in his presence, his body still lying a few feet away, and he had only just avoided a bullet himself. 'He wants the man who pulled the trigger on that copper in Islington.'

'A rogue police officer, then, perhaps?'

'Maybe.'

'It's definitely personal for him,' Conor interjected. 'But I don't think because of Jason Martin.'

Sullivan raised his eyebrows. 'You sound confident of that.'

Conor shrugged. 'Seems to me it's personal to him for another reason.'

Silence for a moment. Then Sullivan said, 'Go on. Say what you've got to say.'

'He said something to me before he left the underground station.' Conor paused, eyes down. 'I planned to tell you in private, but...' He glanced at Ronan's body, whose blood soaked into the rug that had once been a cream colour. 'Perhaps the sooner the better.'

Sullivan nodded. 'Perhaps.'

Conor locked eyes with him. 'He said: *Go back to the man who sent you. Tell him she was my wife.*'

Sullivan frowned. His wife? What the fuck did that mean? Confusion creased his brow, his mind clouded. He brought a hand to his forehead, closed his eyes, rubbed his temples. Then it hit him. He shot out of his seat. 'Clear the room, now!' He locked eyes with Reaper. 'Except for you.'

Everyone did as they were told.

Once they were alone, Sullivan stepped around Ronan's body and approached Reaper. 'You know what this means?'

Reaper nodded. 'The detective I killed before Martin. The one who was getting too close to the old unit in Islington.'

'It has to be.'

'He was her husband?'

'I don't see any other connection, do you?'

Reaper shook his head. 'And if he is, it's an easy ID. Shouldn't take long for me to get the man's name. Then we can dive into his background, learn about him, and decide how best to get rid of him for good.'

Sullivan smiled. 'Get it done and get back to me when you know who he is. I need this man dead, Reaper, you hear? Our Chinese associates – twelve of the most powerful leaders in organised crime – are coming here tonight to negotiate a new deal. I don't want some lunatic, hell-bent on revenge, bursting in and ruining the relations I've worked so hard to build.'

Reaper turned his head to the window, to the activities down below. 'Have you considered calling things off tonight? Perhaps, rearranging?'

Sullivan stepped up close, their noses inches apart. 'The Chinese need to see a display of strength from us. We need to show them we can commit all the crime we want in this city, and still party like celebrities, not hide ourselves away. If confidence in our abilities is to remain, this party needs to go ahead as planned, and it needs to be a flawless display of our untouchable status in London.'

Reaper nodded, turned, and marched to the door. 'I'll get it done.'

'And Reaper…'

He stopped, glanced over his shoulder. Waited.

Sullivan peered down his nose at Ronan's body. 'Send some lads up to clean this mess.' He touched his foot to the thick pile. Blood rose, coating the sides of his shoe, the shag a swamp of death. 'And tell them to buy a new rug.'

26

Drayce pulled the balaclava over his face and activated the Flipper Zero to block the property's Wi-Fi signal, rendering the security cameras obsolete – he'd purchased the hacking device from a computer repair company that kept such items under the counter for customers in-the-know. His gloved fingers clawed the decorative ironwork at the top of the perimeter wall, his boots scraping the brickwork as he clambered up, taking care to avoid the motion sensors as he swung his legs over. He landed with a thud, rolled, and pushed up to the building line. Out of sight of the windows, he listened. No alarms; no doors opening; no movement whatsoever. He hurried to his designated entry point and held the centre punch against the corner of the windowpane.

The address he'd found on Lucy's phone was a big, brick, four-storey structure, with a pitched roof porch over the front door, and an attached garage on the side. It was set back from the road on Parliament Hill, a few houses down from an entrance to Hampstead Heath, the front door separated from the pavement by an immaculate garden paved entirely with pricey-looking slabs of stone, polished to perfection. Rare potted plants that probably each cost thousands followed the brick wall perimeter.

Drayce took one last look through the window, wanting to be sure the room he planned to enter was empty. He'd established the internal layout from architect's drawings he'd found online, and the rest he'd picked up from a physical recce. The ground floor consisted of an entranceway with a staircase dead ahead, a reception room that would be Drayce's entry point, and a hallway that led to a huge open-plan kitchen and dining area at the back. The first floor was dedicated to the guest bedrooms, each with en suites, the second floor to the master bedroom, dressing room, and a family bathroom, and the third floor to a games room and a home office. Drayce had wanted to know precisely what he was walking into and had prepared himself with the equipment he'd need before making the trip. Knocking on the front door wasn't an option. This confrontation would be ugly. He had to be prepared, and leaving behind his fingerprints on furniture and his image on the camera feed was not an option.

Even derelict it would be a seven-figure house, but the occupant had spent hundreds of thousands to make it as luxurious as a home could be in the twenty-first century, hence the alarm with a direct connection to the police, a dozen discreet cameras covering every aspect, motion sensors to warn if anyone climbed the perimeter wall, and a front door and frame made of solid steel, with foot-long, three-inch-thick inter-locking deadbolts.

Excessive for your average person.

But then, the man who lived here had more to worry about than your average person.

Drayce jabbed the centre punch – a small, handheld device that projected a sharp metallic pin, concentrating the force it exerted on the glass to a tiny area – hard and fast, and heard a click as the tool's resistance gave way. The entire outer pane frosted over, cracked in a thousand places. He did the same again to punch through the inner pane. Using a gloved hand he pushed the glass out of the frame, the only noise a muffled tinkle of sparkling jewel-like nuggets raining down on the reception room carpet. He listened. No reaction. So far so good.

He dropped his bag inside the house, used the side of the centre punch to rake the remaining glass out of the frame, and climbed in. The centre punch went back in the bag. His hands searched his jacket, felt the pistol, drew it, his eyes fixed on the door to the hallway.

The interior was immaculate, the furnishings of a quality that could only be obtained with a serious parting of cash. The owner lived alone, no wife or kids, so Drayce could move through the building confident he wasn't at risk of confronting an innocent. Weapon up, he sliced open his view and moved with purpose to the kitchen. Clear. He did a one eighty, came back down the hallway. As he whisked past a phone table, he made a mental note of the car keys resting in a glass dish: a vehicle in the garage – the registration of which had given Drayce the ability to discover the man's address on the Police National Computer app on Lucy's work phone – meant someone was likely home. He made it to the foot of the stairs. Stilled. The creak of a floorboard, second floor. Then another: footsteps of an adult.

Someone was home.

With the ground floor clear, Drayce began his ascent of the stairs, feet placed wide on the steps where they were less likely to make a noise, pistol aimed at his visual limit point. When he got to the landing, he heard more footsteps on the floor above. Just one person. He bit back the urge to skip steps in the process, his discipline preventing him from getting ahead of himself. He took the time to clear the bedrooms, all of them unoccupied.

First floor clear.

He pressed on to the next staircase, slowly, each footstep heal-toe to avoid alerting the person on the next floor up. He paused at the first step. Listened. Someone cleared their throat in the master bedroom, third door on the left, a masculine grunt of a noise.

The man Drayce had come for was home.

Drayce climbed the stairs, moved across the landing, down the hallway, weapon aimed at the entrance to the bedroom. The door was ajar, inward opening, a long vertical sliver of the room visible. A shadow whipped past, left to right. Drayce stopped hinge side and took a breath. This was the pivotal moment, the point of no return. Another step forward and there was no going back. He took another breath, gritted his teeth, and kicked the door wide open.

DCI Paul Territt flinched, his cup of coffee tumbling to the floor, its contents spilling over the cream carpet like an oil leak. He turned to Drayce, a look of horror on his face as he assessed the giant figure in a balaclava. He backed away, hands raised in a pathetic attempt to defend himself, fingers trembling in front of his mouth. His back hit the fitted wardrobe doors and dragged down them until he collapsed on his arse. He brought his knees up to his chest and covered his head with his arms. Drayce thought he heard the man whimper.

'You alone?' Drayce growled.

A panicked nod of the head repeated over and over. 'Yes, yes!' Territt's voice was a high-pitched whine. 'Please don't kill me!'

'Shut up.' Drayce clocked a mobile phone on a desk in the corner of the room. He walked over and pocketed it to prevent Territt from calling for help, then closed the bedroom door, gripped Territt by his ear, and dragged him to the en suite where he knew there wouldn't be any cameras.

'Argh! W… w… what are you going to do?' Territt spluttered. Drayce ignored the question and threw him into the shower cubicle, glaring at him as he slid down the tiles and curled up in the basin.

Drayce shut the door behind him and removed the balaclava. Territt's jaw dropped. 'Alex? What are you—'

'Be quiet. I'm asking the questions.'

Territt rose to his feet, adjusted his suit, a newfound confidence emboldening him. A vicious scowl infected his face. 'What do you think you're doing breaking into my home with a gun? Have you gone mad?'

'Braver now you know it's me, aren't you? Who did you think I was when you were begging for your life a moment ago?'

'What on earth are you talking about? I thought you were some lunatic with a gun who'd forced his way into my home.'

Territt's eyes searched the floor. Seconds later, they snapped back up to stare down Drayce. 'Which is precisely what you are, in fact. You've committed aggravated burglary. You're going to prison!'

Drayce shook his head. 'No, I'm not. Prison is *your* best option if you tell me the truth.' He glanced around the beautiful en-suite bathroom as his voice echoed in the giant space: the marble tiles; the polished copper bath; the giant rain head shower. 'Nice house for a police officer. Care to explain how you've amassed this much wealth on your salary?'

'That's none of your business.' Territt's eyes dipped to the pistol. 'But, if you must know, I collected a large inheritance at the back end of last year.'

Drayce smiled. 'Is that so? For your sake I hope you've got proof of that.'

Territt stuck his chest out. 'I don't need to prove anything to you.'

'We'll see about that.'

Keeping the gun aimed at Territt, Drayce reached into his jacket and pulled out the paperwork from Jason Martin's home. He threw it at Territt. It hit his chest with a *thwack*.

'Read it,' Drayce commanded. 'We'll talk afterwards.'

Territt was hesitant, but after a few seconds did as instructed. His fingers flitted through page after page, from beginning to end, under the watchful eyes of a highly trained marksman. Ten minutes later he straightened them all out and dropped the stack on the floor.

'Where did you get this?'

'I'll come to that. For now, you might want to explain to me why your name's all over those files. Meetings; phone records. You've been working with them for years.'

Territt shook his head. 'Nonsense. It can all be explained. There's something else going on here, Alex. I can assure you I—'

Drayce's knee came out of nowhere, blasting up through Territt's groin so hard it made both his feet leave the ground.

As he withered to the basin, Drayce grabbed his ear again and held him up.

'Do you think I'm stupid?' He slammed Territt's head against the tiles, pressed the gun to his temple to hold him there, and picked up the papers. He scrunched them in front of Territt's face, knuckles white. 'Four years ago, you took over an operation incepted to gather intelligence on an organised crime group run by a man named Daniel Sullivan. Jason and Lily both worked for you on that op. You wanted it shut down from the beginning. Complained it was a waste of time. Said there was no evidence Sullivan was a criminal. Even when Lily died you diverted suspicion away from him. Argued he couldn't be involved in her murder. When you got your way and the op was shut down, Jason left the Met. It's all explained here.' Drayce waved the papers back and forth. 'But Jason didn't leave Sullivan alone.'

Drayce moved the gun from Territt's head and stepped back.

'Jason took a steady job with the NCA,' Drayce continued. 'Something to bring home a wage, but nothing too taxing. With more spare time on his hands, he carried on with the investigation into Daniel Sullivan's criminal empire on his own. He'd taken copies of case files and intelligence reports with him when he left the Met, which he used as his starting point. From there he went on to discover Sullivan's investments: nightclubs, factories, warehouses. He tracked his finances to a wealth management group based in London and Dubai. He discovered Sullivan's contacts, his associates, and even carried out surveillance on his movements around the city.'

Drayce threw the papers on the floor in front of Territt, crouched down, looked him in the eye. 'Sullivan's the biggest trafficker in London, the lifeblood of serious criminality in this city. You name it, he gets it. Drugs, firearms, goods stolen to order.' Drayce paused. Took a breath. 'People.'

Territt hadn't moved. His head was down, shoulders slumped, back rounded, truly dejected. Drayce continued the onslaught.

'When Jason found evidence of Sullivan's criminality, he should have exposed him. Perhaps to a trusted source in the Met, or the NCA, or failing that, an investigative journalist in the city. Someone who would take the evidence and run with it, exposing Sullivan's criminal empire to the world. But he didn't. He wanted more. When a case was finally opened on Sullivan, he wanted the evidence to be so overwhelming there wouldn't be a single crack for Sullivan's defence to prise open. So he pushed on, singlehandedly. He got hold of Sullivan's phone records.' Drayce slammed his fist onto the papers. 'And specific financial transactions.'

Territt turned white. He licked his lips, mouth puckering, as though about to be sick.

'Sullivan made three separate payments of two million pounds to a numbered account online,' Drayce said. 'To any ordinary person, that's where it would have ended. But Jason Martin was no ordinary person. He put the work in, called in every favour he'd ever collected in his career, and revealed who had opened the account.'

Territt shifted, manifestly uncomfortable, sweat building on his face.

'Numbered accounts might offer a good layer of secrecy,' Drayce said, 'but they are not entirely anonymous. The name of the client is held by the bank because it is subject to disclosure in certain legal proceedings. But Jason didn't need an official investigation with a warrant. It turns out some of these banks' employees don't agree with filthy-rich villains hiding their ill-gotten gains. Jason found a whistle-blower, who sent him the name of the person who had opened the account.' Drayce paused. 'You!'

Territt raised a hand as though deflecting a blow. 'No.'

'Daniel Sullivan – a vile human trafficker – sent you a total of six million pounds.'

'This is absurd!'

'What was it payment for?' Silence. 'Binning the operation, perhaps?'

Territt was shaking. 'Now, just wait a second—'

'Or maybe it was for smothering the investigation into my wife's murder!'

Drayce covered the distance between them in a split second. His free hand went to Territt's throat, lifting him to his feet by his windpipe. The man's hands flapped uselessly at Drayce's arm. Drayce choked him until he turned purple, then threw him back to the basin and aimed the gun at him.

'Jason knew someone from Sullivan's organisation murdered Lily because she was getting too close to uncovering the scale of their operation. He feared they would come for him, which is why he was so secretive about his investigation. But they must have found out he was still onto Sullivan, and decided it was worth killing another rogue police officer acting alone in order to protect their interests. Well, now that I'm fully in the picture, I think it's worth killing *them*.' Drayce put the gun to Territt's head. A whisper of fear broke free from Territt's lips. He shut his eyes. 'And all those who helped them.'

'Wait!' Saliva dribbled down Territt's chin. 'You're not a murderer, Alex!'

Drayce took up the slack in the trigger. 'You don't know me. You don't know what I'm capable of.'

'You'd be killing an innocent man. It's all lies. I haven't done anything. I'm being framed!'

Drayce eased the pressure on the trigger. 'Bullshit.'

'It's true! I can prove it!' He opened his eyes, stared up at Drayce, pleading. 'I'll call the police and tell them to come and arrest me.'

Drayce frowned. 'What good will that do?'

'They can take these files and conduct a proper investigation. With Jason's evidence, they can get the warrants to unearth what Sullivan has done, and interview representatives from the bank, who'll have to disclose everything. That way, I can prove my innocence.'

Drayce kept the barrel where it was. He examined Territt's tearful expression. Was he telling the truth, or was he a man in fear of his life, grasping at straws with his lies?

Only one way to find out.

Drayce took out of his pocket the phone he'd collected from the bedroom. He threw it at Territt. It hit his chest and fell into his hands.

'Call them,' Drayce said.

Territt clearly couldn't believe his luck. He fumbled with the device in his hurry to make the call.

'Police,' he said into the phone. His eyes locked on Drayce. 'This is Detective Chief Inspector Paul Territt. I'm at seventy-three Parliament Hill. Send officers immediately.' He hung up and pocketed the phone. Drayce let him keep it. 'Now what?'

Drayce leaned back against the sink, arms by his side, gun pointed at the floor. 'Now we wait.'

Territt's eyes darted around the room, seemingly deep in thought about his plan and how things might progress from here. Drayce decided to turn up the pressure.

'Why would someone frame you?'

'Isn't it obvious? Whoever was paid by Sullivan gave my name to the bank to divert attention from themselves. That way, if the account was ever discovered, the authorities would waste time investigating me, while the real culprit disappeared into the mist.'

Drayce said nothing.

'Think about it, Alex. I've been after Sullivan for years. Why would I help him?'

'This house—'

'Was left to me by my uncle. I renovated it with the money from my father's estate after he passed away last year.'

'Lucky boy. But why all the security? Seems the sort of thing a person might invest in if they were in the pocket of organised crime.'

'I've been a police officer in this city long enough to know how bad the crime can be. I had the money to secure my home in the best ways possible and I decided it was worth it.' He looked away. 'Not that it did much good against you.'

Drayce stayed silent. Minutes ticked by as they waited. Drayce's glare never left Territt, who remained slumped in the shower basin, gazing into outer space, his mind undoubtedly lost in the chaotic turn his life had just taken.

Screeching tyres on the street made the heads of both men turn.

'That must be the police,' Territt said as he got to his feet. 'I'll go down and let them in. Then we can talk about—'

'Not so fast.'

Drayce gripped Territt's jacket and dragged him into the bedroom. He made him sit on the edge of the bed and went to a set of doors that led to a Juliette balcony overlooking the front. He parted the blinds a quarter inch.

A black BMW M5 was abandoned on the street, nose facing the pavement, all four doors wide open. The purposeful movement of predators on the hunt caught Drayce's eye. There were five of them at the front gate, stocky men in dark clothing, long arms strapped to the torso of each. Momentarily stalled by the gate, the circular saw in the hands of the lead man made short work of the lock. Drayce paused, stuck his neck out, squinted: Sean Maack. Three others he recognised from the incident at Angel tube station. The fifth guy was new.

Drayce turned around.

A sickening arrogance infected Territt's expression. 'What's the matter, Alex? Is it not the police after all?' He smiled. 'What now?' His eyes assessed the gun with a newly found confidence. 'Still going to shoot me?'

Drayce tucked the pistol in his waistline, shook his head, and moved away from the balcony doors. 'By the looks of it I'll need all the bullets I can get.'

A quiet alarm sounded, intended to alert the occupant and no one else. A door crashed open on the ground floor. Boots trampled through the house.

Territt was still smiling. 'I'd start running if I were you. The men coming up those stairs might move fast, but they kill slow. You'll die the worst death imaginable if they catch you. And they will, of course.' He chuckled. 'I can't believe you handed me my phone. You idiot. You've walked right into my trap.'

Drayce moved close to him. Bent down. Whispered in his ear. 'They're running to their own deaths. You might think you laid a trap for me with that call, but I handed you the phone for a reason.' Territt's smile wilted. 'The only trap is the one you've led them to.'

Drayce grabbed Territt by his hair and yanked his head back. The man's eyes widened, the whites exposing his bloodshot terror. Drayce turned the man's head and smashed a hammer-fist down on his jaw's hinge, just below his earlobe, dropping his twenty stone into the strike and rotating his hips and torso as he cycled his arm through Territt's head. Everything under his fist crunched. Territt's hands flinched instinctively, but they didn't even make it to shoulder height before he fell unconscious. Broken and bloody chunks of his veneers landed on the carpet. Drayce eased his grip, letting Territt's hair slip through his fingers, and watched as his lifeless body slid off the bed and collapsed to the floor.

Drayce set his eyes on the bedroom door and drew his pistol.

27

The footsteps slowed. An inevitable development. The further they searched through the house, the higher the likelihood of encountering a threat, the heat building, mercury rising, until they reached the last room, where they would know for certain a big angry monster lurked within. But of course, they weren't going to make it to the last room. Drayce would ruin their day long before that.

The internal alarm cut out; these men didn't want attention brought on the house. Not until they'd killed who they came to kill and cleaned up the mess. The sign on the alarm warning potential thieves of its direct link to the police was obviously a ruse. As demonstrated, Territt called upon an entirely different set of people to come to his aid when in trouble.

Drayce treaded carefully to the bedroom door. Listened. The men had stopped on the floor below. Drayce pictured them huddled on the landing, having regrouped before their next ascent. Centimetre by centimetre, he turned the handle and opened the door, pistol up, his left hand cupping his right to steady the weapon as he sliced the pie to ninety degrees. His view opened. Clear. He glided across the carpeted landing without making a sound, barrel trained on the stairs. Still no movement on the floor below. He ducked into a room further along the corridor, left the door open. In a darkened corner he went down on one knee, folded his frame in on itself to appear as unhuman as possible. He admired his cross view of the landing through the open doorway, rested his supporting arm on his thigh, and settled his sight picture on the top step.

He was ready.

The first boot fell on the bottom step.

–

Reaper put a flat hand to Sean's chest. Locked eyes. Shook his head. He raised a single digit in the air: one at a time. Sean nodded. He understood. They watched Brendan climb the stairs, the big man creating enough noise to trigger the ambush, if, as Reaper suspected, there was one set up. Tactics had changed. Necessary, when things are taken out of your hands. The husband was no longer to be captured; he was to be killed. Fuck who he was. Fuck why he was coming after them. He had become a serious problem and needed to die.

Reaper pulled the stock of the shotgun into his shoulder. Listened. Nothing from the floor above. Not yet. But there would be, soon enough. He watched Brendan approach the landing. Reaper aimed his weapon at the ceiling. As soon as their target revealed himself, Reaper would let him have it. The solid slugs and the extra propellant in the 10-gauge weapon would tear through the fabric of the house, through the body of the man they'd come for, and out the exterior brickwork, where they would go on to make a duck jump somewhere on Hampstead Heath. Reaper tracked the weapon from side to side as he waited for the man upstairs to give away his position.

–

Drayce reminded himself of who these men were; what they were a part of; what they had done. There was no rulebook in play here. No challenges would be shouted; no warnings given. This was the real world. They'd come to kill him.

The gesture would be returned in kind.

An indistinct shadow on the far wall was Drayce's next warning of their encroaching presence. He'd heard only one pair of feet climb the stairs. Smart. If they'd come up in a single group, Drayce would have ended their encounter before it even got started.

Drayce waited. Both eyes wide open, he watched the shadow creep higher as he considered his options. The crown of a man's head appeared. Drayce slipped his index finger through the pistol's guard, placed the pad on the trigger. One of the guys from the tube station. Drayce tracked him up to the top step. His trigger finger tightened. Another step and he'd be out of sight.

Drayce let him go.

The group splitting up had created a problem for him: if he engaged the first man, he'd give away his position to the others, the element of surprise ruined. It was imperative he be patient, attacking only when maximum damage would be done.

Drayce eased his finger off the trigger and waited.

—

Brendan made it to the landing. He turned around, stuck his bottom lip out, and shrugged. Reaper sighed, the first noise he'd allowed himself to make since entering the house. Sean, Conor, and O'Brian were behind him. He lowered the shotgun and turned to face them. A flick of the head towards the landing was all it took to communicate his orders. The three men shouldered their assault rifles and pushed past him.

Only once the others were on the landing above did Reaper make the ascent. Brendan was stood in an open doorway, transfixed on something in the room. Reaper moved up to his shoulder and peered around him. It was a bedroom. On the floor, at the foot of the bed, was the body of DCI Territt – Sullivan's rat. He was on his side, eyes closed, curled up in the foetal position. His chest was rising and falling, indicating life, but the unnatural way his mouth hung open suggested he'd been subjected to a brutal amount of blunt trauma, his jaw terribly disfigured, as though he'd taken a sledgehammer to his face.

There was only one man who could be responsible for that.

Reaper skirted past Brendan and stepped into the room, shotgun swaying from side to side as he searched for the man they'd come to kill.

A deafening crack rang out from the landing. He spun around, startled by the gunfire, and caught sight of Sean falling.

28

Drayce tracked Sean's body to the floor with his pistol, ready to shoot him again should there be any indication the first round through his face hadn't done the job. His body came to rest with no signs of life. Drayce moved within the shadows of the room, light on his feet, opening his view of the landing as he danced to the side of the door frame.

Gazing over the top of his weapon's iron sights, he searched for more targets. One of the men from Angel tube station appeared, turning on the spot, assault rifle down at his hips as he fired wildly, clearly unsure where the shot that had killed Sean had come from. The other men joined in. Gunfire cracked off in every direction. Another alarm rang, this from the smoke detectors as plumes of gunshot residue filled the air. Drayce put two in his ear from the side, the rounds puncturing through his skull. As his body dropped, two others were revealed behind him: the guy with long grey hair from the tube incident and his big associate.

They both turned to the room Drayce was in.

Their guns moved with them, eyes searching for something to shoot at.

The big fella with the mop of brown hair gave leave of his discipline and sprayed more bullets, despite not having acquired a target. Rounds punched through the walls, floor, and ceiling. Drayce squinted against the tiny particles of debris floating in mid-air, plaster dust and woodchip raining down on him as he moved into cover. The bullets that passed through the doorway hit nothing but thin air on their way to the wall on the other side of the room.

Drayce dropped to one knee in the dirty corner, took aim at the doorway, and leaned to the side, a tactical probe, to open his view. Two more threats came into focus, weapons sweeping side to side as they squinted through the cloud of burned gunpowder. Drayce gave the big guy the good news first, a double tap to the body and one to the head, followed by the same treatment for his grey-haired friend.

The house fell silent.

Drayce waited. He'd counted five men on the street; so far, he'd dropped four. The other was still active. The one he didn't recognise. The new guy.

Inch by inch, Drayce stood to his full height. Keeping his view of the landing, he stepped out of the bedroom, soft movements, heel to toe, pistol up. Slow is smooth; smooth is fast. Four dead bodies lay at his feet, fresh oxygenated blood soaking into the carpet. He stepped over them, approached the T-junction at the top of the stairs. No way of doing this safely without a team mate to cross arcs of fire with, but there was nothing else for it. Sometimes, you've got to live with the risk.

Hugging the wall line, Drayce opened his view left as much as he could. Clear. Nothing but an empty corridor with several closed doors. That was good. If a threat were to present itself in that direction, he'd at least get a warning when a door opened, giving him time to turn and engage.

Switching his point of aim to the other side of the T-junction, he pivoted around the corner. Clear. A doorway was open to his left: Territt's bedroom. Drayce went to it, gun up, eyes on the crack. No movement in the room. He slowed on the approach. Leaned into the wall to maximise his view of the dirty right corner. The plasterboard creaked against his shoulder. He froze. Held his breath. Had he given away his position to whoever was in the room? He waited. Five seconds. Ten. There was still a threat in the house. He needed to clear that room. He took another step.

'Reaper! He's in the corridor!'

Drayce turned, quick as a flash towards the sound of the man's voice. Sean was alive, barely, a wide gruesome blood trail from the gunshot wound to his face marking out the path he'd crawled so he could warn the man in the bedroom – a man named Reaper, who worked for Daniel Sullivan, and had been sending people after Drayce all day with orders to kill him. Time for Drayce to put an end to that, once and for all. He took aim and shot Sean in the head, twice, then pivoted back to the bedroom door and stepped forward.

The wall he was tracking exploded in front of him. He darted back, ears ringing, and scanned the doorway, pistol up, searching for a target. Nothing. The wall in front of him now had a hole the size of a grapefruit in it. The shot had missed him by inches, and if he didn't get out of sight before Reaper got to the corridor, it was lights out.

A floorboard in the room creaked. Drayce estimated Reaper's position on the other side of the wall and fired as he changed position, punching rounds through the plasterboard. Reaper returned inaccurate fire, putting fresh holes in the walls, the deep *boom* of his shotgun rattling the entire house. Drayce crossed the corridor and slipped into another room, in cover from view, and dived to the floor. Pistol empty, he tucked it away and drew a fresh one. He got up on one knee, eyes on the doorway, and listened. Everything was quiet.

Two men within spitting distance trying to kill each other.

The oldest game of the species.

A *clink* of metal out in the corridor made Drayce's skin tingle. A faint shadow caught his eye, his enemy on the move, creeping across the corridor, approaching the doorway. Drayce took aim at the wall, the source of the shadow somewhere on the other side. He couldn't afford to wait for Reaper to make his entry. Too risky. Drayce removed the slack in the trigger. The shadow slowed. He'd reached his entry point. Any second now and the shotgun barrel would be in the room.

Drayce let rip.

Three neat holes appeared in the wall, grouped as tight as a plug socket. The shotgun answered back, the aim too high, hitting nothing but wall and ceiling. They both kept it up, round after round. Going empty, Drayce made the last switch available to him: the .357 Magnum revolver. The shadow retreated to the bedroom. Drayce held the weapon tight in both hands, the big revolver bucking like a mule as he darted into the corridor, chasing Reaper down. Making a quick assessment on the door, he continued into Territt's bedroom, a metre in, a metre out, searching for a target.

Reaper was crouched by the bed, staring with disbelief into the empty breech of his weapon. Drayce took aim as he closed him down. Centre mass. *End of the road for you, my friend.* The revolver fired, the round striking Reaper in his chest. He fell back, rolled onto his side and continued to spin until he was back on his knees. Reaper glared at Drayce with hatred in his eyes. Drayce stopped and assessed what was in front of him. He frowned. The shot should have cut Reaper in half. Then he saw it: body armour, the mushroomed bullet embedded in the ceramic plate. Drayce raised his sight picture in line with Reaper's forehead.

Click.

Bollocks.

Drayce dropped the empty gun, locked eyes with the man in front of him. Other than their heaving chests, neither moved an inch. Drayce considered the guns out on the landing, in the hands of the men he'd killed. Could he get to one before Reaper rearmed himself?

As though Drayce's mind was being read, Reaper charged at him. Drayce dropped his hips back, tucked his chin, and launched at him. They clattered like bulls, heads butting, arms tangling, both men stopped dead in their tracks as neither relented. Reaper was big, only an inch or two shorter than Drayce, and strong with it. Drayce clinched his neck, slipped an underhook, and turned, using the man's own energy as he rotated him into a throw.

They hit the floor so hard a painting fell off the wall. Drayce kept the dominant top position, wrapping Reaper's head in a scarf hold. He controlled an arm with his legs and began applying a lock, hyperextending the elbow joint. Reaper gritted his teeth, growled, fought with everything he had as he tensed his bicep. But it wouldn't be enough. Drayce had spent years training for situations such as this. Jiu-jitsu was simple physics; Archimedes' concept of leverage. Drayce would break Reaper's arm, then he'd transition into a full mount, and take time with his questions. He cranked the armlock a little tighter, the joint moving past its full range of motion. Reaper's face flushed, glistened, the sinews in his neck strained. His eyes widened.

Nearly there.

Drayce listened for the *snap*.

But then he froze. Let go. Moved like lightning.

The huge blade had appeared in the corner of his eye just in time for him to react. Reaper slashed at him. Drayce felt the air displacement against his neck as the knife's razor-sharp edge missed him by millimetres. As soon as the knife swung past, Drayce pounced back on him, wrapping the arm that controlled the weapon, clinging on for dear life. They rolled together, somersaulting over one another across the room. Hit the wall, bounced off, knocked over a table. Drayce found himself underneath Reaper, who fought hard to free his arm, became frustrated, and threw a punch. Drayce tucked his chin, pointing his forehead at the incoming fist. Reaper groaned on impact, his frustrations taking over. He clamped a hand over Drayce's face, pressing his head into the carpet, palm smothering his mouth and nose, fingers clawing his eyes.

Drayce trapped a leg, bridged his hips, and threw Reaper off him. He flowed with it and ended up on top in a mounted position, the knife-wielding arm still wrapped under his armpit. He climbed up Reaper's body, pinning his chest and shoulders to the floor. A slight adjustment, pulling Reaper onto his side, and Drayce could break his arm, rendering the knife in his hand useless. He moved inch by inch, not wanting to lose control of Reaper's arm, or let him escape.

Either would be disastrous; both were possible.

Reaper knew how to fight. Perhaps not trained to a high level, but he clearly had experience on the street. Drayce had to be cautious.

In the impending doom of his situation, Reaper thrashed beneath Drayce. His eyes bulged and flecks of white spittle fled his clenched teeth. He wriggled, strained, and kicked his legs, trying to get Drayce off him. But it wasn't enough. A black belt in Brazilian jiu-jitsu, Drayce had been in this situation thousands of times before. There was nothing Reaper could do. The process was predetermined, the outcome inevitable.

Until everything changed.

Another knife, in Reaper's other hand, came into play. Drayce grabbed his wrist just in time, holding the blade at bay, but in doing so, lost some control of the original knife-wielding arm. Struggling to control both, Drayce felt himself lose balance on top of Reaper's bucking figure. Reaper's arm slipped a few inches from under Drayce's armpit; if Drayce lost control of it, he'd be cut to ribbons. He stared into Reaper's eyes, a glint of hope cast back at him. Reaper smiled. He knew Drayce was losing it. The arm slipped a little further, now down to his wrist, the blade inches from slicing under Drayce's armpit. He couldn't hold on much longer, and if he changed position, he'd be cut for certain. Time to think of something else.

Drayce dived over Reaper's head, rolling over his own shoulder with enough momentum to get to his feet. He turned and backed away as Reaper stood up, knife in each hand, panting with exertion. Before Drayce could formulate a plan, Reaper ran at him, viciously swinging his arms, a challenge Drayce craved to accept about as much as being invited to stop a plane's propellor with his bare hands.

Drayce dived backwards, narrowly avoiding being cut, and rolled over the bed, collecting a heavy metal bedside lamp on his way. He threw it as he scrambled over the mattress, trying to buy some time, but it glanced off Reaper's shoulder, barely slowing him down. Before he cleared the bed, Drayce pulled the duvet from under him and threw it over his head. The knives punched through the cotton, carving long slits, feathers spilling everywhere. Thinking on his feet, Drayce picked up a bedside cabinet with both hands, raised it above his head, and launched it at his blind attacker. The frenzied figure writhing beneath the duvet took the full force of it in his chest, slowed for a moment, and fell backwards, falling off the bed.

Before Drayce could get past him to the guns in the corridor, Reaper was back on his feet, tossing the shredded duvet to the floor. Blocked from re-arming himself, Drayce searched for an improvised weapon. His best option was the solid wooden chair that was pushed up to the desk. He held it by the seat, legs facing Reaper, a lion tamer in a deadly circus.

The room settled for a moment, the two men weighing up their adversary. Reaper kept his distance, the blades by his hips, pointing forward, weight shifting from one foot to the other. Drayce met Reaper's glare, but held his ground, knowing if he advanced, he risked being stabbed to death. Reaper eyed the chair, no doubt assessing the risk of having a solid wooden leg rammed down his neck. Neither moved. For the first time in their encounter, they properly examined one another.

Drayce memorised Reaper's features. If he got out of this confrontation without bleeding to death, he wanted to recognise his face when he caught up with him in the future. He took in Reaper's flat nose, thick black beard over a square jawline, and his droopy left eye, an old knife wound running vertically through it.

Drayce stopped breathing.

His mind spun through its reel of important information, shone a light through his encounter with Lenny, and projected the man's words in front of his eyes.

...his nose looked kinda funny. Flat, like, you know? As though it'd been broken a few times.

The chair let out a *crack* under Drayce's hands, the wood splitting a hairline fracture under the pressure of his grip.

There was something wrong with one of his eyes. The left one, I think... It just kinda drooped a bit, you know? Like there was a line drawn down the whole thing, through his eyebrow and eyelids, to his cheekbone, pulling it all down, making it sag in the middle.

Drayce stared at Reaper's dark eyes, right into his soul. His pulse pounded in his ears, his body temperature rocketing, limbs tingling, all his senses heightening. His body shook. Another crack formed in the dam, the pressure too much.

Drayce launched the attack, roaring like a lion, charging straight at Reaper, the four legs of the chair aimed at his chest. The dull *thud* of a knife embedding in the bottom of the chair's seat precipitated the wheezing sound of air forced from Reaper's lungs by four wooden legs. Reaper's other arm was wedged over the top of the chair, the knife dangling uselessly in front of Drayce's face as he drove him backwards. Keeping hold of the chair, Drayce prised the embedded knife from Reaper's grip, then used the solid lump of wood to swipe the second knife out of his other hand, kicking it away after the first bounce.

Drayce swung the chair at Reaper's head, but the blow merely glanced off the top of his skull as he ducked under it. Ditching the cumbersome piece of furniture now the knives were no longer in play, Drayce clinched Reaper's neck, and headbutted him square in his face. Reaper's nose exploded, a torrent of blood spraying over Drayce's chest. Bringing his other arm into play, Drayce held Reaper around the neck in a Thai clinch, turned him on the spot, and drove a knee up into his ribcage. Something inside Reaper's chest cracked. He winced, moaned in pain, then came alive, cracking Drayce in the side of his head with an elbow strike as the surprise of Drayce's attack wore off.

Blinded by rage, Drayce changed levels, lifted Reaper in the air with a high crotch hold, and drove him backwards at full speed, forgetting that the doors to the Juliette balcony were only a few feet away. The frame obliterated, splintered wood and shattered glass raining everywhere. Drayce's obsession was so all-encompassing, his momentum so unstoppable, it didn't even slow him down. It wasn't until his hips hit the top of the wrought-iron railing of the bannister that he was forced to change direction, pivoting over the top with Reaper still held in mid-air.

Both men tumbled to the patio below.

29

The universe spun like a washing machine. Drayce hit the roof of the front porch on the way down, bounced, rolled, and continued to the patio with a bodily thud. Broken tiles rained down all around him.

He opened his eyes.

Breathed.

He was alive, on his back, staring up at the ruined balcony doors two floors above. He'd become detached from Reaper during the fall, who could be anywhere; might already be moving, drawing a weapon, closing Drayce down.

Get up!

Drayce moved his legs first: no pain, no numbness. His arms were next, a sensation like a sharp dagger twisting somewhere in his shoulder. Ignoring it, he checked his head: no blood, no discharge from his ears, no soft spots. He rolled onto his front, a blunt trauma injury screaming in his back. Not important; could be dealt with later. He brought his knees up to his chest. Raised his chin.

There was no sign of Reaper.

Drayce got to his feet, blocking out the pain in his back and shoulder. It was imperative he chase the man down. The universe had brought them together, face to face. Drayce would not allow the opportunity to slip from his grasp.

He staggered forward, searching the patio, listening for the sound of Reaper's movements. He couldn't let him get away. Everything Drayce had discovered up to this point told him Reaper was a hitman for Daniel Sullivan's organised crime group. Had worked in cahoots with Paul Territt for years. Had shot Jason Martin dead on his doorstep.

Stabbed Lily to death in the street.

A car door slammed shut. Drayce ran through the open gate, saw Reaper in the driver's seat of the BMW he'd arrived in. They locked eyes through the windscreen. The engine fired up. Drayce ran to the driver's door. The vehicle lurched backwards, stopped, realigned, accelerated at him. Drayce threw himself at the bonnet to stop his legs from being chopped out from under him, rolled up the windscreen, over the roof, down the boot, and rattled along the tarmac for several feet. Tiny chunks of rubber and grit hurtled in his face. He could taste the exhaust fumes, heard the BMW speed off up the road. He rolled onto his stomach, looked up, and saw it disappear in the distance. He pushed his chest off the ground, winced as a cracked rib touched a cluster of nerves. Got to his feet. Scanned his surroundings for something to give chase in.

Nearly every car on the street was a Tesla. The oldest was perhaps three years out of the factory, the security so up to date they couldn't be stolen without keys. But then something caught Drayce's eye: Territt's garage door. On the other side of which…

It took fifteen seconds for Drayce to run back into the house, swipe the Jaguar keys from the hallway table and fire up the motor. As soon as the shutters cleared the roof, he dumped his right foot and rode the power slide onto the street, fighting the back end as he glided it up the road. He worked through the gears to the junction where the BMW had turned left, exhausts popping, tyres squealing as he took the bend at speed. The engine roared, the vehicle devouring another long straight. Fifty, seventy, ninety miles an hour. On the brakes at a T-junction, back end squirrelling, smoke pluming. Drayce brought the Jag to a stop, head pivoting.

No sign of the Beemer.

Did it go left or right?

Fifty/fifty.

After tossing a coin in his mind, Drayce swerved right and booted it. He glanced down the roads at every junction he passed, desperately searching for a black BMW M5.

Nothing.

Nothing.

Drayce felt a sickening pull on his stomach. Had he lost the vehicle for good and with it his chance of capturing Lily's killer?

He pressed on, another coin toss, then another, further and further through London's labyrinth, a man obsessed with the hunt. He ran red lights, ignored keep-left bollards, went the wrong way down a one-way street.

On Haverstock Hill he really pushed it, overtaking everything in sight. At the brow he saw something black, hairs rearing up on the back of his neck. He drove at oncoming traffic, forcing it to move. Cars swerved out of his way. Horns blared. When he hit the crest, the Jaguar got air, landing a few feet later. His view opened.

Something in the distance.

The BMW.

Five cars ahead.

Drayce went to overtake the first, only just made it, swerving in front to a blast of horn from an oncoming car. He straddled the white line to improve his view, ready for the next overtake, cursing under his breath at the sight of solid traffic oncoming.

With the pavement on the nearside clear, he mounted it with all four wheels, foot down, hurtling past the next three cars. Reaper must have clocked him in his mirror. The BMW took off, skidding around the car in front. Drayce heard the ear-splitting sound of steel being violently torn apart, glass shattering, and screams from pedestrians on the other pavement who had dived out of the way of oncoming traffic that had crashed as it was forced to swerve out of Reaper's way.

Drayce re-joined the road, the back end of the Jaguar clipping a lamp post as the wheels thudded off the kerb. He corrected the skid, followed in Reaper's wake, desperately sawing the steering wheel one way, then the other, avoiding a vicious slalom of deadly obstacles.

Congestion at red lights slowed Reaper down, allowing Drayce to catch up. Reaper skittled a dozen temporary bollards, mounting the central reservation as he forced his way through. Drayce saw a mother with her baby in a pushchair approach a pedestrian crossing further on, directly in line with Reaper's current direction of travel. He punched his horn to warn her. She swivelled her head just in time to see the looming danger and lurched backwards, dragging her child out of harm's way in the nick of time.

Drayce chased Reaper through the lights, only metres away from his bumper as they flew down Chalk Farm Road into Camden. Drayce scanned as far ahead as he could see, plotting Reaper's potential route and his own path of least resistance. Everything around them was closing in: people, traffic; there were double the numbers now. Buses, taxis, vulnerable cyclists were all snarled together at the upcoming crossroads. The pavements bustled with footfall. There wasn't room for Reaper to force his way through.

He was trapped.

Brake lights seized Drayce's attention. Reaper swerved left, towards the pavement, clearly willing to mow down crowds of people to get away. Reacting on instinct, Drayce undertook him and steered hard right, slamming into the BMW's rear nearside to stop it from endangering anyone. Reaper lost control, went into a spin, hit a lamp post, and ricocheted into a van. Tipping onto two wheels, the BMW rolled and skidded to a halt on its roof in the middle of the crossroads.

A moment of shock possessed Camden. Someone screamed. Pedestrians took out their phones, made calls, filmed the aftermath. Motorists got out of their cars. Concerned citizens approached the upside-down BMW. Drayce abandoned the Jaguar, ran through the gathering crowd, wrenched open the driver's door.

Empty.

The passenger door was wide open. Drayce peered through the vehicle. Reaper was on his toes, bleeding from his head, an arm clutching his ribs. People tried to stop him, but he shoulder-barged them out of his way and muscled through the crowd, desperate to escape.

Drayce ran around the wreckage and sprinted after him.

30

Drayce chased his quarry, the fleeing figure twenty metres ahead, running full stride along the pavement. Drayce gained on him, avoiding bodies, shoving others to the ground, barely noticing the people he left scattered behind him, his concentration on his target, homing in like a missile.

Eighteen metres.

Fifteen.

Reaper scurried out into the road, disappearing out of sight behind a bus. Drayce stepped out into the stationary traffic, weaving between vehicles, eyes everywhere, waiting for him to pop out. He stayed in the middle of the road, bounding along the line of cars, able to run faster without the slow footfall impeding him. He kept the pace up, eyes searching.

Where the hell did he go?

He should have reappeared by now.

Wondering if Reaper had doubled back, Drayce was about to rejoin the pavement when he was halted by the sight of a biker in helmet and leathers, who staggered backwards from behind the bus and collapsed. Seemingly unhurt, he got to his feet and gesticulated to someone out of Drayce's sight. Drayce pushed on, opening his view, and saw Reaper climb onto a motorbike and ride off.

There was a group of them, the bikes all big, high-powered models. Their body language suggested an assumption Drayce was running over to help them, so they must have been disappointed when he threw the biggest of the group to the ground and stole his huge, matte black Indian Chief.

The wheels spun and the ground shook as Drayce aligned the bike and set off after Lily's killer. Reaper glanced over his shoulder, eyes wide at the sight of Drayce still pursuing him. He dashed off the road, mounted the pavement, and flew under the archway into the pedestrianised Camden Market.

Drayce followed, handlebars rattling, tyres thudding over the cobbled path. Screams accompanied the roar of their engines. People dived out of their way, bodies hurdling benches and tables. A woman fell backwards into a juice stand, collapsing onto crates of oranges that spilled everywhere.

Reaper turned right, narrowly missing a group of people gathered at a Japanese food stall. The rear wheel of Drayce's bike kinked out a touch as he followed him and powered through the open-air market, now only a few metres away. They both accelerated past the horse and cart statue, swerving to avoid the crowds, delving deeper into the bowels of the market.

Drayce stuck to the rear of the bike like glue, following every twist and turn Reaper made. Up ahead, the path narrowed for a long stretch, funnelling the large crowds of people through a bottleneck. Drayce foresaw the hazards early and honked his horn repeatedly, shouting and waving his arm to signal for people to move out of the way. He slowed, working through the crowds with caution.

Reaper didn't.

Several bodies dived to one side to avoid being mown down. Reaper glanced over his shoulder and smiled, undoubtedly because he was putting ground between him and Drayce. With a swipe of an arm, Reaper knocked down a rail of t-shirts, then a tower of bookshelves, scattering paperbacks across the path. With wide eyes, Drayce slammed on his brakes and swerved, the back wheel kicking out as he slowed down. He avoided the wooden bookcase and the metal stand, tyres bumping over the books and piles of clothing.

As Drayce made it through the debris and twisted the throttle, the gap between them had tripled in length. He worked to make up the lost ground, weaving from side to side like a skier in a slalom to get through the crowds, the bike up ahead harder to follow with a heavy footfall in-between, blocking Drayce's view.

At the end of the straight, he saw something dart left at speed. He followed, winding down a ramp to the lower level, and briefly clocked eyes on Reaper, taking a tight turn at the bottom. Drayce raced down and skidded round the hairpin, hurtling after him under a set of arches that led back out onto the roads. He followed left, thudding down off the kerb as he re-joined the road network. A deep growl rumbled in his throat as he lost sight of Reaper.

Willing to risk it all, he opened the throttle up and overtook a bus and several cars on a sweeping blind bend, his eyes never once leaving his visual limit point where the wall met the tarmac. With no sign of Reaper, Drayce risked it all again and went for another overtake, this time a giant cement truck. He moved out, accelerated, and just as he reached the point of no return, was met with the sight of a lorry coming the opposite way.

No time to hesitate. Drayce opened the throttle all the way, engine screaming underneath him, gap closing faster than he was gaining. A flash of lights from the oncoming truck, a puff of smoke as the wheels locked, the machine too big and heavy to slow down in time. Drayce hugged the bike, reducing the drag coefficient as much as possible. The front grill of the lorry loomed ahead, an unstoppable mass of glass and steel bearing down on him. Drayce locked eyes on the front offside corner of the cement truck. Held his breath. Lined up the bike. Said a prayer.

The lorry's air horn screamed at him as he slipped through the gap with nothing more than a clipped wing mirror. He exhaled and leaned to the side to straighten the bike up, throttle still fully open, blasting round the rest of the bend. It opened to a roundabout. No sign of Reaper. He stopped in the middle of the road and looked both ways. A flash of something to the left. His rear wheel spun in a cloud of smoke, the bike turning as Drayce threw his hips into the back end. He worked through the gears, chasing down what he'd seen, hoping it was Reaper. He flew past a parked lorry. Then another. Into the rear delivery yard of a giant supermarket. He clamped down on the brakes. The wheels locked up, rear lifting clear of the tarmac, dropping back down to earth as he came to a stop.

Dead end.

A metal fence blocked his path straight ahead, turning into an L-shape to separate the back of the supermarket from the railway lines. The bike Reaper had stolen lay abandoned in front of him. No rider. Drayce jumped off his big Indian Chief and turned on the spot, three sixty, eyes everywhere, scanning for movement.

Through the slats in the fence, he saw something: the jerky, panicked actions of a man on the run.

Drayce exploded off the spot, arms pumping in rhythm with his legs, ignoring the razor-sharp tips of the fence as he leapt up and swung over. Landing in the dirt with a roll, he was straight back on his feet, sprinting full stride across the railway lines. There were eight of them, spread across a fifty-metre-wide expanse. Drayce locked eyes on Reaper's fleeing figure. The track ahead of Drayce hummed. He saw something in the corner of his eye, approaching at speed, so many carriages linked together he couldn't see the end. If he didn't get ahead of it, he'd be blocked, and would lose Reaper for sure.

Six metres and closing. Couldn't slow down. Had to push on, run faster, get ahead of the speeding train. The humming intensified, the ear-splitting roar of the engine getting closer, hurtling towards him. A deafening horn blared as the driver spotted him, unable to do anything to alter his fate. A squeal of brakes rang out, sparks flying as the metal wheels locked up and were dragged along the lines by the machine's gargantuan bulk. Drayce made one final leap, headfirst, committing everything, eyes closed, milliseconds between success and obliteration. He felt his shoulder hit rocks, a whoosh of air gusting through his hair as the train stormed past. He rolled, came up onto a knee, carriage after carriage whizzing behind him.

Still in one piece.

Still alive.

Time to put it to use.

Back on his feet, he ran hard, leaping over line after line. Another metal fence met him on the other side, taller than the last. Reaper was clambering up, his hands working up the slats, feet scrambling after him. He reached the top just as Drayce caught up. Without slowing down, Drayce jumped at the fence, using one foot to propel himself up, arm stretched, fingers clawing for Reaper's legs. He latched on to an ankle, grip tight, brought his other hand into play and pulled down with all twenty stone of his bodyweight.

A boot to the face from Reaper's other leg made Drayce's grip slip. He dangled from the man's foot by one hand, tasted blood, reached back up and gripped his trouser leg. Drayce braced his feet against the fence and pulled with a rocking motion, trying to break Reaper's hold. When that didn't work, he climbed up his trouser leg, one fist-full of material after another. Something tore – a seam, perhaps – and Drayce felt himself drop an inch. With one hand clamped hard around Reaper's trousers, Drayce reached for his belt, fingers stretched, knowing the leather strap would give him ample purchase. Six inches; three inches; a hair's width away. Reaper tried kicking out again. No chance. Drayce was nearly there. He made one final push against the fence with his feet. The pad of his middle finger crept over the belt, folded it down, allowing the other three to follow suit. Once wrapped around the leather, he clasped down hard and heard Reaper wince as his arms straightened and his grip weakened, his muscles unable to hold Drayce's weight much longer. It was only a matter of time before Drayce would rip him off the fence and control him on the ground. The chase was over. Nothing could stop Drayce now.

Car engines and squealing tyres broke his concentration.

The sounds came from the other side of the fence. Drayce peered around Reaper's legs, in-between the metal slats: three cars; half a dozen men. They fanned out and approached the fence tactically. Hands reached under jacket lapels and slipped to waistlines. Drayce frowned. None of them were cops. Wrong image. Reaper must have called in reinforcements while on the run.

In a split second, Drayce considered his options. A short list. He was an easy target holding on to that fence. No cover; nothing to shoot back with. The only option he had if he wanted to survive was to let go of Reaper and run for it.

But he just couldn't do it.

He told his fingers to relax, but they stayed firm, ignoring the order. Inside he raged, the decision tearing him apart; he was unable to release his wife's killer, but he knew it would do no good if he was blasted off that fence by Reaper's friends and left to die on a railway line. He clamped his teeth together and bit down hard.

Let go, damn it!

The hairs on his arm bristled. Movement on the other side of the fence. Three figures to his left, three to his right. They could see him clearly through the slats, their guns up, taking aim. A shot cracked off, the bullet whining as it spun through the air, missing him by inches. He let go of Reaper's belt, heard another shot. As he dropped to the ground, something kicked up the dirt next to him. He landed feet first, toppled backwards and rolled over his shoulder onto his knees, saw the six men adjust their aim, barrels pointing through the slats in the fence.

Drayce turned and legged it to a building line, his nearest point of hard cover. Gunfire popped off behind him, the rounds whistling past his head, kicking up sparks in front of him as they ricocheted off the train lines. He pumped his legs and arms, eyes focused ahead. Six feet away from the corner of the building he dived, rolled, hit the breezeblock with his shoulder, and crawled into cover.

He glanced behind to check he wasn't exposed, heard the dull thuds of bullets embedding into the breezeblock, plumes of dust spraying out with each impact. He pressed his back against the wall, worked his feet under his hips and stood tall. The shooting stopped. He edged along the wall, dropped to a knee, crept his eyeline around the corner.

The six men were getting back into their cars in a hurry, accompanied by Reaper. Before the doors had even closed, they all did a tight U-turn and sped away. Drayce watched them leave, fists clenched tight. He looked down at his t-shirt. Blood was spattered across his chest.

Not his own blood.

He took out his phone and called Julie.

31

This time, Drayce was the one sat waiting at Starbucks in Vauxhall, his companion's coffee on the other side of the table, cooling by the second. The cafe buzzed with people grabbing drinks and snacks after their day's work. He sipped his own drink, brushed aside the empty sandwich wrappers, and checked the clock on the wall: 6:15 p.m. – quarter of an hour past the time they'd agreed to meet when Drayce had called Julie. She was a busy woman; hardly the nine-to-five type. Often worked crazy hours in a job she loved. But neither was she someone who turned up late. For anything. Ever. Another five minutes and Drayce would call her.

After getting off the train lines, he'd marched to a busy street nearby. With a heavy heart, he binned his ThruDark jacket, the bloodstains so obvious they were bound to arouse suspicion from onlookers, risking a three nines call. He swiped a black suit jacket off the back of a chair outside a coffee house, left abandoned by a careless customer who'd presumably gone inside to order, or perhaps use the toilet. Drayce left some cash on the table so the owner could buy a new one. It was too small, the sleeves riding up his forearms, seams straining, but he could get it on, and he only wanted it to cover the bloodstains on his t-shirt. From there he'd taken a taxi to his hotel, binned the jacket, and changed into fresh jeans, a black t-shirt, and a flannel shirt in black and green check. He stuffed the bloodied shirt into the plastic evidence bag he'd swiped from Islington nick, which now sat under the table, a soft bulge clamped between his feet, ready and waiting.

At 6:18 p.m. Julie walked through the door, saw him, and sat down. Her eyelids were heavy, half closed, the sliver of sclera a bloodshot mess. Her expression was blank. Emotionless. She put her handbag on the table, ignored Drayce, as though he wasn't there, and downed half her coffee in a single gulp. When she set it down, Drayce caught her eye.

'Tough day?'

She wiped her mouth with a napkin, blinked hard, seemingly more alert now. 'No tougher than any other.'

'Still not sleeping?'

She shook her head. 'Doctor wants to put me on medication. Something to knock me out. Told him it can't happen.'

'Because of the job?'

She nodded. 'I have to be able to answer my phone any time of the day or night.'

'Maybe it's time for a change of pace.'

Julie locked eyes with him, wide and unblinking, the caffeine in full effect. 'Maybe it's time you drop the cuddly-care-bear act and tell me why we're here. I can tell you've been busy from the way you're sat.'

Drayce frowned. 'Excuse me?'

'Your upper body is tilted to the left, which tells me you're subconsciously protecting something on that side of your torso.' Julie leaned forward, hands clasped together on the table. 'Been in the wars since we last met, have we?'

Drayce smiled, the expression vanishing in an instant when his broken rib touched a nerve, making him wince. 'Very observant of you.'

'So, let's get to it: why did you ask to meet with me?'

'I need a favour.'

'A legal one?'

Drayce said nothing.

'Silence won't help your case, big guy. Remember: I'm a busy woman. Let's cut to the chase.'

'It's nothing criminal. Just an unofficial, off-the-books, no-one-will-ever-find-out-about-it, breach of procedure.' Her expression didn't falter, eyes set in stone. 'I want something tested for DNA.'

'Why?'

'The less you know, the better.'

Julie rested her elbows on the table, hands rising, fingers steepled like Monty Burns. 'Am I some wet-nosed snow-flake, straight out of university, skipping through the Agency corridors with no knowledge of the real world?'

Drayce contained his sigh. 'Obviously not.'

'No, not obviously. Otherwise, you wouldn't say something so stupid. The less I know the better? Really? After everything we've been through together?'

'I just don't want you getting too involved. This isn't your battle to—'

She raised a hand in front of her mouth, forefinger and thumb pinched together as she worked it across her lips as though closing a zip. 'Shut the fuck up, Alex, and fill me in on the details.'

He frowned. 'Little hard to do both.'

Her expression told him not to be a smart-arse. He took a deep breath, checked over his shoulders to make sure no one was within ear shot, and opened his mouth to tell her everything.

The words wouldn't come.

'I can't,' he said, eventually. 'It's not fair for me to burden you with it.'

Julie shot to her feet, grabbed her handbag, turned to the exit.

'Wait!' Drayce lunged over the table and grabbed her arm. 'Sit down.'

She stayed standing but turned to face him. 'You going to treat me with the respect I deserve? Or are we going to continue with this game, as though we hadn't been through messy times together, wading through murky waters to get the result we want.'

Drayce's eyes dropped to the floor as he thought about it. Of all the people on planet Earth, he could trust Julie the most. But she didn't need to know the details, and as a loyal NCA officer, telling her everything would put her in a terrible position and would ultimately risk Drayce's freedom, and in turn his ability to get his hands on Reaper again.

'Sit down and hear me out,' he said, locking eyes with Julie. 'I'll tell you what you need to know, and you can decide if you want to help. If so, great. If not…' He shrugged. 'I'll find another way.'

She sat back down.

Drayce kicked the exhibit to her under the table. 'I believe the blood on this t-shirt belongs to the man who killed Lily.'

Julie stilled, her face frozen in concentration. 'Why?'

'Information I've gathered.'

'And how did you come across this information?'

'Illegally.'

Silence at the table.

Drayce took out his phone. 'The man who killed Lily works for an international organised crime group. I started from square one and worked my way up the board. Caused trouble. Brought him to me.' He opened the photo he took of the forensic report from Jason Martin's crime scene and sent it to Julie. 'I could be wrong, but I don't think I am.' A ping came from Julie's handbag. She fished out her phone, opened the message, eyes devouring the words. Drayce put his own phone away, rubbed his face, dug knuckles into his eyes. The aftermath of his recent adrenaline dump brought with it an overwhelming fatigue. He needed more coffee.

A sharp pain rang bells in his neck. He rolled his head from side to side, dug his fingers in his traps. His back had stiffened from the fall out of Territt's window. Something in his knee was sore. Inflamed. He could use some strong painkillers; a hot shower; a good stretch and an even better night's sleep. No time for any of that.

'What's up with you?'

Drayce clocked Julie inspecting his squirming antics. 'Tough day. But no tougher than usual.'

Julie frowned as she watched him closely, no doubt wondering what the hell he'd been up to as her mind conjured a series of violent scenarios to explain his discomfort. Her eyes fell back to her phone.

Drayce said, 'If the DNA sequence in that report matches the DNA on the t-shirt, I've found Lily's killer.' He watched her stern face, eyes darting side to side, the screen of her phone reflected in her pupils. 'That's as much as I'm willing to tell you.'

'How'd you get this report?'

'Lucy – my FLO – got sloppy when we first met. I saw an opportunity and took it.'

'Got a name for the killer yet?'

'Not his real one, and I'm not interested in knowing it. I just need you to tell me whether the sequences match. He can die nameless for all I care.'

Julie glanced up at him. 'Die?'

Drayce didn't elaborate.

Julie continued reading. 'How do you propose to track him down?'

'I found him once; I can find him again. His face is imprinted in my memory, a fossil preserved in rock. It's going nowhere.'

She looked up from her phone. 'Going to make him come to you again?'

He shook his head, patted his shirt, a crinkle of paper underneath, stuffed into his belt. 'I know everything about the organisation he works for. I'm going after him this time. I'm going after all of them.'

Julie went quiet, as though she needed a moment to absorb that last statement. 'You go to the police with any of this?'

A shake of the head.

Julie raised her eyebrows. 'You planning to?'

'Of course not.'

She nodded, let out a nervous chuckle. '*Of course not.*'

'It's messy.'

'I'll bet.' Julie put her phone away. This time it was her turn to check over her shoulders. She stared at Drayce. 'You kill anyone since we last met?'

Drayce stayed silent.

'Jesus, Alex.'

'Bad men, Julie. They won't be missed. And I'll slaughter a thousand more and burn this city to the ground if I must. Nothing's getting in my way.'

Julie shut her eyes, massaged her temples.

Drayce gave her time, waited until she acknowledged him again, and said, 'I understand if you don't want to help me.'

Julie's face sharpened, eyes throwing daggers across the table. 'Don't you fucking insult me. It's not about whether I'll help you. Of course I'll help you. In case you forgot what we went through back in January, I'll remind you that this sort of thing isn't exactly fresh ground for us. We've crossed lines before, together, the two of us. I'm more than happy to cross them again, for you, the way you've crossed them for me in the past. But I need to know you've got things under control.'

'Now who's being insulting.'

'This is different. Everything before… that was professional. This is personal. Deeply, deeply personal. If the DNA matches, if this man killed Lily, I need to know you've got it under control. That you'll be careful. Cover your tracks.' Julie's expression softened. 'I don't want to see your face on a bulletin. I don't want you to go to prison.' She paused, took a breath. 'Or worse.'

'Don't worry about me. Just get the blood on that t-shirt tested and tell me if it matches the DNA in the report. I need to be certain this is the guy before…'

Julie stared deep into his eyes, assessing him. 'Before what?'

'You really want to know?'

Julie didn't reply. She put her handbag under the table, stuffed the exhibit bag inside, and zipped it shut. She rested it on her lap, hugged tight to her body. 'You in a rush for this?'

'Of course. I've got things to be getting on with, but the sooner I know, the better.'

She nodded. Slowly. Thoughtfully. 'I know someone in forensics who owes me a favour. I'll cash it in, get this pushed through immediately.' She tapped her handbag. 'You'll know one way or the other by the end of the day.'

Drayce smiled. 'I appreciate it, Jules. Thank you.'

She stood to leave.

'Another coffee?' Drayce asked. 'Something to eat?'

She shook her head. 'I'm busy. Got things to do.' She turned, walked away, then peered over her shoulder as she got to the exit. 'And by the sound of it, so have you.'

32

A deep sigh shot out of Lucy's lungs as she leaned back in her chair and rubbed her face with her hands. She checked her watch – her shift should have been over three hours ago. Her tasks for the day finally completed, she closed the windows she had open on her computer screen and went to log off. She paused at the last one – the results of the searches she did for the phone Drayce had given her. It had been sitting in the back of her mind all afternoon, bugging her. Why on earth would his friend own a phone that was registered to a corporation in Dubai, with intelligence reports linked to the NCA and Interpol? She stared at the screen and hovered the curser over the X, lost in thought as her imagination ran wild, her mind split between two decisions – stay away from him, as she knew getting drawn into whatever he was up to risked both her career and her safety; or get to the bottom of what he was planning to do and put a stop to it.

'Hey!'

Lucy jumped, her hand flapping at the mouse as she hurriedly closed the search result window. She glanced at the doorway and tried to hide the panic that must have been evident on her face.

'Jesus, Susie,' she said when she realised it wasn't Territt stood behind her, but another DC on their investigation team, far younger, prettier, and above all friendlier than their boss. 'You nearly gave me a heart attack.'

'Sorry.' Susie ran her fingers through her long red hair, brushing it out of her face and keeping it in place behind her

214

ear. She leaned against the door frame and frowned. 'What's got you on edge?'

Lucy made a conscious effort to compose herself. 'It doesn't matter.' She forced a smile Susie's way. 'How can I help?'

'Have you heard?'

Now it was Lucy's turn to frown. 'Heard what?'

'The DCI – he's gone missing.'

'Territt?'

'Uh-huh. His neighbours reported hearing gunshots coming from his home, and when the ARVs got there, the place was on fire.'

Lucy felt the colour drain from her face.

'And there's more,' Susie continued with glee.

'More?'

'His car – that flashy Jaguar with the private reg – was involved in a collision in Camden. It had been in pursuit of another vehicle that ended up on its roof!'

Lucy felt her tongue stick to the roof of her mouth. Her lips clung to her teeth like glue. She snatched the bottle of water off her desk and gulped it down.

Susie looked on with a concoction of suspicion and concern plastered across her face. 'You all right?'

Lucy put the empty bottle back and took a deep breath. 'Yeah, fine. It's just been a long day.'

'Better remedies for those than water, let me tell you. Speaking of which, you fancy a drink after work? A group of us are going to swing by a few bars. Nothing crazy.' Susie grinned. 'It is a school night, after all.'

'I'd love to, but I can't.' The image of Drayce's face catapulted to the forefront of her mind. 'There's someone I need to find.'

'Find?'

Lucy inwardly cursed her poor choice of language. 'I meant see. I've got someone I need to see after work.'

Susie pouted. 'Not even got time for a quick one over the road?'

'Sorry, I wish I had. But then again, it's never a quick one with you lot, and I am no longer of an age that allows me to get away with heavy drinking on a school night.' She forced a smile Susie's way. 'You guys go ahead and have fun.'

Lucy logged off her computer, stood up, and grabbed her coat.

'Okay, if you're sure.' Susie backed away from the door. 'Another time, perhaps?'

Lucy begrudgingly produced another fake smile, harder the second time as she did her best to appear unflustered. 'Sure. Another time.'

Lucy shut the door as soon as Susie was out of sight, shrugged her coat over her shoulders, and took out her phone. Decision made, she was grateful she'd given herself this option earlier in the day. Without it, the task of finding Drayce and discovering what he was up to would have been damn near impossible. Her thumb frantically swiped at the screen as she searched for the app she wanted and opened it. The signal was strong, beaming the precise location of the device in real-time. It was on the move, heading northeast, on its way out of town.

Lucy grabbed her car keys and ran out of the station.

33

It was eight p.m. by the time Reaper was able to make it to the club in a fit state to debrief Sullivan. The envelope containing the information he'd unearthed about the husband was tucked under his arm. Other than a bust nose, some nasty bruising, and a few minor fractures, Reaper was fighting fit. A private doctor – held by Sullivan's firm on a retainer for discreet, priority treatment – had patched him up and given him a dozen blister packs of prescription-strength painkillers, which he'd tossed in the bin on his way out of the practice. He despised the numbness those drugs instilled. Pain kept him sharp; alert – aware of how dangerous the man he'd just fought was. Which is precisely what Reaper needed to be if he hoped to survive their next encounter. After what Reaper had confirmed about the man, they most definitely had not heard the last of him.

Reaper crossed the street to the club and spoke to security on the doors. They shook his hand and bowed their heads in his presence. He checked the guestlist. Everything was running like clockwork. Half the guests were already partying, but the main players were yet to arrive. Reaper strolled up the stairs from the main entrance, through the first bar area, and down a neon-lit tunnel, the walls covered in glow-in-the-dark graffiti. Emerging on the other side, he skirted around the dancefloor and podiums and passed the long bar that served the main room, before climbing the stairs that led up to Sullivan's office, carving a path through the crowds as he went.

Strobe lights flashed across his freshly suited figure, all black from his neck to his toes. The bass hummed in his chest.

He glanced up at Sullivan's office window, the giant mirrored rectangle overlooking the dancefloor. He smoothed down his beard, clutched the envelope tighter. Sweat from his palms soaked into the paper. He wiped them on his thighs, ascended the spiral staircase, and marched down the corridor. He paused at the door. Took a deep breath. Knocked.

It opened to reveal Sullivan, dressed in his immaculate new tailored navy suit. As Reaper shut the door behind him, the raucous activities of the club were instantly muted. He walked across the brand-new rug, a carbon copy of the previous thick-piled cream number, and stepped up to the table. He dropped the envelope on its polished surface with a *thwack*.

'You were right,' Reaper said. 'He's her husband.'

Sullivan glanced at the envelope. 'We'll get to that. First, talk me through what happened.'

Reaper explained recent events, starting with the call from Territt, disguised as a 999 call – code that something was very wrong – and ending with his own narrow escape.

Sullivan closed his eyes and pinched the bridge of his nose as though overcome with a piercing headache. He walked to the drinks cabinet, poured a whisky, and necked it in one. Back at the table, he picked up the envelope, worked a finger under the flap, eyes on Reaper, tracking over his wounds with contempt. 'Why d'you only take four men with you?'

Reaper raised his chin, chest out. Defensive. 'It was all I had with me at the time. We needed to act quickly, otherwise we might have lost him.'

Sullivan's finger gradually ran along the envelope, a slow and steady tear the soundtrack to their conversation. He shook his head. 'I don't think you would have done. I think this man, this husband of hers, somehow linked Territt to the killings, drew you clowns into an ambush, and killed everyone but you.' The tearing stopped. His eyes burned into Reaper. 'Want to explain how the fuck that happened?'

'He's not just some angry husband on a vendetta.' Reaper winced, a bolt of pain shooting through his ribs as though coils of barbed wire were tightening around his midsection. 'There's more to him than that.'

'How so?'

Reaper nodded at the envelope. 'It's all there.'

Sullivan upended it onto the tabletop. Four sheets of A4 paper, folded in half, hit the glass surface.

'And I wasn't the only person he didn't kill at Territt's house,' Reaper added.

Sullivan's hand paused mid-air, hovering above the papers. His eyes rolled up to assess Reaper. 'Is that so?'

'Territt survived.'

'Injured?'

Reaper nodded. 'He won't be eating solid foods for a few months, but he's alive.'

'Well, well, isn't he a lucky boy. Not for long, though. If this maniac that's coming after us knows we've got an informant in the police, it makes Territt vulnerable. We can't afford for him to be arrested by his own. With enough pressure, he'll tell them everything.' Sullivan swiped the papers off the table. 'I want him snatched off the street and taken somewhere quiet, Reaper, if you know what I mean?'

'Way ahead of you.'

Sullivan stared at him as though waiting for him to explain his last words. Reaper took out his phone and made a call.

'Bring him in,' he said.

The door to Sullivan's office opened and in walked Territt, chaperoned by two men. Once they were through the doorway, Territt fell in as the middleman in the trio, the other two towering over him as they approached Reaper and Sullivan. Territt appeared different, his face displaying an unusual contour to it. There was almost an underbite to his jaw, the bone jagged, clearly fractured in more than one place. Territt's minders pulled him to a halt a few feet from Sullivan and Reaper, his eyes flitting from one man to the other, wringing his sweaty hands.

'How did this happen?' Sullivan asked.

An indecipherable mumbling was all Territt managed. His eyes were half shut, his blinking unnaturally slow, undoubtedly due to the pain medication he'd been given. A lazy strand of drool crawled out of the corner of his mouth.

Sullivan glanced at Reaper. 'What did he say?'

'No idea, but I doubt it's an adequate excuse.'

Sullivan's eyes briefly skimmed across the folded pages before they locked back on Territt. 'So, he did this to you? The man who wants us dead because we killed his wife?'

Territt answered the question with a series of frantic nodding, his forehead glistening from the build-up of sweat.

Sullivan addressed Reaper. 'The scene at his home?'

'It's been dealt with – burned to the ground.' Territt let out a whimper, this information clearly news to him. 'The only evidence they'll gather from it is a bunch of bullets and bones they can pick out once the ash is cool enough, which will be of no use to them.'

Sullivan pondered this statement for a moment. He gently nodded, then flicked his head in Territt's direction. 'How the fuck did he know this weasel was on our payroll?'

'I don't know exactly.' Reaper nodded at the pages in Sullivan's hands. 'But once you've read those, you'll have a better understanding of how he might have worked it out.'

Sullivan nodded again, slowly, his fingertips caressing the corners of his mouth before he scratched his cheek, no doubt contemplating how he should proceed.

'Get rid of him,' he said to Reaper. Territt's eyes widened and his legs trembled, the crease down the front of his trousers quivering in response. 'Alive, he's nothing but a threat to us.'

Reaper smiled, widely, his teeth bared, glistening like fangs. He approached Territt calmly, sauntering across the room with the swagger of a man who enjoyed his job a little too much. He nodded at the men either side of Territt, who understood the subliminal message and stepped aside. Reaper locked eyes on Territt, who's own had the glassy glint of tears building. His shaking intensified. Reaper leaned towards Territt's shoulder and tilted his head, his lips a couple of inches from the man's ear.

'It looks like you're no longer of use to us, Detective Chief Inspector.' He paused, noticing the hairs on the man's neck stand to attention. Goosebumps broke out across his flesh. Reaper stretched it out a little further, prolonging Territt's suffering, and in turn his own pleasure. When he couldn't wait any longer, he said the last words the man would ever hear. 'And we don't have room for useless things around here.'

He turned his shoulders away from Territt and lifted his arm, fist clenched into a tight ball of bone and muscle. Territt appeared to be frozen, his feet locked in place as though set in blocks of cement. His head, however, was shaking violently from side to side as his central nervous system protested what was about to happen.

But it would do no good.

His paymaster's mind was made.

Reaper swung his arm forcefully at Territt, the punch powered by his hips and shoulders that snapped round, his fist trailing behind, cutting through the air like a rock attached to the end of a baseball bat. Territt shut his eyes a split second before Reaper's fist slammed into his windpipe. He let out a sickening gurgle as his head and neck rocked backwards, as though suffering a formidable bout of whiplash. He collapsed to the floor, mouth puckering silently like a fish out of water, fingers clawing at his crushed larynx as he desperately tried to draw breath. His face turned purple, his lips blue, body writhing, legs clattering against the floorboards as he eked out the last of the life left in him. Moments later, he fell still.

Reaper stood over him, staring at the man's body, panting hard with a smile still on his face. He'd always taken pleasure from killing. It was why he'd never stop. He adjusted his dishevelled suit jacket and turned to face Sullivan.

Show over, Sullivan ignored Territt's corpse and addressed the minders. 'Get rid of the body.'

Both men nodded before one grabbed Territt's arms, the other his legs, and carried him out of the office.

'And in case it didn't go without saying,' Sullivan called out to their backs just before they slipped through the door, 'be discreet.'

Once Sullivan was alone with Reaper once more, he unfolded the papers and began reading.

'That top sheet is a printout of a newspaper article covering the murder of his wife,' Reaper said, dabbing his sweaty forehead with a handkerchief.

'You need a minute?' Sullivan asked him.

'No. I'm fine.' He grinned at his boss. 'Nothing like the excitement of killing a man.'

Sullivan eyed Reaper warily. Reaper knew what his boss was thinking: like an attack dog off its leash, Reaper was a useful asset, provided you kept his nose pointed at the enemy. Sullivan was evidently keen to ensure he didn't turn his attention towards his master.

'I can see that.' Sullivan forced his eyes away from his paid assassin and lifted the article higher to examine it more closely. 'So, tell me, why is this relevant?'

'Skip to the end.' He watched Sullivan do just that. 'Now look at the photograph. The one from the memorial service held by the police.'

Reaper watched Sullivan take in the man's image: a towering presence over those around him. Navy suit, black tie and handkerchief, shoulders back, posture ramrod straight as he recited something from memory.

Sullivan nodded thoughtfully. 'Certainly looks as though he can handle himself.'

'Read the words underneath.'

Sullivan squinted. 'Alex Drayce, husband of the fallen officer.'

'That's his name – the man that's been coming after us. The man who killed the entire crew I took with me and damn near killed me too.' Reaper tapped a finger on the other sheets. 'Now read those.'

Sullivan carelessly tossed the article down and lifted the other pages. Reaper waited until he saw his boss's eyes light up.

Sullivan took a deep breath, exhaled loudly. 'He's one of them.'

'Used to be. Left after we killed his wife. Works as a bodyguard now. I gave his name to a guy I know who's good with computers, and he found his CV for me on some close protection website.'

Sullivan's eyes darted side to side like the platen on a typewriter, devouring each line. He turned the sheet, picked up the other two, his expression souring by the second. 'Well, well, by the looks of it we have quite the adversary on our tails. Boxed and wrestled from a young age, instructor level in Muay Thai, black belt in Brazilian jiu-jitsu. Didn't exactly walk the beat either. Armed Response Vehicles, a Counter Terrorist Specialist Firearms Officer, bodyguard for the Prime Minister. Commendation after commendation. Eighteen years of service.' Sullivan puckered his lips and released a long, drawn-out whistle. 'My, my, he's quite the tough guy on paper, isn't he?'

'Doesn't fall short in real life, I can tell you.'

Sullivan's eyes locked onto Reaper. 'This your excuse for what happened, is it?'

Reaper shook his head. 'I don't make excuses; I give reasons.' He nodded at the sheets on the table. 'This is no ordinary member of the public. He's trained. Very well trained. Brock Lesnar and John-fucking-Wick rolled into one.'

'He bulletproof?'

'Course not.'

'Then he should be dead.'

'Not as simple as that. Not with a man like this. It's going to take a lot to kill this one.'

Sullivan screwed up the sheets of paper and threw them at Reaper. The bundle bounced off his chest and fell to the floor.

Reaper didn't flinch. Sullivan stepped forward, close enough for Reaper to feel the warmth of his whisky-soaked breath. 'Then take a lot. Take whatever you need.'

'If I were to go after this Drayce character again, I'd want fifty men, gunned up, to corner him like an animal and put an end to him. We don't have the numbers to spare. Not right now. Not with the event we're hosting at the club.' Reaper faced the window to the dancefloor, the strobing lights, the strippers, gangsters amassing. The bass rumbled under his feet, vibrating through the soles of his shoes. He turned back to Sullivan. 'May I make a suggestion?'

Sullivan gave it a moment's thought. He nodded.

'This club's flooded with our people, all of them armed. We get this event done, show our guests we're the dominant force in London, that we're here to stay. Then tomorrow, I put all our associates on watch for Drayce, gather up a hundred killers, and flood the city with an order to slaughter the bastard on sight.'

He waited for Sullivan's response.

'What if he comes here?'

Reaper pulled a face. 'Then he's a dead man before he sets foot inside. I've got a ring of steel around this club. No one gets in or out without us knowing.'

'There can't be any drama here tonight.'

'There won't be. If he's stupid enough to come here looking for trouble, we have the numbers to surround him, drag him out of sight, and kill him quietly.' Reaper felt his heartbeat hammering his tender ribcage. He rolled his head. Heard a crunch in his neck. Breathed. 'There's nothing one man can bring to these doors that we can't extinguish in the blink of an eye.'

Sullivan appeared to relax. He walked back to the drinks cabinet, poured himself another. Opened a cigar box, selected a Cohiba Behike, and cut off the cap. 'You joining me?'

'No. Can't. I need to brief the lads before the Chinese arrive.'

'No sign of them yet?' Sullivan lit a long match, held the tip of the flame to the cigar, and rolled it between finger and thumb to ensure the burn was even.

'Not yet.' Reaper peeked at his watch. 'But they won't be long.'

'Show them straight up when they arrive.'

A swift nod. 'I will.'

'And give that photograph to security.' Sullivan pointed to the ball of scrunched-up paper on the floor. 'I want his face burned into their memories. The doorman. The people watching the cameras. Everyone.'

Reaper picked up the ball and turned to leave. 'Leave it with me.' He cracked the door, a thunderous beat greeting him. He raised his voice to be heard. 'That man shows his face here, he's dead.'

Sullivan tugged on the cigar, a cloud of smoke pluming above his head like a crown. 'I hope so, Reaper.' His tongue flicked out and collected a stray fleck of tobacco from his bottom lip, wary eyes observing Reaper like a snake in the bushes. 'For your sake.'

Reaper held Sullivan's gaze with the frosty, emotionless energy of a killer, and let the door gently close between them.

34

Drayce drove the stolen Toyota Hilux towards Abridge: a small village to the northeast of London. The headlights cut a path through the dark country roads. Moonlight cast a silver glow across the fields and woodland. He drove by memory, racking up in his mind a list of what he'd need from the man he was travelling to see.

He'd considered using one of the fake IDs he owned — acquired for use on close protection jobs when an anonymous purchase was necessary — to hire a car. But the risks were too great. Cameras; signatures: even with a fake ID you risked leaving behind a faint track that could be followed by the most dogged of investigators. So theft had become necessary — a ten-year-old Hilux from a builder's yard that wouldn't be missed until morning, when Drayce's plan would be done and dusted, one way or the other. He'd left a bundle of cash in its place, wrapped in cling-film, so the owner wouldn't be out of pocket.

He was on his way to visit an old acquaintance — someone whose expertise Drayce had benefitted from many times since leaving the police. There were occasions when a bodyguard could do their job just fine, and handle the threat more than adequately, without being armed. But then there were other occasions, with more substantial threats, when a firearm to a bodyguard was like a paintbrush to a painter.

Not much use without one.

The Toyota's headlights lit up a sign for the village. Not far now. Squares of light glowed in the distance where houses lined the streets, chimney stacks puffing smoke as families fought the last of the chilly spring evenings before summer broke through. Drayce checked the rear-view mirror, assessed the car lights fifty metres back. The driver had been following him for three miles. Maybe longer. Perhaps a coincidence, but in his current situation, not something to immediately dismiss. He slowed, five miles an hour below the limit. Down to ten, eyes glancing in his rear-view mirror. The headlights closed the gap, but then the driver slowed, keeping an unnatural distance. Strange. It appeared Drayce wouldn't be reaching his destination quite as soon as he'd expected. Some tests were required. Better to be safe than sorry.

He entered a thirty limit, examined the map on his phone, chose a good spot, and memorised a twisty route. Rather than closing the gap between them on this slower road, the car behind maintained its distance. In Drayce's heightened state of awareness, the hairs on the back of his neck twitched. He couldn't even recognise the make and model, never mind a description of the driver, thanks to their dark surroundings and the glare of the car's headlights.

Time to change that.

Into the village proper was a roundabout. With nothing else approaching, Drayce dropped down a gear, swerved right, and floored it across the white markings, contravening a keep-left bollard to carry as much speed as possible. He nailed it down a long straight and switched off the lights. The Toyota disappeared in the gloom of the village. In his mirror, the car behind followed, driving noticeably faster to try and keep up. Using the gears to slow down so brake lights didn't mark the Toyota's presence, Drayce took a left junction at speed, fighting the weight of the big truck and the roll of the soft suspension. Out of his pursuer's sight entirely, he slammed on the brakes, backed down an empty driveway along the side of a house with no lights on, and switched off the engine.

He waited.

Motionless.

Not daring to even take a breath.

Seconds later the car that had been following him shot past, oblivious to his hiding spot. This time he could easily make out the type of vehicle – a BMW 3 Series in black – along with a description of the driver: female; late twenties; slender torso under a white shirt and light blue sweater; black hair tied back in a bun; sharp eyes scanning the road ahead.

Lucy.

Drayce exhaled with a sigh, brow furrowed in a frown, top lip curled. The plastic steering wheel squeaked under his grip. Why had his FLO followed him out of the city? And on her own, as well. Couldn't be anything official, otherwise there'd be a team with her. A few more German saloons. A couple of motorbikes. Full surveillance detail. This was the Met, after all. Hardly short on resources. When they went after a target, they put numbers to the job. So, Lucy's little trip to the outskirts of the city on Drayce's tail was a personal choice.

Why?

He waited in case she decided to circle back, then once happy she hadn't, started the engine, switched on the lights, and pulled off the driveway. He took a different road out of the village than the one he'd driven in on, and got back on track via a long, twisty route, keeping an eye out for Lucy's headlights in the mirrors. For how long had she followed him? Since he left the city? Was it safe for him to carry on, or should he abandon his plans and presume he was being watched?

There was no turning back now, Drayce decided. He'd come this far, and as established, Lucy was on her own, not accompanied by a team. If he kept his eyes peeled, he could avoid Lucy, get what he came for, and be back in the city within a couple of hours.

He skirted around the village and turned down a narrow country lane, making one final check in his mirrors as he did so. Half a mile later he got out of the truck to open a set of gates, paused on the other side to close them, and continued down the lane. Seconds later, the farmhouse appeared ahead of him, windows in darkness, but Drayce knew the man he'd come to see would be home. He drove past a giant tower of hay bales covered in black plastic, a long block of stables, and pulled up in front of the main house.

Security lights activated, flooding him and his vehicle in brilliant white light. He shielded his eyes, stepped out, and rotated on the spot, knowing he'd been watched since turning onto the dead-end lane half a mile back. He removed his hand to give the cameras a clear shot of his face.

A light illuminated on the other side of the wooden front door. It swung open. An old man negotiated the steps in hard-lived boots, the frayed hems of his blue dungarees tickling the laces. His hands were tucked into the Joey pouch, the sleeves of his check flannel shirt rolled up to his elbows with military precision. The hard muscles in his forearms twitched like old rope under tension. Reading glasses dangled from a cord around his neck. He watched Drayce carefully. Old eyes assessed the meaning of this unplanned visit. A hand left the Joey pouch and scratched a patch of stubble high up on his cheekbone that he'd missed on the last half a dozen efforts at shaving. He nodded at his guest.

'Alex.'

Drayce nodded back. 'Henry.'

'Don't have you down for a collection.'

Drayce stepped closer. 'Be a hell of a mind reader if you did.'

'Social visit?'

'Not exactly. More like a last-minute plea for help.'

Henry cupped his chin between thumb and forefinger as though propping his head up. 'Better come inside.' He turned and walked back up the steps. 'If a man like you needs help, it must mean trouble.'

Drayce fetched from the Toyota the gym bag he stole from the three Liverpudlian gangsters and followed Henry. Twice as thick as your average domestic door, it rattled a picture on the wall when it closed behind him. As he did on every visit, Drayce admired the painting in the hall – an original of the Battle of Arnhem. Henry pulled up the handle and turned the key, slid deadbolts into the frame top and bottom. When the old man was done securing his fortress, Drayce followed him deeper into the house.

In the kitchen – a cosy farmhouse style with the obligatory Aga kicking out heat – Henry opened the door to a pantry, switched on a light, and stepped inside. Behind a dusty jar of kidney beans that might have been a hundred years old was an iron lever. Henry pulled it down. A metallic clunk sounded behind the wall. The hidden door opened inwards, taking the shelves of produce with it. Stairs spiralled into darkness.

The two men descended into the basement.

It was pitch black at the bottom of the steps. Henry's hand delved into the darkness and went straight to the light switch from muscle memory, triggering the hum of two dozen fluorescent tubes fixed along the ceiling. As they flickered to life, the giant space, carved out of the ground under the entire footprint of the house, came alive.

Eight steel pillars held up the beams that supported the building above. On either side of the open space were gun safes made of iron, bigger and tougher than bank vaults. At the far end was a steel cage, behind which a selection of weapons was mounted on the wall. Below them, boxes of raw materials were stacked. In a corner was a big V-shaped workbench, with vices mounted to the edge, and a bullet press that nearly touched the ceiling.

Drayce followed Henry across the polished concrete floor to the wooden desk in the centre of the room. His maroon cap badge sat proudly alongside framed medals and family photographs, old and new. Young Henry smiling proudly with his daughter on his knee; older Henry walking her down the aisle. The largest was reserved for his late wife, placed in the centre of the collection, posing for a photograph on their wedding day.

Much of the surface was taken up by a leather-framed blotter. Henry took a seat at the desk, lifted his reading glasses to his eyes, and opened his logbook.

'Not got much to spare you, my friend.' A gnarled finger tracked down the records. 'Everything I've been working on lately has already been claimed.'

Drayce surveyed the weapons mounted on the wall in the cage. 'Who are *they* for?'

Henry removed his reading glasses, turned to face him, followed his line of sight. 'No chance, kiddo.' He shook his head. 'That's part of a special order.'

Drayce walked right up to the cage. Leaned on it. Stared hard through the mesh that bowed from his weight. 'Must be a serious customer to need that lot.'

'They don't come any more serious.'

Drayce's eyes tracked along the wall, left to right, examining each piece. 'Talk me through what I'm looking at.'

'Does it matter what you're looking at? I told you. They're spoken for.'

Drayce turned to him and smiled. 'Just humour me.'

Henry stayed seated, his tired, irritated face doing the talking for him. His bushy eyebrows camouflaged his squinted eyes, the corners of his mouth turned down to complete the hostile look. Anyone else would have turned and walked away from an expression like that. But Drayce knew Henry well. Beneath their professional relationship, they were friends. When Henry had been in trouble in the past, Drayce had been by his side within the hour. The old man wouldn't turn his back on him.

Henry stood. 'From left to right you've got a Colt C8, the CQB version, chambered in 5.56 and fitted with a suppressor, a laser illuminator, and ACOG scope for magnification, with a mini red dot reflex sight for the up-close stuff.' He ambled over to Drayce and stood by his shoulder. 'Next is the Benelli M4 shotgun with pistol grip. Unlike earlier Benelli models, this one uses an auto-regulating gas-operated system, meaning there's zero chance of a stoppage. Works as smoothly as an AR, and the solid slug 12-gauge ammo I've made for it could stop a charging rhino faster than a cannon ball.' He raised a hand in front of Drayce's face, pointed a finger at the pistol on the wall. 'Last but not least is a little something I've been working on for a while. It started life as a Glock 19, but I developed an interchangeable grip and backstrap system to make it ergonomically designed to fit perfectly in the hand of the shooter. I also extended the mag release button, the slide release, and the magazine to allow for faster reloads.' He nodded at the boxes on the floor. 'Most of the weapons for the job are boxed up, ready to go, along with a portable tool kit and covert listening device, some abseil rope, body armour, and tactical belts with D-rings. Then there's the ballistic helmets with ear defenders and night-vision goggles, the blocks of plastic explosive, the frag grenades, stun grenades, and of course the ammunition.'

Drayce pursed his lips and let out a high note, which dropped low in a long, drawn-out whistle. He was impressed. 'What do they need plastic explosive for?'

'For blowing doors off their hinges and making holes in walls big enough for the team to walk through.'

Drayce nodded, slowly, surveying it all. 'Nice.'

Henry hooked his pointed finger inside the mesh and leaned on it. Drayce felt the man's eyes on him, saw the smirk in his peripheral vision, face beaming with pride. Drayce turned to face him.

'Impressive order,' Drayce said.

'You bet. Got to be when it's for a group of ex-SBS guys who've taken on a private military contract in Somalia. Only the best will do for the best in the world.'

Without saying a word, Drayce nodded his head at the door to the cage and smiled.

Henry pushed off the mesh, stood up straight, and frowned. 'What the hell is that smile for?'

'You know.'

'No, I don't. Otherwise, I wouldn't be asking.'

Drayce focused on the door. Henry followed his gaze.

'Oh no.'

'Just hear me out.'

'Absolutely not.'

Drayce walked past him. 'When are these ex-SBS guys coming to collect?'

'Doesn't matter, Alex.'

Drayce stopped at the door. Locked eyes with his old friend. 'Come on, Henry. After everything we've been through, you owe me that much.'

Drayce watched the old man consider his options and obligations.

'In three days.'

'Perfect.' Drayce dumped the gym bag at Henry's feet.

'What's that?'

'Open it and see.'

Henry frowned, hesitated, then bent down and yanked the zip. He stepped back, eyes wide. 'What the hell? You can't be serious.'

'I've never been more serious.' He nodded at the bag. 'I haven't counted it, but there's six figures there for sure. I had to take some out to recompense strangers for a jacket and a truck I stole, but it's still an excellent little earner, considering I'll have everything back to you in twenty-four hours.' He shrugged. 'Minus some ammunition.' His eyelids narrowed. 'And some of the plastic explosive.'

Henry glanced at the bag for a fraction of a second, his eyes soon flashing back to Drayce. 'Sorry, friend, but I can't risk letting these lads down.' He pointed at the weaponry. 'That lot isn't going anywhere until they come to collect.' He placed his hands on his hips and regarded Drayce with wonder. 'Besides, what kind of a job have you taken on for your team to need all this?'

'There is no team. I'm on my own for this one.'

Henry shook his head. 'Come off it, mate. You can't expect me to believe you need this lot for something you're taking on by yourself.'

Evidently, Drayce's hard, unforgiving stare was enough to tell Henry he did.

'Jesus,' Henry said. 'What's the job?'

'It's not a job. It's personal.'

Henry didn't respond. He watched Drayce with wary eyes.

'I think I've found Lily's killer,' Drayce said.

Henry stilled, frozen in time, lost in the implication of Drayce's words. When he snapped out of it, he pulled his shoulders back and stuck his chest out, a fire in his eyes. Drayce thought his old friend had never looked so serious.

'You perhaps should have started with that information,' Henry said, before turning away and strolling across the room. 'I'll go get the keys for the cage.'

–

Just outside the village, Drayce parked the stolen truck in a deserted layby. He stood in the cold night air, his surroundings illuminated by nothing more than the vehicle's side lights and the grey tint of the moon. The engine was off. He listened for approaching vehicles. With silent countryside all around, he turned to the tarpaulin that covered the bed, and undid the ties holding down the weaponry and explosives.

Having filled the truck's bed on the farm, Drayce was asked by Henry to make tracks; with another customer due any minute, he didn't want Drayce there when they arrived. In Henry's line of business, clients crossing paths was unwelcome. They were the secretive types, who wanted as few people as possible to see their faces while they were acquiring the necessary tools and equipment for their high-risk jobs.

Meet Henry; make the order; return to collect the goods: that was the process.

Bumping into others within that process added their faces into the minds of a third party, which might be enough for Henry's client list to rapidly diminish.

So Drayce was politely ordered off the farm as soon as the last item was placed on the truck's bed, which meant he needed to stop somewhere nearby while he ensured everything was strapped down tightly. Shedding a load of guns, bullets, and bombs across a dual carriageway on his route back into the city would be a bad day at the office.

With the load checked, tarpaulin tucked around the corners as neatly as a sergeant major's bedspread, and ropes so tightly tied an experienced sailor would be impressed, Drayce walked back to the driver's door.

He stopped, the hum of something mechanical approaching. He turned. Headlights in the distance. Bright LEDs. He waited for the vehicle to pass, then cursed when he saw the red reflection of its brake lights in the branches that hung over the narrow lane. It pulled into the layby and came to a stop, headlights forcing Drayce to squint. He didn't move. No point.

The truck couldn't out-run a BMW as powerful as that.

35

Drayce waited for Lucy to alight the vehicle. He tucked his hands into the pockets of his jeans and resisted the urge to glance at the tarpaulin. No use drawing attention to it. Lucy ambled up to him, face as serious as a doctor with bad news. She stopped well out of his reach, her shadow from the BMW's headlights cast up to Drayce's feet, and surveyed him with the same suspicion and hostility as she would a suspect.

'What are you doing out here in the middle of nowhere?' she asked through the gum she was chewing, jaw working hard as though burning up a nervous energy.

Drayce was a statue; solid as a rock. No shuffling of the feet; no nervous fidgeting of the hands. Eyes locked on the detective.

'Just enjoying a drive in a free country.' His stare deepened. 'Or so I thought.'

Lucy didn't respond.

'Care to explain why you're following me?' Drayce asked.

'Not yet.' She jutted her chin at the Toyota pick-up. 'Where d'you get the truck?'

'It's mine.'

'Since when?'

'Since I bought it.'

Lucy pouted. 'Mind if I run the registration through PNC?'

A pang of worry hit Drayce. He knew it wouldn't have been reported stolen yet, but if Lucy discovered he wasn't the registered keeper, he'd have a tough time convincing her it was legit.

Should I be defensive? Drayce thought. *Or call her bluff?*

'Do as you please,' he said, after a moment's deliberation. He waited for Lucy's reaction, but the only parts of her that moved were her eyelids, which narrowed to wary slits.

'What's in the back?' she asked.

'Supplies.'

Lucy held his gaze, waiting for him to expand. After an awkward count of five, he obliged. 'Just some of life's essentials.'

'You going to show me?'

'You got a warrant?'

'Don't need one, and you know it.'

Drayce stepped forward, putting himself firmly in-between Lucy and the bed of the truck. 'If you want to search this vehicle without a warrant, you need reasonable belief that I'm carrying stolen goods, illegal drugs, or prohibited weapons.' He somehow managed to say those last two words without a change in the pitch of his voice. 'And we both know you don't.'

'I could arrest you.'

'For what?'

'You're up to something.'

'And what section of which act of law is that, exactly?'

Lucy's lips quivered, but her brain fumbled for the right words.

'Precisely,' Drayce said. 'Now why don't you answer my question and tell me why you've followed me all the way out here past the Met's border?' Lucy dithered, shifting her weight from one foot to the other. As Drayce watched her, a thought struck his mind. 'And more importantly – how? You can't have been following me all day, I'd have picked you up long before now, which means...' His eyes widened, which was noticed by Lucy, who displayed the first sign of real worry he'd seen on her face all day. He reached into his jacket pocket and took out the phone she'd unlocked for him. Stripped the back off the case. Held it up for her to see. 'You planted this before you handed the phone back to me.'

She crossed her arms, sinewy muscles flexing in her neck. 'I don't know what you're talking about.'

'You're a terrible liar, Lucy.'

Taped alongside the battery was a small chrome circle the size of a thumb tack, inside which was the circuitry that had allowed Lucy to track Drayce. He thought about everywhere he'd been since he'd taken that phone back from her. Everything he'd done. A hot flush of anger rushed through his body, burning his face up.

'Why?' he asked.

'I needed to know what you were up to, in case you were lying about your "friend in need". And after what I've found out, I'm glad I did.'

'What are you talking about?'

'I know you lied to me about who's phone that is.'

Drayce was ninety percent sure he hadn't flinched. 'What makes you say that?'

'It's registered to some corporation in Dubai that has known connections to organised crime, and there are NCA and Interpol intelligence reports linked to it.'

'Which say what?'

'They're restricted, and I can't ask for permission to view them because then people will know what I've done.'

Drayce concealed his relief with a big shrug. 'Well, I guess you'll just have to trust me then.'

She stuck her neck out and let out a nervous chuckle. 'Trust you? No chance. You're up to something, and I want to know what it is.'

Drayce kept his mouth shut for a moment while he worked his brain hard and ironed out the kinks in the events that had transpired. If Lucy had been following him all day, she'd know he'd committed murder, and wouldn't have confronted him on a dark road, in the middle of the countryside, on her own. Too risky. Which meant the tracker must have a live feed only, without the ability to record. Perhaps when she found the intelligence reports linked to the phone's number, she checked the tracker, saw he'd left the city, and decided to get out on the road and follow him in person.

Drayce took a deep breath, confident she didn't know what he'd been up to since he'd landed back in London.

'Territt's gone missing,' Lucy said. 'There was a fire at his home. They're sifting through the ashes, but they're pretty sure he isn't amongst them.'

'So? Why are you telling me? We weren't exactly friends.'

'Did you have anything to do with it?'

Drayce picked the tracker loose and flicked it deep into the verge. With the back of the case replaced, he returned the phone to his jacket pocket. 'I've had just about enough of you accusing me of crimes, Lucy.'

'I'm not accusing you; I'm just asking the question. This happening the same day you come back to town is just too much of a bloody coincidence.'

'Then gather some evidence and come back to me with it. Until then, stay out of my way.'

'It's being done as we speak. They might not get much from his house, but they will his car.' She paused, her eyes scanning Drayce's face for any hint of a reaction. 'It was involved in the pursuit of another vehicle. Forensics are checking it for fingerprints and DNA.' Another pause. A narrowing of her eyelids. 'Think they'll find anything of yours in there?'

Images of earlier events flashed into Drayce's mind. He homed in on the gloves he'd worn – no prints would have been left behind. But he'd been bleeding from his fight with Reaper. Not badly, but still, it would only have to be a tiny splatter of blood for them to link him to the crash. And the chase had been a ferocious one, so there was every chance he'd left behind strands of hair and skin cells during the numerous impacts he'd taken.

'Of course not,' he said, trying to hide the concern from his face. 'Unless I leaned in it when he pulled up to me earlier today outside Islington Police Station. Hmmm, can't remember. But I could have done.' He stared Lucy down. 'Which would mean my DNA might be in there for completely innocent reasons.'

Lucy's mouth curled into a half smile, but her eyes stayed angry. 'Getting your defence in early, are we? Smart. Better hope it holds up when we check CCTV.'

'Do as you please, Lucy. Nothing matters to me after today.'

Drayce turned away and opened the driver's door.

'You're involved in Territt's disappearance!' Lucy said, her voiced raised. 'I'm sure of it, and that phone you gave me did not belong to a friend.'

Drayce said nothing as Lucy assessed him. He looked over his shoulder, her eyes burning into his, his lack of a defence apparently enough evidence to convince Lucy she was right.

'I should have known the moment you fed me that pack of lies. A man like you wouldn't bother hacking into a phone if a friend was in that situation. You'd just break the husband's neck and bury him out in the woods.'

Drayce watched her closely, waiting for her to come to her senses and calm down. 'You don't know me half as well as you think you do. But let's say you're right about the phone. Why does it matter?'

'Because I want to know the truth.'

'The truth?' Drayce sighed. 'The truth is I needed that phone unlocking, and you need your husband out of your life. So, we made a deal.' He put one foot into the truck's cabin. 'Now, if you'll give me a brief moment's respite from your illegal surveillance, I'll be getting on with my plans for the evening.'

Lucy covered the gap between them in three long bounds and grabbed him by the shoulder. He turned. Her expression had altered: harder and colder than before, her eyes cast the energy of someone not to be messed with.

'If you've involved me in something illegal,' she said, 'I'll make you pay.'

Drayce stared her down, patiently waiting until she took her hand off him. 'Go home, Lucy. Forget about me. Forget about what I may or may not be doing.' He climbed into the driver's seat, started the engine and held the door open, staring at her over his shoulder. 'It's in your best interest to leave me alone. Nothing good lies behind the door you're trying to force open.'

–

Drayce slammed the door shut. Lucy watched his eyes in the wing mirror. As soon as he was focused on the road ahead, she spat her gum into the palm of her hand, rolled a fresh tracker up in it, and slipped her hand under the truck's bed, pressing the wad of gum and circuitry onto the metal as the tyres turned and the vehicle moved off.

She'd let him leave with the last word.

For now.

But she wouldn't be far behind.

36

From the shadows of an alleyway across the street, Drayce watched scarred men in black suits loiter either side of the wide, double-door entrance to Sullivan's nightclub in Mayfair. Curly wires slithered from their earpieces to the backs of their thick necks and disappeared under their strained shirt collars. Their faces showed no emotion, eyes soulless and guarded as they assessed the hordes of guests piling into the venue. An orderly queue of scantily clad young women stretched down the street. Every so often a car would pull up and a group of men would pile out, straighten their attire, and swagger inside, ignoring the queue while exchanging head nods and fist bumps with security.

Drayce leaned back in the driver's seat of the truck, out of sight behind the B-pillar, and flicked to the section in Jason Martin's notes that described the interior of Sullivan's club. Past the double doors was a wide staircase to the first floor, twenty-eight steps, no cover. At the top it opened into a large area with a square bar in the centre, tables and chairs scattered among the space, and booths lining the walls. Beyond the bar was a tunnel leading to a dancefloor, with several small stages to accommodate the pole dancers. A high ceiling helped to accommodate the light fittings, speakers, and the balcony that ran around the circumference of the venue on the second floor, access to which was gained via one of two spiral staircases that bracketed the dancefloor. Judging by the constant stream of partygoers, Drayce was sure it would be stretching its capacity of eighteen hundred tonight.

Sullivan had an office on the second floor, with giant one-way windows that overlooked the dancefloor. If he was at the club, that was where he'd be. From Martin's observations, Drayce had noted there was only one way in, and one way out: a heavily fortified, bulletproof door, accessed from the balcony. The walls and windows were thick enough as to make them bulletproof also, when it came to nearly all conventional calibres of ammunition. With that office being simultaneously the safest place for Sullivan within the walls of the club and the only spot in which he could be quietly confronted, Drayce didn't need to just get past the cameras and security teams; he also needed to get to the other side of that office door without being confronted by Sullivan's goons, delaying the inevitable gun fight.

Drayce needed a cast-iron plan.

And an angel on his shoulder.

He tucked the notes back into his pocket, closed his eyes, and thought of the time he'd said goodbye to the only angel he'd ever known.

–

Lily's chest rose and fell with the robotic rhythm of the ventilator. Tubes, dozens of them, snaked around her chest and arms, pumping her lungs with air and dripping fluid into her veins. Drayce sat hunched over on the hard plastic hospital chair, caressing her hand. He hadn't moved in hours; hadn't slept in more than seventy-two. His back ached and his eyelids scraped his pupils with every blink. The constant beep of her heart monitor threatened to send him mad. The nurses came and went, worked around him, had long since given up on any conversation. He wasn't sure he could still speak. Everything felt like a dream. A nightmare. A vision of Hell. Something he desperately wanted to wake up from.

The sound of a door creaking on its hinges jolted him. A blue uniform hovered in his peripheral vision, the blurry outline of a nurse's presence. She walked to the opposite side of Lily's bed and checked the connections to the monitors. She took her time, meticulous with everything. Drayce felt eyes on him.

'You okay?' she asked.

'She can't hear you,' Drayce replied, his voice a croaky mess.

'I was talking to *you.*'

There was a delay in Drayce's response. 'Oh.'

'You need to look after yourself. Why don't you go get yourself a sandwich and a cup of coffee. There's a decent cafe down on—'

'I'm not hungry.' In the awkward silence that followed, Drayce remembered his manners. 'But thank you.' He looked at her: blonde hair framed green eyes on a stern face. A badge told him her name was Stephanie. She focused on the task at hand.

'Maybe just go get some fresh air then, while I check your wife's bandages.' She examined the dressings with delicate fingertips. 'No point you being here for—'

'There's every point.'

A sigh from Stephanie. Unsubtle. And deserved.

'You combed her hair again,' she observed.

Drayce glanced at Stephanie as she stared down at his wife.

'Of course.'

'And put on some make-up.'

'Just the dusty, paste stuff.'

The nurse smirked. 'You mean concealer?'

Drayce shrugged. 'Probably. I've watched her apply it before; seemed simple enough. Wasn't sure what the rest was for.'

'I could give you a crash course, if you like?'

'Thanks, but even with all the training in the world, I'd still mess it up. If she woke up looking like a clown, she'd kill me.'

They both smiled.

'Besides.' Drayce stroked Lily's cheek. 'She doesn't need it.'

Stephanie placed a gentle hand on Drayce's shoulder. 'If you need anything, press the call button. And remember what I said about looking after yourself. You can't care for others if you're not caring for yourself.'

Drayce nodded. 'I will.'

Stephanie walked off, then paused in the doorway. 'And by the way, she *can* hear you. Every single word. So make sure you keep talking to her.'

Drayce listened to Stephanie leave the room. Heard the door close behind him. Once again alone with his wife, he kissed her hand and leaned forward, his lips so close they almost touched her ear.

'If she's right, and you *can* hear me, then that means you can pull back from this.' His grip on her hand tightened. 'Don't give up.' He kissed her cheek. Stroked her hair. 'You're not dead yet.'

Something twisted in his chest. It was the first time he'd said that word out loud at her bedside, a step closer to accepting it as the terrifying potential reality of her near future. He kissed her hand again, held it to his own cheek, something he'd done nearly every day they'd been together, now acutely aware that sometime soon it might be the last. It had always made her smile. Now, her mouth was contorted into a soulless half grin by the ventilator's tube. Every muscle in Drayce's face strained at the sight of what a monster had done to his beautiful wife.

'I'll find who did this to you. I promise.' Tears coated his eyes. 'Do you hear me, Lily? I promise you I will not rest until I've found who did this.' His shoulders trembled, fighting to hold it in. 'Come back to me, sweetheart.' A tear fell. Landed on their clasped hands. 'I'm not sure I can go on without you.'

He clamped his jaw shut. Held the emotions at bay. He needed to be strong, a rock for his wife to cling to in her fight back to the real world. He sat up straight, ran his fingers through her hair, something else that had always made her smile. He watched her eyelids, held closed by clear tape.

'I love you so much.'

A flicker against the tape. Movement. Life.

Drayce stood up as though a current of electricity had passed through his seat. The back of his knees struck the chair, flinging it across the room. He kept hold of her hand. Breath fluttered on his lips.

'Lily?' Nothing. Had he imagined it? 'Sweetheart? Can you hear me?'

A piercing alarm struck him like a knife. The door burst open, an entire team of nurses and a doctor suddenly crowding Lily's bed. Words, indecipherable, as though a pack of animals were barking at one another. A hand on his shoulder, gentle at first, then as hard as steel. Another on his arm, both arms, trying to pull him back. Failing.

'Wait!' He clung to Lily's hand. 'Is she okay?'

They worked around him. Someone started chest compressions while another prepared the defibrillator, removed her gown, and slapped the pads to her bare torso. Drayce felt a heatwave flush his face. Anxiety, bold and fierce, gripped him by the throat. He had to concentrate to breathe. He stepped back, the space between him and Lily immediately filled by uniforms. Her hand was still in his, her arm stretched out. He couldn't let go.

'Lily?' he said. 'I'm still here.' They worked on her like ferocious mechanics, pushing and pulling and twisting and jabbing. His beautiful wife, the love of his life, manhandled in front of his eyes, the most precious person on the face of this Earth reduced to an object that needed to be fixed.

'Lily?' He forced himself to move back even further, his grip sliding down her fingers, knowing when he let go, it'd be for the last time. 'I love you!'

Her fingers slipped out of his grip. The team of people crowded around her, blocking his view. He watched them work, the robotic voice from the defibrillator rising above the chaos.

Evaluating heart rhythm… Stand by…

The team backed away from Lily, leaving her lying there, eyes closed, naked body limp, unresponsive.

Helpless.

Everyone clear… Do not touch the patient.

The delay was unbearable as the entire room waited. Drayce had to force himself not to barge through them to get to her.

Delivering shock.

Lily jolted, a cruel mimicry of life that was nothing more than a spasm against the electric current, the movement a mere fallacy. The team dived back on her a moment later to commence chest compressions. Amid the turmoil, Drayce wasn't sure how many cycles the defibrillator went through, but he knew all hope was lost when he heard its last prompt.

No shock advised.

The energy of the team faded, the inevitability of the situation spreading quickly through their consciousness. Soon they weren't doing much of anything.

The ventilator was switched off. Lily lay still, as still as Drayce had ever seen her. It wasn't until someone put their hands on him that he heard the flatline of her heart monitor. The tears came. Someone started screaming. He buried his face in his hands to block out a sight more painful than anything he could ever have imagined. He staggered backwards, desperate for an escape from the Hell he was in. His shoulder blades hit a wall. He slid down, his buttocks thudding against the floor. He dropped his hands from his face, saw that a crowd of nurses had formed in front of him, and realised he was the one screaming.

–

Drayce opened his eyes, wiped tears from his cheeks. He turned to the club: more women had joined the queue, teetering on high heels, ogling at a procession of expensive cars that had just arrived. They shielded their eyes from the dazzling headlights. Brake lights reflected off the wet tarmac. Hard men of Asian origin, dressed in expensive suits, alighted the motors and crossed the entrance. More of Sullivan's muscle joined the security team. Drayce counted eight in total, plus six cameras: fourteen pairs of eyes just at the front. Watching. Waiting for him to arrive. He couldn't just walk through the front door. With everything they knew about him, and everything he'd be taking with him, there was no chance of being inconspicuous.

But did it need to go down now? Or would waiting for a different location another time, with more in-depth planning, be wiser?

His phone buzzed: a message from Julie. He hurriedly opened it, skipped past her attempts to pull him back from the brink, and focused on the only part of the message that mattered to him.

The DNA results are a match.

Drayce froze. He'd expected it, but to have it confirmed for him, without a shadow of doubt, was overwhelming. His eyes bore into the club's entrance. His mind once again considered whether he should go after Sullivan and Reaper now or bide his time.

A flash of Lily in her hospital bed made the decision for him.

One more glance at Jason's notes confirmed the only viable entry point.

He backed the truck up the alleyway, got out, and ripped up the tarpaulin.

–

Reaper opened the door to the security office. A bank of CCTV monitors covered an entire wall. Radio equipment hummed in the background. Each of Reaper's men wore an earpiece so any trouble could be communicated precisely and stamped out quickly. On a normal night, the room served as a hub for everything his men might need to ensure the club operated smoothly, without hassle from rival criminal enterprises. But tonight, circumstances were a little different. More than a dozen heads turned to face him as he walked in, none of whom were his usual staff. They were stood tall, muscles bulging beneath sharp suits, their shoulders pulled back, chests out, ready to receive their orders. Every man in the room was an experienced killer, sourced from all over London just for this one event. Reaper closed the door behind him and addressed the extra security detail for the evening.

'As you are all aware, tonight is a little different to our usual events, which is why I've brought you in on top of our usual security.' He surveyed the room, meeting the eye of every hardened face before him. 'I'm aware this is far below your skillsets; every one of you is massively overqualified for mere nightclub security. But I wanted you here for a reason. We have a group of Chinese associates joining us for the evening. They'll be sitting down with Mr Sullivan. All indications suggest this will be a calm meeting of minds, planning how our organisations move forward together without bloodshed, but nonetheless, we must be prepared for every eventuality.' He glanced at the wall opposite the CCTV monitors, normally bare, now fitted with a collection of what these men might need should things turn sour. 'I've had these brought in for your use, should the evening's events require it.'

The men all followed Reaper's gaze and admired the racks of weaponry mounted to the wall.

'Pistols, shotguns, assault rifles,' Reaper continued, 'each with hundreds of rounds of ammunition.'

One in the group turned to face him, an inquisitive expression on his face. 'If these guests are so dangerous, why bring them to the club when it's packed out?'

'It's been mentioned to Sullivan, who had considered the point, but ultimately disregarded it. The meeting is vital for our business to be successful in the long term. He doesn't want it delayed.' Reaper paused, giving himself a moment before moving on to the next threat. 'But the weaponry isn't merely for our Chinese associates.'

'So, who else is coming?'

'Perhaps no one, but we need to be ready if he does. He's hell-bent on revenge against us and our organisation. If he does come here looking for trouble, we need to be ready to give it to him. Think you boys can manage that?'

A wave of nods and murmurs of agreement came back at him.

'Good,' Reaper said. 'Familiarise yourself with the arsenal, then make your way to your designated points.' He handed a stack of papers with Drayce's face printed on to the nearest man, having copied it from the newspaper report covering his late wife's memorial. 'And you all need to memorise that man's face. If you see him here tonight, radio it in, and keep your eyes on him while everyone else comes back here to collect the guns.'

'Then what?' another in the group asked.

Reaper regarded him sternly. 'We kill him.'

37

Drayce adjusted his rucksack and assessed the climb.

After driving a loop to the back of Sullivan's nightclub, he'd parked out of sight of any cameras, pulled a balaclava over his face, and with a rucksack full of weaponry, leapt the wall into the courtyard and sprinted to a camera blind spot on the building line. An old, steel-framed sash window on the third floor was his entry point. It was made of a dozen small panes of glass, intersected by the iron framework, and led to a storage room, the door to which had a flimsy lock that a swift kick would quickly destroy. From there, he would have access to the network of corridors that would allow him to navigate down to Sullivan's office.

After donning gloves, he gripped the iron guttering with both hands, jammed the toe of a boot in the brickwork, and began the climb.

The gloves helped him gain purchase on the pipe, which was wet and coated with thick black shiny paint that made it especially slippery. He took his time and ignored the burning muscles in his hands and arms. As he passed the first floor, he paused to check the building's cameras. He was still in their blind spot, but another couple of feet and he'd be in view of at least two as their line of sight crossed over one another. Six feet above that and he'd be in cover again. He had to be quick, knowing those cameras would be regularly monitored. He pulled on the pipe, legs braced against the wall, and prepared for the explosive movement that would be needed to complete this next stage as fast as possible. He locked eyes on where his hands must reach before he was hidden again, took a deep breath, held it, and launched up the pipe.

The climb went quicker than expected; just fifteen seconds. But it felt slow, as Drayce was aware of the cameras that were pointing at him every reach, pull, and step of the way. As soon as he clasped the final hold, he pulled himself in close, cheek touching the brickwork, and caught his breath. By his own calculations, he was out of sight again. He waited. Listened. The fire doors below hadn't crashed open. There were no alarms, or shouts, or car tyres screeching to a halt in the back alley. He gazed up at his entry point. Ten feet. Six hand placements. Twenty seconds. No time to waste. He reached for the next hold.

A moment of unexpected weightlessness stripped his breath from his lungs. His grip had given way, his body tumbling, fingers clawing the brickwork for something, anything, to grab on to. He spun, the night sky and the dark city streets interchangeable. He grunted, the straps of his rucksack yanking against his chest. The pack had snagged on something. He hung there, feet dangling above the rock-hard concrete that might have been his executioner. He shook his head to dispel the fog of adrenaline and assessed his position. He was caught on a bracket that fixed the guttering pipe to the wall, just between the first and second floors.

In direct view of the cameras.

—

'Boss!' The security guard leaned forward, eyes just inches from the monitor's screen. 'You need to see this.'

Reaper turned to him. There were only four of them in the room: two to monitor the cameras, one the radio channel, and Reaper there to oversee everything. The others were scattered around the club, eyes peeled for Drayce. Reaper stood behind the man who had spoken.

'What is it?'

The guard pointed at one of the monitors. 'I was flicking through the different feeds and saw this. Someone's climbing up the building. Nearly missed him, but it looks like the guy fell back into view.'

Reaper placed his hands on the desk and leaned forward. The footage was paused, a man's figure clearly visible, dressed all in black with a big rucksack on his back, clinging to a drainpipe as though in desperation. The guard was right: he did appear to have stopped himself during a fall. He wore a balaclava, his eyes not visible because he was facing away from the camera, but Reaper knew who it was. There was only one man who had reason to be breaking into the club.

'Do you think that's the guy you were worried about?' the guard asked.

'Play the footage,' Reaper commanded, ignoring his question. 'I want to see where he goes.'

As the footage ran, Reaper watched Drayce climb back up the building until he was out of sight. 'He's going to the top floor.'

'But there's nothing up there other than storage.'

Reaper considered this observation, running through his mind what he might have planned if he was in Drayce's shoes. 'It's a quiet entry point for him, and once he's inside, he might get to the main rooms without being spotted.'

'How do you want to play it?'

Reaper considered the question. To go after Drayce with all guns blazing straight away would ruin Sullivan's meeting with the Triads before it had even got started. In those quiet rooms on the top floor, Reaper's men stood a chance of dealing with Drayce quietly, without any disruption. Reaper snatched a radio and pressed the transmit button.

'I need three men to contain the third floor while another two come to the armoury and collect a silenced pistol each.' He waited for confirmation from those who were closest, then pressed to transmit again. 'We've got company.'

Drayce was quick to collect himself mentally after the fall. He took hold of the pipe, spun to face the building and tore the rucksack from the bracket as he clung to it with both hands. He moved with a purpose unlike before. If he was spotted on camera, they could surround him, putting him entirely at the mercy of men who had none, and all of this would have been for nothing. He practically ran up the side of the building, his hands and feet finding the holds from memory, his adrenaline drawing everything into focus. He passed the second-floor windows, muscles screaming, his mind so focused he was unsure if he'd even taken a breath. But he didn't stop. Not until he reached the big sash window on the third floor. He pulled out the centre punch, quietly shattered one of the small panes of glass, reached inside, and unlocked the window.

He slithered inside headfirst, moved across the storage room to the door, paused, and listened for activity out in the corridor. Nothing. The people he hunted were gangsters, not trained professionals; if they were coming for him, at the very least he would have heard footsteps.

He swung his rucksack around to the front, dumped it on the floor, and began emptying the kit.

He froze.

Somewhere on the other side of the door he heard a handle turn. Then came the squeak of a hinge, the creak of a floor-board, followed by the heavy breathing of more than one large man.

A team had just entered the corridor.

38

Drayce considered the rucksack full of guns, contemplated how this confrontation might play out, and quickly disregarded them. Sullivan's office might be soundproof, but there was nothing in Jason's notes to suggest anywhere else was, and although there was a chance the noise of the nightclub would drown out any gunshots, he didn't want to take the chance of an all-out war breaking out this early on. He would have to deal with these men with his bare hands in the hope they were merely a scouting party, as opposed to a full-scale gangster-assault-team.

Drayce hid his rucksack, pressed his ear to the wall, and listened.

The footsteps ended just the other side of the door, suggesting they knew he was in that room. Drayce moved along the wall line, backing away from the door, vanishing deeper into the shadows.

A splintering *crack* rang out, light from the corridor bursting into the room as the door was booted open. Shadows hesitated in the corridor, Sullivan's inexperienced, untrained thugs hesitating, wasting the element of surprise. Drayce watched intensely. A suppressed pistol was the first thing to come into sight, causing Drayce to curse his decision to leave his guns in the rucksack. Never mind. Nothing he could do about it now.

He watched the first man enter.

The guy was huge, your typical underworld thug. He walked forward far enough to allow his friends to enter behind, but then continued deep into the room, beyond the light and into the shadows. A mistake. Drayce moved silently in the darkness, using a head-height stack of spirits as cover as he approached. He paused behind those boxes, crept his line of sight around them, and waited until the entire team was in the room.

There were five of them. Two had pistols in their hands, one had a knife, and the other two were empty handed. Drayce heard the guy closest to him move again. He must have been less than three feet from the other side of those boxes. Another footstep: two feet. Then another: one. Drayce waited in the shadows, confident his vision had adjusted to the low light better than theirs. He bent his knees, one foot behind the other, hands out in front, fingers spread, ready to begin the violence. The pistol came into view. A hand. An arm. It was now or never. No more time to wait.

Drayce launched the attack.

He grabbed the pistol's barrel and twisted it out of the man's grip. With his free hand bunched into a fist, he pivoted around the corner of the boxes and threw a heavy hook at the guy, aiming for his chin, but with his accuracy diminished due to the darkness, he felt his knuckles slam into the man's throat. The giant figure stumbled backwards, staggering into the light as his hands shot up to his crushed windpipe. Drayce moved back into cover before he was seen by the others. The man he'd punched collapsed to his knees, face reddening, eyes bulging, unable to breathe. The two who were unarmed went to him, unaware there was nothing they could do to help. The guy with the other pistol stepped forward, waving the gun at the shadows, his friend with a knife right behind him.

Drayce backed up, keeping the boxes between him and them. He did a quick press-check on the weapon in his hands, his natural night vision good enough to spot the glint of a brass round in the chamber. He crouched down, opened his view, pistol up, finger on the trigger. The guy with the other pistol was moving forward, carefully creeping into the shadows, travelling along the same line as the first guy. Drayce ran through his options, determined to keep things as quiet as possible. He stood up and moved as close as he could to the encroaching threat without showing himself. He paused, gun up, and waited for the other pistol to come into view. As soon as it did, he pushed it out of the way and punched his weapon forward, burying the tip of the suppressor into the man's chest as he pulled the trigger.

The combination of both the suppressor and the proximity of the weapon to the man's body meant it hardly made a sound as it fired, the gases that were released mostly contained by the man's clothing and flesh. Drayce gripped him by his throat with his free hand and drove him backwards, using him as a shield against the man with the knife, who froze, panic on his face, unsure of what he was witnessing, his friend's retreating figure staggering backwards from the shadows the only clue he had as to what was happening. As a result, he hadn't seen Drayce. The knife lowered to his side, his empty hand rising to his friend's shoulder to stop him, presumably so he could turn him around, speak to him, find out what he was backing away from. But he didn't get a chance to do any of that.

At the last second, Drayce shoved his shield to the ground and followed through with his pistol, shoving the muzzle into Knifeman's chest in a carbon copy of what he'd done to the other guy. He pulled the trigger twice, both shots no louder than a child's cough. Knifeman fell backwards, the blade clattering against the floor, his hands clutching the wounds to his chest.

Drayce found himself fully illuminated in the glaring light from the corridor. The remaining two men turned away from their friend with the crushed windpipe, who was now nothing but a corpse, and charged at Drayce. Unable to smother the gunfire as he had done with the others and wanting to keep this encounter as quiet as possible, Drayce tossed the gun into the shadows and launched himself at his attackers. The first guy stopped dead as Drayce checked his bunched-up fist and slammed a forearm into his neck. The other guy threw a hook punch, fast and tight, whipping it round with the power of his hips. Drayce weaved under it, which set his weight on his left foot, allowing him to drop the guy with a ferocious liver shot. The man buckled to one knee, face a grimace, arms protecting the right side of his torso as the organ was no doubt lacerated from such a powerful blow. Drayce felt his pain; he knew from his many years of boxing training how devastating liver shots were. He placed a hand on the crown of the guy's head, teeing him up as he slammed a knee into his face, putting him out cold, and out of his misery. He turned back to the last of the thugs still standing, who was just beginning to recover from the forearm strike to his neck. Drayce clinched a single leg, lifted it up high, and swept the man's supporting limb from under him. He hit the hard wooden floor with a *thud*, his groans vanishing as Drayce stamped on his neck.

The room fell silent.

Drayce surveyed the ruined bodies that lay before him; no way was this all Sullivan had to offer. Drayce snatched a radio and earpiece from one of the bodies. There would be more for him to deal with on the floors below, and being able to listen in on their comms would come in handy.

He retrieved his rucksack and hurriedly got kitted up. The plate carrier body armour went on first, the chest plate stacked with four pairs of fully loaded magazines for the Colt C8 carbine, which he clipped to a single-point sling, hanging in front of him where it would always be in reach. Four stun grenades sat in pouches next to the magazines, and alongside those was a pouch containing the detonator for the wall charge – which, for obvious reasons, couldn't be kept in the same bag as the plastic explosives. With the Glock holstered to his right thigh, on his left he clipped a drop leg containing a dump pouch for empty magazines, above which were four spare magazines for the pistol, slotted into pouches that were attached to his left hip. A small daysack containing the portable tool kit and listening device, along with the prepped PE wall charge, went over his shoulders. The shotgun went on his back, strapped to him with a two-point sling, enabling him to swing the weapon round to his front in a heartbeat. The black face covering and ballistic helmet with NVGs and ear defenders completed the ensemble.

With the rucksack empty, he tossed it into the corner of the storage room. No point carrying around dead weight, and he'd wiped it with bleach before packing it at Henry's digs, so was confident there was no one's DNA on it; he would never risk getting Henry in trouble.

Drayce stood tall and pressed the carbine's stock into his shoulder, the *thump-thump-thump* of the nightclub's beat vibrating through the floor.

Time to make these people pay.

He marched down the corridor to the stairway.

39

Sullivan led the eight men from the Chinese Triad into his office, each man dressed in his finest suit. Tattoos and gold jewellery peeked out from their cuffs and collars. Reaper brought up the rear with two of his goons, weapons hidden under sharp suits, wary eyes held on their guests. Strobe lights pulsed behind them, their presence accompanied by the monotonous drumbeat from the club's music, silenced as the door swung shut.

'Take a seat, gentlemen,' Sullivan said, gesturing with an open hand to the eight seats that faced his desk, arranged in a half-moon shape. 'Drinks?'

Lao Chen nodded, communicating for the entire group. His eyes caught sight of the small spider-web pattern of cracks in the window, in the centre of which was an embedded bullet. He flashed Sullivan a look, the beginnings of a wry smile taking shape. 'Had some trouble, have we, Mr Sullivan?'

'Just one of the many occupational hazards that come with our line of work, Mr Chen.'

Sullivan took a seat at his desk and gestured to one of Reaper's thugs, who stepped forward and poured champagne for all eight guests. Once seated, they sipped from their flutes. Sullivan took a glass of his own and locked eyes with Reaper as he sat. He nodded at the door. Reaper didn't move, his stare held steadfast as though to say, *you sure?* Sullivan nodded at the door again, more forcefully this time, a frown cut deep in his expression. Reaper's eyebrows raised – *you're the boss*. He tapped his men on their shoulders, and they left the room.

'Mr Sullivan,' Lao Chen began, 'let me open our discussions by issuing an apology. The latest container you received from us was… unacceptable.'

Sullivan inspected Chen, a man whose meek stature camouflaged the formidable power he wielded over his organisation. 'I'm glad you see it that way.'

'We've done business together for a long time now. I hope you understand this sort of oversight is not common for us. Those responsible have been punished and replaced.' Chen fixed Sullivan with steely eyes. 'It won't happen again.'

'That's good to hear, Mr Chen. I commend you for your honesty, and I graciously accept your apology.' His gaze swept the group, making eye contact with each person. 'Thank you all for agreeing to meet with me tonight. It's hard for men of our calibre to be in the same room as one another. So many powerful men, all in one location. If they knew, it would be Christmas for the authorities.' He nodded at Chen. 'I appreciate the effort everyone has made to be here.'

'Good business is worth the risk,' Chen said.

'Indeed it is.'

'On behalf of my people, I would like to congratulate you, Mr Sullivan, on your successful dominance of the smuggling trade in this city.'

Sullivan couldn't hold back the smile. 'Thank you, Mr Chen.'

'I was reluctant to meet with you, but after much contemplation, I have come to realise the advantages of strengthening our working relationship as we move forward. Bloodshed is costly. United, we all thrive.'

The others were plainly willing to let Chen do the talking. Their keen eyes assessed Sullivan: his replies; his body language; his overall demeanour. A sheen on the forehead, a rosy complexion to his cheeks, would indicate unease. Nervousness. Weakness. It was imperative he kept his cool.

'It's been a long road,' Sullivan said, taking a sip of his drink. 'But we're finally approaching where we aimed to be. Our deal today will seal our two organisations at the very top of London's criminal hierarchy for decades to come. And whoever runs London—'

'Controls the flow from Europe.'

Sullivan nodded. 'Indeed.'

'Then let us get down to business. I want to explain our goals, our expertise, and our plans for London's drug market.'

Sullivan leaned forward. 'I'm all ears.'

'London is one of the largest cocaine markets on the planet. My people control more than a quarter of it. It used to be closer to half, but thanks to growing competition from our Russian and Albanian counterparts, our market share is rapidly diminishing.'

'Do you know why?'

Lao Chen nodded. 'We cannot put the same number of soldiers on the streets as the Russians and Albanians. They blend in better. Inconspicuous until they speak, and even then, with work done to diminish their accent, in London they go unnoticed. They have their people at the ports, in the taxis, at the clubs, in the restaurants. You name the route to market, and I guarantee they have their people inserted within. We are being smothered.'

'So where do I factor into your plans?'

'You move a huge amount of product for our competitors.'

'And you'd like that to change? You want to use my smuggling operation to get *your* product to the customer, and for me to cut ties with your rivals?'

'On the contrary, I want you to move as much of their product as possible.'

Sullivan scratched his cheek. 'I'll need you to expand on that a little.'

Lao Chen exchanged glances with the man next to him. 'I want to hit our competitors on two separate plains. Firstly, we ramp up our business with your organisation, to get our product to market without the cost and hassle of bribing officials and inserting our people into official organisations. Secondly, we give the customer a reason to come to us, and us alone.'

Lao Chen grinned. Sullivan waited with no idea what was coming.

'We want to use your access to our competitor's product to enable us to steal from it, replacing what we take with fentanyl from our laboratories in China.'

Sullivan froze as he assessed the man opposite him. 'Fentanyl?'

Chen nodded. 'It is one hundred times more potent than morphine. An extremely dangerous opioid.'

'I know what fentanyl is,' Sullivan said, a frosty tone having crept into his voice. 'What I want to know is why?'

The group chuckled. Sullivan smiled out of politeness alone.

'Our plan is to destroy our competitor's reputation. We want every regional distributer in the United Kingdom to be terrified of buying their product.'

'Leaving a void in the supply chain that you will quickly fill.'

Chen nodded again. 'Precisely.'

Sullivan locked eyes with him. 'People will die.'

'Some, initially.' Chen's eyebrows peaked. 'Does this concern you?'

'Well, it is only prudent I consider my own preservation. When the authorities find your rival's cocaine is cut with fentanyl, they'll throw everything they have into finding out where it's coming from and destroying everyone involved. That increases the risk to my organisation. And with additional risk, must come extra reward.'

'We would of course recompense you handsomely for your cooperation, exceeding by far what those Slavic dogs pay you for your services.'

'And what about my reputation? If word were to get out through the underworld as to how your rival's cocaine became poisoned—'

'It won't, I assure you.'

'How can you possibly assure me of such a thing?'

'My people are extremely reserved. No one will suspect you of a thing.'

Sullivan sat in silence for a moment, contemplating his decision. 'If I am to seriously consider this, I will need more than a simple pay-off.'

Chen's eyelids narrowed. 'What did you have in mind?'

'A percentage of the revenue you make from the cocaine I smuggle for you.'

The muscles in Chen's jaw tightened. 'How much?'

'Twenty-five percent.'

'Out of the question.'

'Then so is your plan, Mr Chen. Without me, you'll be bullied out of the cocaine business in less than six months.'

Chen raised a hand to his lips, stroked the corners of his mouth as he contemplated a strategy. 'Ten percent.'

Sullivan sighed. 'Take the piss like that again and I'll withdraw my offer and have you escorted off my premises.' He slouched in his chair and carefully examined Chen's blatant discomfort. Sullivan enjoyed the power play. 'I will not drop below twenty-five percent. The offer is non-negotiable.'

Chen's hand clenched into a fist, the knuckles pressed into his chin. 'For how long do you want to be paid this percentage?'

'Indefinitely.'

Chen's fist dropped to his lap, his face sagging in disbelief. 'You can't be serious.'

'I've never been more serious, Mr Chen. You currently pay for monthly shipments with my organisation for a variety of goods. If you are successful with your takeover, those shipments will need to become weekly to keep up with demand, of which I will take a quarter for as long as we continue to do business.'

A moment of silence passed between them. Neither man moved an inch, both as rigid as stone statues.

Chen exchanged confident glances with his men. 'I suspected this would be an issue.'

'How could it not be?' Sullivan replied. 'You expect me to risk my business being discovered and dismantled by the authorities without making it worth my while?' Sullivan locked eyes with Chen. 'I have ways of mitigating the risk to myself, if you decide this is how you want to proceed, but I must demand a fair cut of the takings for the trouble it'll cause me.'

Chen placed his clenched fists on his armrests and regarded Sullivan with a calm anger.

Sullivan picked up on Chen's barely restrained contempt for him. 'Nothing in this world is free, Mr Chen. A man in your line of work surely understands that.'

Something changed in the room – a shift in the power dynamics. A further layer of tension materialised in the air. It was so quiet, Sullivan could hear the faint beat of the club's music despite the soundproofing, its fast, powerful rhythm matching his heartbeat.

'I feared it would come to this,' Chen said. 'Which is why this is not the first meeting I have had regarding the future arrangement between our organisations.'

Fast hands moved under clothing, producing several guns aimed Sullivan's way.

–

Drayce entered another dark storage room with his weapon on aim, the environment tinged green thanks to the NVGs, and efficiently cleared the space. With no threat to deal with, and no other doors or windows to be concerned about, he knelt next to the brickwork that made up the far wall, on the other side of which was Daniel Sullivan's office.

Drayce slung his rifle and got to work setting up the explosive.

Out of his daysack he removed two slabs of plastic explosive, taped together, which would form the wall charge, and propped them up against the brickwork using an extended telescopic camera pole. From the pouch on his plate carrier, he retrieved the detonator, which was attached to a reel of shock tube, and taped it to the det cord tail that was already prepped inside the PE. Crouching down, he shuffled back to the doorway that he would use as hard cover, unravelling the shock tube as he went. Happy the charge was set up, he moved back to the wall and used a drill from the tool kit to burrow a small hole, into which he slid the tiny microphone from the covert listening device Henry had given him. Once in place, he lifted his ear defenders, fitted the earpiece for the surveillance equipment, and closed his eyes, concentrating hard to ensure he could hear everything.

He needed to be sure Sullivan was on the other side before he made his presence known.

Drayce hadn't drilled all the way through; that would have risked giving the game away on the other side. Instead, he'd gone just far enough to allow the microphone to pick up all the tiny vibrations from within the room that were emitted when people spoke. He kept his eyes closed, heightening his other senses, and listened to the conversation taking place.

–

A prickle of fear hit Sullivan suddenly as he stared down the barrels of snub-nosed submachine guns.

'Are you insane?'

Chen shook his head, slowly, his grin widening. 'The complete opposite. I am a calculating man.'

'Then you must have calculated the odds of you leaving this building alive if one of your monkeys pulls the trigger.'

'Yes, yes, Mr Sullivan, I have. Which brings me back to the first meeting I had with your organisation.'

Sullivan was hit by a sudden thud of anxiety. The memory of Chen mentioning another meeting a few seconds ago pushed through the shock of having guns drawn on him. 'What meeting?'

'Mr Ryan was very accommodating. He understood the immense potential that our union would bring to his operation in Liverpool, and was far more accommodating than you have been. I'd hoped you too would see the potential, negating the need for me to take such actions so soon, but it appears your greed has let you down. With you gone, John Ryan will run both operations, north and south, incorporating our plan for a percentage far lower than the selfish twenty-five you arrogantly offered.'

Rage swarmed through Sullivan. He glanced at the panic button under the lip of his desk that would alert Reaper, who would know to storm in, guns blazing.

Chen's eyes flashed down at the desk, then back to Sullivan. 'I wouldn't bother trying to push that. My men will gun you down before your finger covers half the distance.'

'And then what? Fight your way out of here, outnumbered and outgunned?'

'We'll walk out of here without a shot being fired and be back in our hotel before your men find your body.'

'With the noise those guns will make? I don't think so.'

Chen laughed. 'You don't think I've noticed the sound-proofing that encases this room? The music on the other side of that door is deafening, but in here it is barely audible. The gunshots that kill you will be lost in the noise like the pops from a teenager blowing bubble gum at a rock concert.'

Sullivan broke into a sweat. 'You can't trust Ryan. He's a coward. He'll betray you eventually.'

'Not before I do him, Mr Sullivan. My plans for your organ-isation only involve Mr Ryan for a short period. Eventually, my people will control everything.'

Sullivan clamped on to the chair's armrests with all his might, nails embedded in the wood, the muscles in his forearms cramping from the fear-induced exertion. Chen's men stood up and fanned out, their point of aim never leaving Sullivan's chest. He had no words left. No options. His legs trembled, shoes rattling against the chair legs. The last thing he saw was the smile on Chen's face, before his entire world collapsed in front of his eyes.

—

An argument was taking place, their voices raised and angry. Things weren't going well for Sullivan. He was outnumbered, like prey backed into a corner by a pack of wolves. Threats were issued. He'd been betrayed. Drayce heard bolts being racked on firearms as rounds were chambered. The meeting had turned bad quickly, but now it had escalated to a knife edge, a violent death on Sullivan's horizon any second now.

Drayce couldn't allow that.

Killing that man was his job, and his alone.

He backed away from the wall until he reached the end of the shock tube, attached it to the initiator-firing device, lowered his ear defenders, and after giving himself a quiet 'stand by, stand by', pressed the initiator's trigger.

40

A palpable, all-encompassing wave of shock rocked Sullivan's entire body. He convulsed, a deafening wave of air pressure flying past him, debris cracking the window to the dancefloor in numerous places, camouflaging the original spider's web from the bullet that killed Ronan. With his eyes shut tight in a blind panic, Sullivan's lungs emptied, on the tail end of which he let out a gentle whimper, which soon died to nothing as his hearing shut down, totally overwhelmed by the noise of the blast. A high-pitched ringing sang in his ears. His shoulders sagged, head lolling forward as his eyes opened.

Am I dead?

The familiarity of the room and his sweating, heart-pounding presence, answered the question for him. He patted his chest, arms, and legs; no blood, no pain. He peered through the thick dust that hung in the air and stared at the other men in the room, noticed the terror in their eyes, and felt the confusion that must have been portrayed in his own expression.

A thin laser cut through the air from nowhere, its thin green beam shimmering in the thick smoke as it tracked from one man to another. Cracks of gunfire preceded the thuds of bodies as they hit the polished wooden floor where they stood, Chen and his band of merry men dropping like mere puppets with their strings cut. But Sullivan heard none of it, was merely a spectator, deafened by the explosion.

The assault was over in seconds, a barrage of precise carnage. The ringing in Sullivan's ears subsided, making way for a deep and profound silence that made him wonder if he was still deaf.

He noticed a huge hole in the wall, fragments of which were riding on a wave of gunshot residue, tiny particles of the sound-proofing glistening in the air like snowflakes. Sullivan wanted to stand but wasn't sure his terrified jelly-legs would support his weight. He stared at the panic button, reached forward to push it, but was stopped in his tracks by the sound of footsteps. As heavy and ominous as they were, it was nonetheless a pleasant sound to Sullivan, confirming, to his relief, that he hadn't been permanently deafened by the explosion. A dark figure material-ised through the smoke and appeared suddenly in front of him, freezing him on the spot with the green lenses of night-vision goggles, above a black rifle that was pointed in his face.

—

With one hand on the grip of his gun – safety off, finger on the trigger – Drayce lifted his NVGs and lowered his face covering, noting the sheer incomprehension on the face of the man sat in front of him.

'You?' Sullivan uttered, his voice almost a whisper.

Drayce pulled Jason Martin's notes out of his pocket and dropped them on the desk. 'We have something to discuss.'

Sullivan glanced at the papers and sat back in his chair, confidence growing, almost smiling as he rode the wave of euphoria he was no doubt experiencing, thanks to still being alive. 'Seems like you've got a real hard-on for me. Thorn in my fucking side all day long!'

'A little appreciation wouldn't go amiss. I just saved your life.' Drayce dipped his muzzle at the notes. 'Now read it.'

Sullivan assessed the chaos that surrounded them. 'How about you fuck off before my men rush in here and shoot you dead. Think that explosion and those gunshots will have gone unnoticed? My people will be assembling a team on the other side of that door as we speak.'

Drayce pushed the tiny speaker a little further into his ear. 'No communications from your security yet, so it seems the explosion wasn't very loud from the other side of that bullet-proof, soundproof glass. And any noise it did make, has likely been drowned out by the music.'

Sullivan's confidence lost its edge. He casually took hold of his armrests and shuffled his chair forward. Drayce grabbed the desk and pulled it away from Sullivan, keeping the panic button out of his reach.

Drayce picked up Jason's notes and threw them into Sullivan's lap. 'Read.'

With an air of reluctance, Sullivan did as he was told. Minutes later, he tossed them back on his desk. 'So fucking what? You think this is proof of anything my barrister can't dismantle?'

'Barrister? That's a mighty big assumption for a man who's just watched me gun down eight men. You think I'm here to put handcuffs on you?'

'Well, you were once a police officer, Mr Alex Drayce.' Sullivan must have picked up on the reaction that registered on Drayce's face. 'That's right. And I know a lot more about you than just your name.'

'Good. Then you'll know why I've pursued you so relentlessly.'

'You have indeed. Quite an unsubtle creature, aren't you, Mr Drayce? Which makes me wonder how you expect to get out of this alive?'

'What makes you think I care about living beyond your destruction?'

Sullivan gazed up in contemplation. 'Well, I may have ordered the murder of your *bitch* wife.' A flutter of something travelled up Drayce's spine. He demanded his trigger finger hold fast. 'But someone else did the deed.' Sullivan locked eyes with Drayce. 'And you want that person dead every bit as much as you want me dead. Which means it can't end with me. You can't allow yourself to get backed into a corner here. You need to get out alive, so you can go find the man who stuck the knife into your precious Lily.'

The conversation broke, the only sound in the room that of Drayce's heavy breathing. The dam wall bowed; the cracks spread. His heartbeat pounded in his neck; his finger tightened on the trigger. He forced himself to stay in control.

'Hand over your phone,' Drayce demanded. When Sullivan didn't move, Drayce shrugged. 'Fine, have it your way.' He dipped the muzzle down to Sullivan's groin.

'Okay, okay!' Sullivan took the device out of his jacket pocket and flung it on the desk.

'Unlock it.'

Sullivan didn't move, so Drayce pulled the trigger. The bullet travelled between his legs, smashed through his chair's seat, and embedded in the floorboards with a splintering *crack*, the hole it had created a mere inch from his reproductive organs. Breathing hard, Sullivan leaned forward and unlocked the device. Drayce went into its settings, removed all the security so he could access it as he pleased, and put it in his pocket.

'You have no idea what lies on the other side of that door,' Sullivan said.

'Nothing I can't handle.'

'May I remind you what Jason Martin discovered in his one-man investigation?' He nodded at the notes. 'I have the resources of every major criminal organisation in this country at my fingertips, Alex. They come to me for everything they need. I have an unlimited number of soldiers to send after you.'

Drayce collected the notes, folded them up, and stuffed them into his pocket. 'Is that supposed to alter what I'm going to do to you?'

'You're out of your league.'

'I doubt it.'

'The men I have in this nightclub are trained killers. They've got more guns than you. More guns than anyone else in this city, in fact. Even more than your former colleagues, Alex. Your only chance of leaving here alive is to hand over everything you've got and—' Bored with Sullivan's speech, Drayce stepped forward and leaned over the desk. 'What the fuck are you doing?'

Drayce reached under the lip of the desk and pushed the panic button. Almost immediately he heard orders being delivered over the security team's radio channel.

Sullivan's head cocked back, shoulders rocking as he laughed to the ceiling. His face reddened. Pretty soon, tears streamed from the corners of his eyes. Seconds later, the laughter diminished enough for his gaze to settle back on Drayce. 'You mad bastard!'

Drayce didn't reply. He pulled his face covering over his mouth and nose.

'You're fucking done now, boy,' Sullivan said, the smile still stretched across his face. 'I give you ten seconds before that door opens and you get cut to ribbons by machine guns.'

Drayce backed into a dark corner of the room, went down on one knee, slipped a stun grenade from a pouch, and with the lever pressed firmly into the webbing between his thumb and forefinger, pulled the pin. Sullivan wouldn't know it, but under Drayce's face covering, he was smiling too. When Sullivan eventually registered what was in his hand, Drayce was the only one smiling.

The door handle turned.

'Wait!' Sullivan bellowed. He was on his feet, eyes like saucers, his arms outstretched, palms facing the door. 'Stay out! Don't come—'

The door swung in as though it had been hit with a battering ram and clattered against the wall, the lights and music from the club crashing into the office like a tidal wave. Six of them entered in a clumsy fashion: big, hard, rough men with guns in their hands, heads on swivels, but they were poorly trained. They loitered in the fatal funnel of the door frame, their room assessment wholly inadequate.

The grenade went off at their feet before they'd even seen Drayce. On the second explosion, Drayce opened fire with his carbine, sharing the fresh thirty-round magazine with the centre mass of each man. The other four explosions from the grenade intermingled with the sound of the gunshots, the *thuds* of their bodies dropping, and the barely decipherable tinkling of brass landing on the floorboards.

In the aftermath, Drayce glared at Sullivan. Strobe lights from the club cut through the smoky haze that thickened the air between them. The gangster who had ordered Lily's murder stared open mouthed at five of his 'trained killers', lying dead on his office floor. Rivulets of blood tracked the joints in the floorboards. Drayce stood up and walked towards him, carbine in high port, reloading as he moved. Sullivan turned, his face aghast. He held his arms out, palms open in a pleading gesture. When Drayce reached the desk, he planted his feet in a shooting stance and flicked the weapon's setting to full-auto.

Sullivan fell back into his chair. 'Wait—'

The first bullet cut straight through the middle of his palm, tracked up his arm, and embedded in his shoulder. He cried out in pain, a squeal bursting from his lips like steam from an old-fashioned kettle. Drayce held the trigger down, riding the gun like a cowboy on a bucking bull as the muzzle spat flames. Sullivan took all thirty bullets in a little over three seconds, his body convulsing with every impact, the force tipping his chair back, sending him crashing to the floor. The assault over, he lay slumped on the ground, blood oozing through his punctured suit like soup through a colander, eyes lifeless.

Drayce exhaled, releasing a breath he hadn't known he was holding.

Movement in the open doorway made him turn. His eyes lit up when the man came into view through the smoke, his face paling with shock when he looked past the scattered bodies of his men and saw Drayce.

Reaper.

41

A surge of adrenaline coursed through Drayce. Out of pure, blind instinct, he shouldered his carbine, took aim, and pulled the trigger.

Nothing.

The expectation caused Reaper to react as though he'd been shot. He stumbled back, a hand rising to his chest. Drayce tilted the Colt to examine the breech and saw the bolt was locked back, the magazine empty after his execution of Sullivan. He cursed his stupidity and went to draw his pistol. Realisation he was unharmed quickly gathered pace in Reaper's body language. He snapped out of his incomprehension, turned, and ran.

A bullet from Drayce's pistol clipped the stairs as Reaper went out of sight. Drayce holstered the pistol, reloaded his carbine, and hurried to the doorway to give chase. Frenzied voices barked commands over the radio: it sounded as though an army was closing in. Reaper leapt down the stairs, jumping the last three steps and breaking into a sprint. Heart pounding, Drayce took aim again. Held his breath. Settled his sight picture. Squeezed.

Four figures rounded a corner up ahead, distracting Drayce enough to ease off the trigger before it discharged. Reaper slipped through the men, flinging an arm behind him at Drayce as he shouted an unintelligible instruction. The men lifted their guns. An open target on the staircase, Drayce slipped to the side of the doorway into cover. Gunshots rang out, a barrage of bullets tearing through the walls. Drayce dived, chest pinned to the bloodied floorboards. He spun to face the doorway, pulled a stun grenade from his body armour, and pulled the pin. Rounds flew over his head. Brick dust rained down on him. He held tight, waiting for the right moment.

The gunfire stopped, footsteps on the stairs and the clattering of empty magazines on the floor indicating the men were reloading and coming to finish him off. Drayce got to his feet and threw the grenade down the staircase.

On the first bang, he pivoted the corner and opened fire, sweeping the carbine across the group. Distracted by the grenade's explosions, they were sitting ducks. Drayce descended the stairs, shooting as he moved. Once he got to the last step, every man had fallen. He pushed to the corner, rounded it with the carbine up, focused on his visual limit point. Dozens of the party's guests were running for their lives. Others had frozen on the spot, transfixed on the emerging chaos. Some loitered in their groups, cocktails in hand, in denial at what was unfolding around them. Drayce caught sight of Reaper's figure through the crowds, legs and arms pumping. He lifted the carbine's sights to eye level and searched for a shot. No good. The angles were all wrong, too many bystanders at risk of getting hit in the crossfire.

Reaper disappeared down the spiral staircase to the dancefloor.

Drayce ran after him, his Colt in high port, darting around guests as he tried to catch him up. At the top of the staircase, he saw Reaper reach the dancefloor, which was packed out with revellers who didn't know of the gun fight, thanks to the volume of the music. More security guards were crashing through the crowds, pushing on their earpieces to better hear the radio communications from the others. Drayce counted nine, weapons in hand, barging guests to the ground as they fought their way to Reaper. Words exchanged with his thugs about the looming six-foot-six, twenty-stone threat to their lives, Reaper scurried off to a neon-lit tunnel lined with graffiti that led to another bar, leaving his men to do the fighting for him. The atmosphere on the dancefloor rapidly changed as people spotted the gunmen and backed away, glancing at their friends to see if this was real, or perhaps some sort of an act.

Their denial won't last much longer, Drayce thought.

He dropped down to one knee and opened fire.

The dancefloor erupted, bodies scattering in all directions, the screams so loud they almost drowned out the music. The reaction of Sullivan's men was better than before. They instantly starburst, all nine running off in different directions to try and find cover behind the iron pillars that surrounded the dancefloor. Drayce hit one, sending him staggering to the ground, clutching his side as he crawled to safety, but the others became too embedded in the crowd to risk any further shots.

Drayce seized the opportunity and sprinted down the staircase, making it to the dancefloor just as the gunmen reached the pillars and turned to engage with him. One of them got a shot off, the round whizzing past Drayce's head. He quickly fired back, aiming high to avoid the mass of hysterical clubbers. A flare of sparks indicated his shot placement on the pillar, close enough to make the shooter duck his head out of sight. But others appeared, eyes and gun barrels peeking out from behind their cover, less concerned than Drayce was about hitting bystanders.

Bursts of gunfire cracked off all around him. He ducked and ran, moving like lightning, carbine in high port to enable him to move faster. He saw a booth, the structure made of poured concrete, and dived for cover inside, the shots tearing chunks out of the back supports. He lay flat on the seat and reloaded the Colt. He tried to manoeuvre into a position that would allow him to shoot back, but it was no use. The barrage of bullets was too relentless, their firepower too ferocious. Any attempt to take aim would result in him getting his head blown off. He shuffled to the floor and under the table as rounds clipped the top of the seats above his head, stuffing and leather raining down on him. They were working out his position, drawing their fire closer to him as they arced round to the booth's opening. If he stayed much longer, he'd get hit.

Movement caught his eye. One of them was coming into view, trying to get a clear shot. He was close, maybe only a couple of steps away from the mouth of the booth. The others stopped shooting to give this assaulter a chance to finish Drayce off without getting shot by his own people.

Mistake.

Drayce seized the opportunity, lifted the table like a shield, and charged at him. Wide eyed and in a fluster, the man wasn't expecting the sudden attack. He tried to aim his gun in the panic, but he was too slow; too clumsy. Drayce bowled him over, trampling on his body as he ran through him, leaving the table behind as he carried on sprinting to the bar. The others opened fire again, but they clearly hadn't been prepared for Drayce's reckless burst for freedom. They missed, the bullets going high, crashing into the bottles behind the bar as Drayce dived over it into cover. He lay flat on the floor, being showered by broken glass and spirits as he assessed his new position, and quickly realised he'd made a critical mistake under the pressure of escaping the booth. He was now pinned behind the bar by their gunfire, just as he'd been trapped inside the booth. But rather than the one opening to the booth that they had to cross to get a shot at him, they now had the entire length of the bar they could simply lean over.

Drayce noticed their arcs of fire change as they moved closer to him, fanning out now they were confident he was snared. He tried to cover the length of the bar with his carbine, but it was hopeless. He would always leave his back to at least one of them when they eventually leaned over to kill him. He held his ground, waiting, hoping for an idea. They were close now, their bullets shredding the bar into a flurry of splinters as they upped their rate of fire to force him to keep his head down.

Drayce shouldered his Colt and scanned the lip of the bar, expecting a kill shot to come his way any second.

42

A pause in the gunfire was the sign Drayce had been dreading. One of them was about to lean over and kill him. He scanned his surroundings one last time in the hope of instigating a moment of vital inspiration. A small stool tucked under the bar caught his eye. With only seconds to spare before their final attack, he grabbed it by one of its legs and hurled it down the length of the bar into the glass door of a refrigerator, a last-ditch effort to cause a distraction.

A gun appeared over the bar, followed by the head and torso of one of the late Daniel Sullivan's men, mercifully aiming his weapon at the broken fridge where he thought Drayce lay hidden.

Drayce took the shot.

The sight of one of their own getting his head blown off was markedly enough for the others to back off. Drayce kept up the momentum, pulled the pin on his last grenade, and threw it over the bar. On the first bang he stood and opened fire. The ones still facing him got shot first, but some had turned their backs on him and were running into cover. He pulled the trigger until the bolt locked back, reloaded, then let the working parts forward and vaulted the bar to give chase.

As soon as his feet landed, the world was pulled out from under him, the room spinning as he flipped in the air and fell, his back hitting the floor, winded as the air was forced out of his lungs. A gunman had been hiding just behind the bar, too close to have retreated with the others, and had kicked Drayce's legs out from under him. As he spun on his back to face his attacker, he saw a gun being levelled at his face and kicked out wildly, his boot colliding with the man's forearm just as the trigger was pulled. The bullet missed, slamming into the floor just above Drayce's head.

The muscle memory ingrained into him from his years of jiu-jitsu training kicked in without him having to think about it. As the man stood to his full height, preparing to beat down on Drayce, Drayce hooked his feet behind the man's legs and used the leverage it afforded to spin behind him. From there, he grabbed the man's belt, swept his legs from under him, and sat him down on his arse, where he slipped a chokehold around his neck.

As he strangled the man unconscious, another gunman fired from across the room, the bullet missing Drayce's head by inches. He rocked his hostage onto his side, using his body for cover as more shots were fired, the rounds thudding into his living shield. He let go of the chokehold, drew his pistol, and returned fire, forcing the shooters to duck out of sight again. Seizing his narrow window of opportunity, Drayce got to his feet, flicking the empty magazine out of the Glock's grip as he reloaded, and darted sideways towards the graffitied tunnel, lit by neon lights, where he'd last lost sight of Reaper. He ran like lightning, shooting as he moved, the fifteen-round magazine lasting until he made it across the room.

In the cover of the tunnel, he breathed hard as he reloaded the pistol again, holstered it, then slammed a fresh magazine into the carbine. The stock in his shoulder, he hurried down the tunnel and opened his view into the next room.

Galloping boots chased him down the tunnel. No time to hesitate. He entered the next room tactically, weapon up, searching for a target.

A bar ran along the length of the wall to his right, the open space decorated with a smattering of high tables full of abandoned drinks. Drayce spotted Reaper slipping through a set of double doors at the other end of the room that led to the main foyer. He took aim, but there wasn't enough time; Reaper slipped through, the giant slabs of wood and metal slamming shut behind him.

Drayce ran after him, tossing tables to the floor in his wake to slow down his pursuers. Once across the room, he turned and let rip into the tunnel, forcing those chasing him to back off. Keeping eyes on the tunnel's opening, he mule-kicked the double doors behind him, but they didn't budge: Reaper must have locked them from the other side. Firing another couple of shots at his pursuers to buy him some time, he let the Colt hang from its sling, swung the shotgun round to the front, turned, and blew out the hinges. Holes big enough to fit his arm through appeared in the wake of the explosions, a smattering of splinters, sheered metal, and ball bearings hurtling across the foyer on the other side.

A bullet *whizzed* past his head from behind. He turned to face the tunnel and shot the man who'd fired, sending him flying back into the wall as the buckshot thudded into his chest. More gunmen appeared from the tunnel, their muzzles breathing fire like dragons as they shot at Drayce, forcing him to stagger backwards through the doorway as he returned fire. Once through, he side stepped into cover, ditched the shotgun on its sling, grabbed his carbine, and turned.

What he saw made him instantly realise his mistake.

Reaper stared at him from the top of the stairs with those dark, soulless eyes, aiming the same pump-action shotgun as earlier directly at Drayce's chest. Drayce began to lift his carbine, but there was no time.

The gun bucked in Reaper's grasp, a brilliant burst of flame exploding from its barrel.

43

Drayce felt as though he'd stepped into the path of a speeding truck. The breath shot out of his lungs with the immediacy of a burst balloon. The world slipped from under him, his feet leaving the ground for what felt like an eternity, his body suspended, floating backwards as the crushing power of the impact resonated within him. He hit the floor, the room above him spinning. He tried to breathe. Couldn't. His chest had seized up. Panic threatened. No time for that. If he didn't get out of sight before Reaper took another shot, he was finished. He crawled backwards, reached for the door frame, and heard the crunch-crunch of the pump-action shotgun as Reaper chambered a fresh cartridge.

Drayce pulled himself through and got into cover just as Reaper fired a second shot. The wall exploded above his head, scattering him with debris, leaving behind a hole the size of a dinner plate. Back in view of those chasing him through the tunnel, Drayce braced himself on his back, aimed between his legs, and fired a volley of shots at the neon-lit opening to hold them back from entering the room. He finally managed to draw breath, his hand patting down his body armour. The plate lay ruined within its Kevlar pouch, broken into a dozen or more pieces. He reached underneath, felt his chest, and was hit with a boost of energy when he realised it hadn't gone through.

Frantic movement at the mouth of the tunnel caught his eye. He got to his feet and opened fire before they'd clocked his position, dropping two and sending another three scurrying back into hiding. With the magazine in his carbine empty, his transitioned to a pistol and walked a lazy arc to open his view of the tunnel, firing as soon as the bodies of the remaining gunmen came into view. All three dropped where they were standing, hands clutching fatal wounds, in too much shock to offer any comeback.

With the threat behind him dealt with, Drayce holstered the pistol, reloaded the carbine, and came back on aim at the doorway to the foyer. He took as deep a breath as his traumatised chest would allow, pulled his weapon's stock tight to his shoulder, and stormed into the foyer.

Reaper was nowhere to be seen.

Drayce moved to the top of the stairs with caution, heel to toe, each step as quiet as possible. He tracked the wall line to gradually open his view and aimed down the staircase, finger on the trigger. But there was nothing to shoot at. All he saw were the entrance's double doors, swinging back and forth under the momentum of the club massacre's most recent escapee.

44

Lucy had parked out of sight and nestled herself in a dark corner of the street to watch Drayce's truck. She'd followed the tracker's coordinates from a distance through the city, then pursued him on foot to the back of a nightclub, Drayce too focused on the task at hand to notice her shadowing him. She watched him leap the wall with a giant rucksack on his back, no doubt on his way inside the club, and doubled back to wait for his return, at which point she'd have a decision to make.

Confront him, or not?

The answer depended on what kind of state he was in when he got back to his truck. If Lucy clocked anything suspicious about his demeanour, as though he'd done something illegal at the club, she'd intervene; if she didn't, she'd continue to follow him until he slipped up.

Because he was up to no good, she was certain of that much, and if by following him she could find out what he was conspiring to do, then depending on how serious it was, she could either stop it from happening, or gather evidence of his wrongdoing, and use it as leverage to make certain he kept their plans for Barnaby a secret for the rest of his life. A favour for a favour wasn't enough, she'd decided. As things stood, she had far more to lose than he did, should anyone find out about their agreement.

That needed to change.

She leaned against the wall, wondering why he'd been sneaking around the back of a nightclub with a giant rucksack on his back. Bizarre. Just what the hell was he up to? Maybe she should confront him when he got back, regardless of his demeanour. Perhaps she should grab him when he went to climb in his truck and demand he tell her what he was doing.

She screwed her eyes shut and shook her head. The stress in her life was killing her brain cells. Trying to physically dominate Alex Drayce was not a bright idea. The interaction would likely mimic a koala pouncing on a grizzly.

Goosebumps broke out across her bare arms. She pushed off the wall, stuffed her hands in her pockets, and marched on the spot to get her circulation going. There was a chill to the night air. Other pedestrians rushed past the other end of a nearby alleyway, hugging themselves and shivering, the mild spring daytime weather having lured the city's residents into a false sense of security.

It had only been an hour, but Lucy was already sick of waiting. A nervous apprehension encouraged her to go find out what Drayce was up to at the club. She wasn't exactly dressed for clubbing, but what the hell. She could make it work. Shorten her skirt, let down her hair, and with a cocktail in hand she'd blend right in. Then she could search the building, find Drayce, and see what he was doing in there. She could film him on her phone. Maybe get footage of who he'd gone there to meet. Perhaps she'd capture something she could hold against him, to keep his mouth shut about their plans for Barnaby. Motivated by her change of plan, she set off for the club, running through the streets.

Minutes later, she jogged down an alleyway and slowed to a walk. Before the venue came into view, she heard a commotion. She carefully moved to the junction ahead and creeped her line of sight around the corner. Erratic shadows danced in the streetlights. Bloodcurdling screams echoed off the buildings. Heart in her mouth, Lucy instantly knew Drayce had something to do with the chaos unfolding. She held fast on the corner and gingerly peered round to get a full view.

The nightclub had spilled out in a chaotic evacuation. Crowds of revellers ran for their lives. The doors at the entrance to the club swung violently, exposing strobe lights and loud dance music from within.

A noise made Lucy jolt as though a current had passed through her.

Gunfire, cracking off inside the club.

The goosebumps came back, this time covering her entire body. She seized up, in shock and unable to move, wondering what to do. She took out her phone, the adrenaline dump making her fumble, slowing her down. She swore, stamped her foot, forced herself to be calm; to get a grip, to think, to act. With a firm hold on the device, she entered her PIN and tapped on the call icon. The keypad came up. She went to press the first nine.

Everything went dark.

The hand that had grabbed her from behind was huge. It covered her nose as well as her eyes, the man's moist palm emitting the stench of something that might have been gunshot residue. She shrieked, her phone slipping from her grasp and tumbling to the ground. She felt it bounce off her knee and heard it clatter in the street. Her hands flailed, desperately lashing out at the figure behind her.

Did someone hear me cry?

Would they help me if they had?

She screeched again, hoping to draw attention. The man's other hand clamped over her mouth, turning her screams into the muffled cries of the helpless. Panic overwhelmed her; she couldn't breathe. Desperately, she yanked down on the hand over her mouth, trying to make space. She managed to open her mouth, allowing her to draw breath. Flesh was instantly pressed between her teeth. She bit down hard. He grumbled in pain but kept his hand where it was. His forearms crushed her ears, muting the world around her. He pulled her back, her feet dragging on the cobbles. She lost a shoe, her bare foot slipping uselessly against the power of his phenomenal strength. Eventually, the tips of her nails found the back of a hand. She dug them in and clawed down his skin.

This time, the pain was enough. His hand moved from over her eyes, just enough for her to see she was still being hauled backwards, deeper into the dark alleyway, away from witnesses, and responders, and anyone who might help her. The hand in front of her eyes had three lines of old scar tissue running down the back of it, now accompanied by two fresh gouges. Blood trickled down his arm. She inhaled through her nose and screamed with everything she had, but the effect was muted, drowned out by the giant hand still pressed over her mouth. Worthless. With the mayhem that had spilled out of the club, no one would have heard it.

She thrashed, bucked, kicked, but he was too strong. They rounded a corner, into shadows even darker than before. The hands came free from her face. She gasped for the air she'd been denied, her equilibrium settling now she was no longer being dragged backwards, blind and suffocating. She could breathe, hear, think.

See.

The man towering over her was a giant, his eyes demonic, his presence terrifying, stilling Lucy as a monster would a child. She fought the shock, told her body to move, flinched sideways to get to her feet. But she was instantly pulled back, those thick, grotesque fingers searching her scalp, before yanking her hair. She yelped. A grin bloomed across his face, putting a kink in the scar that ran over his right eye, clearly enjoying the fact he'd hurt her. Her nails clawed at his hands again, but it was no use.

Something flew out of the darkness, as solid as a lump of iron, and hit her above her right eye. Woozy, she noticed the monster pull his knee back. The smile on his face widened, indicating he was pleased with his efforts. The earth moved beneath her, turning slowly, before building to a spin. She felt sick. Her eyes closed of their own accord, too heavy for her to resist. She collapsed backwards but didn't hit the ground, held up by the monster's grasp of her hair. He wrapped his arms around her waist and dragged her backwards again, then lifted her clear off the ground. She tried to focus on what was happening to her, the only senses left her hearing and movement: the hiss of a car boot being opened; the sudden drop as she was tossed into the void; the digital snap of a lens shutter, as a photo was taken on a mobile phone.

The boot lid was slammed shut, plunging her into absolute darkness. Exhaustion overwhelmed her. She just had time to hear the engine start up, and feel the vehicle move off, before her consciousness was torn from her weakened grasp.

45

Drayce waited until he was back at the truck before he risked removing his face covering. With his wary eyes keeping watch on the streets, he tossed everything – weaponry, rig, body armour – into the vehicle's bed, apart from a frag grenade, pistol, and a spare magazine, all of which he either clipped onto, or wedged into, his beltline. He strapped the tarpaulin down and checked his surroundings. Bar him, the street was deserted. In relative safety having survived the assault on Sullivan's nightclub, exhaustion threatened.

He climbed into the driver's seat, the only sound that of the long, deep breaths he drew through his nostrils. The sweat that had poured from him in the club had almost dried, and the adrenaline dump he'd experienced had fizzled out to nothing. Consequently, his core body temperature was plummeting. He turned on the engine, set the blowers to hot, and slid his hand up his t-shirt, tentatively feeling the area around his sternum where the shotgun round had impacted. He pressed lightly with his fingers. It hurt, but it wasn't agony. Unlikely to have broken bones under there. Without adrenaline to focus his mind on a specific task, events in the club flashed to the forefront: gunning down the Triad members; confronting and killing Sullivan; fighting his way out.

Reaper escaping.

Drayce punched the dashboard. Something plastic cracked under his fist. This was the second time his wife's murderer had escaped. Had been right there, in his sights, but had somehow got away. With Sullivan and his henchmen dead, Reaper would likely vanish. Perhaps change his appearance drastically. Maybe skip the country. Everything indicated he'd worked as an enforcer within organised crime for decades without his DNA landing on any police systems, so the man was evidently an expert at hiding. Drayce felt as though he'd wasted the last opportunity he was ever going to get to kill Reaper.

Heavy eyelids made their presence felt. Drayce ignored the tiredness that swamped him. Adrenaline was wonderful when it was flowing, but the comedown was brutal. He rubbed his eyes, his face, held his head in his hands, pressured his mind to come up with a plan for where he went from here.

Something vibrated in his pocket: Sullivan's phone. With how focused he'd been on chasing Reaper down, he'd forgotten he'd taken it. He rushed to get it out. A message from Reaper.

You make it out?

Drayce frowned. Reaper's view of Sullivan's body must have been blocked from his position at the top of the stairs when he came to the office's doorway. He didn't know Sullivan was dead. Drayce opened the keypad, considered his options, and went with:

Yes. Just. Where are you?

Heading to the unit. Meet me there.

Drayce took out Jason's notes, cast several pages aside in a hurry, and found the section he wanted. Sullivan had an industrial unit to the southeast of the city, right on the bank of the Thames, which he used to process the goods he smuggled into the country. That must be it. He put the address in the truck's sat nav, stuffed the notes away, then returned his focus to Sullivan's phone.

> On my way.

A *read* confirmation flashed up instantly. Drayce stared at the screen. He hoped for more but knew fishing for it risked arousing Reaper's suspicions about who he was actually talking to.

Reaper is typing…

Drayce waited. From somewhere in the city, sirens wailed, testing his patience. He had to get moving, but he desperately wanted to know what else Reaper had to say.

> How did you get out?

Drayce's mind went to work, hard and fast. He had to be quick with his reply, to propagate the illusion it was Daniel Sullivan typing.

> After Drayce killed Chen and his men, he got distracted by you. Tunnel vision, I think. He knows you killed his wife. Now he's obsessed with killing you.

As soon as Drayce hit send, he thought of something Sullivan would undoubtedly want to know. He hurriedly typed another message.

The sirens were much louder now. Drayce tossed the phone onto the passenger seat, started the engine, and set off at speed. The phone buzzed. He snatched it up and opened the message.

A sick feeling invaded Drayce's gut. He typed on the move.

Flashing blue lights illuminated the buildings up ahead. Drayce took a hard left and raced through the streets, as fast as the big heavy truck would allow. Sullivan's phone buzzed in his hand. He slowed down, driving normally to blend in, in case a cop car suddenly got sight of him. Reaper had sent him a photo, the image blurred as it downloaded. Drayce waited, time ticking by in slow motion. He glanced between the road ahead and the screen, waiting for the image to come into focus.

When it eventually did, Drayce was transfixed. His surroundings faded away, driving no longer a priority, the image the only thing his brain could process. The photo sharpened into brilliant clarity, while everything around it blurred into insignificance. The enormity of what it meant hit him like a rocket. He felt himself plummeting, his world collapsing.

A horn sounded, forcing his attention back to the real world. A bus, oncoming. He swerved left, back into his lane, missing it by inches. He pulled over, eyes boring into the phone. The photo was of Lucy, stuffed into the boot of a car, bleeding from the head, her eyes half closed. As Drayce tried to process this nightmare, another message from Reaper appeared.

Drayce felt as though his head was about to explode.

Reaper is typing…

Drayce held tight, the wait unbearable, one hand crushing the steering wheel, the other cracking the phone.

Drayce turned red hot, his skin burning up. He knocked the blowers down a few settings and reduced the temperature, breathing deeply to calm himself enough to type his last message.

He tossed the phone onto the passenger seat and pulled out into the road, his mind back in focus, sharp as a blade, energy firing through him. He changed up a gear and floored the throttle, following the sat nav eastbound.

His adrenaline was back.

46

Lucy woke in a basement.

The first sensation to hit her was the pain in her head. She told herself this was a good thing, that it meant she was still alive. Able to think; to move; to fight. After blocking it out as best she could, she summoned the courage to open one eye and assess her surroundings.

She was on her side, sprawled out on the floor, which was rock hard, ice cold, and wet. Her wrists were tied behind her back, ankles bound together with rope. She tried to move, managed to shift her position a little, then lay still again. Everything hurt. Dirty, oily liquid sloshed into her mouth. She retched, forced herself to sit up and open her eyes fully.

A single bare bulb hung from the ceiling. The room was partially flooded, an inch or two of fetid water having pooled around her. Stone steps led up to a steel door, old and rusty, but undoubtedly far too solid for her to force her way through. She inspected the walls: solid brick. No windows; no vents. As bleak as a medieval dungeon, and just as impossible to escape from.

Her head whipped round to face the steps. Goosebumps prickled her flesh. A cold shiver scurried down her spine. From somewhere in the guts of the building had come the sound of a heavy door's mechanics, echoing down to the basement. She held her breath and listened. Bolts were racked, hinges squeaked, before it was slammed back into the frame with a noise like a gunshot. Lucy had known she wasn't alone in the building, but hearing her kidnapper skulk around out there produced real terror. Was he coming back for her? And if he was, what did he have in store for her?

Prepare yourself, she ordered. *Don't go down without a fight.*

She brought her knees to her chest and examined the rope. It had been tied in a hurry, leaving slight gaps in the knot. If she could get the tip of a nail in there, she might be able to loosen it, get to her feet, and put up a fight. What did she have to lose? She had to try something. Waiting for the monster who had kidnapped her to come back was not an option.

She stretched her arms, lowered her wrists as best she could, then lifted her bum up and shuffled her hands underneath her, the rough fabric burning her skin as she fought to get her hands and arms in front of her.

Eventually, she managed it. The restraints around her wrists were tighter than the ones that confined her ankles, but still, there was room to work. She tried to get a nail to the knot. No good; she couldn't contort enough to get at it. Cursing, she reached for her ankles. Now able to touch the rope down there, she realised there wasn't as much room as she'd first thought. The water had soaked into the rope and made it swell, filling any gaps in the knot there may once have been. She clawed at it, but it was no use.

The fear, frustration, and sudden loss of hope got the better of her. She clenched her teeth and stomped her feet on the floor. Her soles hit something metal, the rope around her ankles snagging on something sharp. Intrigued, she moved her legs out of the way to get a closer look.

Beneath the water was a manhole, covered by a grate. One of the bars was broken, its edges sticking up, jagged and sharp. It struck Lucy that this was where the water had come from. Maybe it was part of the building's drainage that had backed up, or perhaps what she was observing was rising ground water, climbing through the old building's plumbing.

Another door opened, somewhere beyond her prison, closer than the last. Someone was coming her way. Heart pounding, she stared through the grate into the pitch-black water, down into the abyss. Did she have the courage to explore where it led to?

Damn right I do.

She placed the rope around her wrists against the sharp edge of the broken grid bar and got to work, sawing back and forth. Threads separated and came loose. She smiled; it was working. Motivated by the sight of the rope being damaged, she pushed and pulled even harder, dropping her weight into every stroke.

Snap.

The severed rope fell through the bars of the grate, vanishing beneath the inky black water. She lifted her legs, placed the rope around her ankles against the sheared bar, and repeated the process.

This time, progress was much slower. The motion needed to be carried out by her legs was awkward and clumsy, making it difficult to get a rhythm going. She persevered, grunting with every stroke. Cramp in her hamstring forced her to stop. Gritting her teeth, she straightened her leg and rubbed the muscle until it eased.

Get back to work, she told herself. *You've no time to waste.*

Barely a quarter of the way through the rope, the cramps came back, worse than before. She stifled the cry she wanted to let out; it felt as though her muscle was about to tear. Straightening her leg again, she dug her knuckles into the tissue, trying to relieve the spasms. It worked, but the back of her thigh was so tight she knew any more exertion of that muscle and it would go again, perhaps tear next time.

Footsteps made her blood run cold.

Someone was approaching the basement door. They sounded close, perhaps only a few strides before a key would be inserted. Lucy had to hurry: if she still had her ankles tied when they entered, she'd be entirely at their mercy. Her legs back in position, she went hell for leather, hacking through the threads twice as fast as before. The cramps returned, but she didn't care. Freedom was more important.

A jangle of keys; the rattle of an insertion.

She ignored the door, her focus entirely on cutting that damn rope. Something in her hip cramped. She blocked it out, determined to persevere. Beads of sweat trickled from her brow and stung her eyes.

Crank!

A bolt was pulled out of the door frame, the handle turning.

Nearly there, Lucy. Don't stop now. Just… a little… more…

Her ankles separated. She exhaled in relief, the split rope vanishing underneath the black water. She hurried to her feet, rotating her upper body to the opening door, preparing to mount her defence. Her foot caught the grate's broken bar. The whole thing rattled, clearly loose from its fittings.

Was it really a viable escape route?

No, Lucy decided. She had no idea where it led to, if anywhere. For all she knew, it was a dead end, the entire tunnel flooded. And even if it did lead to safety, if she got stuck, she'd certainly drown. Her only option was to fight her way free.

A man appeared in the doorway, the same disfigured thug who had dragged her down an alleyway, knocked her unconscious, and thrown her into the boot of a car. He hesitated at the top of the stairs, evidently shocked by the sight of her without restraints, poised like a jungle cat about to attack. She clenched her fists, ready to give a violent burst for freedom her best shot.

Her hope diminished.

Another man appeared behind the first, and then another behind him. The one at the front pulled a knife, the blade huge, perhaps a foot long, glinting in the light. Lucy's strength evaporated. She felt ready to collapse, to give up, to resign herself to whatever hell they had planned for her. Against one, she had a chance. But three? One of whom was armed with a giant knife?

No chance.

She retreated, her feet sloshing through the water until her back collided with the wall: nowhere to go. Her dire predicament registered on the faces of the three men, all of whom smiled at her. The one with the knife took his first step down the stairs. Fear made Lucy's limbs tremble. She turned to the manhole cover, its dislodged grid at a haphazard angle.

Could it really be any worse than what's coming down the stairs?

She locked eyes with Knifeman, glanced at the manhole cover, back at Knifeman. His widening eyes told her he understood her intentions. She dived for the grid as he leapt down the steps. Her palms hit the broken bar, knocking the entire thing clear of the opening. Capitalising on the momentum from her dive, she slid headfirst into the water, gulping in a big breath before she submerged.

It was so dark she couldn't see her hand in front of her face, but she could feel the solid walls of the tunnel around her, just wide enough for her to fit. She shut her eyes tightly and kicked her legs to swim forward. Something grabbed her ankle: a hand, reaching down from the basement floor, its giant fingers like talons. She tried to pull her leg free, but it was no use. She could feel herself being pulled back to the surface. She clawed at the tunnel walls, felt a nail snap as she fought to drag herself forward, away from the opening. With her free leg, she kicked at the man's arm, colliding with what she presumed must have been his wrist.

To her relief, his grip gave way, allowing her the freedom to kick both legs. She pulled and kicked herself through the tunnel and felt the man's hand swipe at her legs again. Gratefully, this time he missed, his fingers glancing off her foot as she kicked with all her might. She delved further into the abyss, with nothing but her imagination to paint a picture of what lay ahead. With how tight the tunnel was, she knew the men wouldn't be able to follow her. But now came the next hurdle in her fight for survival.

The need for air.

She pulled herself through the tunnel as fast as she could, stroking its walls in the search for another opening. The worsening pain in her chest reminded her that the harder she swam, the faster she burned through the oxygen in her bloodstream, invigorating her body's desire for fresh air.

But what choice did she have?

Her desperation escalated with every second that passed. What had once been a tingle of claustrophobia when she'd first entered the tunnel was now becoming a throat-closing, heart-stopping panic attack. Being poisoned by carbon dioxide, her brain screamed at her to breath out. But she kept her lips clamped firmly together, knowing she would be forced to inhale water if she exhaled before she reached the surface.

If a surface even existed.

Terrible thoughts invaded Lucy's mind. Was this a mistake? Should she turn back? It felt as though the tunnel was getting narrower, but she hoped it was just a figment of her imagination. She pushed on, committed. Even if she decided to take her chances with her kidnappers rather than drown in that tunnel, she wasn't sure she had enough air left in her lungs to retrace her route with how slow moving backwards would be, and she certainly didn't have enough room to turn around.

A bubble of air escaped her lips, her diaphragm taking over after her brain's final call for oxygen, spasming in its attempt to draw breath, despite its commander's unwavering discipline. Soon, her body's mechanics would take over, and Lucy would be forced to breathe out whether she wanted to or not, with nothing to replace the carbon dioxide in her lungs other than fatal water. Seconds later, the pressure peaked, her chest about to explode. Several bubbles of air pushed their way out of her mouth. This was it: the end. She couldn't hold it in any longer. Her eyes bulged, forced to open them.

Light, up ahead, just a few metres away.

Lucy clambered forward, leaving behind a trail of air pockets as her lungs finally gave up. She felt as though she was hardly moving, the progress torturously slow. She reached for the light, which was shining down from the top of the tunnel, fingers searching for a break in the surface. But she was still some way short, her perception of distance ruined in that dirty water. Lungs empty, she strained to not inhale, her muscles screaming against the urge to breathe. Her vision worsened, her surroundings merging into one giant blurry mess. She felt sick, her equilibrium shot. With enough energy left for one final kick, she reached for the light again, knowing it was her last chance before she passed out.

Her hand broke the surface, a cold breeze wafting over her palm. Her fingers closed around a metal bar. She pulled herself closer. It was another grid, covering a different manhole. She pushed but it wouldn't budge. The light faded, her world darkening. She was slipping under. Couldn't hold on any longer. Her lips parted and her chest heaved, drawing water into her lungs. Choking her. Drowning her.

With her back against the bottom of the tunnel, she gave the grid one final shove.

It moved.

She pushed it to the side and sat up, her head bursting to the surface. She retched, vomiting the water she'd just taken on board. The world came back to her. She climbed out of the tunnel, crawled along the concrete, rolled onto her front, and convulsed in a horrendous coughing fit. She pushed herself up onto all fours, back rounding as she retched. More water shot up from her throat. She came up onto her knees, focused on her breathing. She assessed her surroundings, shivering in the cold night air; she was outside, in the middle of a brightly lit yard. A metal fence marked the boundary, coils of barbed wire running along the top. There was an old industrial building in the direction from which she'd come. She must have been in its basement. She swept her hair back.

Time to get moving.

Torch lights came into view as she got to her feet. A group of men rounded the building's corner, their movements hurried. Lucy ran, heading for the fence line. Loud voices echoed across the yard like barking dogs. They'd seen her. She didn't look back, not even when the torch lights illuminated her from behind, their heavy boots slapping the concrete as they chased her down. She hit the fence with her palms, the chain links rattling from the impact. She pulled herself up, fear, and excitement, and adrenaline all working together to push her on.

The men reached the fence just as she got to the top, the structure swaying as they hit it at speed and climbed after her. With no time to take care, she swung a leg over, the coils of barbed wire snagging onto her clothes. She tried to tear them free, but they just became even more entangled and caught her flesh, the barbs burrowing into her skin like ticks. She screamed from the pain as she swung another leg over, determined to get free even if she tore herself to pieces.

With both legs over the other side, she let go of the fence and allowed her bodyweight to sag, using it to pull herself free from the clutches of the barbs. Her trousers, her jacket, her shirt: they all ripped free from the wire at once. She plummeted to the ground, landing on her back.

Winded, she got to her feet and stared daggers at the men through the fence. The one who had kidnapped her off the street was at the front of the group. She glared at him. He scowled back, his feet planted firmly on the ground, unwilling to sacrifice the same pain as she had to get over.

Pussy.

With a defiant smile on her face, Lucy gave him the finger and turned to run.

Which is when she realised why he hadn't bothered trying to climb over.

Another group of men were fanned out in a semi-circle, blocking her path. Tears filled her eyes, the hopelessness of her situation killing her spirit. She collapsed to her knees as they crowded her, took her roughly by her arms, and dragged her back to the building.

47

'Put her somewhere more secure this time!' Ryan bellowed from the front and centre of his group of heavies.

'What does it look like I'm doing?' Reaper replied. He dragged the detective across the rough concrete floor of the warehouse, around the fully loaded pallets of merchandise, to a radiator on the wall. 'I've got chains this time, and these pipes go deep underground. She's going nowhere without our say so.'

Ryan placed the flat of his hand against his forehead. 'If she'd got away—'

'But she didn't.' Reaper latched her to a pipe and smiled down at her. Pretty thing. He'd enjoy himself when the time came for him to kill her. 'Did you, darling?'

She lunged at him, the chains rattling against the metal as the slack was pulled tight, keeping him out of her reach. Evidently frustrated, she resorted to spitting at him, thick goblets of which peppered his trousers, like a cornered cobra firing venom as it lashed out.

Without so much as a frown, Reaper stepped forward and backhanded her across the cheek, a slap of flesh echoing throughout the giant room. She glared at him, her sodden blonde hair clinging to her brow, defiance and hostility person-ified.

Reaper smirked, reluctantly impressed by her courage. He turned to Ryan. 'So stop worrying, old man.'

Ryan dropped his hand and stared at Reaper in disbelief. 'Stop worrying? After what's just happened? Are you insane?'

'She barely got out of the compound. No one saw her.'

'I'm not talking about her little burst for freedom. She's just a small turd on the giant fucking mountain of them we currently have stacked in our back yard. Do I have to remind you of what just happened at Sullivan's club?'

'Of course not.' Reaper approached Ryan and stood square on to him. 'I was there, don't forget.'

'And you're sure Sullivan survived?'

'I messaged him while travelling here. He's alive, and he's on his way, so we need to be ready for him when he arrives.'

Ryan stuffed his hands in his trouser pockets and paced back and forth. 'I can't believe those Chinese idiots fucked it up. We put him alone in a room with them. They had him on a fucking plate and still couldn't get the job done.'

'In their defence, they were interrupted, and it cost them their lives.'

'And the man who interrupted them? He know about this place?'

'No chance.'

'Bet you thought the same about the club a few hours ago, didn't you? Well, I for one will not just sit around here waiting for that psychopath to arrive.' Ryan delved into his jacket pocket and produced a revolver. The six men on his shoulder stood a little taller, their hands among their clothing, no doubt clutching weapons of their own.

'Calm yourself. He's the reason I snatched her off the streets.' Reaper flicked his head in the detective's direction. 'To use as a bargaining chip if he finds out where we are, or as bait when we decide we want to lure him in. He's an ex-copper. They look after each other. He won't be able to resist trying to save her life.'

Ryan's mouth hung open in shock. 'You saw what he did to Sullivan's firm. Everyone apart from you and Sullivan is dead, and you want to lure Drayce back in?'

Reaper nodded. 'When the time's right.'

Ryan rubbed his face with his free hand, plainly exhausted. 'You're mad.'

'I'll kill him with or without your help, but first we've got Sullivan to deal with.'

Ryan checked his watch. 'How much longer before he gets here?'

'Could be any minute.'

'Then we need to get ready for him. He might already suspect something. If the Chinese said too much before they got—'

'I doubt they had the chance. The alarm went off minutes after the door was closed. Sullivan trusts me. All we need to do is wait for him to get here, and then—'

'And then what, exactly? Kill him? Act like we didn't plan to use a powerful Triad to overthrow him? How exactly do you want to play it now that we don't have an army of Chinese gangsters on our side?'

Reaper didn't have any good answers, but he went with the best one available. 'When Sullivan gets here, I'll kill him, and then I'll run the London operation myself, and you can fuck off up north to get on with things up there.'

Ryan's mouth hung open. 'You can't be serious. So, what? We just carry on as we have been doing? Me in Liverpool and now you down here?'

'It's our only option now that we don't have the Chinese to assist us in expanding our reach. After the hit we've taken at the club, the only other thing I'll need from you is some borrowed manpower until I've been able to recruit some extra muscle.'

'So, it's *we* now, is it? What happened to me being merely an investor in this city?'

Reaper fixed him with a hard glare. 'Those were Sullivan's words, not mine. Things will be different now I'm in charge. We'll need to work together if we're to rebuild our workforce in London back to the formidable presence it was before tonight's massacre at the club.'

'And if Drayce hunts us down in the meantime?'

'I'll be ready for him. Now make yourself useful and call Tommy for an update. He's on high ground on the edge of the compound, watching for Sullivan's arrival.' Reaper drew his hunting knife, inspected its razor-sharp edge in the glint of the ceiling light. 'I want to know as soon as that man gets within sight of this place.'

Ryan reached for his phone. As his hand delved into his pocket, Reaper noticed him stop suddenly, a shiver coursing through him before he froze. And Reaper understood why, because he'd heard the same thing from outside. Tyres had screeched up to the compound, followed by the unmistakeable sound of a vehicle smashing its way through the unit's gate. Then something more distinctive, and far more worrying, had presented itself above the chaotic racket.

The *crack* of a rifle.

48

Tommy shivered in the cold wind, the wooden stock of his rifle like ice against his neck. Sprawled out on top of a pile of pallets, thirty foot high, he had a clear view of the approach road through the weapon's magnified scope. He wiped the drizzle off his beard, pulled his jacket tight around his neck as a buffer for the rifle's stock and to keep the breeze out, his keen eyes never leaving the road. One hand on the rifle, he clutched his phone with the other. As soon as headlights appeared, he was to make the call to Reaper, so they could be ready for Sullivan the moment his only exit was cut off behind him. It's how Reaper wanted it: no delay, and no opportunity for escape or negotiations afforded to their old boss.

A lorry was parked on the service road, just out of sight from anyone approaching. When Tommy saw Sullivan arrive, he was to phone the man in the lorry and instruct him to pull out and block the entrance – a nice little contingency, one Tommy had thought of all by himself. There was no guarantee the gate would stop a car if Sullivan smelt a rat and tried to reverse his way out.

Tommy shivered again, so violent an experience it felt more like a convulsion. When his view settled back on the road, he saw headlights, just one pair, hurtling towards the compound. Hard to judge in the dark, but the vehicle was perhaps a hundred metres away, eating up the road as though it were in a drag race, so fast he struggled to follow it through the rifle's scope. Able to make out that it was a Toyota Hilux, Tommy judged that there were seconds until it was at the entrance. It wasn't going to stop for the gate to open. This was not how it was supposed to go down. Sullivan must know something.

Tommy fumbled with the bolt to get a round chambered as his thumb jabbed at the screen of his phone, rushing to call the lorry driver.

But he wasn't quick enough.

The speed of the Hilux didn't diminish at all as it smashed through the compound's gates. The lock obliterated on contact, sheared metal rocketing up into the windscreen, cracking it in a dozen places. The gate passed over the roof to the hellish sound of its chain links being ripped apart. Strands of barbed wire entangled the truck's rear bumper, tearing the gate from its hinges and dragging it along in the truck's wake.

Tommy fired at the driver, the high-calibre round hitting the windscreen a split second later. Tiny shards of glass sprayed out from the impact, but the truck's direction of travel stayed true. Tommy chambered another round, took aim, and fired again. A flash of light burst out from the windscreen, a cloud of tiny broken shards showering the front of the truck as the glass exploded in almost the exact same place. This time, the vehicle shifted, its course altering, swinging a wide arc towards Tommy's position. Smoke billowed from the tyres, leaving a black trail across the concrete, snaking out behind, marking its journey, the rubber screeching against the driver's demands.

But his efforts were evidently not worth it. The truck lost control, its back end swinging out wide as it began to spin, still hurtling towards Tommy.

'Shit!' he shouted when he realised what was about to happen, his hands abandoning the rifle, feet scrambling for purchase as he tried to make a run for it.

But he wasn't quick enough.

The truck's back end clipped the pallets, swiping the bottom two rows out from underneath the stack. Tommy felt his world shift underneath him, his legs wobbling as the pallets began to tumble like a giant game of Jenga. Mercifully, he slid down the outer stack, rather than plummeting straight down the middle where he would surely be crushed by the imploding mound of wood. He tried to cling on to something to slow his descent as a hearty scream roared from deep in his chest. His fingers clawed uselessly at the pallets, unable to gain purchase. Five metres from the ground, a lump of wood cracked him on the shoulder, knocking him sideways onto the flat top of a pallet, which he rode all the way to the concrete below. The corner of the pallet was the first thing to make impact, obliterating it into a hundred pieces and throwing Tommy forward, headfirst. He rolled, uncontrollably, tumbling over his shoulders, legs clattering against the ground like a ragdoll with every rotation until he eventually came to a stop. He curled up into a ball, arms protecting his head as broken shards of wood rained down all around him.

Once the avalanche fell silent, Tommy tried to move, thanking God when he was able to get to his knees and realised he wasn't buried under the broken pallets. He clambered over the obstacles, patting himself down as he fought his way out of the debris, dusting off some of the thousands of tiny splinters he was covered in. He searched for his rifle but soon gave up: no use wasting precious time; it was lost under the giant pile of wood and would take a week to recover. Once free, he scanned the compound for the truck and spotted it thirty metres away, stationary, on its roof. Steam hissed from the engine bay, a dark pool of glossy liquid expanding across the concrete. His head pivoted to the lorry driver, who having blocked the entrance – albeit too late – was now leaning out of the open door to his cab. He made eye contact with Tommy.

'Get over there and check that truck!' Tommy shouted. 'I lost my rifle in the fall!'

The lorry driver nodded, reached back in for his pistol, and jumped down, both boots landing with a thud on the hard ground below. He jogged up to the wreck and aimed his pistol at the driver's door. A quick glance at Tommy with trepidation written all over his face instigated a swift nod from his superior to encourage him on. He reached for the handle with his free hand, the other ready to aim the gun between door and frame when it opened. Tommy watched him take a deep breath, the quiver in his pistol evident even from that distance away. The door flew open, his gun waving erratically at the interior. Tommy held his breath as he anticipated the simultaneous *pop* and *flash* of the shot that would indicate Sullivan's execution. But it never came. The lorry driver stepped back and exhaled, a smile materialising on his relieved face.

'Sullivan's not in it!' he shouted to Tommy, his grin widening as he wiped the nervous sweat off his brow. 'It's empty!'

Tommy felt his face drop and the corners of his mouth wither. The dreadful realisation of what the empty truck likely meant filled his stomach with butterflies. Speechless, he watched the lorry driver reach inside the vehicle.

'This must have been holding the accelerator down!' the lorry driver shouted as he stood tall and raised a brick that he'd retrieved from the interior.

Tommy opened his mouth to shout a warning, but his voice was lost beneath the *boom* of the gunshot that erupted behind him. The driver's head snapped back, a puff of pink mist wafting into the air. He fell, dead before he hit the ground. Momentarily frozen from shock, Tommy composed himself and moved to turn his head so he could get a look at the shooter. But he didn't make it far before the red-hot muzzle of the weapon that had killed the driver was pressed to his cheekbone, stopping him dead. He winced against the burn, his determination not to do something that would get him killed preventing him from pulling away. He rotated his eyes as far as he could to get a look at the shooter. As soon as he did, the man spoke, his voice deep and calm, as though at the tail end of a perfectly executed plan.

–

'Evening,' Drayce said.

'You're not Sullivan,' the sniper replied, confusion creasing his brow.

'No. I'm not.'

'How d'you find us here. No one knows about this place.'

'I know everything about your organisation.' He regarded with an inquisitive expression the man stood before him. 'Except your name.'

'I'm Tommy.'

'So, Tommy, why were you shooting at that truck if you thought Sullivan was in it? I'm no expert, but I'm pretty sure that sort of behaviour from an employee is frowned upon by a boss.'

A drop of sweat broke free from his temple and trickled down his cheek. 'He's not my boss anymore.'

'Reaper taking over, is he?'

'How'd you—'

'I told you; I know everything.'

Tommy managed a smile. 'You'll know what's waiting for you inside that building then, won't you?'

'Yes.'

'You're not leaving here alive.'

'I've heard that before.' Drayce pushed the carbine harder into Tommy's face. 'And what-do-you-know, I'm still breathing.'

Tommy's phone rang from somewhere on his person. He assessed Drayce's reaction through the curtains of damp hair that dangled in front of his face, eyes defiant. 'That'll be them. They'd have heard the gunshots. They'll be ready for you.'

'It won't make a difference.'

The phone went silent. Exhaustion took hold of Tommy's features. 'You really kill all those men at the club?'

Drayce nodded.

'What about Sullivan?'

Another nod.

Tommy smiled. 'So it was you who messaged Reaper after the shootout in the club? You pretended to be Sullivan?'

'Very perceptive of you, Tommy.'

'Well, let me tell you what else my perception tells me: you've played right into Reaper's hands. He was planning on killing Sullivan today anyway. Had it all lined up with the Chinese so he could take over and give them the deal they wanted. Make us all rich, instead of Sullivan creaming it off for himself. You've done Reaper's job for him, mate. He'll like that. The man loves it when a plan comes together.'

Drayce took the slack out of the trigger. 'He won't like my plan for him.'

The Colt kicked in his hand, a cloud of gunshot residue burning Tommy's face around a neat hole that appeared instantly in his cheek, the splatter of brain matter that exploded across the tumbled stack of pallets behind him an indication of the chaotic exit wound.

Drayce applied the safety catch, stepped over Tommy's body, and approached the building.

49

'Tommy's not answering,' Ryan said, his face red and gleaming from a nerve sweat, revolver quivering in his jittery hand as he stomped back and forth in the unit's warehouse. 'What the actual fuck do we do now?'

'We stay calm.' Reaper stood between two columns of merchandise, offering him cover from every entrance to the room. 'Panicking around this man will get us killed.'

'Fuck not panicking! Did you not hear it out there? Sounded like a battle in a war zone.' Distracted by one of his men, who had turned to face his evidently terrified boss, Ryan waved his revolver at him. 'Never mind ogling me, son! Concentrate on your fucking job, which right now consists of locking eyes on that doorway!'

They had a man at every access point to the room, gun in hand, having concluded that sending anyone out there on the hunt would have been suicide.

Reaper's cold eyes met Ryan's. 'It's been quiet out there for a few minutes now, and we don't know who's left standing. Maybe Tommy shot him.'

'Then why isn't he answering his phone?'

Reaper didn't have a good answer to that question.

Ryan levelled a stiff finger at his face. 'You know as well as I do that Drayce has killed Tommy, and probably Sullivan as well.'

'If that's the case, he's done us a favour, and all that's left is for us to kill *him*.'

Ryan regarded Reaper as though he were contemplating the world's greatest fool. 'You make it sound so simple.'

Reaper closely inspected Ryan's body language. He was brimming with frustration, a man unaccustomed to being on the back foot, trapped, with no option but to wait for his enemy's next move. His feet were dancing on the spot, anxiety preventing him from keeping still.

'Control yourself, John,' Reaper said.

Ryan ignored him, marched to one of the columns, and tore at the black wrapping with his nails. 'I'm not just standing around, waiting for this man to come and kill us. Get over here and help me get this pallet open.'

'What for?'

'There're guns and ammunition in these. If we can arm ourselves properly, maybe—'

Ryan stilled and went mute. He gazed up as though he'd heard something. Reaper had heard it too: a scratching sound on the exterior brickwork, high up, near a window just underneath where the wall met the ceiling. Reaper tucked himself tighter into cover, locked eyes with Ryan, and shook his head. 'It's too late for that, John.'

The window exploded inwards.

–

Having spotted Lucy safe behind the cover of giant stacks of loaded pallets, Drayce went through with his plan and smashed the window, before throwing the fragmentation grenade through the shattered pane, the device plummeting to the warehouse floor among a thousand tiny shards of glass, glistening in the ceiling lights as they descended like flakes in a snowstorm. He waited for the explosion, tucked into cover to the side of the window. A blinding flash of light preceded a deafening boom, the building shaking so hard it was a miracle it didn't collapse. Feet braced against the wall, abseil rope taut between the D-ring on his tactical belt and his anchor point, he swung to the broken window and gazed down the ACOG sight on the Colt C8 carbine, zooming in on the warehouse's interior.

Six men were in view. They'd been dotted around the room in defensive positions, guns in hand, expecting him to use a door, with no cover from the grenade as it landed.

Mistake.

Two were plainly dead, the other four alive, their clothes shredded, bodies peppered with blast injuries. Drayce settled his sight picture on the centre mass of the first one to spot him, held his breath, and squeezed. The reticule jumped as the firearm bucked in his grip. The figure dropped. Drayce let the weapon settle, pivoted to the next man, and repeated the process.

Sight picture, squeeze; sight picture, squeeze.

Three more dead bodies were sprawled out on the ground by the time the last man standing returned fire. He was older than the others, his movements slow as he ran for cover, impeded further by recent injuries: the entire left side of his face was a burned mess from the grenade, and blood gushed down his neck and chest from several shrapnel injuries. The revolver in his outstretched hand kicked wildly, his limp wrist flapping against the recoil, attempting to shoot on the move. The stray round collided with the glass that clung to the window's frame, showering Drayce in fragments. But he barely noticed, too focused on the task at hand. He calmly tracked the man with the Colt, sight picture just ahead of the fleeing figure's skull. He fired. A cloud of pink mist sprayed in the air. The man's legs gave way under him, his ruined face colliding with the ground. There had been no attempt to break his fall. He lay motionless, not a quiver of life in him.

Drayce put another round in him, just to be sure.

A quick scan of the room confirmed no sign of any further threats. Drayce tilted the Colt to check the breech: the bolt was locked back, the magazine empty. He let it hang from its sling, pushed his feet off the wall, and abseiled down the outside of the building, a heavy smell of singed leather in his nostrils as his gloves smoked. With no more ammunition for the carbine, he ditched it on the ground, along with the belt and damaged gloves, then drew his pistol and moved to the warehouse's nearest door. It was open a crack, showing a sliver of vertical light. Gun up, Drayce pushed it open and sliced the pie, pivoting across the opening to get as much of a view inside as he could before he entered. With no threats, he crossed the threshold, a metre in a metre out, and planted his feet, scanning for a target.

The only bodies in sight were the six dead ones. Drayce worked the wall, opening his view between the pallet stacks. He saw Lucy. They locked eyes, hers wide with terror, lips snarled as though about to shout something.

'Alex! He's behind—'

Movement caught Drayce's eye. He turned, a dark figure in the shadows, forty metres away, stepping out from the cover of a pallet-stack. A gunshot rang out. Drayce felt something clip him on the leg, the dull trauma soon amplified to a burning sensation. He danced off the spot and fired back, his target on the run. Both guns bucked repeatedly in their hands, bright flashes of light bursting from the barrels as they exchanged fire, both hard targets with pistols at that distance. Drayce hurried to a loaded pallet, his nearest cover, pulling his trigger throughout the journey. The figure buckled at the waist, hand instinctively clutching his chest, but it wasn't enough to stop him; he continued shooting with one hand.

Another bullet caught Drayce's arm. At full sprint, he hit the loaded pallet with his shoulder, spinning him like a tossed coin. Mercifully, he fell into cover, the last shooter's rounds thudding into the giant bulk of merchandise. Drayce rolled onto his front, checked his pistol: slide locked back, magazine empty. Completely out of ammunition, he ditched the weapon and got to his feet.

The room was silent. Drayce opened his mouth, which in turn expanded his ear canal, giving him the best chance of hearing his adversary's manoeuvres. Nothing. Drayce cautiously stepped to the corner of the loaded pallets, eyes locked on his visual limit point. He edged round, opening his view.

The man was down on one knee, head bowed, both hands now grasping his chest. The pistol he'd fired at Drayce was discarded at his feet, breech wide open, both magazine and chamber empty. Drayce stepped out of cover. The man looked up, his angry face square on to Drayce.

Reaper.

They locked eyes. The fact Drayce wasn't aiming a gun at him was apparently enough to signal there was no need to hurry into action. Reaper gradually got to his feet, making no play to reach for another firearm that plainly didn't exist. His hands left his chest, the prominent extra bulge an indication of the body armour under his black shirt and jacket.

Drayce stopped ten feet away, head up, shoulders back, hands balled into fists. Warm blood ran down his arm and leg, gathering in his boot and trickling between his fingers. Reaper swept his hands through his black hair and straightened his suit jacket, as though preparing for the inevitable bare-knuckle fight on the horizon.

'If it's any consolation,' Reaper began, 'she was good at her job. Too good. If she hadn't been such a determined copper, she might still be here.'

Drayce stepped forward, halted by the glint of the knife Reaper pulled out.

Reaper smiled. 'Easy now, fella.'

The blade was huge; longer and wider than Reaper's forearm. It twinkled in the bright ceiling lights as he turned it over, its edge razor sharp.

Drayce held his ground. For now.

'I don't do easy,' Drayce said.

A prone figure, lazily crawling along the floor, came into sight from behind Reaper, who turned after hearing the man's fingernails clawing the concrete, but only halfway, ensuring he kept Drayce in his peripheral vision while he assessed the dying man.

'Reaper,' John Ryan uttered, the word hardly audible beneath the thick blood that oozed out of his mouth. Drayce recognised him from a mugshot in Jason Martin's notes. The headshot Drayce had landed evidently hadn't killed him, but it had left a mark that, if Ryan survived, would stay with him forever. His right cheekbone was missing, having been obliterated by the exit of the 5.56 round Drayce had put through him. He couldn't see the entry wound in his left cheek, lost as it was amid the terribly scorched and blistered skin from the grenade blast. A long trail of blood marked the path Ryan had crawled across the warehouse, most of which had gushed from the bullet wound to his chest that Drayce had fired in an attempt to ensure he was dead. 'Please,' he spluttered. 'Help me.'

Reaper sighed; having evidently presumed his associate to be dead, he was plainly frustrated at this additional complication. He shuffled to Ryan, sideways, like a crab, so he could keep an eye on Drayce at the same time, and stood over the dying man's body.

'Your revolver,' Reaper demanded as he held out a hand to receive it.

'I… don't have it. I dropped it… somewhere.'

'Any other gun on you?'

'What? No. I…' Ryan's eyes pleaded with the merciless man. 'Please… I need an ambulance.'

'And I need a gun, but you don't have one.' Reaper squatted down to him, took a handful of the man's hair, and lifted his head off the ground so he could growl into his ear the last words Ryan would ever hear. 'So, what fucking use are you to me?'

The attack was so fast, all Drayce saw was the glint of the knife as it cut through the air on its way to Ryan's neck. The tip of the weapon punched through Ryan's flesh just below his earlobe and was quickly followed by the rest of the blade as Reaper buried it in him up to the handle, a satisfied grimace displayed on the assassin's expression. He drew his arm back, the knife retreating from the wound, his wide eyes easing back to the dark, dead ones so often displayed by the experienced killer. Ryan's eyes, on the other hand, had rolled back into his head, lifeless. He slumped forward, the ruined flesh on his face clapping the concrete as the last embers of his being withered to nothing.

Reaper turned to Drayce. Thick crimson globules dripped from the tip of the knife and splashed on the dusty grey floor. The assassin walked towards Drayce, but halted several metres away, visibly cautious of getting too close. 'I suppose you want to know what happened to your wife before I kill you as well.'

'Her name was Lily.'

Reaper's face contorted into a scowl. 'I don't give a fuck what her name was!'

Drayce's foot hovered in the air, about to take a step, everything in his being pushing him forward to end the man's life. He breathed deeply to control himself, holding on to his discipline with fingernails alone. He put his foot down. 'I already know what happened. What you did to her.'

'Not fully, you don't. The screams, the things she said as she lay dying at my feet.' A smirk infected Reaper's hateful expression. 'Want me to paint you a pretty little picture?'

A burst of high-pressure water exploded through the crack in the dam, its entire structure crumbling. Drayce quivered on the spot, the energy unstoppable. He took another step forward.

'That's it.' Reaper waved him on. 'Walk over here and get what's coming to you.'

Drayce held off, his last measure of discipline gripping him, reluctant to get drawn into the trap. But it was the hardest thing in the world. His fists trembled from the adrenaline, every bit of his soul demanding violence. His battle-hardened DNA, passed on over hundreds of thousands of years, screamed at him to run forward. To maim. To kill.

'All in good time,' he said.

'What are you hesitating for? Look at everything you've done to get to me.' Reaper held his arms out wide, the tip of the bloody knife pointed up at the ceiling. 'Now's your chance.'

'I've waited three and a half years for this moment. No point rushing now.'

'Sounds like you've got something to say. Better spit it out before I get bored of this little stand off and come over there.'

Drayce glared into his dark soul. 'I've been a mess since you murdered my wife. You can't imagine the emotions that build up in your head when you lose the person you love in such a way. It's as though there's a physical being inside you, a gremlin, tearing your heart to pieces, destroying your mind, sending you mad.' Beads of sweat trickled down his face. 'I tried to bottle it up, to hold it down, to bury it.' He shook his head. 'But it's no use. It's too powerful, the emotions, the pain, all of it too strong to control. I've come to realise the only way for me to get rid of that energy is to burn it up, by putting a bullet in every man linked to Lily's death.' He pointed a finger at Reaper. 'You're the last one left, and the one who deserves to die the most. Which means a bullet's too good for you. Too quick. You need to feel your death.' Drayce pounded his fist on his own chest. '*I* need to feel it.'

Reaper pointed the tip of the knife at Drayce, bared his teeth, and stepped forward. 'Well let's get to it, then, tough guy! You need to put your words into action! I'm not exactly going to kill myself, now, am I?'

Drayce walked forward. 'You killed yourself three and a half years ago.'

'Shut up and get over here so I can gut you with this knife! Just like I did your bitch wife!'

The dam fell apart, its entire structure collapsing like an avalanche, the rubble riding an unstoppable tidal wave. Drayce ran at him, arms and legs pumping with fury, a battle cry erupting from deep in his chest. Reaper sprinted forward, knife at the ready. Drayce grabbed his arm in the clash, holding the blade at bay as they collided heads like horned beasts. He rocked back and headbutted Reaper square in the face, scooped up one of his legs in his arms, teeth clenched as he swept the man's standing leg out from under him and dumped him on the ground.

Reaper's back *thumped* against the concrete, a *whoosh* of air rushing from his mouth. Drayce pinned him with a knee on his belly, still grappling with the man's knife-wielding arm, the blade slicing the air in front of him. He got two hands on Reaper's wrist and drove it to the floor, arms locked out, bearing down with his full weight. Reaper groaned, saliva spraying from between his clenched teeth. Red-faced, a vein pulsed in his neck. Drayce transitioned into a full mount, high up on Reaper's chest and shoulders, constantly keeping two hands on his wrist. He ideally wanted to strangle him, but would take destroying his elbow with an arm bar or his shoulder with a kimura as a close second. He crept into position, little by little, Reaper unable to counter Drayce's grappling ability.

A bolt of lightning fired up Drayce's leg. He whipped a hand off Reaper's wrist and reached back, felt the man's firm grip on his flesh, his thumb digging into the bullet wound to his thigh. Drayce growled from the pain and was forced to move, switching back to a knee on belly as he batted Reaper's hand away.

In his haste to relieve the pain in his leg, Drayce lost control of the knife. Reaper slashed at him, the blade cutting through his clothing, carving a shallow ridge across his chest. He rolled away, but Reaper followed him, lunging with the knife as Drayce landed on his back. He caught the man's wrist just in time, stopping the blade's tip inches from his throat. Reaper pushed forward, clambering between Drayce's legs as he pressed the knife down with his bodyweight.

Drayce tensed every muscle he had in his fight to hold the knife at bay. He cinched his legs tightly around Reaper's torso and locked his ankles together behind Reaper's back to take some control of the situation. But it wasn't enough. The back of Drayce's skull scraped along the ground, trying to create distance. Triceps burning, he tried to press the knife away with all his might. But it kept coming. Six inches; four inches; two. The tip touched his windpipe, a sharp sting as it broke the skin. He closed his eyes, focused his energy, the pressure building in his head as he held his breath and gave it everything he had. But the knife just wouldn't budge. Reaper was too strong, his position above Drayce too dominant. Weakening, Drayce felt his arms give way, unable to hold the knife back any longer.

A trickle of blood ran down the side of his neck.

50

Reaper's eyes were wild, grin devilish, his expression the epitome of evil. His teeth were stained red from the impact of the headbutt, blood oozing out of his damaged nostrils, dribbling from the corners of his mouth and galloping down his chin before falling onto the knife's blade. The tip was edging deeper into Drayce's throat, the slow, torturous infliction almost unbearable. Thick ropes of muscle strained in his neck as he tried to fight off the assault. He focused on the fact he could still draw breath, so the damage wasn't fatal. Yet.

Crimson bubbles formed on Reaper's lips as he spoke. 'How about I paint that picture for you now?' His smile widened, his tone taking on the sing-song quality of a fairy tale narrator. 'Twas a cold winter's night…' He laughed, the knife jiggling inside the puncture in Drayce's throat. 'Do you want to know something?' Reaper stretched his neck out, their noses now inches apart, his voice a whisper. 'This is the exact same knife I used to kill your precious Lily.'

The hairs on the back of Drayce's neck stood up. Something awoke in him, something on a different dimension to the physical.

'See those old scars on the back of my hand?' Reaper continued. 'She did that, trying to claw the knife out of my grip.' His smile widened. 'Didn't manage to, though. And neither will you!'

Drayce felt an energy beyond the creatine and glucose his muscles had burned through, a fuel from an unknown element, firing him up, demanding results, despite the horrendous build-up of lactic acid in his arms. He felt the knife's progress halt.

Reaper sneered at Drayce. 'I'm going to stick this knife in you, just like I did her. Only, you won't be able to beg the way she did.'

Drayce's heart ached at the thought of Lily suffering. The pain must have been evident on his face.

'You didn't know that, did you?' Reaper asked. 'You weren't aware of her pleas.' He came closer. 'She called out your name. Begged for you to help her.' A single tear broke free from the corner of Drayce's eye and ran across his temple. 'How does it feel to live knowing you weren't there for the woman you love?'

A deep, animalistic growl erupted from Drayce's chest. The knife retreated, its blade sliding out of the shallow puncture wound, lifting free of his neck. Reaper was aghast, eyes on stalks, confusion wiping the menace off his face. The knife kept moving: two inches, three inches, five. Reaper grimaced, trying to fight back. But it was no use.

Drayce locked eyes with him. 'I'm here for her now.'

Drayce launched his hips up and rotated into an arm bar. He hooked one of Reaper's legs and rolled him over onto his back, his knife-arm clamped firmly between Drayce's legs. Controlling the wrist, Drayce thrust his hips up at the same time as pulling Reaper's arm down, hyperextending the elbow joint. Reaper fought back, flexing his bicep to fight Drayce's efforts, his resistance pointless. A sickening *crack* rang out, as though five pencils had been snapped in half at once.

Reaper screamed, the ear-piercing howl echoing back off the walls repeatedly.

Drayce took the knife out of his limp hand, sat up, and stabbed it down into his windpipe. Reaper made a gurgling sound, his body seizing in response to the trauma. After transitioning into a full mount, Drayce stared down into Reaper's wide eyes, which were bloodshot and bulging, his own knife pulsing against his attempts to draw breath. His slack jaw opened wide, lips curling back as a torrent of blood rose from his throat and poured down his cheeks. His eyes seemed to plead for mercy. Drayce reared up, drew his arms back, and slammed his fists into the man's face, beating him repeatedly. When one arm fatigued, he switched to the other. Once Reaper's face was a broken mess, Drayce slammed the heel of his palm into the bottom of the knife's handle, ramming the entire blade into Reaper's neck, the tip punching through his spine until it met the resistance of the concrete floor.

Reaper went limp.

Drayce got to his feet, slowly, exhaustion threatening. He knew his body was riddled with injuries, but he could barely feel them, such was the effect of the monumental adrenaline dump he'd just experienced. He put a hand to his throat, fingertips assessing the damage. It was bleeding, but only minimally, the puncture wound mere millimetres deep. A good clean, maybe a stitch or two, and he'd be fine. His attention moved to the bullet wound in his shoulder, and the one in his leg. He breathed a sigh of relief. Neither was a direct hit. Surface damage only. No danger of bleeding out any time soon.

He searched the dead man at his feet, found a set of keys, and walked over to Lucy.

51

The warehouse glowed brightly, the flames reflected in the choppy water of the Thames, the dark London skies tinged a burnt orange. They were in the truck, having used a forklift they'd found on site to flip it back onto its wheels. Drayce was in the driver's seat, Lucy the front passenger's, and they were parked just outside the compound, both spectators to the fire's consumption of the building. She was wrapped in his coat, so much material she could use the garment as a duvet. Eyes forward, they gazed through the cracked windscreen, their faces glowing in the warm hue of the blaze.

'What now?' Lucy asked.

Drayce resisted the urge to look at her, focusing instead on the flames that licked the frame of the broken window, on their way to consuming the roof.

'That's up to you,' he replied.

The truck's interior fell back into the comfortable silence of before, nothing to hear but the cogs in Lucy's brain whirling as she contemplated her choices. When she eventually broke it again, Drayce could feel her eyes on him. She jerked her head at the inferno.

'There's a lot of evidence being destroyed in there.'

'No one left to put it to, though. Sullivan and his entire gang are dead.'

'Thanks to you.'

'You say it as though it's a bad thing.'

'Isn't it?'

'They made their choices; they suffer the consequences. The world's a better place without them.' He met her eyes. 'Tell me I'm wrong.'

Lucy said nothing, her face, her body language, her energy uncertain, as though she found herself on another planet to the one she'd previously occupied, her moral compass no longer able to guide her in this strange new gravitational pull.

Drayce pressed the reality of the situation home to her. 'They kidnapped you, held you hostage, and would almost certainly have killed you if I'd died in there. They've been smuggling weapons, drugs, *people*, into London for years, and every time a cop got too close, they murdered them.' Drayce paused before he drove this last point home. 'One of whom was my wife.' He looked away, sat back, and gazed at the burning building – the collapse of an evil empire. 'So go ahead and tell me why your rules mean I did a bad thing here.'

Lucy licked her lips, pulled his jacket tight to her neck. 'Well, when you put it like that.' She glanced at the fire. 'I suppose you may have a point.'

'Which brings us back to the original question.'

'The "what now" issue?'

'That's the one.'

A sigh whistled through Lucy's front teeth. 'Throughout all your antics today, have you left any trace the Met could use to link you to the murders of these men?'

He shook his head. 'I've been careful.' He nodded at the warehouse just as the roof crashed in on itself, consumed by tall fingers of bright yellow flames twisting up to the sky. 'The only evidence of my involvement was bled out in that building, and I think even today's forensic examiners would struggle to pull anything worthwhile out of there now.'

'What about Territt?'

'What about him?'

'Are you responsible for what happened to him?'

'No. Not all of it. Territt had been Daniel Sullivan's rat for years. I went to his house, confronted him with evidence of his crimes, and set a trap for Sullivan's people. When they arrived, there was a shootout. One of them – the man who kidnapped you – escaped. I stole Territt's Jaguar to chase him through town. But I didn't set Territt's house on fire – that must have been Sullivan's people, covering their tracks.' Drayce took a deep breath, conscious of how much he was revealing to a serving police officer. 'I left a few of their bodies behind; evidently, they didn't want the police finding them there in a state in which they could be easily identified. It would have brought too much heat, far too quickly, onto Sullivan and his gang. But as for Territt, he was still alive when I chased Reaper out of his home.'

'Who's Reaper?'

'The man who kidnapped you. The man who killed Jason Martin.' Another deep breath. A long, drawn-out sigh. 'The man who murdered my wife.'

Lucy's shock was evident. She stared hard at the side of his face, his gaze forward, locked onto the flames. 'How do you know?'

'His DNA.' Drayce thought about Jason Martin's notes. 'Among other clues.'

'So, where's Territt now?'

'If his ashes aren't inside his burned-out home, I'd say Sullivan and his people thought of another way to dispose of him. Once they knew his corruption had been discovered, he would have been seen by them as more of a threat than an asset.' Drayce turned to face her. 'I wouldn't bank on him turning up alive.'

Lucy's hands appeared from beneath the jacket. She rubbed her face and swept her hair out of her eyes.

'So, Detective,' Drayce said, observing her carefully. 'What do you want to do now?'

'My choices?'

Drayce considered her options. 'You only have two: either we wait here for the first responders to arrive, I tell them the entire truth as to what happened, and they arrest me.'

'And my second?'

'Is that we leave before they get here.'

He watched her, waiting for her response, the fire reflected in her pupils.

'Then we leave,' she said.

Drayce waited a beat. 'You sure? I don't want you doing something you'll regret. I can handle the consequences of my actions, whatever they may be.'

Lucy faced him. 'You don't deserve to go to prison for what you've done, so get us out of here before I change my mind.'

Drayce started the engine. 'Will do.'

'And we never mention any of this to anyone.' She leaned towards him. 'Ever.'

'Fine by me.' He pulled a U-turn and drove off. 'I'll get out of London. Keep a low profile for a while.'

'Good idea. But first, there's something you need to do for me.'

Drayce peered at her out of the corner of his eye as he navigated the road network to leave the industrial estate. 'And that is?'

Despite her traumatic experiences, Lucy managed a smile. 'Don't tell me you've forgotten about the deal we made?'

52

The following week

Barnaby's legal practice was in a gleaming white, five-storey Kensington town house, the enormous black door furnished with a shiny brass plate to identify the company name: Fitzgerald's Solicitors. Intelligence gathering on the internet had determined his office was on the top floor, with double doors leading to a balcony overlooking the garden, where he held a summer party every year for the wealthiest of his criminal clientele. The front of the property overlooked a park in the centre of the square, sealed off by wrought-iron fencing painted jet black, a key to the gate issued to every resident.

The lock hadn't been hard to pick.

Drayce was sat on the bench that gave him the best view of Fitzgerald's front door, wearing his finest tailored navy suit, the latest Gregg Hurwitz novel in hand, killing time with a good story while he waited for his target to return. Barnaby had left for lunch at 11:30 a.m. It was now 1:45 p.m.

Not the hardest worker in the room.

With Orphan X midway through a shootout, Barnaby returned to the office, a swagger in his gait as he alighted the taxi and marched up the steps to the front door.

Drayce reluctantly slid his bookmark between the pages, stood up, and left the park.

The receptionist was easy to get past. In his suit, Drayce appeared to belong, and capped it off with the confident stride of a man who was late for an important meeting, brushing off the lady's attempts to get his attention with an arrogant wave of the hand. He rode that same energy up the stairs, all the way to the fifth floor, a purpose to his step that, on a man his size, meant no one challenged him about his presence.

He knocked on Barnaby's office door.

'Come in!'

Drayce did just that.

The room was huge, panelled in wood everywhere apart from the sliding glass balcony doors. A large wooden desk with a leather topper faced the entrance. A big luxurious leather wingback chair sat on the far side for Barnaby, and two slightly smaller ones on the opposite side for visiting clients. Barnaby was stood facing the balcony doors, his back to Drayce, gazing down at the garden.

'I've told you before, Anna. Use the intercom.' Barnaby turned. 'You know I hate being inter—' He stiffened at the sight of a six-six, twenty-stone man in Anna's place. The skin around his nose ruffled, lips fractured in a grimace, as though a bad smell had entered the room. 'And you are?'

'Who I am is irrelevant. It's why I'm here that's important.'

Barnaby's eyebrows peaked. 'Well then, please do hurry in your attempt to explain why you *are* here, in my office, without my authorisation.'

Drayce smiled as he put his paperback down on the desk and took a seat in a wingback, the leather creaking. He moved a picture frame to the edge of the desk so he could see Barnaby clearly. He was going to enjoy this even more than he'd imagined. 'I'm here to remind you of something.'

Barnaby frowned. 'I'm sorry, you're here to do what, now?'

'You heard.'

'Did Anna send you up?'

'No, she did not.'

'Well, do you have an appointment? Because I certainly don't have anything in my—'

'Nope. No appointment. Thought I'd just pop by. Keep this little chat of ours nice and casual.'

'What little chat?' Barnaby stepped forward, putting the desk squarely between him and Drayce: a subconscious defence tactic. He adjusted his shirt cuffs, puffed his pigeon chest out, confidence growing. 'I demand to know who you are!'

Drayce regarded him with the same demeanour as a lion sizing up an irritating hyena. 'Lucy sent me.' He paused a moment to let those words sink in. Barnaby was clearly confused. His eyes scanned the floorboards, openly trying to digest this information. Just in case there were other Lucy's in Barnaby's life, or the subtext wasn't obvious, Drayce said, 'Lucy Fitzgerald nee Gardner. Your soon to be ex-wife.'

Barnaby's eyes nearly popped out of their sockets. He reached for his intercom.

Drayce yanked its cable, ripping it out of the wall. He did the same with the landline and sat back with his elbows on the armrests, fingers interlocked, waiting for the man's next reaction.

Barnaby's breathing rate visibly increased. 'You don't scare me.'

'Liar.'

A nervous shuffle of the feet, a raise of the chin, defiant on his sugar pedestal that was about to be melted back down to earth. 'What could *she* possibly want? She's already got everything that's hers.'

'But that's just not true, is it, Barnaby? Lucy's entitled to half the equity in the house you jointly own, which you're refusing to sell.'

'There's a legal process to—'

'Yes, there is. And once that process has played out, you'll be forced to either pay her the money that's hers or sell the house to release her half of the equity. But at this rate it'll take years to play out because you're delaying things at every step.'

'No, I simply—'

'Even though you're more than able to send her the money she's owed, you're dragging this painful divorce out for as long as you can, because it gives you a tie to Lucy, and that enables you to act out the disgraceful methods of manipulation and control you clearly enjoy so much.'

'I… I…'

'So let me tell you what's going to happen now I'm involved.' Drayce reached into his trouser pocket and took out a slip of white paper with an account number on it. He placed it on the desk, pinned it with an index finger, and slid it forward. 'You're going to transfer what Lucy is owed to that account, right here, right now, in front of me. Then,' he delved into his jacket pocket, pulled out a folded stack of papers, and tossed them onto the desk, 'you're going to sign those divorce papers, in front of me, and I'm going to take them back to Lucy.' Drayce regarded the man in front of him with all the contempt he deserved. 'She wants to move on. And you're going to let her.'

Barnaby clamped hands on his lapels, back ramrod straight, oozing self-righteousness. He glared down his nose at Drayce. 'I'll do no such thing. Now get out before I call the police.'

Drayce sighed. He pinched the flesh between his eyes. 'Okay. If that's how you want it.'

The desk was lighter than it looked, Drayce thought, as it left his grip and flew into the wall. His paperback landed next to him and the divorce papers fluttered in the air, drifting gently to the floor. Drayce stepped on the picture frame that had fallen off, the reflection of the sole of his shoe an indication it was a mirror, not a photo, that he'd moved to the edge of Barnaby's desk. It crunched under his weight as he took a grip of Barnaby's suit jacket and marched him onto the balcony.

The wind ruffled Barnaby's tightly combed hair. His hands pawed at Drayce, tugging on his jacket helplessly. 'What are you doing? Wait. Please. Just wait a second!'

At the wrought-iron balustrade, Drayce grabbed Barnaby's belt with one hand, kept hold of his suit jacket, lifted him in the air, and pressed him clean over his head.

'No! Wait!' In response to the dread at what was forthcoming, Barnaby turned as rigid as an ironing board. 'Oh fuck! Oh shit! Oh-fuckitty-shit!'

Drayce looked him in the eye, smiled, then dangled him headfirst over the garden.

Barnaby's jaw locked tight, paralysed by fear, a whiny squeak forced through his clenched teeth like pressurised steam.

'Right then, let's have this conversation again,' Drayce said, 'now that the correct power dynamics of our relationship have been established.' The squeaking continued unabated. 'There are levels in our species, Barnaby, and knowing on which level we truly stand is a key aspect of safely navigating our way through life. You see, all this time you've believed that because you had money you could do as you pleased, too powerful and important for anyone to dare challenge your behaviour. Well, this is your reality check. You are not on the level you thought you were, and above the level you are on, are many thousands more. I stand here looking at you from one of those higher levels, many miles above your head, reminding you to be more respectful to the people with whom you cross paths in life. Understood?'

The squeaking dialled up to a higher pitch.

'I'll take that as a yes. So, what's going to happen now is you're going to come back inside, transfer the money, sign the papers, and try to live the rest of your life a better man. Sound good?'

The squeaking intensified further. Drayce sighed. 'I need an answer in English, Barnaby.' He thought about his gunshot wound. 'And I'd hurry if I were you. I'm recovering from a shoulder injury. Not sure how much longer I can hold you up like this.'

Barnaby's jaw relaxed. His lips trembled. 'O... O... Okay.'

Drayce lifted him back over the rails, turned him the right way round, and set him down on his unsteady feet. He dusted him off, examining him as he did so. The man visibly shook, his collar damp with sweat, his expression suggesting he was about to burst into tears. The message had been received loud and clear, but physically he was unharmed.

Lucy would be pleased.

Drayce placed a hand on his upper back, the other stretched out to the office with an open palm, inviting Barnaby back inside. 'Shall we?'

Barnaby staggered forward. Drayce followed him in, righted his desk, placed the papers and a pen in front of him as he took a seat, and watched him let go of his only remaining tie to Lucy. The signature was a little off because of his quivering hand, but it would do the job. Papers back in Drayce's possession, he picked up his novel, stood the broken mirror on the desk, and watched Barnaby send Lucy her money.

Once confirmation of the transaction had been received, Drayce turned to leave. As he walked out of the office, he glanced over his shoulder and took his last view of Barnaby in the mirror's reflection, disfigured like a Picasso painting due to its cracked surface, his dour face depicting a cruel man forced to re-evaluate his approach to life.

Ego broken; spirit humbled; the ability to change forthcoming.

Mission accomplished.

53

One month later

Drayce adjusted his suit jacket and rang the doorbell, eyes on the frosted glass.

Clutched in his hand was an article he'd cut out of *The Daily Telegraph*. Initial reports had attributed the shooting at the nightclub to an act of terrorism, but the Met were quick to quell the public's fears, and released the bare bones of what they knew of the incident: that armed men had exchanged gunfire inside a nightclub owned by a businessman with ties to organised crime, and that no one outside of those actively involved in the shooting was hurt in the crossfire. In a similarly downplayed fashion, reports covering the blaze at the warehouse were limited to a few small articles detailing an act of vandalism committed at a disused factory, the heavy police presence explained as the Met's desire to ensure it didn't turn into a series of arsons. The media bought it, their attention soon diverted to fresher, shinier stories.

Until Jason Martin's notes landed on their desks.

Drayce had written them up, made several copies, and sent them to all the major newspapers. Within twenty-four hours, the full story hit: the breadth of Daniel Sullivan's smuggling operation; the reason why Lily Drayce and Jason Martin were murdered, and by whom; Detective Chief Inspector Paul Territt's ties to Sullivan, and how his corruption helped the criminal enterprise go from strength to strength. With little other evidence to assist enquiries, Territt's missing person investigation had gone nowhere. Both the police and press had attributed his disappearance to him either skipping the country to avoid arrest and prosecution for his crimes, or him having fallen victim to murder by Sullivan's people, before they themselves were killed by an unknown suspect.

Drayce examined the article in his hand, the most comprehensive of all that had been written, his attention drawn to the headline. He smiled.

The Demise of the Sullivan Cartel.

Movement caught his eye, a silhouette hovering at the other side of the frosted glass. He wiped the smile off his face as a key turned and the door opened.

Sam Carleton filled the gap, his formidable stature a less aggressive presence than on Drayce's last visit. Sam pivoted his torso to allow his wife to pass. Elizabeth stepped outside, hands clasped in front of her chest as though clutching something precious. Her gaze searched Drayce's face, waiting for answers. Drayce handed her the article. She took the pages in both hands and immersed herself in the report, her husband peering over her shoulder, both hungrily absorbing the words.

Finished, they looked up at him, an understanding in their expressions. Elizabeth opened her arms and threw herself at Drayce, knocking him back a step. She held him tightly, her arms around his waist, the newspaper cut-out scrunched in her clenched fist, face buried in his chest. When she eventually released him, there were tiny damp patches on his shirt, marking where her eyes had been. She retreated into her husband's embrace. Sam reached out to Drayce. They shook hands, their grips fierce, extinguishing the last flame of resentment that had burned for so many years within Lily's father.

Without a single word exchanged, Drayce left the couple with the best closure he had to offer, and walked away to his next visit.

54

At the gate to the graveyard, Drayce spent five minutes stood next to a parked car, checking his reflection in the window: his freshly cut hair styled; face wet-shaved that morning; three-piece tailored navy wool suit dry-cleaned; brilliant white shirt immaculately ironed; navy tie with white polka-dots perfectly folded; a matching handkerchief carefully tucked into his chest pocket; polished black leather Lanx shoes pristine, reflecting the dull sky back at him.

In one hand was a bag of cleaning equipment; in the other, another copy of the same newspaper article he'd delivered to Lily's parents, the pages laminated.

He turned away from his reflection, took a deep breath, and walked through the gates.

Lily's place of rest was in an area for those who'd been cremated, in the centre of the front row. Drayce took a clean towel from the bag, laid it out in front of her plaque, and knelt on it. He admired the engraving, each letter painted gold, the colour dulled from the slight build-up of grime since his last visit.

Always loved. Never Forgotten. Forever in our hearts.

He poured soapy water from the plastic bottle he'd prepared earlier onto the plaque and scrubbed it with an old toothbrush. After a rinse with clean water, the bright lettering stood out from the dark-grey granite. He took out a pair of secateurs and pruned the lavender plant he'd placed at the head of the plaque last year, taking care not to disturb the bumble bees busily gathering their pollen. He gave it a drop of water and scrubbed its cream pot with a wet wipe from the cleaning bag.

Maintenance done, he tidied everything away and began the ritual he'd planned for. He laid the laminated newspaper article on the plaque and weighed it down with a rock that had waves of white marbling over its smooth surface – something he'd collected from the beach where he'd proposed to Lily and kept as a memento. Next, he took a trowel from the bag, removed a small square of turf from the foot of the plaque, and dug a shallow hole. He reached into his pocket, fished out the pieces of his wedding ring, and placed them inside – after the beating he'd given Reaper, his hands had swollen up so badly he'd needed to cut it off. From another pocket, he removed his necklace and opened the locket.

Lily gazed up at him, her shoulder-length brown hair framing her bright green eyes, one side swept back behind her neck, the other continuing down past her smile, the back of a hand delicately placed under her chin. He removed the photo, kissed it, and placed it in the hole. He locked eyes with her as she lay in the loose soil, struggling with the next goodbye. The locket shook between his quivering fingers. He needed closure, something to draw a line under the gut-wrenching tragedy. Lily smiled up at him.

It's for the best, Drayce told himself. *They belong together.*

He forced his eyes back to the locket.

Underneath Lily's photo was a small, folded square of white card. Drayce took it out and opened it: an ultrasound image, their first, captured the week before Lily was murdered. He stared for a long time, so engrossed in the power of it that he didn't notice his legs go numb, or the rain pattering against him, his mind lost in the thought of what might have been.

Sometime later, the dreary skies having darkened, he kissed the image of his unborn child and placed it in the hole with Lily. He dangled the necklace and slowly lowered it in, shovelled the soil over everything and replaced the square of turf.

A single tear broke free from his eyelashes and landed on the plaque among the raindrops. Thunder rumbled overhead, the deafening crack of lightning erupting seconds later. Drayce felt the pain gather pace within him, the same stab in his heart he experienced during every visit to Lily's place of rest now a bludgeoning pickaxe. He let it come, abandoning the hatred he'd carried with him these last three and a half years. He cried for what he'd lost: the lives taken; the love stolen; the future that might have been and the family they could have had. Horizontal rain stung his cheeks. Fierce gusts of wind stole his cries.

As his emotions settled, so did the storm. In its aftermath, the graveyard was silent. Drayce gathered his things and stood tall, his suit dripping wet. A flock of geese flew overhead in a V formation. The flap of their wings and a single honk broke the silence. Drayce couldn't take his eyes off Lily's plaque.

Always loved. Never forgotten. Forever in our hearts.

Movement ahead caught his eye: a woman in a flowery summer dress, walking among the headstones. Drayce lifted his chin, wiped his eyes and patted his drenched jacket, suddenly self-conscious about his appearance now he realised he wasn't alone. The lady had her back to him. Drayce squinted. Her hair, her dress, they appeared to be bone dry, and she wasn't carrying an umbrella. Had she sheltered during the storm? Drayce surveyed the graveyard. There wasn't any overhead cover within a hundred metres and the rain had only just stopped. How had she stayed so dry? He looked her way again. She turned to face him.

His heart missed a beat.

Lily brushed her hair back as she walked towards him, the dress now familiar, something she'd worn on their honeymoon. He knew the figure before him was a figment of his imagination, but it didn't diminish the strength of his emotions. His chest burned with delight; butterflies danced in his stomach. She stopped a few feet away, her eyes never leaving his, the two of them admiring each other as though nothing else in the world mattered.

Drayce was overcome with the fear that if he were to reach out and touch her, she would disappear, the illusion shattered. He kept his feet planted firmly on the ground, took a deep breath, touched his fingertips to his lips, and blew a kiss in her direction. She smiled, that gorgeous kink of her lips that never failed to make his heart melt. He smiled back. A warmth spread through his chest that felt like pure happiness. The same feeling he'd had when they first met; as they had their first kiss; when he watched her walk down the aisle. The kind of love that never diminishes. The kind of love so powerful it leaves an imprint in the universe, rippling through time.

The kind of love worth killing for.

Lily's image faded, a hand rising to her lips, blowing a kiss back as she vanished.

'Until we meet again,' Drayce whispered.

He set off for the gate to live the rest of his life a good man in her honour, principles unwavering, character unbreakable.

Promises always kept.

Acknowledgements

Thanks, as always, to my agent Kate Barker, without whom the Alex Drayce books would never have seen the light of day. Thank you to Kit Nevile, Thanhmai Bui-Van, and Kate Shepherd at Canelo, who have all worked so hard to help get my books into the hands of readers. And to you, the reader, thank you once again for joining me on another adventure with Drayce. I hope you enjoyed what I did with this third book – the deeply personal and traumatic nature of Drayce's motivations in this story meant he ended up being even more brutal than he was in the first two. But that's the nature of the beast. It was never going to be a peaceful story when he's exacting revenge on the people who murdered the love of his life.

Special thanks go to Wayne Hamer, whose medical expertise helped me to make sure Lily's hospital scene was accurate; and to my close friend and jiu-jitsu training partner, Adam, whose time as a Tier 1 operator and demolitions specialist helped me to get my use of language spot on when it came time for Drayce to blow a big hole in a wall.

And now, the time has come for me to get back to work, so I can find out what trouble Drayce is going to get into next. I hope you'll join me for the ride once it's finished.

Many thanks,

Max.